A SOCIOPATH'S GUIDE TO A SUCCESSFUL MARRIAGE

A SOCIOPATH'S GUIDE TO A SUCCESSFUL MARRIAGE

A Novel

M. K. OLIVER

ATRIA BOOKS
New York Amsterdam/Antwerp London
Toronto Sydney/Melbourne New Delhi

ATRIA BOOKS

An Imprint of Simon & Schuster, LLC
1230 Avenue of the Americas
New York, NY 10020

For more than 100 years, Simon & Schuster has championed authors and the stories they create. By respecting the copyright of an author's intellectual property, you enable Simon & Schuster and the author to continue publishing exceptional books for years to come. We thank you for supporting the author's copyright by purchasing an authorized edition of this book.

No amount of this book may be reproduced or stored in any format, nor may it be uploaded to any website, database, language-learning model, or other repository, retrieval, or artificial intelligence system without express permission. All rights reserved. Inquiries may be directed to Simon & Schuster, 1230 Avenue of the Americas, New York, NY 10020 or permissions@simonandschuster.com.

This book is a work of fiction. Any references to historical events, real people, or real places are used fictitiously. Other names, characters, places, and events are products of the author's imagination, and any resemblance to actual events or places or persons, living or dead, is entirely coincidental.

Copyright © 2026 by M. K. Oliver

All rights reserved, including the right to reproduce this book or portions thereof in any form whatsoever. For information, address Atria Books Subsidiary Rights Department, 1230 Avenue of the Americas, New York, NY 10020.

First Atria Books hardcover edition February 2026

ATRIA BOOKS and colophon are registered trademarks of Simon & Schuster, LLC

Simon & Schuster strongly believes in freedom of expression and stands against censorship in all its forms. For more information, visit BooksBelong.com.

For information about special discounts for bulk purchases, please contact Simon & Schuster Special Sales at 1-866-506-1949 or business@simonandschuster.com.

The Simon & Schuster Speakers Bureau can bring authors to your live event. For more information or to book an event, contact the Simon & Schuster Speakers Bureau at 1-866-248-3049 or visit our website at www.simonspeakers.com.

Manufactured in the United States of America

3 5 7 9 10 8 6 4

Library of Congress Cataloging-in-Publication Data is available.

ISBN 978-1-6680-9690-1
ISBN 978-1-6680-9692-5 (ebook)

Let's stay in touch! Scan here to get book recommendations, exclusive offers, and more delivered to your inbox.

*To my mother, who would have loved
and delighted in all of this so much*

A cat, in its own interest, sometimes hides its misanthropy under the guise of amiable gentleness; instead of tearing what it desires from its master's hand, it approaches with a caressing air, rubs its pretty little head against him, and advances a paw whose touch is soft as down.... That artfulness in it is called hypocrisy. In ourselves, we give it another name, politeness, and he who did not use it to hide his real feelings would soon be driven from society.

EMILY BRONTË, "Le Chat," 1842

PART ONE

Relapse

When we are struck at without a reason,
we should strike back again very hard.

CHARLOTTE BRONTË, *Jane Eyre*, 1847

1

Visitor

Friday, November 15

Muswell Hill is a leafy suburb on a hill overlooking North London. It's not Hampstead or Highgate, of course, but a five-bedroom house on one of its prime roads will still set you back over three million.

I live with my husband and two children at 44 Ennerdale Avenue, a highly desirable tree-lined road close to the shops of the Broadway and the open green spaces of Alexandra Palace. It's within walking distance of three good schools, and in the spring the street is full of cherry blossoms.

Our home is a double-fronted Edwardian villa with all its original features. Marble fireplaces, stained glass panels, and ornate cornices abound, to which we've added the requisite architect-designed kitchen extension. It's the perfect blend of period charm and contemporary style.

The house boasts panoramic floor-to-ceiling glass doors, a generous south-facing garden, five well-appointed double bedrooms, three exquisite bathrooms, and two light-filled reception rooms—one of which currently contains a dead body.

I've not called the police because it was I who stabbed him. Seven times in all, which no doubt the authorities will call *overkill*. The truth is, it's surprisingly difficult to kill someone with a vegetable knife. But as I was preparing carrot sticks at the time, it's all I had to hand. Wounds two through seven, therefore, were more to do with an eagerness to avoid any interruptions to Nathan's birthday party than any deranged psychopathic impulse.

To be clear, I'm not of diminished responsibility, nor am I drunk or under the influence of any kind. I can assure you that I couldn't chair the junior school winter fair committee unless I was absolutely on my mettle at all times. Besides, any forensic pathologist worth their salt would confirm that the axillary artery was severed rather precisely—a surgical rather than an impassioned incision—and I'm rather proud of my steadiness after so many years of self-restraint.

The specific blood vessel in question is hidden just under the armpit and usually quite inaccessible, but when someone grabs you around the neck and tries to strangle you, it presents a decent target. You thrust your blade upward, drag it backward, *et voilà*.

It's only fair to say that I've been slightly overwrought recently: Nelly's admissions tests, for one thing, my mother-in-law's interference in our lives, for another. Not to mention Stephen stopping all conjugal activity, which really hasn't helped my mood.

In case you're wondering, the dead man is not my husband. I do resent the lack of sex, but I wouldn't kill him for it. Not yet, anyway. More annoying is his lack of grit. I set him the task of making partner a year ago, and he's still trying. It's unsettling when you work hard to build a successful marriage and your husband can't keep up his side of the bargain. The uplift in income is essential to my plan to move to Hampstead and have a third child. Our marriage depends on it.

Speaking of children, Nathan, who's four today, slept through the whole affair, which is a relief as he's moody if interrupted during a nap. My friends and their offspring arrive in under thirty minutes and I've got to finish the party tea, fold the organic napkins, and bring up two bottles of Chablis from the cellar. And now I also have to change my outfit and somehow dispose of a corpse.

This presents something of a dilemma. Do I cancel and face the wrath of Sophie, who believes that regular access to chilled white wine is an inalienable human right, or simply close the door and deal with the corpse after I pick up Nelly from school? As we chose not to extend our open-plan kitchen-diner into the living room, I do have the option of sealing the area off with a Do Not Enter sign.

I chastise myself for being indecisive but, in my defense, I've not had to deal with this kind of situation since Stephen and I were married, seven years ago now, and, since the children came along, well, I wouldn't have had the energy anyway. I've often wondered whether becoming a mother has softened me, but looking at the ravaged corpse at my feet, I think this is hard to argue.

After considering my options, I decide to go ahead with Nathan's birthday party. The cake alone cost nearly £400, and I'd hate to waste the opportunity to pass off someone else's talent as my own. Anyway, the deceased isn't going anywhere, and if I let something slip from my to-do list today, there's no telling where I'll be by the end of the week.

I just need to tidy myself up a little as I look like I've been visiting an abattoir on Ladies' Day. By my estimation, there are several pints of blood all over my Persian rug and parquet floor, not to mention my Oscar de la Renta dress. I unzip and let it fall in a puddle of silk at my feet. The blood has soaked right through to my underwear, and that will have to go too.

Kicking off my splattered heels, I stand completely nude amid these human remains. For a moment, I feel a bit sorry for myself, because I did love that dress, and no amount of dry cleaning will remove all the forensic evidence. The same goes for the nine thousand pounds' worth of dyed Persian sheep's wool.

As I leave, I notice a fine spray of arterial blood on the wall that has almost dried to a Tuscan red, and suddenly I'm looking at the paint job, which was done last year in Little Greene's Pompeian Ash and Lute, and realize this is a wonderful opportunity for a whole new color scheme.

2

Monsters

The doorbell rings persistently. I rush downstairs with Nathan struggling in my arms, holding his ears dramatically. If it's the Metropolitan Police, I'll take back everything I've ever said about their capabilities.

I've managed a quick shower and changed into a silk cream blouse with dark wide-legged trousers. Not a party outfit, but sometimes corners have to be cut. I even tried some new facial expressions in the mirror as I reapplied my makeup. Looking delighted when your child receives another plastic monstrosity is a challenge, but YouTube helps enormously.

I find Sophie jiggling on our stone steps, wearing a slightly stained puffer jacket, a tired pink roll-neck, faded blue jeans, and scuffed Chelsea boots. On the positive side, she has beautiful long hair, and eyes that make you feel like she adores you.

She's holding Jethro up to the bell with one arm while carrying a Sainsbury's bag full of gifts in the other. She pulls a face that I don't immediately understand. There are sixteen major facial expressions in the human repertoire, and I've learned to read them all when used individually, but even now I struggle when people use several at once. While it's acceptable to ask people to repeat words, asking them to repeat facial expressions is considered odd.

"Sorry, Lalla darling, I desperately need the loo."

"Who doesn't love an insistently pressed doorbell?" I reply, and remove Jethro's grubby finger from the bell. Just seeing Sophie floods me with calm. Although she says I'm *on the spectrum* a little too often, I do like her. I think it might be because she's so unsuccessful.

"If I did that at Tor's, she'd have me arrested for damaging the ears of her *musically gifted* children." Sophie mimics Tor's vowels to a T.

"You're welcome to press my bell anytime." I wink at her. "Anyway, Tor's still recovering from her 'spa break' in Switzerland."

"I'm running a book on what she's had done," says Sophie, kissing my cheek. I smell eau-de-motherhood—coffee, crayons, wet wipes, and white wine.

"I'll put twenty pounds on Botox. She's been bemoaning her neck bands for weeks," I say.

"Not being rude, darling, but Nathan's left half his lunch in your ear," Sophie says, laughing and pointing.

"Nathan loves spitting his Tom Toms all over the place," I say, hastily picking off a crusty flake of what I presume is dried blood. I jiggle Nathan in a gesture I hope conveys motherly affection. He squeezes my cheek in return, but I feel only mild irritation. In truth, I'm still trying to bond with him, and it's infernally difficult.

Sophie loves easily and undiscerningly. She's even bonded with her partner's annoyingly perfect child. My children and I get by through familiarity and routine. But if love is the irrational continuation of affection in the face of continual disappointment, then I do love my children. And perhaps even Stephen too.

Loving anything as demanding, noisy, and erratic as a child seems quite heroic to me. Mothers are expected to react with joy and delight from the moment a child is born. All I felt was a vague resentment that this parasite had lived inside me for so long without paying a penny in rent.

"Happy Birthday, little Nate, you're so adorably cute." Sophie squeezes his fat cheek and Nathan buries his head in my chest.

"Sorry—he's no good for anything till he's had his first shot of organic almond milk."

"Oh, I'm exactly the same," says Sophie. "Now while I'm in the loo, open a bottle, and we can get one in before Aisha arrives and starts guilt-tripping me."

"Everyone has a cross to bear. You have wine, Cait has Owen, Aisha has yoga, and I have astonishing beauty," I say. Sophie laughs even though I am quite serious, then she thrusts the bag of poorly wrapped presents into my free hand and darts into the loo.

I put Nathan down and pat his head as kindly as I can. He runs off to the kitchen with his presents. I expect Jethro to follow. Instead, he smears snot across his cheek and yanks on the handle to the toilet door (mothers are not permitted loo breaks). He then spots Purdy, my blue-eyed Turkish Angora, slinking down the stairs like a debutante arriving at a ball.

"Cat!" shouts Jethro and runs toward her. Purdy is unamused, increases her gait elegantly, and pushes open the living room door. Her fluffy tail disappears through the gap as she heads to her favorite sun spot. Jethro bolts after her and shoulder-barges the door.

Unless I stop him, he's about to face his first significant trauma.

"No!" I bellow. He stops dead, turns, and stares at me, his face a cubist miasma of fear and shame.

"There's a monster asleep in there," I whisper, pulling the door closed. "If you wake him, he'll be extremely hungry. Do you know what he likes to eat?"

Jethro's eyes widen as he shakes his head.

"Little boys," I say, with a cold blank expression.

Jethro shivers, his eyes glued to the door, when we hear a faint scratching sound from the other side.

"You've woken the monster," I say, my face exaggerated with mock fear.

Jethro's eyes crease, and he runs down the hall screaming. I open the door, and Purdy walks out imperiously, leaving a trail of little red paw prints across the shiny tiles.

3

Chablis

We're all gathered around my large kitchen island (Italian marble). There's an open bottle of chilled 2020 Chablis Montmains between us, which is possibly too good for Sophie, but you try to improve people where you can. If it were a drinking race, Sophie would be dipping for the tape, Aisha would be jogging slowly in her Lululemons, while Cait would be at the starting line tying her laces.

There's a scattered mass of abandoned presents on the brightly colored party table. The children have all charged outside, following Nathan, who has a cardboard box on his head. An unruly pile of wrapping paper is making everyone feel guilty (three comments so far, two from Aisha), and we quickly cycle through the "Can you recycle wrapping paper, or have you tried reusable Japanese wrapping cloth?" conversation again, which probably saves several forests all by itself.

As we're chatting, I fold each piece of wrapping paper into a neat pile and tie it with a ribbon. I tell my friends I'll reuse it, which I won't. This leads to a discussion of how everyone's parents used to save pieces of string, make meals out of leftover animal fat, and share baths. Halcyon days.

"Can you hear someone calling?" says Aisha, and we all go quiet. There's a plaintive cry coming from the direction of the hallway.

"It's just Purdy," I say, more in hope than expectation, but she does meow sometimes like she's in the last act of an opera.

After a quick check on the man in the living room, who has not moved one inch, I decide I need to focus on happier things and fetch the cake.

Homemade birthday cakes are directly proportionate to parental love, so it's important to devote appropriate resources. A supermarket cake, even if you choose the pricier option, just won't convey the necessary level of motherly devotion. I baked and discarded a small Victoria sponge earlier—the aroma adds authenticity to the masquerade.

I return to the kitchen and place my masterpiece on the table for everyone to admire before the children arrive to undo all the good work. It's a Winnie-the-Pooh extravaganza with Pooh, Piglet, and Eeyore at Eeyore's birthday party. My friends coo in approval. There's even a low gasp.

There are two kinds of children's parties—the couture and the diffusion line. The diffusion line involves inviting every member of your child's class, is inevitably crowded and stressful, and relies on ultraprocessed snacks and a supermarket cake. The couture party is for select friends and characterized by fine wine, dips, self-entertaining children, and a showy cake.

"Oh my god, Lalla, that's absolutely amazing!" gushes Sophie. "How did you do it?"

"Trial and error . . . It's not quite as good as it seems, but marzipan and butter icing hide many flaws," I say with a self-deprecating shake of the head.

"The glaze on the honey pot looks almost real," says Aisha, leaning in closely with an artist's eye for detail. Even in November, Aisha is a vivid picture of health—flawless skin, dark glossy bob, sculpted cheekbones, and boundless energy levels. She dresses permanently in Lululemon, which shows off her impressively toned physique. She has three overly clever children, runs her own design business, and is married to a cardiologist. She's also unfailingly nice to everyone, so we do our best not to hate her too much.

"Trade secret," I reply, and put my arm around her shoulders in the way I've seen Olympic gold medalists hug the losers. However,

Aisha's replica of Hogwarts Castle for her son's sixth birthday still reigns supreme. I don't think any of us had ever seen a lighted candelabra inside a cake before.

"I love Piglet," says Cait, staring longingly at the little pig in a striped shirt with a sniffle of self-pity. Cait is like the character but without the energy or enthusiasm. She's short and thin, and her affection for Toast's oversize peasant clothes doesn't do her any favors at all. With her pale skin and long red hair, she looks like a struck match.

She was supposedly happily married until she revealed that her charming and witty husband, Owen, was a systematic abuser. He was arrested, a court case followed, and he was given a suspended sentence and restraining order, which keeps him away from her now. She's left with her twin flame-haired girls, an untidy house, and almost permanent paralyzing fear.

"We all love Piglet," I say, and smile at her. Cait tries to smile back, but her expression is more the look of someone about to tell you they've been diagnosed with an incurable disease, so the impact is limited. On a cheerful note, Cait does have a passion—a morbid true crime obsession that she pours into an earnest podcast that has two subscribers (one is her mother).

I don't tell my dear friends that I had the cake made, bespoke, at great expense, from GC Couture in Mayfair. I asked them to make it look slightly homemade so that it was more believable. Apparently that's not an unusual request. They even had it delivered in an unmarked van to avoid detection.

We sip Chablis, observe our children in a rare moment of blissful calm, and admire the beautifully landscaped garden designed by the charming Luca, although his efforts have been ruined by an assortment of slides and swings, as well as the new trampoline Stephen bought for Nathan's birthday. We openly objectify the poor man, but it's not our fault Luca speaks in an Italian accent and knows how to handle an axe. Meanwhile our husbands get increasingly angry at car parking infringements and garbage collections.

Nathan is digging up tulip bulbs with Jethro. Cait's twins are trampolining together and giggling hysterically. Aisha's son is completing the Sudoku from last Saturday's *Telegraph* that Stephen failed to finish. It's a rare sunny mid-November day; even the trees seem elegantly poised.

"Your garden's still looking smart," says Aisha, staring out. "Ours is completely covered in leaves."

"Luca does most of it, but Stephen attacked the privet rather aggressively at the weekend," I say. "The pressure of the bank's partner process is probably getting to him."

"I think he just likes a well-pruned bush," says Sophie, half-pissed, pointing at our denuded hedge. Everyone giggles. All except Cait, who's still staring down at her phone, probably finding holes in some police investigation as armchair detectives are so adept at doing.

"Anyway, I can't mock, I'm meeting an old flame tonight, so I'll have to get the razor out," says Sophie. She's a part-time secondary school teacher, which explains her drinking of course, but also why someone with such a beautiful figure would dress in clothes that seem disappointed to be there.

"Oh, and how is that going to help things?" says Aisha, our icy moral compass. "You don't throw oil on a fire, you cover it in a blanket."

"Oh, I don't want a blanket. I want to remind him that you can't take *this* for granted!" Sophie thrusts out her chest and raises her wineglass. "But making him jealous would be a lot easier if men were a bit more effing impressive."

"Why don't you ask him yourself, if it bothers you that much?" says Aisha.

"Ask him to marry me?" says Sophie, astonished. "It's below my dignity."

"Why does being married matter?" says Aisha.

"Because he married *her*," says Sophie, the drink allowing more honesty than usual. Her partner, Paolo, is also a teacher (head of geography, aged forty-seven, but not as unattractive as that makes him sound), and his first wife died, which had nothing to do with me (it was cancer). Sophie met Paolo when he was still grieving, and she became pregnant with Jethro soon after, but Sophie still feels second best to the dead wife.

"You should try couples therapy," says Aisha.

"I don't want anyone fiddling with parts of me that I can't fiddle with myself," Sophie says, arching her eyebrows.

"I would've thought that's exactly what you're after," I say. Some of my jokes are successful and many are not. Sexual innuendo is an easy win in social situations. Less so in a job interview, as I once found out.

Everyone is laughing when Cait suddenly jumps up and gasps. A short panic attack, or maybe an itch. She cradles her phone as if she's foreseeing doom.

"What is it, Cait?" says Aisha.

"He was in my fucking house last night!" she says.

4

Owen

About eighteen months ago, Cait and I were sitting in the sunshine, watching our children playing together in the sandpit in Highgate Wood, when I asked her, "What'll happen to the girls if he ends up killing you?"

Cait looked quite surprised by my question, but I have a nose for such things, and Cait's habit of covering up even on the warmest of days meant she was hiding either an eczema outbreak or bruises. With a child's pink spade in her hand, Cait explained quite matter-of-factly and completely tearlessly how Owen punched and kicked her and, more recently, had started to strangle her.

I suggested various quick solutions using everyday household items (bleach, iron, even the kettle, a favorite of mine), but these were all rejected. I even offered to do it myself at one point and Cait laughed. As she was unwilling to do anything, I told her to take pictures, make notes, and record as much as she could, which she did with impressive thoroughness and hid rolled up in her headboard until required by the courts.

I met them some time later, at a school fete, working side by side on a secondhand stall. A picture of familial unity. I asked Owen, quite loudly, why he beat his wife and whether he intended to stop. He tried to shout me down, but I had so much detail that Cait had shared with me, and such a large audience of other parents, that I didn't stop until the police arrived. He never much liked me after that, but someone tried to hurt me once too. The difference being, with me, it was only the once.

"Who was in your house?" says Sophie, her arm already around Cait's shoulders.

"Owen," says Cait, shaking now. "He texted me a photograph he took of me asleep in my bed."

"He's not supposed to be near you, is he?" says Aisha. "You've got a court order."

"The number is anonymous. He sent me another text last week, asking for money. He says he's in debt to some bad people. Probably gambling again."

"So this picture is a threat?" I say. "He broke into your house, right?"

"What else could it be?" Cait stifles her tears, then presses her finger to her nose. "He was probably searching for money while we were all asleep."

"Fucking bastard," says Sophie. "He should be locked up."

Cait looks up, her face etched with fear, nails scraping across her red neck. Sophie is hugging her tightly.

"You must tell the police right now," says Aisha, sensible as ever.

"But there's no proof it's him."

"Does he still have a key?" says Sophie.

"I was going to get the locks changed, but it's two hundred pounds. I thought the court order would be enough," says Cait.

"It's never enough with men like that," says Sophie, stroking Cait's long red hair.

We don't get into too much more detail, as Jethro decides he wants Nathan's spade and Nathan objects by throwing soil in his mouth. Other children take sides, and a small skirmish breaks out on the patio. We all rise to intervene.

"Drinky-time!" I call out, trying to keep my mood light and cheerful. A horde of small people stop fighting and career toward me as I stand between our voluminous double-fronted fridge (my husband seems to think we're American) and the rather quaint old-fashioned butler sink, diluting some blackberry and raspberry juice.

If I didn't dilute, at least two of the mothers here would react as if I were feeding rat poison to their children.

My mind wanders to the dead man as I pour the bright red drink into their little organic bamboo beakers. At first, I presumed he was just a common burglar after cash, jewelry, or the key fob for the Porsche. But he didn't seem like a burglar. He was dressed quite smartly, but perhaps they go upmarket when raiding Muswell Hill. No, it was something else. The way he looked at me, with recognition. And why did he strangle me? Why not just run?

As I muse, Jethro grabs at the tray and a beaker tips over. I feel a strong urge to tip the rest of the beakers over his head. I often have such urges, but I have learned to resist and now have excellent self-control. If I didn't, I'd probably be a widow by now. Instead, I mouth the word *monster* and Jethro starts to howl again. Nathan, who's consumed too much sugar, starts to cry along with him. Sophie rises, looks at her son, and then turns away and heads over to her handbag for her vape.

I'm rushing toward my son when I hear Cait's phone ping again and, out of the corner of my eye, I see her jump up and run into the hall. I suspect Owen has texted something even more unsavory, but I can't follow her because I've just grabbed hold of Nathan and he's struggling the way sheep do when they're about to be shorn.

"Not the living room, Cait!" I call out. Even if I had Aisha's creative powers, I don't think I'd be able to come up with something believable if Cait stumbles across a fresh corpse.

"Stop," I say harshly to Nathan as he pulls my lip down with his grubby fingers. I can taste soil. I put him firmly on the floor and dart for the door.

I am only halfway across the kitchen when a piercing scream echoes from the hall.

5

Rabbit

Human beings are adept at distinguishing between different types of scream. They each awaken several of our senses, but only the scream of genuine fear grips your nervous system by the throat and applies sudden pressure.

At least, that's what I can gather from Aisha's and Sophie's frozen stances as their faces drain of color. Each child, a moment ago lost to their own squabbles and antics, stops dead. A short silence is followed by children sobbing.

I'm pleased that no one sees the faint smile on my lips. It's just as quickly gone, however, as I need to contain the situation. Although this discovery could land me in prison for several years, I'm palpitating with excitement. I've always been excited by danger. I lick my lips and rush to the hall.

"Leave it to me," I call over my shoulder, although I've no idea how I'll silence Cait if she's face-to-face with the man I've turned into a sieve. Cait is standing outside the living room door, visibly shaking. I can practically hear the thump of my pulse, and I feel goose bumps tingling.

"What's the matter?"

Her shoulders heave up and down. I want to put my hand over her mouth to stop her whimpering, but I've learned to resist my first urges. They are rarely acceptable to others. I breathe deeply, count to four (there's no time to get to ten), and approach her.

The living room door is still closed, so I conclude it's just Owen again. I put an arm on her shoulder. It's the acknowledged way to comfort people in distress, but Cait flinches.

"Has he texted again?"

"It's not him." Her frightened eyes stare into mine.

I glance over my shoulder and see Aisha and Sophie at the kitchen door, holding subdued children in their arms. "Cait needs some space. She's got another text, that's all," I lie.

I turn back to Cait, look her dead in the eye, and whisper, "Did you go into the living room?"

"There's ... something ... in there," she says, her voice rasping.

"You're overwrought," I say. "It's just the horrible shock about Owen."

"No, no," she says quietly. "There's blood everywhere ..."

Cait's hair is tangled and her top lip is lined with sweat. She looks slightly postcoital. I take her hands in mine. They feel like porcelain against my warmth. I sense she'd break into pieces with the slightest pressure.

"Listen to me carefully, Cait. The mind plays tricks sometimes, especially when we're scared."

"Please just look!" She withdraws her hands and wrings them like a child.

I have no choice. I open the living room door and peer into the room.

"Oh," I say, then shut the door quickly, my mind racing through ideas, a slot machine of turning possibilities. I know something will turn up.

"I told you!" says Cait. "What is it?"

I wait for the reels. They stop turning, one by one.

"It looks like Purdy disemboweled our pet rabbit."

"A rabbit?" says Cait.

"Just a rabbit," I say. Her brow wrinkles in disbelief, but I remain firm. "Please don't mention it or Nathan will be inconsolable."

Cait's expression changes again. She nods conspiratorially, as if she's understood something.

"Now let's get you a cup of tea. Not a word or we'll have the worst birthday ever."

With Cait's distress ruining the party mood, everyone finds their children and party bags and starts packing them away. We smile and hug, even though we'll meet at school pickup in an hour. Aisha supports Cait with a motherly arm and agrees to take her home so she can arrange to have the locks changed and call the police.

I head to the living room and tape a hastily constructed sign on the door to repel Aimée, our feces-intolerant nanny—

Cat Accident—Do Not Enter

6

Hamster

The school playground is pitted with unrepaired tarmac and criss-crossed with faded lines. I stand along with another thirty mothers and three fathers, two of whom have found each other and are talking about the best route to Lord's Cricket Ground. Sophie, Aisha, and I are waiting by the classroom doors for our elder children to be personally delivered back to us by their class teacher. Cait, we discover, has gone to her mum's to wait for the police to call back. As far as I can tell, she has not yet spilled the beans about the "rabbit."

Sophie's partner's annoyingly precocious daughter, Ellie, runs out first, her long light brown ponytail swishing as she shows us all a rather good copy of a Matisse. Sophie opens her arms and hugs her like a woman who hasn't seen her child in several years. I squeeze Nathan's hand at my side. He shows me a worm he's carried all the way to the school.

"Don't eat it," I say.

"Can I play for five minutes, please, Sophie?" asks Ellie, patting Jethro on the head.

"Of course you can," says Sophie, who can't take her eyes off Ellie as she runs across the playground and within a moment is hanging upside down on a bar alongside two other girls.

"She's so talented," says Aisha, looking at the painting in Sophie's hands. I sigh inwardly.

"No sign of Tor," says Sophie, spotting Tor's nanny waiting for Hero.

"Healing takes time," I say.

Aisha's eldest zooms out of the classroom next, side-swerves his mother, leaps up the grassy bank, barges into another boy, and starts wrestling. We watch to see if this is an act of camaraderie or a vicious assault. A moment later, the two boys are kicking a ball against a wall together and all is well.

No sign of Nelly. She's six years old but won't be rushed, even by a teacher. I think being last helps her to avoid other children. She finds friendship difficult, as I did at her age.

Nelly finally walks out holding the one thing in the world that she seems to love, an aging blue-eyed doll, with a filthy gingham dress and a fixed expression, which has been passed from mother to daughter. A visible bond between us.

Her teacher follows her over to me, which is unusual, as they do tend to keep their distance since my animated lecture to Nelly's previous teacher on why she deserved to be at the top table despite her poor showing in maths tests.

I turn swiftly to make my escape. I not only want to avoid small talk; I have a lot to do before Stephen gets home for Nathan's family party.

"I wonder if we might have a word," says Miss Hammond. She's wearing a shapeless corduroy smock dress. The floral embroidery on the collar is the only sign of life I can see.

"About?" I say.

"About Nelly."

"I think we should make a fast getaway," a smirking Sophie says to Aisha.

"What about her?" I watch Sophie making a crucifix symbol behind Miss Hammond's head and smile. Miss Hammond glares at me disapprovingly, then looks down at Nelly.

"We had a little accident today, didn't we, Nelly?"

My daughter stares up at her teacher, her angelic expression devoid of understanding.

"Do you remember what happened in class? Do you want to tell your mummy?"

Nelly shrugs.

Miss Hammond turns to me. "There was an incident with the class hamster."

Nelly has decided to appear nonchalant and starts swinging her hips and rocking her doll in her arms.

"I might need a private word with Mummy, Nelly. Can you play?"

We watch Nelly wander off to a bench, sit down alone, and place her doll beside her as a kaleidoscope of children in colorful coats cascade all around her.

"So, Miss Hammond, I'm glad of the opportunity to speak. I wanted to ask if you could give Nelly some more demanding homework. Her entrance exam for Adams Prep is approaching at pace."

"Please call me Rosie," she says, which I won't. "And Nelly doesn't do any of her homework, which I've mentioned a number of times."

"She throws her homework in the bin because it's too easy for her," I say. "That's at the root of her behavioral challenges. Nelly is not like other children."

"Well, yes, I can see that," she says in a tone that is close to the bone. My guts churn. I know what it's like to be locked away from opportunity and friendship just because your mind works differently, and I don't want that for Nelly.

"Praise works. But she's thick-skinned, so you have to praise her wildly for minimal effort."

"Mrs. Rook. I don't know how else to say this. Your daughter drowned the class hamster."

"But she loves animals."

"She filled the art sink with water, put the hamster in it, and just walked away."

"I'm sorry to hear that, but it's hardly the fault of a child if a hamster can't swim."

"I found it floating there," says Miss Hammond.

"Just to be clear, she made it a swimming pool, presumably in the belief that the hamster would enjoy it. Nelly loves swimming."

"Hamsters don't."

"Is this something you taught her?"

"What?" says the teacher, her face screwed up quite melodramatically.

"Is it in your class plan?"

"No, it's not," says Miss Hammond, looking flustered and turning around as if looking for support. "She's the pet monitor this week. Her job was to look after the hamster."

"I think she was clearly trying to, Miss Hammond. We all make mistakes."

"I'm concerned about her lack of basic empathy."

"And I'm concerned about your lack of basic pedagogy," I say, quite firmly.

"When I told her it was dead, she smiled at me," she says, wringing her hands.

"Do you want me to pay for the hamster?"

"It's not about money."

"Well, the learning point here is that you should teach the children about risks if you give them responsibility. I mean, that's your job." I shake my head and look the teacher straight in the eye. "I hope she's not traumatized by your accusation. I don't want to make a complaint against you, Miss Hammond, so let's just put it down to experience, shall we?"

7

Tapping

Returning from school with Nathan and Nelly, plus a little shopping from Sainsbury's (bleach, garbage bags, Marigold rubber gloves, and parcel tape), I discover Aimée in her bedroom in the loft extension. I know she's there because the boiler is going at full blast, which means someone is showering. She doesn't respond to texts, so I turn off the boiler.

Not too long after, my disgruntled employee arrives with her hair wrapped in a towel and gives me a withering look. I respond with a gesture of my hand to the stacks of party dishes that she was tasked with clearing, push Nathan and Nelly into her arms, and point outside. Aimée makes a noise that sounds like a growl and tells me it's too dark. I flick a switch, and the garden lights up like a stage set.

I rush straight upstairs, take out the bag of clothes awaiting the charity shop, and change into an old pair of pajamas. I head down to the utility room, tie my hair back, pull on the new Marigolds, grab the bleach and garbage bags, plus a mop, several old sheets, and a bucket of water.

The living room smells like a bus shelter on a Saturday night—a heady mix of blood and urine. I stare at the man's bloody face and wonder who he is. In truth, I've been preoccupied with the task of clearing him up rather than wondering about his identity.

I kneel beside the body and search him. I find a white handkerchief, which is stained dark red, and a car key fob and phone in his jacket. I put the key fob back and try to open his phone.

The home screen shows a photograph of a grinning woman and a child, probably his family, but no one I recognize. I try to open it using face recognition, but his features are too bloody. I take a sheet, dip it in the bucket, and start to clean. As his eyes and nose reappear, I feel I've seen him before, and recently too. I try to place him but nothing comes. I point the phone at him again, but it won't open. I imagine it's designed to reject the dead to avoid situations just like this.

I switch off his phone in case it can be tracked and put it in a Jiffy bag. I use the sheets to mop up the blood, although the Sarouk rug has done an excellent job of absorbing most of it—a quality the man at Liberty failed to mention. I stuff the bloody sheets into bin liners, tie them shut, then wipe up the residue and turn to the body.

Time is of the essence, not least because I've got a spaghetti Bolognese to make before six and have to get rid of the corpse and change before Stephen arrives home. He's not been himself lately, in fact not since his father died a year ago, and there's no doubt that a dead body would exacerbate his rather tiresome morbidity. When most men find life meaningless, they play golf, but Stephen prefers to mope.

I've no idea how to remove the body. Strictly speaking he's "organic waste," but he certainly won't fit in the little green bin that Haringey supplies for the purpose of composting.

There's no time to dig a pit, and even if I did, I imagine Purdy would investigate—she's dug up several of Nelly's deceased guinea pigs, which seem to die at an alarming rate.

The only option is to remove him from the premises, which is difficult because he's heavy and rather messy. Wrapping him up carefully is vital. I find that the cling film is almost out and the trash bin liners I bought are only eighteen gallons—I'd need one for each limb.

I search the kitchen for larger garbage bags and see Nelly and Nathan bouncing on the new trampoline. Nelly is throwing Nathan about like a rag doll, but he seems to be laughing. Aimée is less engaged. She's sitting in the vicinity of the children, staring at her phone with her head still in a towel.

I don't know why Nelly dotes on her. It might be because she lets Nelly use her makeup, but I think it's because Nelly's attitude is so similar to Aimée's own Parisian disdain for the world.

Stephen thinks Nelly is more like me than Aimée, which means he thinks she's cold and detached, and his mother, Madeleine, actually refers to Nelly as the "maniacal" one.

As I stare into the garden, I have a sudden thought and head for the garage. I rejoice as I see that Stephen hasn't taken the gallons of thick plastic wrap from the trampoline to the dump. I've found my body wrap. I now realize my single role of parcel tape will be inadequate and search for duct tape. I come back with half a roll of masking tape and three rolls of Sellotape, one of which has a Christmas theme.

In the living room, I flatten the wrapping as it's not very malleable, then begin the dance of the dead. I lift his legs, drag the plastic under them with my foot, and, with a heave, slide it just under his buttocks. It's rather like changing a diaper, but significantly larger.

I wriggle and tug the plastic under his torso, pull the plastic under his head, and pause for a moment to dwell on my accomplishment when I hear three sharp taps on the window.

8

Corpse

I don't know how long Cait's been staring in at me, but her ghostly face suggests she's seen everything. I smile as casually as possible, which I realize is inappropriate when wrapping up a dead man, but then, what is the right expression?

Presumably Cait didn't believe my story about the dead rabbit. I wipe my hands and pull a sheet over the body, which will at least hide the stab wounds—damage limitation.

I answer the door dressed in bloodstained Liberty pajamas. If it were Halloween I could justify the outfit, but that was weeks ago. Cait stares at me intensely. I'm not sure what approach she'll take, but I wonder if professional interest brought her back. I mean, what better for her podcast than a real-life corpse?

"Are you on your own?" she whispers.

"Aimée's with the children in the garden."

"I knew it wasn't a rabbit," she says, and pushes past me into the living room, which is quite un-Cait-like.

I follow her in, intrigued by her brisk, confident tone. She stands at the fireplace fixated on the dead man under the sheet, biting her lower lip and taking everything in, slowly and methodically. I'm expecting her to take out a roll of crime scene tape, but she just stares.

"It was an accident," I say, to interrupt her reverie.

"Did he hurt you?" Cait turns to me and holds my gaze.

"Yes," I say, as it sounds better, given the nature of his injuries.

"I'm so sorry. I should've known." Cait wraps her arms around me and hugs me tightly, without a care in the world for the forensic integrity of the crime scene or her Toast linens. I can feel her skeletal frame pressing against me and want to fetch her a slice of birthday cake.

"I'll do whatever I can to help you. I won't tell," she confides, stifling her low sobs.

"No?" I say, surprised. I wonder if she's afraid of me, but the hug suggests female solidarity.

"It can happen to anyone. I always wondered about you," says Cait, rubbing my back. "You're always so perfect, but perfection is just a mask. We're all hiding from something. And the way you knew instinctively about Owen's abuse, I knew you understood how it feels."

Cait is so understanding that it crosses my mind that she's found something out about my past and I'm angry at myself for letting the memory back in. I remember sitting for so long in the cellar that I couldn't distinguish myself from the darkness, listening to the world above—carpet-muffled footsteps, the drone of television, clinking cutlery, my mother sobbing.

"Perfection isn't a mask, it's full body armor," I say, and prize her arm from my back.

"When did it happen?" she says, leaning over the corpse.

"Just before Sophie arrived."

"And you just went on with the party?"

"I had no time to think, Cait. I just went on automatic," I say, steering her away as her foot steps in a pool of blood.

"I used to do that," she says. "Owen would punch me, then the children would come in and I'd be weeping in a corner one minute and singing jolly nursery rhymes the next. You just put on a face, right?"

"That's exactly what you do, Cait. You put on a face."

"How long's the abuse been going on?" she asks.

"The abuse?"

"Stephen," she says, gesturing toward the corpse. "How long's he been hitting you?"

"Stephen?" I say. "Stephen doesn't abuse me, he's a kitten. I mean, I sometimes wish he was a little more forceful, to be honest."

"If that's not Stephen," she says, her face a caricature of confusion, "then who's dead?"

"I think he was a burglar. He didn't say. It all happened so quickly."

"He was in your house?" says Cait.

"I was getting ready for the party and heard a noise. I went to investigate and he attacked me. He had a knife," I lie, realizing that this story works better from a legal perspective. In truth, I think he realized I'd heard him and then hid behind the door, but when I came in, he panicked and grabbed me.

"Oh my god! How did you escape?" She is trying to be sympathetic but is shaking with prurient excitement.

"It's a blur, Cait. I'm still in shock."

"Have you called the police?"

I shake my head.

"Why not?" she asks slowly.

"Well, there was the party," I say. Her expression indicates I might have said the wrong thing. I reach out, enfold her tightly in my arms, and pretend to sob. "I couldn't call the police. They'll send me to prison. I'll lose my children."

"They won't send you to prison. It's not murder, Lalla, it's self-defense. He attacked you."

"I know," I say. "I fought back and he fell. He must've fallen on his knife."

"Well, that's not even self-defense. That's accidental death. You've got nothing to worry about."

Cait focuses on the corpse with a little glint in her eye. Her shoulders twitch and her tongue touches her top lip. It's clear that her anatomy is enjoying this, even if her mind is still resistant to the idea.

"Can I look at it?" she says. "I've read so much about dead bodies, but I've never actually seen one."

I nod as Cait picks up the corner of the bloody sheet with her thumb and forefinger and peels it back with a low squelch. She stares, completely still, at his dark red clothes and clean face.

Cait leans left and right, to get a clearer sight of the body, then pulls back the rest of the sheet and stares at the torso, a quizzical look on her face.

"How many times did he fall on his knife?" she asks.

9

Soap

I spot a box of Lindt on the bookshelf left over from Stephen's birthday. Cait is counting knife wounds, and I am thinking about chocolate. I walk over, open the box, and take one. It is the right decision. It removes the taste of blood from my mouth.

"Do you want a choccy?" I hold the box out toward Cait, but she glares back.

"Lalla, I don't think he could've fallen on his knife seven times, do you?" she says sharply.

"Who knows what happens in those fleeting moments?" I shrug, which doesn't appear to appease her curiosity.

"The police'll ask these questions. I'm just trying to help."

"Police? You said you'd do anything to help, and I need help wrapping him up." I kneel down and pick up a roll of adhesive tape from the floor as she peers closely at the knife wounds.

"You definitely shouldn't move him, Lalla. You have to leave everything exactly as you found it . . . for the police." She seems to have decided to take on the role of head girl at a crime scene.

"The oak parquet will stain," I say, but even this concern doesn't move her.

"Did you stab him all those times?" she asks. "Is that why you didn't call the police, Lalla?"

"Well, he wouldn't stop fighting. I had to fight back," I say.

Her small hand reaches out for mine and she squeezes my fingers. I pull her down and she kneels beside me. I think this is a good sign.

"It's manslaughter at most. But you'll need a good lawyer."

"You know how courts are with women. How they were with you even though it was Owen on trial. Insinuating you were a liar. We're women, Cait, the law doesn't work for us."

"But a man's dead. You have to tell the police."

"How will that look now? A mother stabs an intruder seven times and carries on with her son's party. I can see the headline already."

"Just explain that you were traumatized," says Cait quietly. "It does happen. You block things out that you can't cope with and just carry on for the sake of the children."

"So traumatized I spent the next two hours laughing and drinking with friends?"

"They'll find out eventually," says Cait, scratching away at her neck.

"Not if you help me. You know all about crime scenes. You're an expert."

"No," she says, slightly preoccupied. I see that she's staring at the knife that's still embedded in the man's chest like a sacred object.

"Pass me the knife," I say, realizing additional leverage might help.

"No! I don't want *my* fingerprints all over it. It's a murder weapon."

"It wasn't murder."

"Sorry," she says. "I mean a manslaughter weapon."

"I'm going to scrub it anyway. Just pass it over." Cait shakes her head so vigorously it really annoys me, so I reach over, grab her hand, pull it across the corpse, and close it around the knife handle. She shrieks as I force her to pull the knife out of his chest, then let go of her hand.

"There. Not so difficult, was it?"

Cait stares at the bloody knife in her hand and looks like she's going to be sick.

"How does that feel?"

"Not good," she says, but her face betrays passion rather than revulsion. Even so, she drops the knife. "I could never do what you did. It's wrong."

"You might need to if Owen breaks in again," I say.

"I'm not brave enough," she says. "I never was."

"Cait, look, just help me get him out of here. We can dump his body somewhere in Wood Green, the police'll think it's just another everyday London stabbing. What do you say?"

"You can't just dump a dead body on the street," she rails. "It's teeming with your DNA, clothes fibers, saliva, hair... And my DNA now! They'd have our genetic fingerprint within hours."

"You see, that's the kind of thinking that'll help us get away with it. You're so good at this," I say, smiling at her enthusiasm.

"I can't do this. I won't," she says, and stands quickly. One foot slips on a sticky trail of blood and she lurches forward. She manages to stop herself by grabbing one end of the sofa, but not completely, and her other hand lands on the dead man's chest.

"Blood!" she cries, and stares down at her hand like an amateur Lady Macbeth, her whole palm dark crimson like an autumn leaf.

"It washes off, Cait. A little bit of soap and water and it's gone," I say, trying to calm her down.

"I'm going to the police," she shouts unhelpfully.

"Cait, your fingerprints are all over this knife. They'll arrest you," I say, and take her arm.

She acts as though she's going to be my next victim, recoils from my hand, shoots me a terrified look, and rushes to the door, holding her bloody hand out in the air, looking rather guilty, I can't help thinking to myself.

10

Wrapping

As soon as Cait's gone, I fetch a freezer bag from the kitchen and put the knife inside without touching the handle. I then text Cait a quick text message, 🔪 💀 🤐, and return to wrapping the corpse.

I grab the edge of the plastic sheeting and pull it up as high as I can until the corpse rolls into the middle. It's like making a sausage roll but with polyurethane and a dead body. I look at my watch. I see that time is quickly slipping away, and also that I've already done fourteen thousand steps, which is fantastic news.

I grab the scissors and parcel tape, and I've soon forgotten about the contents of the package because I'm utilizing my gift-wrapping techniques courtesy of a tutorial that Liberty offered last Christmas. The shape of the package is a challenge, but with the right number of pinches and folds, I do a good job. I'm about to search for a ribbon to embellish the parcel but come to my senses just as the children arrive in the kitchen, accompanied by a stream of Parisian invective.

I rush upstairs, remove my bloody pajamas, get dressed again, reapply lipstick, go back downstairs, put the pajamas and charity clothes on a hot wash, and enter the kitchen.

All is not well there either. There's a Mexican standoff. Nathan is threatening to drop Nelly's doll in the sink, Nelly is threatening to throw Aimée's phone out of the window, and Aimée is threatening to put Nathan's slug in the wastebasket.

"Stop," I say calmly and assertively, as the parenting guides tell you to do. I walk through the chaos, pick the doll out of Nathan's hand, give it to Nelly, take the phone out of Nelly's hand and give it to Aimée, pick the slug out of Aimée's hand, place it in the sink, and turn on the hot tap.

"Now, let's cook," I say.

Aimée slinks away (probably for a quick afternoon absinthe), and I hand Nelly an onion, as she's deft with a knife, and Nathan a piece of garlic and a garlic crusher, which he adores as the garlic turns into so many wiggly worms.

I take a pound of Waitrose Native Breed ground beef, slice open the packet, and find myself wrangling with bloody plastic, not for the first time today. Nelly browns the onions, Nathan adds the garlic, and I add the meat as we sing "He's a Funky Kind of Monkey," which they still love even though it's been over a year since we last went to Monkey Music.

I add a generous splash of red wine and grind in some salt and pepper. Nelly tips in bright red dollops of Duchy Originals organic chopped tomatoes. Nathan throws in bay leaves and scatters a handful of dried oregano all over the stovetop like confetti. Cooking done, I kiss each child and thank them, then call Aimée to supervise some craft and coloring activities. Arguments about the red felt-tip begin almost immediately, and I leave Aimée to utilize a little of her international relations degree.

Back in the living room, I try dragging the body but I lose my footing after a few earnest tugs. I turn to Google. I refrain from typing "how to move a corpse" as that's inadvisable when you have an actual corpse in your house. So I type in "ancient stone-moving methods" and become absorbed by the ingenuity of Egyptian engineering. Rolling the body over logs seems plausible, but the ones in the log basket are all cut into angular shapes, and the three-part pulley would work but is beyond my capabilities.

As I'm thinking about this, I remember our gardener's new

wheelbarrow with an enormous orange front wheel in the shape of a ball—not what you see the gardeners use at Polesden Lacey, but Luca is difficult to refuse.

The ball barrow is stable and light. I roll it from the garden shed into the living room, right through the kitchen (no one bats an eyelid), and once in the living room I tip it on its side and roll the body into the center of the barrow. Then I tip the wheelbarrow upright and feel pleased with myself.

I leave him in the living room for later and go back to the kitchen; there I wash my hands, put on a pan of water, admire my children's utter concentration, put the pasta on, and then order Aimée to take the children to wash their faces and hands, while texting Stephen, who should be home by now.

The children troop off with a barrage of complaints, and in the short window before they reappear, I carry the rug to the garage, lean it against the door to save time, and race the wheelbarrow out into the garden and into the garage. I lock the garage door, then hide the key and the spare to avoid Stephen stumbling across the body. I do worry for him since his father passed away, and I don't want to trigger a Hamlet's ghost moment—he's indecisive enough as it is.

I'm feeling super proud of my multitasking when Stephen texts to tell me he won't make it home for dinner with Nathan. He's forgotten about it, of course, but I don't admonish him—minor squabbles can ruin a successful marriage, and I'm actually pleased that he's forsaken his family to focus on becoming a partner. I send back three little words, three hearts, and three kisses. I really am a perfect wife. I go to my to-do list and add four satisfying ticks (of course, all incriminating lists are destroyed once complete).

✓ *Prepare dinner*
✓ *Wash charity shop clothes*
✓ *Secure incriminating knife*
✓ *Wrap corpse and rug and remove to garage*

I can't abide an empty to-do list, so I sit in my study for a moment, and in addition to the standing item (make love), I add four bullet points to my list:

Clean living room
Flatter Stephen's masculinity
Move corpse from garage
Order more Sellotape

11

Fathers

Friday—Evening

Stephen sits opposite me, pushing green beans around his plate under the large brass downlights in our bespoke German kitchen. He hasn't thanked me, even though I've hosted his son's birthday party, cooked two meals, and saved his family from a violent intruder. Par for the course for a busy mum, but thanks is appreciated.

"Do you want to talk? Or we could have an early night," I say, looking over the top of my wineglass.

"I'm not good for anything except sleeping." He gives me the woeful look of a dog sitting outside a shop waiting for its owner.

"You'll soon be claiming you've got a headache."

He sighs demonstrably. Ever since his father died, Stephen's behavior has been depressive and slovenly. *Unacceptable* is another word for it, but I've been cautioned by previous partners against apportioning blame, even when it is entirely someone else's fault.

"I'm ... just not feeling much about anything. We've been through this. I think it's probably depression."

"Well, I'm here for you," I say, and pat his arm. What I really want to say is that I don't feel anything, either, and my father was a brute, but you won't find me moping like a lovestruck teenager. The problem is, Stephen didn't ever tell his father what he really felt about him, and if you don't stand up to your parents, you'll always live in their shadow.

My parents were respectable people, of course. Pillars of the community. But once the door was shut and the curtains were closed, my father was an altogether different man. You could never say he was lazy. He put a lot of effort into creating just the right level of menace and fear. Of course, it's all water under the bridge now. I explained how I felt as clearly as possible just before I turned fourteen and that was that. It's surprising how even the worst of situations can be turned around in a moment.

"I've never missed Nathan's birthday before. I just forgot. Work was crazy," Stephen says, picking up his phone and reading something, which doesn't help to convey particularly strong remorse. I feel my inner ratchet click two teeth tighter.

"Oh, you should've said. I thought it was something selfish and superficial. I mean, Nathan worships the ground you walk on, but if you *forgot* . . ." I grab his phone and slap it down on the table.

"Look, I said I'm sorry." He stares at me, then his phone again. I sense guilt or an out-of-control *Candy Crush* habit.

"Your mum called earlier to speak to Nathan, apparently. She said she'd tried you at work, and they said you'd left."

"What?" he says, his tone a little high, like someone's just stepped on his testicles.

"Where were you?"

"Okay, look, I wasn't working. My bad. I went straight to the gym after work. I should've said. I always go on a Friday. It was just habit."

"Your son sat staring out of the window for two hours, asking if every car was yours."

"I'm a selfish idiot. I'll make it up to him."

"Is this still about your dad?" I ask. He misses his dad, of course, but you have to grieve quickly, or it's bound to depress you. "Or is it your mum? Is she pressuring you to leave me or something?" I put my hand on Stephen's arm. I hope he finds it comforting, because if he looks up he will see my eyes are burning and not with desire.

"She's still grieving."

"Or is she just using the opportunity to get her claws into you again?"

"She's lost her husband, Lalla. They were married for forty-three years."

"I know, and it seems she wants you to take his place."

"Don't be crude, it's not nice. She's just lonely," he says. "And anyway, she likes you."

"Rubbish. She only ever liked Georgie," I say, a reference to his former fiancée, a lithe golden-haired product of Anglo-Saxon breeding and elite girls' schools that Madeleine Rook handpicked as her son's helpmeet since she was the daughter of a baronet, no less.

"I don't want to go there, Lalla." He pulls his arm away, slips his phone into his pocket, then places his hands on his knees to avoid any further sympathetic gestures.

"Me neither, darling, but sometimes you have to put your hand in the water to clean the U-bend. Listening to James Blunt doesn't equal introspection. It's fine to indulge male myths, but let's not confuse them with thought."

"Oh, fuck it," he says and drops his fork. It clatters onto his plate. I am slightly concerned that he might've chipped the china and peer over his hand. Stephen doesn't swear except in the bedroom, so this strikes me as important. I head toward the red wine.

"There's nothing we can't do together, you know that," I say as I pour him a generous glass. He sips his wine and stares into space as I massage his shoulders and take the opportunity to tick off one of my to-dos.

"The gym's working wonders. Your shoulders are so strong," I say, which is entirely untrue—he's been going to the gym for a year and I don't think he's gained an ounce of muscle. "Would you like a rubdown?"

He shrugs my hands away and makes a low growling sound.

"Or a quick blow job instead, if you're too busy?" He doesn't crack a smile. He might be about to tell me that he's dying or that he's scuffed the alloys on his beloved BMW. I simply can't measure the magnitude of the man's misery.

"It's just a work thing. I fucked up on a deal, again. That's why I went to the gym. I know how much you want me to make partner," he says.

"I want it for us, for the children, not for me. I'd be happy living in a hut together, wearing secondhand clothes." He nods. Bless him, simple creature.

"It's just that there's a lot—holidays, mortgage, your clothes, the cars, ballet, piano, Mandarin, the nanny, the cleaner, the gardener... It feels like the more I earn, the less I have. Does that make sense?"

"If you make partner, Stephen, those pressures will evaporate. Your salary doubles and you get a share of the executive bonus. It's just a short-term investment of your time and energy, but the benefits are extraordinary."

He has to understand that his role is to earn money so that we can live in the manner I prefer. In return, he gets to be married to one of the most beautiful and brilliant of wives, who never looks anything but her best while offering scintillating companionship and indulging enthusiastically in his rather workaday lovemaking.

"I always wanted my dad's approval," he says, sipping his wine. "At school, I only got good marks because he would call me his 'smart boy.' And now he's gone, I don't know why I'm doing it. You work your whole life, and then you die. What's the point?"

"The point is progress," I say.

"But where does it end?" he bleats. "Learning to ride a bike, breaking into the first eleven, getting my A levels, running that bloody marathon, degree, MBA, bank. It was always just to gain his approval, and it was never enough."

"Have a drink," I say. I could tell him that Roger only supported our marriage after I discovered his visits to a woman in Baker Street who specialized in "submissive services," but why tell the truth when Stephen prefers his misery serviced with lies?

I pour him another glass of wine in the hope that it will help to relax him, but I'd be lying if I said I wasn't also aware that moving the body from the garage would be a lot easier if Stephen was out for the count.

12

Cul-de-Sac

With the majority of a bottle of wine inside him, Stephen doesn't shrug off my affection as I hug him in the en suite. He's still fully dressed, but I don't want to wait. I let my hands slip under his shirt. Not only do I enjoy the pleasure of physical contact, I gain the additional advantage of mentally ticking off my to-do list.

Without the distraction of romance, married love is simply a rational business choice based on intellectual compatibility, economic benefits, housing prospects, propagation of the species, and reasonably reliable sexual gratification (current period excluded).

I fell for Stephen for the normal reasons—he was attractive, he worked in an investment bank, his parents were wealthy, he had no siblings, and he was keen on marriage. Of course, he was already engaged, but I stepped in with an improved offer. Gazumping happens in marriages as well as in house hunting.

Prior to meeting Stephen, I learned how to behave in his circle by becoming a nanny to a wealthy upper-middle-class family. I used the opportunity to purloin clothes, jewelry, shoes, and handbags—my costume. When I was ready, I road-tested my new self on half a dozen young bankers and found that they rarely saw beyond what they wanted to see, then I went in pursuit of my chosen host.

Within five minutes, we're on the bed (Stephen's sense of propriety moved us out of the bathroom quite quickly) and I'm straddling him, but Stephen's hands are roving without enthusiasm, and circling farther and farther from any recognized erogenous zone, until he's gently stroking my elbow.

"You're drunk," I say with sudden irritation.

"I am," he says. "Can we just . . ."

"No excuses," I say, and with steely determination and some well-chosen words I get him over the finish line. He seems relieved it's over, even though I did 95 percent of the work.

I roll off him, lie on my back, and notice that he's not even taken his shoes off. I think about the dead man's loafers and, for a moment, wonder if I've killed a real estate agent. I mean, Foxtons are forever sending unsolicited letters asking if we want to sell, so it wouldn't surprise me if they were measuring up without our consent.

I look at my husband lying there staring blankly at the ceiling and think back to when this all started. Not long after his father died, despite my being an almost faultless wife, mother, confidante, lover, caregiver, cook, emotional crutch, and career adviser to my beloved spouse, he became withdrawn. He lost his passion for work. He neglected the children. He even lost interest in sex, which is astonishing, given that I have read widely and practiced tirelessly in this area.

I thought that the plan (make Stephen partner, move to Hampstead, have third child, and get children into private school) would provide him with his lost motivation and save our marriage, but almost a year later, I have to admit it, we're failing. Stephen's not made partner. Hampstead is still a pipe dream, Nelly is stubbornly committed to being less bright than she needs to be, and I'm not even pregnant—the simplest of tasks. I've even booked an appointment with a fertility specialist to check all is well.

As I'm lying there, quite depressed about the state of our marriage, I have a moment of inspiration about how to get rid of the body and feel like Sherlock Holmes and Anaïs Nin at the same time. As I head downstairs, I stop to peer in on Nathan and Nelly. The smell of their room captures me for a moment and I stand there looking at them sleeping so peacefully.

I know I'm waiting for the feelings to come. I can stand like this for hours. Sometimes, I almost feel something connect within me, like a small flame igniting, and then it gets lost like a forgotten word. I'm sure I do feel things for them, but it's always in a language I don't understand.

13

Toyota

Friday Night
It's pitch-dark outside, but no ravens are cawing, and the corpse is waiting patiently for me in the wheelbarrow. I pull off the parcel tape and cut and pull back the plastic wrap until I reach the body. I reveal just enough of his torso to push my hand down inside his jacket. It is not easy as he is stone-cold and stiff as a board. I reach his pocket and pull out the car key fob.

Something inside me is whirring with pleasure. There's only so much adrenaline one can squeeze out of not following washing machine instructions. I spend another fifteen minutes wrapping him up again with the last of the tape. It's like having to rewrap Christmas presents because you used the normal wrapping paper instead of the Santa wrapping paper—a thankless task.

I open the garage door and feel the sting of the night air. Our little corner of Muswell Hill is unnaturally quiet. I'm pleased it's cold, as that will slow down decomposition. I put on Stephen's old gardening coat and a muddy pair of wellies and walk up our road, discreetly pressing the button on the key fob every few feet.

Nothing beeps all the way to the bottom of Ennerdale Avenue, so I turn into Muswell Road and then right up Braithwaite Avenue. I stop as a police car turns and cruises slowly toward me. I put my head down and walk purposefully until it passes.

The wind is whispering in the treetops and the clouds are moving fast across the sky. Unwittingly, I find myself at Cait's house. It looks ghostly in the orange streetlights. With no lights on, the windows look like gaping eye sockets and the ivy resembles tears running down its cheeks. I need to make sure we're still on the same page, so I take out my phone and type:

> Thanks a million for today. You're the best. Friends need each other so much, especially women. Please remember 🙈🙈🙈 ... let's talk tomorrow. xxx

No luck all along Keswick Road either. I turn back into Ennerdale Avenue. I know I should try a larger circuit but it's too cold. I head home and click again. Some twenty feet ahead of me, a car flashes its lights and beeps. It's a blue Toyota Corolla hybrid. Not the kind of vehicle I was hoping to use to transport a corpse around London in the dead of night. I was holding out for a G-wagon.

It has a child seat in the back, and all the sticky evidence of a family—wipes, chocolate stains, and lots of sand. I'm no detective but I hypothesize that this man has recently taken his family to the seaside and is too fucking lazy to clean his car. It reminds me how much I detest both the seaside and untidy people.

I pull on a pair of gardening gloves from my coat pocket, open the trunk, and realize that it isn't designed to hold a sizable corpse (not something mentioned in the brochure, I imagine), and no amount of folding will help. I try to create some extra space by taking out the engine oil, a five-quart bottle of windshield washer fluid, a poorly folded picnic rug, and a child's lunch box with an uneaten Twix bar inside. Still too small. I feel hungry, so I admit I eat the Twix, but it doesn't improve matters.

I throw the lunch box, picnic blanket, and oil back in the car and walk home. I decide to take the windshield wash as it's amazing how quickly you get through it in the winter. I realize there's only one option left. I fetch my own key fob, reverse my white Porsche Cayenne up to the garage door, and park it just outside.

All the nearby households seem to be sleeping or watching TV with curtains drawn. A dog walker farther along the street stops at a lamppost as his dog defecates. He glances idly but will forget he's seen me by the time he's put his hand in the green plastic bag to grapple with fresh dog shit.

I create a small ramp using two old pieces of teak shelving that Stephen is saving for some unknown future need and, with a run up, push the wheelbarrow right to the lip of the rear cargo trunk space, then tip with all my might. It works momentarily, but then the corpse falls back into the barrow and I have to start again.

I've packed this car for a two-week holiday in Cornwall before and fitted in a buggy, cot, two suitcases, diapers, and a high chair, so I'm not going to be defeated by six feet of stubborn flesh. I try again by tying the corpse to the tie loops in the trunk and using a spade as a lever.

After a brutal wrestling match, I manage to push him into the trunk. The rigor mortis doesn't make this an easy task, but with nearly twenty-eight cubic feet of trunk space, the Porsche is up to the task. I sprinkle him with some patio cleaner, in the hope that this will help disguise any unpleasant smells, and close the rear tailgate.

14

Hampstead

Saturday, November 16

To-do list:
Morning swim at Heath Pond
Foxtons house viewing, Hampstead
Lunch with Tor
Relocate corpse

Hampstead Village sits on a hill right beside Highgate. It's a mix of cobbled lanes and Georgian town houses right next to the beautiful Hampstead Heath. It's only a few miles from Muswell Hill but a detached family home in Hampstead can go for twenty-five million.

The village is known for its intelligentsia, artists, and celebrities. There are ancient trees, traditional pubs, and an abundance of private schools, including Adams Prep. John Keats died of syphilis and mercury poisoning here. Harry Styles lives here. Muswell Hill, on the other hand, has Tony Hadley (exactly), someone who used to be on *Coronation Street*, and a small private school quite unlike Adams.

The house is an imposing six-bedroom, redbrick Victorian villa set behind electronic gates on a quiet lane just moments from the Heath, and it's on the market for a reasonable £8 million. It has been extensively remodeled, bringing cutting-edge design to Victorian grandeur. There are views of lush greenery and village rooftops from every window and a self-contained apartment for two staff. The large south-facing garden even features a wellness center with sauna, steam room, and pool. One up on Tor, for the moment.

Stephen went into the office first thing, as we agreed some extra hours might help his cause, but he promised that he'd meet me here. I've known this is *my* house ever since I first saw it, almost a year ago, just as I knew Stephen was my husband the moment I found out how rich his father was.

Esmae, our articulate and manicured real estate agent with glistening hair and abundant enthusiasm, arrives on time. I decide to wait for Stephen before going into the house, so Esmae shows me the garden and wellness center. The pool is thirty-nine feet long and has a blue safety cover that Esmae rolls back automatically to reveal an expanse of blue tiles and clear water.

I imagine my daily dip and an hour in the sauna with friends. In my musings, I would have new friends, of course—my Muswell Hill companions wouldn't be quite right for my new life, so they would probably have to go. Perhaps I could keep Sophie, though, to show my new friends that I enjoy helping the less fortunate. The only downside is that Tor would be a near neighbor.

As we're admiring the pool, I have a sudden brainstorm. Since last night the parcel in the back of my Porsche has leaked a dark, foul-smelling liquid. Two dogs were sniffing about the rear tailgate this morning and getting excited. I need to relocate the corpse, and if we have an offer accepted and they stop showing the property, the pool might be the perfect temporary solution as the cover will be closed all winter.

We hear Stephen's car pull up on the gravel drive, and I rush to meet him. I throw my arms around old misery-face, tell him he looks dashing in his V-neck sweater and checked shirt, and suggest that Esmae won't be able to resist his rugged off-duty policeman look. He pulls a face, and when I suggest that we sneak to the pool house for a little extracurricular, he winces.

"We're not in a position to do this, Lalla. You do understand? This can't happen," he says with the shrill urgency of a parakeet.

"I don't agree," I say. "You'll make partner later this month, I just feel it, and it's such good value for money."

"It's eight million quid, that's one point six million per bedroom. In what universe is that good value?"

"Oh, you little pessimist. I know we can do it. I have a really good feeling about it."

"A feeling? Well, in that case..."

I kiss his cheek and say, "Thank you, darling."

He tries to argue with me, but I'm too full of the joy of property. Putting aside the decomposing corpse, Cait's knowledge of the murder, Stephen's depression, and Nelly's disregard for the sanctity of life, I feel certain this will be the thing that changes everything. Pressure cookers must have safety valves, and there's only so much Pilates can do for you.

Perfectly manicured Esmae patters away in a bold yellow suit with large flares and larger lapels. I fear she's watched too much *Selling Sunset*. She's only in her early twenties but could earn fifteen thousand commission on this house alone. No wonder she's glowing.

This is a magical moment for me, the culmination of a serious piece of reconstructive surgery on my life, and testament to holding on to a tiny vision that I've kept locked in my heart (or the space therein) for so long. I've looked at Tor many times over the years and thought, *If someone so limited can achieve this, so can I.*

Stephen's passive-aggressive approach to house hunting is exceedingly tiring, but even his undisguised annoyance can't take away from this moment. He is simply the means, or will be, just as soon as he makes partner.

"What do you think?" I hold on to his arm as we stand in a glorious glass atrium, staring out at manicured lawns and topiarized bay trees.

"Too expensive."

I nudge him and he turns to me, but his face sags with thoughts of bridging loans and mortgage repayments.

"Plenty of wow-wow-wow factor," says Esmae, wafting us into the generous oak-floored drawing room. "There's over four thousand square feet of living space, plus the wellness center. It's a dream home."

I love the sound of my heels on the polished wood, the vast sweep of the bow windows, the voluminous kitchen with two huge walls of glass, the sunken garden, and the view of the Heath. I could hit ten thousand steps just making coffee.

"What are the heating costs like?" asks Stephen. It has only just occurred to me that I married a man who would look at a Titian and ask how much it cost to insure. But Esmae likes him—he's good-looking, and she can just smell money.

"All the windows have been double glazed in thermal glass, and there's a ground-source heat pump, so it's also environmentally sustainable."

"Why don't you show Stephen upstairs?" I say. "I just want a moment to imagine myself in the kitchen."

"Of course, of course," chirps Esmae, then lowers her head to one side, looks up at Stephen, and says without any irony, "Shall we explore the bedrooms, Mr. Rook?"

I know something about human psychology and when a man is with his wife, whom he perceives to be profligate, he will dig in his heels, but alone with a younger woman, who carries none of the complexity of his primary relationship, and who is, into the bargain, flirty, attentive, and attractive, he will want to show off his impressive plumage.

I head toward the kitchen but am drawn to a narrow door on the right. I can't resist the temptation to look and find myself staring down a set of low-lit stone steps. I descend, my hand steadying myself on the bare brick walls.

I feel memories fighting for air as the darkness thickens and sounds deaden. I stand in a grotto with a deep bath in the center. From a cold, dirty cellar to water glistening against a domed mosaic ceiling. I smile at the difference I have made to my life.

Some would imagine romantic candlelit evenings in such a

place, or the more adventurous might even consider an unusual end to a dinner party, but I am thinking of how easy it would be for Madeleine to drown accidentally here. No one would even hear her scream.

I hear Esmae's singsong voice chirping endlessly and feel a little sorry for Stephen. We rejoin in the back garden.

"Do you like it, darling?" I trill like some submissive wife from yesteryear.

"It's an investment really," says Esmae. "Many of my high-net-worth individuals see property as the best way to secure their assets."

"I know how finance works," says Stephen sharply. I realize I misjudged the depth of Esmae's charms.

"Isn't it perfect?" I say.

"As a money pit," says Stephen.

Esmae, detecting tension, subtly moves away from us.

"We'd have to sell first, raise another million in cash, and then borrow a barrow-load. Do you know the monthly repayments on a five-million-pound loan?"

"I'm sure you do, darling, you're so clever with money," I say. "But your bonus will cover it all."

"There's no guarantee I'll make partner."

"I hear you, darling, let's reflect," I say, deciding that discussion is futile at this point and will only further entrench his position. A successful marriage is about many things, not least knowing when to give your husband the impression that he has won.

15

Tor

Tor has a driveway. In Hampstead. We don't have a driveway and still live in Muswell Hill, but there's no point bemoaning life's injustices. Tor is from reasonably old money (textile industry before interfering politicians put an end to low wages and cruelty) and believes that she just barely makes ends meet.

Their Saab Estate is seventeen years old, she wears an ancient Barbour with a tear in the sleeve, and boots with real mud attached, and yet she has four children, three in the most elite private schools, employs four staff, and lives in a six-bedroom mansion on a private road. She would have you believe it's all down to only ever using second-class stamps.

I sit in my car, with a rare five minutes to myself as I'm early and Tor won't answer her door until the exact time that she expects you. The identity of the man in my trunk is playing on my mind. I open the Ring app on my phone and watch the recordings from yesterday. Aimée leaves the house and doesn't shut the door fully. A minute later, the intruder arrives; his face is hidden with a hoodie and face mask. He's clearly been watching the house, so I wonder if he's been doing that for days.

I search through the history but can't find anyone coming to the door, so I change the filter to motion detection, which captures the front path and gate. It takes a few minutes and then I spot him, two days earlier, coming up the path, quickly scanning the door and windows and leaving. I pause on the best image of his face.

As I look at him, I remember where I've seen him before. He was at the school gates. I'm sure of it. You notice unusual people hanging around a primary school and I'd clocked him. He wasn't an opportunist intruder; he was following me. I take a screenshot and head to the house with questions buzzing in my head.

"Hello, Lalla, darling, you look gorgeous! Is that a new dress? Oh, you needn't have dressed up for me," says Tor. She gets in first both with flattery and hints of a social faux pas. Her face is designed to look as if it hasn't been touched by the hands of man although it's had more work than the M1. Her style is wealthy socialite meets ten-year-old girl—neat cardigans, long straight hair, and velvet Alice bands.

"You look relaxed. Switzerland must've been gorgeous," I say. "And the house looks stunning, so it was all worth it."

"Oh, but it's a trial, isn't it?" says Tor, the thought of owning so much weighing heavily on her. "The builders finished the kitchen, which is a blessing, but they're bringing in a hundred tons of concrete for the footings of the pool house on Monday. The neighbors are complaining, but we only want a tiny thing so I can have my daily dip. We're not planning LA pool parties."

"Neighbors," I say. "You can't live with them and you can't bulldoze them."

I spy Lawrence in his study, a toadlike Tory politician of the port-and-gout school. He's wearing half-moon spectacles and hunched over some learned policy, no doubt condemning the poor to further penury for their own benefit.

"So sorry to miss Nathan's birthday," Tor says.

"Not to worry, so did his father. How's Cait getting on?"

"She seems distraught. Aisha dropped her off this morning and explained the whole Owen situation. She also mentioned your marvelous cake!"

"Well, it's good of you to put her up. Her mum's too far from the girls' preschool, and I think Cait is safer here, away from Muswell Hill."

"How dangerous is Owen? I don't want him coming here. I never liked him, even before I found out he was a wife-beater."

"You've always had such good instincts."

"Oh, and Aisha also told me that Sophie's embarking on an affair. I think that's bad form," says Tor.

"I think it's a double bluff," I say. "She adores Paolo. She just wants him to propose."

"Well, she should try drinking a little less. Anyway, come through."

I follow the effortless linen-blend white trousers hanging from her tiny waist as Tor wafts through her marble hallway and into the white kitchen. The ceiling is made almost entirely of glass held up by an ornate metal framework.

"It's like the Royal Opera House," I say, staring at the huge dome.

"Funny you should say that," says Tor, picking a piece of celery from a bowl, turning it in her fingers, then putting it back. "When Neil, the chief architect, was thinking of design cues, he took us to the Floral Hall. That's the feel we wanted." She waves a hand in the air. "It's criminally expensive, but this is where the memories happen."

"That's certainly true for me." I think of Nathan spraying me with pureed carrot and Nelly smearing cat feces on the floor.

"And then, there's this ridiculously large garden to manage!" she says, gesturing beyond the wall of glass.

"So difficult to know what to do with so much land," I say.

Tor narrows her eyes, then heads off to her extravagant coffee machine. We sip carbon-neutral coffee from an approved Rainforest Alliance producer as she narrates her problems with the nanny and housekeeper. Fortunately, there's no need to listen as I can tell the general tone of dissatisfaction and distress from her arm gestures.

"We've been looking at houses nearby," I say.

"In Hampstead? Really?" she says, her expression finely balancing mockery and surprise.

"It's my dream."

"It's everyone's dream, Lalla. But it's not like Muswell Hill. There's not something to fit every budget."

"We've found somewhere, actually. About to make an offer."

"I had no idea. Be a love and pass me the almond milk," she says as a means to move the conversation back to her. She is much nearer to the fridge than I am, so I give her a quizzical look. In response, Tor nods rather quickly to indicate that I need to follow her instruction.

I walk to her double-fronted fridge. It is covered in charts monitoring all kinds of activities, labeled with the kind of names only possible if you know your child will go to the most elite of schools: Ptolemy, Ulysses, and Poseidon (shortened to Toli, Uli, and Psi), and their daughter, Hero. Clearly not Christian in nature, but it does provide Tor with a daily opportunity to explain that she read classics at Oxford and went back to do a summer school in art history. If you ask her where she went to university, she says, without hesitation, "Oxford, twice."

"Are these charts new?" I ask.

"No. I used to keep them in the snug because Law's a bit prudish about bowel movements, but I no longer monitor that now they're all older, so he's happier."

"I didn't know Psi played the harp," I say as I open the fridge and find the almond milk.

"Yes, and they don't even have a school harp, so that cost us five and a half grand," she says. "And we have to transport it too."

I hand her the milk with a poorly executed look of sympathy.

"I'm not going to have milk, actually," she says with a shake of the head. "But thank you."

I put the milk back, admiring Tor's habit of making everyone serve her, even in her own home.

"Is Cait around?" I ask. "It'd be nice to see how she is."

"Oh, she's in the studio."

"In the garden? She's not in the guest room?"

"Well, if Owen does turn up, I don't want him in the house with the children around. It wouldn't be safe," says Tor. "It's cozy enough, and I gave her as many blankets and cushions as I could find."

"Can I see her?" I interrupt, fearing another long tale.

"You do that. I can't visit myself as the planks the builders have left are quite unstable. Wellies outside in the welly hut—help yourself."

16

Accomplice

I find a pair of wellies in a small knee-high shed that looks like an Icelandic troll house. I pull them on and wander up the garden path, through patios and arbors, and across wooden planks that crisscross six long trenches. The studio is usually reserved for relatives that Tor doesn't like and has one double bedroom and a small en suite. It is quite idyllic, sitting alone under the leafless trees.

"Cait, darling, how are you?" I say, pushing the door open.

She is sitting on the edge of a camp bed. She shushes me and points to the red-haired twins, who are fast asleep on the double bed.

I lean down and hug her shoulder, hoping it creates a sense of camaraderie, but she doesn't smile.

"How are you keeping?" I whisper.

"Not so good as you'd expect."

"Do you want to come outside and talk?"

Cait puts on a pair of wellies and follows me to the large bare beech tree.

"Did you get my text last night?" I touch her arm. I'm pulling out all the stops here, but she still pulls away.

"I've been moving. I've not had time to reply."

"You must be exhausted. You had two big shocks yesterday—Owen's texts and then the body. Anyone would feel stressed."

"It's not good," she says firmly.

"Well, positive news first. On the home front, I've cleaned things up and booked the decorators. Second, the man's not even been missed. Nothing at all in the papers."

"An adult wouldn't be counted as a missing person for some time," she says flippantly.

"No, but it does mean no one realizes he's dead, which is good, right?"

"What have you done with him?" Cait chews her nails, which doesn't help her look.

"He's safe and sound in the car. The trunk, I mean." I decide not to tell her that I found out he was following me just yet, as she'd use it as further reason to tell the police.

"In *your* car?" she says with a withering look. "So that's now contaminated too. Well done, you."

"I've been scoping out potential disposal sites."

"So you're really not telling the police?" Her outraged tone is accompanied by a castigating glance.

"It's too late, Cait. I can't report that I killed a man yesterday, wrapped him up in plastic, and stuffed him in my car. It wouldn't help my defense one little bit."

"I didn't sleep a minute last night, Lalla. All I could see was the bloody knife and my hand covered in blood." Cait looks down at her hands, but they're perfectly clean now, so I'm not sure what all the fuss is about.

"Just put it out of your mind. I'll look after everything. You know I've always looked out for you, right?"

"Right," she says, slightly reluctantly, which is quite rich, given the selfless support I lavished on her during the Owen drama. If it wasn't for me, she'd still be his punching bag. And she's not an easy person to help, I can tell you that quite honestly.

"It's all in the past now," I try, reassuring her. "We just need to bury him somewhere and it'll all be forgotten."

Cait shakes her head. "You can't just sweep a dead body under the carpet. They'll find out eventually, they always do."

"Well then, what's your suggestion?" I say with a glib smile that is not at all well received.

"To tell the truth, I don't know," says Cait, quite forgetting that she hid her own *truth* for several years. One rule for her, and a completely different one for everyone else.

"You want me to call the police?" I say firmly, and take out my phone.

"It's for the best. Just explain to them that you were scared."

"Of course, and the important thing is, it's the right thing to do, never mind where it will lead," I say, and dial 999. I look at Cait as I listen to the ringtone. "Just so you know, you need to get your story straight. The police will want to question you."

"Question me?"

"Police, please," I say into the phone.

"Why me?" Cait repeats, her voice rising.

"Your fingerprints are all over the body and the knife, for one, and your clothes are contaminated with his blood. You'll need to explain that."

"I fell. You saw me! And it was you who made me hold the knife," she says.

"Yes, exactly. You be sure to tell them that. Let's just hope they'll believe you."

"Why wouldn't they?" Her eyes were now watering in distress.

"Sorry? Yes, police, please," I say into the phone, then turn back to Cait. "They're just connecting me. I'm just being careful. I want to make sure you're not arrested."

"Arrested?"

"I'm sure they won't, but it's already been twenty-four hours. They'll want to know why on earth *you* didn't tell the police."

"You told me not to."

"I know that. But it's hardly going to stand up in court, is it? 'My friend told me to keep my mouth shut, Your Honor!'"

"Yes, hello. I'd like to report an incident. Well, an accident really," I say into the phone.

"Stop," Cait whispers harshly.

"Please, could you hold for a moment, thank you," I say.

"They record these calls," she whispers urgently, pointing at the phone.

"What?" I say loudly. "Caitlin, you'll have to speak up."

She rushes up to me, grabs the phone, and disconnects.

"You told them my name! They can trace phones, you know, and now they've got all that information recorded!"

"I thought you wanted me to report it," I say, my face a picture of innocence.

"They'll think I did it!" Cait says, walking in a circle, her head bowed.

"I'll phone back and explain. I'll say that you didn't actually kill the man, you were only an accomplice."

"Lalla!" she half screams, holding on to a tree trunk for support. "I wasn't an accomplice!"

"Well, whatever you call someone who helps a murderer and obstructs justice . . . I thought it was called an accomplice."

"I didn't help you," she says.

"Oh, you're being modest, of course you helped. You were hugely reassuring, and you pulled out the murder weapon. You even discussed getting rid of the corpse in Wood Green and, most helpful of all, you kept this crime from the authorities."

"That's not how it was at all!" she says, grabbing at me with both hands.

"Don't panic, Cait," I say, and rub her back. "I know you're innocent, but you know how the police are. They want everything to fit into place. The worst-case scenario is that they see you as an accessory after the fact."

"But I didn't kill anyone!" she shouts, then glances at the studio and stops herself.

"No one thinks you did. I'm just trying to protect you. Now, I'm all for getting this out in the open, but I'm scared for you and the twins."

"What have the twins got to do with it?" says Cait, rising toward me, her expression taut and knotted.

"We don't want to do anything that might risk custody. Would Owen get them if you weren't deemed a fit mother?"

"Oh god," she says, her body shrinking.

"Look, I'm so grateful you didn't tell anyone," I say. "I bought you a Terry's Chocolate Orange as a thank-you. It's in the car. I want to avoid any possibility of an experienced detective thinking you're up to your eyeballs in this."

"All I did was look in through the window," she says, sobbing. "I thought you'd killed Stephen."

"Of course you did," I say, and hold her hands. And then a thought occurs and Cait sees me frown.

"What is it?"

"It's just the door camera," I say. "They'll see you running from the house with blood all over your coat."

"Oh god . . ." she whimpers, and throws her hands to her face.

"But if we don't tell . . ." I prize her hands down. "No one knows anything. The girls are safe. It's our little secret."

My phone rings, which startles Cait. It's a withheld number, but I answer anyway.

"Hello," I say.

"This is the Metropolitan Police. We just received a call from this number and wanted to check that everything's all right."

I look across to Cait.

"*Is* everything all right?" I ask.

17

Concrete

Sunday, November 17

The rain has thankfully held off and I'm standing by my car outside a depressingly cheerful superstore with a shopping cart full of bunting, paper plates, cups, and wooden cutlery for the school's winter fair—the PTA have ordered enough to run a small café for a year.

I'm not doing it out of kindness—it's on my to-do list, under "being a good person," which is the section including motherhood that involves doing unpaid tasks and receiving absolutely no thanks at all.

On the press of a button my car tailgate opens theatrically, and I look in at the large parcel wrapped in plastic. I gag as a little aroma of fermenting flesh has leaked out. I scatter the body with the air fresheners I've just bought, and the car fills with the smell of a beautiful Norwegian pine forest.

I look up at the large building site between Pets at Home and DFS. No doubt it will soon become another homage to the astonishing beauty of British warehouse architecture. The compound is dusty gray and surrounded by wire fencing. It's possibly because I find paper-plate shopping so dull, or it might be Stephen's lack of connubial reciprocity, that my attention is drawn by the sight of several weathered builders parading their unreconstructed masculinity in front of me and wearing their high-visibility vests and hard hats rather provocatively.

I pile the shopping bags into the back seats, then put my handbag and coat on the front seat. I release two buttons of my silk blouse, ruffle my hair, check my makeup in the door mirror, and walk to the site entrance, where a blond with alluring stubble and ample chest hair is twisting a pencil suggestively between his lips.

"I wonder if I might take a look around your compound," I say with a coy smile.

"It's a restricted site, love; you can't come in here without a hard hat," he says, playing hard to get by pointing to a large red-and-black safety poster.

"Well, flouting the rules can sometimes be fun." I lightly touch his hairy forearm.

"There's nothing fun about being clouted with a scaffolding pole," he insists, and he then lifts his hard hat to reveal a sexy scar across his forehead.

"I'm asking if you'd like to . . . Oh, never mind," I say. A man who can't excite my mind isn't going to satisfy my body. I glance beyond him at another tantalizingly tattooed specimen shoveling concrete from a long metal chute into a wide trench. My mind goes to places that it really shouldn't and I scold myself, but I tingle all over as the huge tube shudders and suddenly erupts with thick gray sludge.

I think it's the first time I've been turned on by a cement mixer. I really do need to convince Stephen to take his marital responsibilities more seriously, and then, just as it happened in bed, my sexual frustration leads to a moment of inspiration.

"How long does concrete take to set?" I ask the foreman.

"It can take a month until it's fully set," he says, almost proudly.

"And how long does it stay malleable for?"

"A few hours at most. A bit longer if it's cold."

"Thank you, that's helpful," I say as I spot a security guard looking at my car for some reason. I worry that he's been attracted by the heady scent of pine needles and putrefaction.

I hurry back and explain to the middle-aged man in uniform that I'm just leaving. He tells me that I'm parking in a mother-and-child space and asks for evidence of a child. I tell him that I can show him stitch marks if he's interested.

He says that these bays are reserved for parents with children present. I tell him that if he's suggesting that I'm trying to defraud Tesco by parking in the wrong bay, then he has a dim view of my criminal capability.

He asks if I'm threatening him. I tell him that if I were threatening him he would know about it. He tells me that he's going to report this as verbal abuse. I ask him if he'd like me to make that physical abuse. He asks for my name and address. I decline and ask for his name and address so that we can continue this argument at a time that is inconvenient to him as well as me.

I feel the urgent need to get in my car and test its pedestrian safety rating on his legs. Fortunately for all, at that moment an abandoned cart starts rolling dangerously toward a car. He runs off, heroically preventing minor paint damage to an old Volvo. Random murder avoided, we part on good terms.

In the car, I run things through my mind briefly, then call Cait.

"Hello," she says, her voice decidedly unfriendly, but that's really to be expected.

"You've not been responding to my texts, Cait, are you okay?" I ask, keeping things chirpy.

"I'm having panic attacks," she says, with a shrill little emphasis on the word *panic*, as if it needed to be acted out, which it didn't. I'm actually good with language.

"Well, until Owen's arrested, I'm sure you'll feel a certain degree of anxiety."

"About the dead body, Lalla," she says loudly.

"Well, don't shout about it; it's quite triggering for me too."

"Really? It doesn't seem so," she says.

"Look, you're the expert, Cait, and I need your help. Can't you turn your forensic eye on this case positively? I've found a picture of him from the door camera. I wonder if you could do an image search online. I've just texted you a screenshot."

"And created indelible digital evidence of a murder victim on both our phones. Well done."

"Manslaughter. Anyway, I think he might've been following me," I say. "I found an image of him scoping out the house two days before he broke in. And then I remembered seeing him at the school gate."

"I can see the image now," she says. "He's too far away. I don't think that would lead to anything online."

"Worth a try? I want to know who he is and why he was following me."

"He was probably just scoping out your house. It's what thieves do," says Cait, a little disdainful.

"Then why was he at the school, Cait? What if there's more to this?"

"You could be mistaken. Or maybe that's how he finds his marks. I'll look online for missing person reports."

"Thank you," I say. "Oh, while you're on the phone, Tor said she's having concrete delivered tomorrow. Can you find out what time the builders are arriving?"

"How would I do that?"

"Just check Tor's schedule. It's in the kitchen. She's got things mapped out second by second. We're thinking of having some work done. I just wanted to catch them."

"Right," says Cait suspiciously. I hear the creak of the door opening in the background, then silence. Eventually, Cait comes back on the line, panting.

"It's being delivered tomorrow. Three p.m. to four p.m. And I know what you're thinking," she says in an accusing tone. "Concrete, dead body... I'm not a fool. And no, you can't bury him under Tor's new pool house."

"Well, where else? I've got to get rid of the body. There's nowhere safer. It's your DNA I'm burying as well as mine, Cait."

"What about Tor?" she says after a good thirty seconds.

"Leave Tor to me. I'll get her out of the house. Tell her I've found a copy of the Adams Maths entrance paper. I drive round at about four p.m., we carry the body to the garden under the cover of darkness, and plop, it's done. No mess, no trace. No more panic attacks."

"This is so wrong!"

"Life happens, Cait. Burglars steal. Husbands abuse. It's time to even the score. So be a fucking woman for once in your life and bury a fucking body, won't you?"

18

Letter

Having failed to get pregnant over the past year, I booked Stephen in for a physical with a private health center to check everything was in working order. He was deemed healthy with a strong sperm count. I repeat this to him often, in the hope that he will feel more manly.

The doctor suggested a medical intervention, but Stephen doesn't believe in chemically induced arousal, so Viagra was off the table. I tried it anyway, by putting some in his muesli. He returned from work highly embarrassed, having been unable to rise from his chair at the end of a meeting. I had no idea it worked so quickly, and that while it produces a physical effect, it doesn't create the desire to go with it. What's the point of keeping the light on if no one's at home?

Running out of options, I just thought: Why not try nature's own Viagra? So I hired Aimée, a twenty-four-year-old Frenchwoman, as our nanny. I didn't choose her for her personal charm, her ability to cook, or her nurturing nature—she has none of these—but because she is stunningly pretty and very much Stephen's type.

I hoped that the sight of a nubile young woman around the place would get his juices flowing and his testosterone levels would revive. But if it worked they've not been flowing in my direction and I haven't seen him even glance in hers.

This evening, after Aimée has put the children to bed and

grunted at me, Stephen is sitting in the kitchen and I'm feeding the dishwater its daily diet of plates and cutlery.

"Police were around today," he says casually. "When you were out shopping."

I scrape congealed carbonara into the organic waste bin and hold myself still for a moment. "The police?"

"Yeah."

He says no more. I wonder if that's because it's of no interest or if he's gauging my response. I rinse the creamy remains from the plate and put it in the rack.

"What did they want?"

"They're doing a house-to-house. Missing person."

"Anyone we might know?" I turn, but he's scrolling through his phone.

"A man. They showed me a photo. Not anyone I've ever seen."

"Did they say who he was?" I ask.

"Jason Mercer," he says.

"What did he look like?"

"Midforties, close-cut brown hair, mean-looking, green eyes. Said he was about six foot two."

"Could describe a million people," I say, although it's an accurate description of the man I last saw staring up at me through thick plastic. My heart jumps and my skin tingles. "Why are they searching for him? Is he dangerous?"

"They said not to approach him. He's on the run for something and was last seen in this area."

I feel my mouth go dry, but my head is both relieved and concerned. He might be a criminal, which explains the break-in, but it's not great to hear the police are already out searching for him and have Muswell Hill as his last known location. I want to ask more, but Stephen turns to me, pulls an envelope from his jacket pocket, and says, "There's something else."

"What?" I ask.

"This was posted through the door today," he says. "Addressed to me."

"On a Sunday?"

"Hand-delivered," he says, staring at my face now.

"What is it?" I say.

"You'd better read it," he says.

With my pulse still racing from the revelation about Jason Mercer, I take the envelope. It is one of those you buy in packs of thirty from WH Smith's and it's warm from its proximity to Stephen's armpit. I pull out a piece of ruled A4 paper and read eight short words:

Your wife isn't who she says she is.

"Came about an hour after the police were here."

"You don't know who it's from?" I ask.

"No idea."

"She didn't sign it, then?" I say.

"Who?"

"Your mother. There's only one person I know who'd stoop so low as to try to drive a wedge between us."

"That's absurd. My mother wouldn't do a thing like that. What does it mean, anyway?"

"Oh, don't be so naive. She's always questioning my background, isn't she?"

"That's only because you never share anything about yourself."

"It doesn't matter what I share; in her eyes, I'll never be good enough for her little boy."

"She's not going to send anonymous letters, Lalla. Anyway, she wouldn't know what to do with a ballpoint pen."

"That's a fair point," I say, looking at the scrappy note. "But who else would do such an unpleasant thing?"

"Sounds like a threat, doesn't it?" he says. "Whoever sent this thinks they know something about you that I don't. What might that be, Lalla?"

"Well, darling, if I was having an affair, which I'm not, I'd have good grounds, wouldn't I?"

"And what does that mean?"

"You barely touch me anymore, unless you're drunk."

He looks at me guiltily, then looks down at his phone. "I'm under a lot of pressure."

"I know," I say, and fill his wineglass. "When you make partner and we're in our new home, you'll feel so different."

"Not this again, please," he says. I put my hand on his leg. He stares at it like it's unprofessional conduct. I don't know quite why, given he's being such a shit, but I want him now.

"Let's make love," I suggest, as it's not escaped my notice that I'm at my most fertile this week.

"What for?"

"Do I need to spell it out?" I say.

"Let me do it for you," he says. "N. O."

To-do list:
Go for long run
Prepare for Adams activity day
Lunchtime Pilates with Sophie
Research Jason Mercer
Bury body

19

Burial

Monday, November 18

I arrive at Tor's in the Porsche as it's getting dark. Given the increased stakes, I've bought burner phones for me and Cait. I call Cait, hoping she's not heard about the police search, as she'd freak out. I've done an online search for Mercer but there's about a million results, and I couldn't find a picture matching him anywhere.

"Hi, I'm at the front. Just saw the concrete truck leave. Anyone else around?"

"Not as far as I know," she says. "Not done this kind of thing before."

"No, me neither," I say.

"True, but I've also not killed a man. You did."

"Let's not split hairs—we're both involved now, so can you please stay calm," I say.

"If you stop trying to make me bury someone, I could," she says.

"I'm doing this for both of us. To keep you and your girls safe."

"You're just covering your own bottom," she says.

"I've texted you something," I say. "You may find images easier to understand." 😷 🔪 🐾 🧬 🍃 💀 🙈 ❤️

There is a long pause, after which Cait says, "I don't know what the paw prints mean."

"I couldn't find a fingerprint emoji," I say.

"Where is the knife, by the way?"

"It's with the body," I say, lying through my teeth, as I've kept the knife hidden in the car, should I need it. "So we're actually burying evidence of your involvement, thank you very much. Now, come around and help me," I say, and end the call.

I get the car into position and Cait appears with the wheelbarrow. I see that she is wearing a large white T-shirt with the words *Not an Accomplice* hand-painted across the front.

"You'll be a victim all your life, Cait, unless, at some point, you acknowledge that you're here by choice," I say as I open the hatch and start dragging the corpse out of the cargo space.

"This isn't my choice," she says, watching as I groan with effort.

"Oh, Cait. You're free. Everything is a choice."

"Ha! As long as you're not being blackmailed."

"Please, can you pull!" I instruct.

She grabs the body with some determination and yanks it powerfully. The corpse shifts. His buttocks cross the lip of the back end and drop into the wheelbarrow.

"Well done, you!" I say. We drag the rest of the body out of the car in silence and then stop to stare at the long cylindrical object wrapped in thick plastic and sealed with masking tape and Christmas-themed Sellotape.

"Do you think I chose to be Owen's victim too?"

"No. And I didn't choose to be burgled, but we do choose how we respond. And it's time to say fuck all of them."

"Fuck them all," she says as we grip the wheelbarrow handles and lift. It's surprisingly easy with the two of us.

"Cait," I say, and look up suddenly.

"What is it?" Cait says fearfully.

"Isn't Hampstead beautifully quiet?" I say. "Muswell Hill always has a background buzz of traffic, but here, you could imagine you were in the countryside."

Cait has nothing to add to this observation. I ask her to push the wheelbarrow up the passage on the side of the house as I need to put on plastic booties to protect my shoes. She gives me a disapproving look.

In the dark of the side passage, the front wheel hits an abandoned brick and the load nearly topples over. Fortunately, the security lights come on as we get to the back garden, so even though Cait has to wheel the body across a thin scaffolding plank, there are no further mishaps.

I inspect the different footings, trying to discern the order they were filled in, but they all look exactly the same. I find a stick and poke each of the footings in turn. The trench nearest the house is freshest.

"We'll put him in here," I say.

Cait, always one to put problems above solutions, says, "But that means reversing backward."

"That's a tautology," I point out. "We're rather pushed for time, so saying things twice is a little unhelpful."

She bites her lip and, if I'm not mistaken, raises her eyebrows to the CCTV camera as if she's on *Candid Camera* and wants an imaginary audience to side with her. I make a mental note to keep out of camera shot and delete any incriminating footage as soon as we're through.

Cait's making rather heavy weather of reversing the wheelbarrow across a narrow plank. She ignores my advice to keep her eye on the body rather than look behind her, and she shrieks as the wheelbarrow tips to the right and the body rolls lethargically into the concrete.

We stare down as the head dips beneath the gray sludge, while the legs stick on the plank.

"Well," I say. "He seems content to go here."

Cait gets down on her knees and tentatively attempts to roll the rest of the body into the footing.

"Use your legs," I suggest.

She doesn't seem pleased with being told how to push a dead body into a puddle of concrete, but she follows my advice and his legs roll in. Cait stands and I take her arm.

"Bravo, you've buried your first body."

Cait can't help smiling.

"Do you want the chocolate orange now?" I say. "You've earned it."

20

Uniform

Tuesday, November 19
The following day, I see Aimée committing another heinous crime. Her task, which was repeated twice, was to have Nelly in her school uniform with her neat brown bob combed to perfection. The child who appears in front of me is wearing a blue party dress with bright red patent leather sandals. Her hair is tied with a ribbon on the side. I have no idea where the sandals have come from, but I suspect the Wicked Witch of the West.

Nelly is absolutely beaming. She is happiest when dressed as something she's not. Between the ages of two and four, she refused to wear anything but a succession of historical and fancy dress costumes—shiny polyester princess dresses, a Victorian orphan brown smock with a white apron, and a full Mary Poppins ensemble.

"She looks so sophisticated," says Aimée, looking admiringly at her work and smiling not out of pride but because she knows how much this outfit will annoy me.

"For a Moulin Rouge trainee, not a girl going for a prep school activity day."

"I don't believe in uniforms for children. This looks better."

"Nelly, go and change. School uniform, black shoes," I say, raising both eyebrows.

Nelly's beaming smile becomes a fierce pinched pout, and her eyes blaze at me. She keeps her anger wrapped up tight and will hold it, sometimes for months at a time. She stomps across the wooden floor as loudly as possible and turns at the threshold.

"You're the most horrible mother in the whole world," she declares primly, then slams the door.

This makes Aimée's smile widen.

"I expect in France, being pretty is a vocation in itself, but it isn't a career option here."

"Maybe that is why everyone in the UK looks so dreary," says Aimée, and she leaves. Nathan, who is sitting on the floor with several dinosaurs, looks up and wiggles his *Tyrannosaurus rex* toward the door with a loud roar.

"Quite right," I say.

Gaining entry to Adams is harder than being made partner. Today is euphemistically called an "activity day," ostensibly to make your child feel at home before they return for the dreaded entrance exams, but it's clearly a carefully disguised social suitability test. Although mimicry along with a good wardrobe disguises many things, you can't imitate the depth of privilege that some, like Tor and her kind, possess, which is only detectable beyond the visible spectrum.

Nelly reappears in a new outfit and stares at me with a broad delighted smile.

"It's school uniform," she says, daring me to argue.

"Yes, but it's Hermione Granger's school uniform," I reply, and march Nelly to the bedroom as she explains how Aimée is better than me in every respect. We return downstairs, Nelly in shirt, tie, and blazer, and me covered in her barbs.

I worry, of course, that wearing her current school uniform may look too earnest and that the more privileged families will allow their daughters to wear anything at all.

I text Tor:

What's Hero wearing to Activity Day? Nelly moaning about wearing uniform.

Adams is one of the top prep schools in London. The children all have their own named wellies, and they have over a hundred clubs to choose from each week. The headmistress creates the grand illusion that she knows every child and makes each parent feel that their little one is truly special. It's like Claridge's for small people.

Tor texts back:

Uniform is absolutely perfect.

"Nelly," I call out. "Wear what you like." I know not to trust Tor's advice. She's a friend, but Adams is a competitive process, and every tiny advantage matters. I haven't even considered my own outfit, so I text Sophie as Ellie (brains of Britain) is going for a scholarship:

What are you wearing to the ball, darling? Chanel or Dior? x

Sophie replies:

It's a means-tested scholarship so I'm going for the workhouse look—gingham dress, apron, shawl, and bonnet. xxx

On my to-do list I note that I should ask about Paolo:

How was the date?

Sophie replies:

Good and bad ...

I text back:

Can't wait to hear all about it! xxx

I'm sure I could say more, but I decide I've done enough to tick it off my list.

There are four Mercedes SUVs, a Porsche Panamera, three BMWs, and a generous helping of Range Rovers corralling the prep school.

They're trying to park but there is no parking to be had. Like cornered beasts, they're agitated; their red lights are glowing and their horns are beeping frantically. Inside the air-conditioned, leather-seated cockpits, the glossy-haired owners glitter with gold as they gesticulate at each other over a spot of grass verge.

I tend not to get anxious and spot a parking space quite easily. Admittedly, it's not a legal space and belongs to the owners of a rather handsome house, but I don't mind being someone else's headache. If it ends in an argument, I will win, and if there is a parking fine, what's a few pounds when you are about to commit over twenty thousand per year to support a six-year-old's hand-painting, ukulele, and social-climbing lessons?

Before I can reverse into the space, a large red Jaguar SUV appears from nowhere and sneaks in behind me. I grip the steering wheel. Rage trickles down my spine.

I stare at the woman and she pulls a face back at me. I can't read the expression but it looks tigerish—black slashes of mascara, gold necklace, and bright white teeth. These entitled women see fault as something belonging to the rest of the world, not themselves. She doesn't back down and parks impressively in a single speedy motion. She leaps out of the driver's seat (skinny jeans, short leather jacket, spiked heels, large handbag clinking at her elbow), skips to the rear doors, and extracts her pristine daughter.

They stride off together, noses held high, her daughter in a cream wool beret and matching woolen coat. The beret is a magnificent touch and I'm sad I didn't think of it. I look down and see that my knuckles are white against the steering wheel.

I watch them cross the road, one hand raised commandingly to stop the traffic, then I reverse up to the side of the Jaguar and wind down my window. I find my nail scissors in my handbag, and drive past her SUV, slowly digging the steel tip into the paintwork. It makes a delicious screeching sound and leaves a deep white line in the shining paint.

I pull away, quite pleased with myself, but a few moments later I feel like I've let myself down and experience an overriding sense of regret. I reverse, open my car door, lean out of my seat, and push the blade deep into her front tire. I pull it out, watch the tire quickly deflate, and leave satisfied.

I join the other frantic mothers in a circus ring of circling SUVs. As time is tight, I mount a high curb and drive onto the grass between two trees. The space isn't large enough for a car, but one of the trees is a sapling, no more than five feet high, and I simply drive over it. I'm sure it'll spring back up when I drive off.

21

Adams

Nelly will not move from the car. Both praise and threat fail, so I take out my purse and show her a ten-pound note. She unsnaps her seat belt immediately and gets out. All the other mothers are walking hand in hand with their darling daughters. Nelly prefers single file with a four-feet distance between us.

We are overtaken by a tall blond in a Chanel suit with a ponytailed, blue-eyed girl in either hand, looking like an advert for an Aryan eugenics program.

"Excuse me!" she says dramatically, barging against my shoulder as she tries to avoid the muddy verge.

"We're all heading in the same direction." I smile as broadly as possible and barge back. She stumbles and her right foot lands in a puddle. It is a good thing to be polite but you can't be a pushover. How would you sleep at night?

We arrive at the gate and are greeted by a round-faced woman with an enormous smile, dressed in what I imagine M&S might describe as "modern elegance." It's neither of those things, being of no discernible color or shape. I smile beneficently at her and hope it helps.

I begin to wonder if this is going to be so difficult. I've chosen a velvet-trimmed Fendi blazer, which is a bit showier than some of the mothers, but who wouldn't go the extra mile for their little one?

"Welcome to Adams. And may I ask your name?" says the woman, leaning down toward Nelly.

"Her name's Nelly."

"What a lovely name, and how are you today, Nelly?" she says, bending down and offering her hand. I could have warned her if she'd asked. Nelly doesn't touch people.

My daughter cradles her terrifying doll, since she point-blank refuses to leave home without it, and stares at the hand fiercely until it is removed with slight embarrassment. I nudge her with my knee-length boots. She kicks me back.

I imagine a clip around the ear would be frowned upon in these surroundings, so I smile and say, "She's so excited about Adams. Such a bundle of nerves. Didn't sleep a wink."

"Did," says Nelly.

"It's going to be just fine," says the woman. "We've got games and painting. Do you like painting?"

"No," says Nelly.

"She does," I say, and with a firm hand on her back, I guide her quickly through the gate.

We're greeted a second time by two girls looking resplendent in perfect uniforms on the pillared portico, standing beside a glossy black door that's shining so much it appears white in the sunshine.

"Good morning and welcome to Adams. My name is Elspeth, I'm the head girl," says the first prefect, holding out her hand to shake mine. "I do so hope you enjoy your visit."

"And I'm Luciana, the deputy head girl. The headmistress will be so delighted to meet you."

They bristle with pride as we walk past their badge-laden lapels into the gleaming marble lobby.

"Stop growling," I say under my breath.

"Don't like them," she replies loudly.

"Well, I want the best for you, Nelly, so please smile. There's another ten pounds for you if you behave."

The headmistress is at the far end of a long corridor, designed to instill fear, as you have at least twenty steps to make under her watchful gaze. I enjoy a game of chicken, so I make eye contact and don't break it. By the time we meet, I haven't blinked and she's only slightly tilted her head. An unusual act of bravery.

"Welcome to Adams. I'm Mrs. Pembury."

"Lalla Rook," I say, shaking her hand firmly. Mrs. Pembury smiles at me and grips even harder. "And this is Nelly. She's so excited to meet you."

"Hello," says the headmistress. "What an interesting outfit."

I look around. Every other girl is in their uniform. I have been double-bluffed by Tor. I curse myself for underestimating her guile.

"So pleased to make your acquaintance," says Nelly. As soon as she says it, she tries to open my handbag for her payment.

"*Magna est veritas et prævalet*," says the headmistress. "That's our school motto. Now, can you tell me what it means?"

I look hopefully at Nelly, who's been studying Latin each Saturday for two years because her primary school doesn't offer classics.

"If you're the headmistress, and you don't know, I'm certainly not going to tell you," says Nelly.

The headmistress touches a pearl earring. "Is that a reference to Pippi Longstocking, by any chance?"

"I do apologize. She's such a big reader." I have a sudden vision of Nelly throwing the headmistress onto the school roof.

"No need to apologize," says Mrs. Pembury. "Some children do find it difficult to be polite. Have a lovely day."

I hurry Nelly through to the reception room before she can argue. She's immediately engulfed by a cascade of attentive girls and washed downstream, where she's seated at a little table.

The child in the cream beret is sitting calmly at her activity desk, engaging in her "creative" task, which is to sculpt something out of Play-Doh. She's created a rather impressive pink dolphin.

Nelly is given a ball of soft blue clay and asked to make whatever she wants. That's an error. She flattens the Play-Doh with her fist and shapes what's beginning to look like a dog turd.

While no one is looking, I approach Nelly's desk and pick up her Play-Doh. She snaps, but I'm too quick. I walk up to the girl with the dolphin and with feigned interest ask if I can look at her sculpture. She hands it to me proudly.

"It is a good effort but probably only a B grade, sadly," I say. Her face crumples into an expression I recognize as the precursor of tears. "Crying is minus one grade, so why don't you try to do another one instead. An elephant might get you an A."

I take the dolphin and replace it with Nelly's bright blue turd. The girl looks crestfallen for a moment until a steely determination returns to her eye and she starts to mold an elephant. I return to Nelly and place the pink dolphin on her desk.

"Now, don't you touch it, or you'll be sent to a school for disturbed youths."

As I leave, I hear a teacher lavishing praise on Nelly's dolphin. Much deserved, I think, as she resisted the desire to destroy it. I leave the room feeling extraordinarily proud.

22

Police

Wednesday, November 20

The doorbell rings in every corner of the house. Stephen has anxiety about missing parcels and has plugged in Ring extensions everywhere. I'm with Nathan in the kitchen, teaching him basic baking skills, but he's yet to understand the important of neatness. Whenever I tell him off, however, he hugs me because he thinks I'm sad. I sometimes find myself telling him off just to get him to throw his arms around my neck.

I pop into the downstairs loo on the way to the door and straighten my hair. I expect to see a harried delivery guy annoyed because I've made him thirty seconds late. Stephen continues to buy unnecessary items from Amazon. The last thing was a tactical torch with ten thousand lumens of light, which I can say with confidence he will never use.

It isn't Amazon.

"Good afternoon, madam. I'm Detective Sergeant Birch and this is Detective Constable Mattoo."

"Oh god, what's she done now?" I say instinctively, staring at the two plainclothes police officers holding out their badges for inspection, although the name Jason Mercer jumps to the front of my mind.

"Who?"

"My daughter. I thought she might have run away from school again."

"This isn't about your daughter," says DS Birch, an athletic woman of indeterminate age with bleach-blond hair. "Are you Mrs. Lalla Rook?"

"Yes, how can I help?" I say.

"May we come in?" she says assertively. "We need to speak to you about a missing person case."

"If you must," I say, but my mind is trying to work out why they're back here. Do they want to ask every adult directly about Mercer or is it something else? If Cait has broken down and blabbed, I have little sympathy for any repercussions that may occur in a moment of blind rage. It's unfortunate because I've yet to find someone to sand the floors, and although I've done a deep clean, they only need one tiny speck of blood these days.

I lead them into the living room and they sit on the sofa, their feet on a new Persian rug, which Liberty delivered only yesterday. I angle myself toward the detective sergeant and ignore her gangly assistant, who seems to have no purpose whatsoever.

"Now, what's this about?" I say and tilt my head to one side. "I'm in the middle of making cupcakes for the school charity bake." This is a lie, but I want to inject pace into the proceedings.

"What's the smell in here?" says DC Mattoo, sniffing quite rudely.

"It's paint," I say, with as kind an expression as I can muster.

"Doesn't smell like paint," he says, doubling down.

"Well, it's not Dulux, if that's what you mean. It's nontoxic—made from antique horse dung and the ground-up bones of Victorian philanthropists."

"Posh paint," says the woman dryly. "Mrs. Rook, we're making inquiries about a missing person, you may have heard. His name's Jason Mercer."

"Yes, my husband spoke to the police, but what does this have to do with me?" I say, scanning their faces and finding nothing revealing.

"Did you have any visitors here on the morning of the fifteenth of November?"

"Yes," I say bluntly. "All of Nathan's friends, average age four, and my friends Sophie, Aisha, and Cait."

She looks at me, unblinking, possibly waiting for me to add another name. If so, she will be waiting a long time.

"Did Jason Mercer visit you on that day?" says the detective sergeant, finally.

"Why would he? I don't know who he is," I say, watching the woman's face, which expresses disdain and suspicion at once.

While I enjoy the feeling of risk, I do recognize the jeopardy of this situation. If Detective Sergeant Birch were to glance to her right, she might notice a tiny drop of blood on the velvet cushion. If she moved the new rug with her foot, she might notice a faint pink blush where blood seeped into the wood.

"Perhaps this picture might help jog your memory. He might've called on another day or used another name. Any information would be helpful." DS Birch hands me a photograph of the man I stabbed to death, wrapped in trampoline packaging, and buried in my friend's concrete footings. I decide not to mention this.

I shake my head, squint as people do in films, hold for a moment, as if I'm searching my memory bank, then shake more emphatically. I've always enjoyed pretending more than expressing what I feel and am happy with my performance.

"No, I've never seen him before in my life. Can I ask why you think he would visit me?"

"We have information that suggests he was here on the fifteenth of November."

"What information?" I say, trying to prevent my hands forming a fist as I seethe at Cait's deviousness. Is anyone honest anymore?

"We're not able to reveal the source at the current time," says Birch.

"An anonymous source," says DC Mattoo helpfully. DS Birch gives him a withering glance.

"Well, your informant is wrong," I say. Anonymous source! I can't believe Cait's gall. "Look, is this man dangerous, is that what this is about?"

"Jason Mercer is a police officer," says Birch, her stern expression moving from iron to steel. "We have no reason to believe he's a threat to the public."

"A police officer?" I feel my eye twitching and can't quite understand what I'm being told. "My husband said he was a criminal. On the run."

Birch stares and says nothing. An old interrogation technique, I imagine, to encourage me to fill the silence with a sudden confession. It doesn't work.

"Jason Mercer was not on active service. He was due to stand trial on Friday afternoon and didn't show up. There's a warrant out for his arrest, but he's not been found guilty as yet."

"On trial for what?"

"The charges were for various alleged criminal activities."

"Not a poster boy for the Met, then? Why would a disgraced police officer be here?" I say, although I marvel at his time management in fitting in a little bit of burglary on the same day as his trial.

"We think he's hiding out with someone, and we found your name and address in his desk drawer."

I feel a strange sense of disorientation as they are leaking information piece by piece and watching me like hawks. "Why did he have my name and address?" I ask.

"We were hoping you'd know the answer to that. From mobile phone records, we know his last known location was in this area and that he'd been here several times in the last month."

"So he's stalking me? Is that it?"

"His wife believes that he's having an affair and is likely to be with his latest girlfriend," she says, and looks me up and down with the expression that mothers use when their teenage daughters go out for the night. "I therefore have to ask—are you or have you ever been in a relationship with Jason Mercer?"

"You think I'm his lover? Oh, dear me." I laugh at the ridiculous assumption that I'm an adulterer indulging in a bit of rough. "Don't take this the wrong way, but I wouldn't consider anyone below chief inspector level."

"It's not a laughing matter," DS Birch says coldly.

I'm about to assure her that it's not a joke, but I sense she thinks very poorly of me already, so I smile sweetly.

"You can look around, if you like. No secret lovers here, I can assure you," I say. "Just cat, rabbit, children, husband, and nanny. If you think I also have the capacity to conceal a fugitive, I fear you underestimate the demands on my time."

"Perhaps you can explain why he had your address?" says DS Birch.

"I have no idea. Never seen him in my life," I say. "You found my name and address in his desk, his phone shows he was a regular visitor to Muswell Hill, and some shadowy informant says he was at my house . . . is that it?" She nods slowly, and I can't resist adding, "I mean, you're just guessing, Detective."

She doesn't like being patronized and stares at me. DC Mattoo leans forward as if to get up, then clocks his boss and leans back again.

"Not guesswork, madam, a carefully considered hypothesis based on the available evidence and key assumptions."

"Well, your assumptions are faulty. If he failed to turn up to court, I imagine he had good reason to run, dumped his phone, and drove to darkest Scotland."

"His car is still in his driveway, madam, which suggests he may have access to another vehicle. Do you have a car yourself?" she says, and takes out her notebook.

"I do. It's outside, so no, I haven't lent it to a runaway policeman."

DS Birch takes the registration number of my Porsche and tells me with some glee that they can track registration numbers.

"Will that be all?" I say abruptly. The good news is that they don't seem to be looking for the blue Toyota, which is full of my DNA, most probably. I can only surmise that it was stolen or borrowed.

"You understand that it's a criminal offense to assist an offender and help them evade prosecution?"

"That's not relevant," I say, just as my son wanders in, face covered in soil, as he's been digging. I am, however, concerned by DS Birch's persistence and the anonymous tip-off.

"Nathan, these police officers are looking for someone." I take Nathan on my knee. So useful to present oneself as a loving mother, but Nathan disagrees, wriggles away, and stands in front of DC Mattoo.

"You don't have a police helmet," says Nathan.

"No, we're detectives," says DC Mattoo.

"Do you want to borrow mine?"

Mattoo smiles at Nathan, who is beyond delighted and runs off. Birch glares at me as if I'm going to break, and we sit in awkward silence. Fortunately, Nathan runs back in with the police helmet and hands it to Mattoo, who kindly perches it on top of his head to hilarious effect.

"If you remember anything at all, please get in touch," says Birch, rising quickly and handing me a card. She takes the hat off Mattoo's head, hands it back to Nathan, looks around the room with an air of suspicion, and sniffs dismissively.

I close the door as they leave, with Nathan waving wildly, and quickly open my Ring app to watch Mattoo and Birch on my screen. I turn up the volume just in time.

"What did you think?" says Mattoo.

"Guilty as hell," says Birch, and then glances directly at the camera.

23

Research

Thursday, November 21

"Right, darling, well done! Great workout," I say to Stephen as we arrive home after a morning run around Ally Pally. As he's gasping for breath, I decide the time is right.

"I think we should make an offer on the house," I say. This is a little disingenuous as I've already made an offer, but it's important to make him feel in charge.

"We can't offer because we can't afford it," he says, in such a depressive tone that I wonder if the early run was worth it at all. I was hoping the dopamine hit would make him more optimistic.

"An offer doesn't hold us to anything, at this stage, so let's have some fun," I say. "We could even ask your mum for help."

He looks at me, handsome but forlorn, shakes his head, and trudges up the steps in his running shorts; his calves are spattered with mud, which, sadly, arouses me slightly.

I am showered, dressed, and out within thirty minutes, heading toward the blue Toyota, which is a godsend. Until you have an untraceable car, you never know how useful it can be. Especially living somewhere like Muswell Hill, as you're so visible. I mean, you can buy lemongrass in the morning and by the afternoon someone at yoga will ask if you're making Thai curry for dinner.

I park outside Tor's in my hat and shades. It's not that I don't trust Cait, but who else could've told the police that Jason Mercer had been at my house? When I make a promise, I stick to it, but when Cait makes a promise, it feels conditional. That's emotions for you. Better without them, frankly.

I know she's had to flee her own home, is having to endure Tor treating her as if she's infectious, has a vicious estranged husband threatening significant harm, and buried her first body this week, but even so, trust is everything. I imagine she couldn't sleep after burying him and called Crimestoppers at four in the morning.

It's not myself I'm worried about; it's the children. Nathan would probably be fine. Boys have their needs for food, activity, company, and hierarchy, and that's it. They're like dogs in this respect, and any decent owner would do. Nelly needs something else and would take revenge on the world when it didn't bend to her will. And we all know how that ends.

As I wait, I call Sophie. She's on her way to work but sounds strangely cheerful.

"Just wanted to check in and see how Paolo reacted to your date?"

"Well, there's a story!" she says. "I got all dolled up—new dress, matching underwear, the whole shebang—flaunted it around the flat before I went out. Paolo was asking all kinds of questions, but I batted them all away and left, humming Beyoncé's 'Single Ladies.'"

"Go, girl," I say, and Sophie tuts at me, which I think is for my poor American accent.

"I went to the bar, but I couldn't go through with it."

"Always disappointing to find you have moral boundaries," I say.

"I realized I didn't want to spend an evening with anyone else. It made me feel grubby," she says sweetly. "So I went for a long walk and took in a late film at the Everyman. When I got home, he was waiting up, head in hands."

"Poor Paolo," I say. "Oh, wait, Cait's here!"

I have to wave three times to Cait as she doesn't recognize the car. Eventually, the car door opens, and Cait gets in. No happy smile from her—just a glum look of what I imagine is guilt sitting like a lump of lead in her stomach. I tell her Sophie's on the phone telling me about her date, and put it on speaker.

"You're on speaker now," I say. "Go on with the story."

"Hi, Cait!" Sophie calls. Cait barely responds. "Anyway I thought Paolo was angry, but he was crying. He said he didn't want to lose me." Sophie pauses. "And . . ."

"He threw you against the wall and . . ."

"He proposed!" she shouts.

"Oh, that's wonderful," I say. "One fake date and he's in the bag. Good on you."

"Congratulations," says Cait more quietly.

"More later, the kids are staring at my ring," Sophie says as we hear the chatter of children in the background.

"Isn't that wonderful news?" I say to Cait.

"Yes," says Cait. "I suppose the wedding will be nice, although, sadly, we'll be in prison."

"Oh, you little cloud of gloom," I say. "Of course we won't."

I drive Cait to Muswell Hill, explaining all about the identity of the dead man. The fact that he's a disgraced policeman, had my address in his home—that the police are now actively searching for him and they've already been to my house—all seems to make Cait feel jittery. When I explain that the Toyota is his stolen car, we have to stop on Bishop's Avenue while she leans out and vomits.

We go to Sable d'Or for a quick cup of sweet tea to put her right and then head for the library to conduct some research. I leave Cait at the bank of computers next to an old man who keeps asking her what a mouse is and head for the self-help section.

After I spend forty-five minutes reading a book about how to save your marriage, Cait appears and sits next to me on the stained foam sofa.

"He wasn't a nice man," she says. "A long-serving Met officer in the Serious and Organized Crimes Command. Multiple disciplinary issues. He was suspended pending his trial for sexual harassment and assault, bribery, fraud, and witness intimidation."

"But why was he in Muswell Hill, and what was he doing in my house?"

"No idea," says Cait. "But I know why they're so keen to find him. The Met is facing criticism for letting him get away with it for so long. They wanted to set an example, and now he's on the loose."

"That's good news," I say.

"How is this good news?" says Cait. "They think you're his girlfriend. One search warrant and they'll find evidence that he died in your living room."

"Think about it, Cait, it's actually perfect. He's disappeared because of the trial, right? No one's wondering why he's gone missing, and they'll never find him anyway. They'll think he made it to the Costa del Sol."

"At the moment, they think he made it to your house."

"Did I tell you that they'd had an anonymous tip-off too?"

"About what?"

"Someone told the police that they'd seen Mercer at my house."

"But he had your address anyway."

"Whoever blabbed didn't know that, did they?" I say.

"Why are you staring at me?" she says. "You don't think it was me, do you?"

"Well, who else could it be, Cait?"

Cait throws down her notebook and leaves in a mood, slamming the library door—which pleases no one. From her carefully handwritten notes, I find out that Mercer has three children from three different relationships, was a gambler, drinker, and philanderer as well as a serial sex attacker and bully. He wasn't working on a case as he'd been suspended for over four months. He was either making a living as a burglar or he was a serial sex offender looking for his next victim. Perhaps he was trying to kill two birds with one stone.

I leave the library feeling an overwhelming sense of moral pride that I dispatched him so forcefully.

24

Aimée

Later in the afternoon, thinking of ways to inspire my husband to feel more positive about the house purchase, I head upstairs to see Aimée. Love is a strategy to keep people close to you, and to make those you use feel that their support has value, but even love needs to be sweetened sometimes. My approach might be unconventional, but treats work with dogs, so why not husbands?

As I walk past our bathroom, I hear the sound of water running and glance sideways. The door is ajar and I see Aimée's on the toilet scrolling through her phone.

I open my mouth to speak. She looks up at me. No change in her facial expression, no surprise, no embarrassment. I think, fundamentally, it's laziness rather than a political statement.

"Aimée, may I have a word?"

"While I'm peeing?"

"We tend to close the door in this country."

"Doors, minds, legs," she says, with a flamboyant gesture.

"When you're ready, do come down."

Eight minutes later, Aimée flounces into the kitchen and drags a stool across the floor, as I suppose lifting is also a terrible British time-waster. I am stroking Purdy, who is purring loudly.

Having consulted the finest minds on the topic (*Cosmopolitan*), it seems likely that Stephen's sexual deterioration is due to a debilitating cocktail of stress, depression, bereavement, and financial concerns. I have, therefore, created a plan to reanimate our love, spark his testosterone production, and reengage him with our primary projects, namely, Hampstead and a third child. For this, I need Aimée's help. She stares at me with barely disguised boredom.

"What now? Is the jam jar lid not on tightly enough?"

"The jar is not correctly closed, but it's something else."

"What? The fridge door is slightly ajar?"

"Sometimes, in all types of employment, you need to go the extra mile."

"No," says Aimée, with the same defiant expression Nelly uses.

"But you don't know what I mean," I say.

"I don't do extra miles. No miles more. You want me to clean. Non! I have said already."

"It's not cleaning. It's Stephen. He's going through a difficult patch."

"He seems happy."

"Yes, but that rather proves my point, doesn't it? If he's reached Gallic levels of happiness, we're at crisis point."

"This is not misery!" she says, gesturing to her visage. "This is intelligence. Life is tragic because we think. That is why we are second only to Finland in suicide."

"Something to be proud of, I'm sure, but we're getting off the point. Stephen used to be more enthusiastic, attentive—loving, even. But since his father died, he's just gone limp."

"Limp? What is limp?"

"The opposite of stiff," I say. "He's lost his desire. He stares into the distance. He shares increasingly liberal views. He doesn't look after business."

"Maybe he's unhappy with his marriage."

"Yes, but more importantly, *I'm* unhappy with our marriage. He's like a car battery that's gone flat, and I was wondering if you might help recharge him?"

"I'm not a battery charger."

"You're a beautiful young woman, and he's suffering a premature middle-age crisis. I wonder if you would show interest in him—flirt, catch his eye, say nice things about his eyes or muscles. Maybe even dress provocatively. You're French, I'm sure you'll find such things come naturally."

"You want me to seduce your husband?" she says, with a serious expression that seems to suggest that this is not an unusual request.

"No. Just pretend you find him attractive, you know?"

"But I don't. He's not. He's a suit. He's a bore. He's got too much nasal hair."

"That's why I used the word *pretend*."

"Why would I do this?"

"I'd pay you extra. A surcharge, so to speak."

"How much?"

"An extra hundred a week, and if he becomes attentive again, a bonus."

"What must I do for this bonus?" she asks as Purdy raises her head to inquire about the cessation of stroking.

"I'm not asking you to sleep with him, just to awaken his senses. Make him desire you."

"And what do I do with him when he's unable to resist me?" she says, and purses her lips as if this is a foregone conclusion.

"You just walk away and let me take over."

"You're taking a big chance. He will fall in love with me," she says, pouting. "Everyone does."

"I can only imagine how terribly difficult it must be to be so attractive, but it would really help."

"Two hundred," she says, and flounces out.

25

Suspicions

Friday, November 22
Muswell Hill possesses some fine establishments (Le Creuset, Sweaty Betty, Martyn's, the Hampstead Butcher), but sadly, the center is also host to a chilling number of fast-food outlets, charity shops, and coffee shop chains. Add to that a flotilla of Deliveroo drivers, hordes of schoolchildren walking eight abreast, and several aggressive chuggers, and it's like Oxford Street.

You don't read about that in real estate agents' brochures, nor about Muswell Hill's notoriety as the onetime home of Mr. Dennis Nilsen, who dismembered people in a flat on Cranley Gardens, on the market at £500,000. House hunters in the "jewel in Haringey's crown" are clearly not put off by high prices or serial killers. Hampstead beckons like a siren.

We were expecting the Adams letter this morning, but nothing arrived. Sophie received her letter, telling her that Ellie has been taken through to the written examinations. Tor said that Hero had gotten through. Nelly hasn't asked but I know she's thinking about it. She might not want the prize but would like to refuse it herself.

Having spent the morning in some distress, in the afternoon I became convinced it was Cait who tipped off the police. Who else knew about it? Only Mercer himself, and he's rather incommunicado currently. I expect she wanted evidence that she'd reported the crime, while also not telling them too much, as she wants to be a good friend. Just like Cait, to position herself so cleverly between self-interest and kindness.

It's harder to explain why Jason Mercer was in my house, and in the area. His poor wife's suspicion of another affair (I say "another" as men rarely disappoint just the once) suggests that he might have been romantically (I use the term loosely) involved with someone close by, but that doesn't explain why he had my name and address. I'm also alarmed by the detective sergeant's conviction that I'm "guilty as hell." I've been staring into the mirror for some time, wondering what it is about my face that would make someone think, *Here's a woman who likes roughing it with abusive policemen.*

The first possibility is that Mercer needed cash, identified Muswell Hill as an easy target, scoped the area for a few weeks, and identified 44 Ennerdale Avenue as his next job. A workable hypothesis but it doesn't explain why he had my *name* as well as my address.

The more worrying possibility is that he wasn't after cash at all and was in the area solely to target me and find information. There's no evidence that he was actually a thief. He hadn't taken anything from the living room, and there were no stolen goods or housebreaking tools in the Toyota.

When I think about the noise I heard that day, I remember it was rather loud—like the sound of a drawer slamming shut. It was such a thump I thought it could only be Aimée, who appears to think that British furniture needs a firm hand. Mercer was an experienced policeman, used to stealth, but he was clearly under some stress with all his other problems. He knew he'd made a mistake because he was behind the door when I entered. I think it was panic, or maybe he was going to threaten me until he got what he wanted. Maybe some identifying document to tie me to the past or something else?

Sexual depravity? If so, why target me? And why would a man about to face prison for sexual abuse risk worsening his sentence by stalking a woman with a view to committing another heinous crime? And I can't help wondering if it's normal behavior for a depraved sexual pervert to keep someone's name and address carefully written down. What for? To send flowers afterward?

No, Detective Sergeant Birch doesn't think Mercer was randomly stalking me. She thinks he was connected to me, and so do I. She's wrong to think that the connection is romantic, but what if Jason Mercer was being paid to find out information about me or even frighten me?

There are several people from the past who might have an interest in my current whereabouts. It's true to say I've crossed a few lines and broken one or two laws here and there, but I can't think of anyone bright enough to have tracked me down, which leaves me with one main suspect.

Someone with the resources, a grudge, a devious mind, and a questionable overattachment to their only son and heir. There's only one person in my mind as I beep aggressively at the queue of stationary cars—Madeleine Rook.

After getting through the traffic on Muswell Hill's congested Broadway, I arrive at Cait's house. Real estate agents talk enthusiastically about curb appeal, and I have to shake my head—the front gate needs painting and a new set of hinges, the concrete path is ruptured by tree roots, the window frames are peeling, and there's a faded 2010 election poster for "Building a Fairer Britain."

I drive to the road behind Cait's and park the car at the house directly behind hers. The prevalence of Ring doorbells and security cameras means that you're seen wherever you go these days, and I'd prefer not to be captured planting evidence in Cait's house.

I get out of the car and take the Le Creuset knife from my handbag, still safely secured inside a freezer bag. It's dark, and in my large puffer coat, cap, and oversize sunglasses, I look more like a minor celebrity than a thief. I saw Lauren Laverne the other day in Snappy Snaps in a similar outfit.

In my experience, the best way to stop someone being afraid of something (prison, for instance, or your violent estranged husband gaining custody of your children) is to make them more scared of something else. Cait hid her secret abuse journal quite effectively in the headboard of her old-fashioned bed frame. I'm going to plant the knife there and warn her that any further contact with the authorities will backfire spectacularly.

I climb the fence into Cait's garden and make my way to the house, shaking my head at the abandoned bikes, buckets, and balls. There are many things to like about Cait, but I can't think of a single one right now.

I put my gloves on and try the back door. Strangely, it's not locked. The door creaks ever so slightly as I slip into the kitchen.

I look at the children's drawings on the fridge, the kind of pictures only a mother would keep, and the unwashed dishes—no excuses. I'm thinking about cleaning up myself, when there's a noise from above. I stand deadly still and hear the unmistakable sound of footsteps.

Cait's here! So that's why the door was open. Tor mentioned that she was going to pick up supplies and children's clothes. I consider what to do. It'd be easy to slip back into the night, but I feel I'm being presented with a unique opportunity. Perhaps I could silence Cait more directly.

Owen would get the blame, no doubt. In some ways, I might be doing Cait a favor. Her life is one long series of disappointments, and it would help her achieve her goals, too, as Owen couldn't get custody of the girls if he was in prison. Always look for a win-win.

As I think this, I realize, oddly, that I would miss her.

I take my shoes off at the bottom of the stairs and slowly make my way to the first floor, placing my stockinged feet carefully on the outside of each step. I head toward what a real estate agent would call the "principal bedroom," although it's far from deserving of the title.

As soon as I open the door I'm hit with the unmistakable stink of gasoline. I put my hand over my mouth and step back. Through the half-open door, I can see Cait's bed is soaked with it. A green fuel canister is lying on its side on the floor.

What stupid idea has Cait got into her head? Suicide? Insurance fraud? I can leverage either.

The moment I enter the room, the door slams behind me and a rough hand shoves me. I stagger forward, only just stopping myself from falling, and then turn quickly to see a man standing there staring at me, wild and unshaven, his hands toying with a box of matches.

26

Matches

"Hello, Lalla," says Owen O'Donnell. He smiles, leaning his bulk against the door. There's a bed with a gasoline wet patch behind me. I feel the knife in my pocket and slowly remove it from its plastic bag in readiness. Sadly it will remove Cait's fingerprints, but needs must.

"Cait sent you, did she?" he says, glowering with menace. "Ask you to do more of her dirty work?"

"The question is, what are you doing here? Planning to burn your wife's house down? That's romantic."

"Fuck you. If it wasn't for you, we'd still be together."

"If it wasn't for me, she'd be dead, Owen, and you'd be in prison, you disgusting little coward."

He lurches toward me, kicks me hard in the stomach, and I fly back onto the gas-soaked bed. I lie there, feeling the pain course through my body, but it immediately turns into anger. My hand slips back into my pocket. I will enjoy cutting his throat.

"You speak like that again and I'll kill you," he says. I notice he's slurring his words and swaying slightly.

"What do you want?"

"Money!" he shouts. "I told Cait I needed five grand today, and she didn't even reply. Stupid bitch."

"You think burning her house down will help?"

"I'm dead unless I get five grand, so I'm making my fucking point."

"What point is that?"

"I'm burning her bed. This time without her in it," he says, and laughs. "Next time, who knows?"

"You'll burn down the entire house, Owen. It's gas. Are you pissed?"

"Not pissed enough," he says.

"Let me go," I say, pushing myself to my feet. I grab the handle of the knife as he strokes the match against the matchbox. Even if I pull the knife, he could probably disarm me. I might cut him once or twice, but unless I catch an artery, his strength and size would leave me at his mercy. I need to get closer somehow.

I take a step toward him. "This has nothing to do with me, Owen. You need help." I stare up at him, eyeballing, and take another step. I'm close enough to smell the alcohol on his breath. He puts the matches in his jacket pocket, raises a hand, and holds my chin.

"I might like to help you." He smiles.

I take the knife out of my pocket. He holds my face so firmly I can't even glance downward. If I stab now, I could hit his coat, bone, or muscle, and I can see in his eyes what this scared and humiliated man would do to me.

I look up at his neck. It would be difficult. But the decision is taken out of my hands as his hand moves from my chin and he gropes my crotch.

My hand rises. One fast blow. I stab, but he feels the attack coming. His head jerks back, and the knife slices across his neck rather than into it. Blood cascades from the wound. He grabs my arm and twists it so violently that I drop the knife. His other hand grabs my neck and squeezes. He shoves me hard, and I fall back onto the bed. He stands over me, holding the gash on his neck.

"You cut me, you fucking bitch." His eyes burn as they move over my body. Lust or hate? Both, I imagine.

I'm calculating distances and force, but a well-aimed kick to his crotch might just make him angry. I have to find another way. I need to switch him from one mode to the other.

"I can get you five grand," I say.

"I don't want your money, I want to hurt you, like you hurt me," he says, climbing on top of me. His weight crushing me, gas fumes choking me, and blood dripping down onto my face.

"I've thought about this many times," he says.

"I know you have, Owen," I say, "and so have I." A good magician must distract their audience effectively and I make some flattering remarks while my hand slips into his jacket pocket and pulls out the small rectangular box.

He tries to force his knee between my legs. I know I have one opportunity. As he's off balance, I raise my knee with as much force as I can and connect with his crotch. He shrieks in pain and tumbles onto his side.

I jump off him and, in a single quick movement, strike the match. The teardrop of red sulfur bursts into flame. His eyes take half a second to work out what's happening. He tries to get up, words and arms flailing, but I'm not going to give him a second chance.

I drop the match. It tumbles through the air and, instantly, flames engulf the bed, along with Owen O'Donnell.

PART TWO
Recalibrate

If I cannot inspire love, I will cause fear.

MARY SHELLEY, *Frankenstein*, **1818**

27

Laughter

Saturday, November 23

We gather at Sable d'Or, a pretty café on Muswell Hill Broadway with excellent pastéis de nata. Sophie smiles and doesn't notice a blob of guacamole drop onto her top. Tor stares at it, visibly distracted, her expression straining against her Botox-assisted forehead. We've discussed "the fire," but no one has walked around to see which road or house it was as yet. It was the talk of the Broadway this morning, and the acrid smell of smoke still hangs in the air like a low fog.

"How's Cait?" says Sophie, scraping the guacamole from her lapel and into her mouth. "She's not responded to my texts."

"Oh, she dashed home last night to collect things for the girls and headed off to her mum's for the weekend," says Tor. "It's easier for her there, I think."

Easier for you, I want to say, but I suspect Cait's decision to relocate was also to avoid seeing me again, as she says her eczema flares up whenever she hears my name. I suspect that the fire brigade will have found Cait and relayed the unfortunate news. Poor thing, she's having a real time of it.

"What've you been up to, Lalla?" says Sophie, tapping my arm.

"What do you mean?" I smile, wondering if I smell of gas. I showered three times and had to throw away another set of clothes. Murder is so expensive; people probably don't realize.

"You're all glowing. You look like you had mind-altering sex all last night," says Sophie with a playful nudge.

"Yes, the sex is pretty nonstop at the moment," I say with a coy smile. Sophie claps her hands in joy as Tor curls her lip over her coffee.

Obviously I haven't had any sex at all. Despite Aimée's valiant effort at flirting (she tried to strike up an intimate conversation about the fruit on his muesli), Stephen was glued to his phone when I tried to seduce him after the trip to Cait's house left me feeling quite excited.

Tor puts her cup down. "Surprised you two can concentrate on anything but your Adams letter. I'd be going round the bend."

Aisha leans toward me and holds my arm. "Did you call them?"

"No, I've not called." This is a lie. I've called so frequently that they no longer pick up when they see my number.

"It's so odd you haven't heard anything," says Tor, tossing her thinning hair with a twisted little smile. "I don't know how you can be so patient. Hero was bouncing off the walls till the letter came yesterday."

"I'm sure it'll be there on Monday," I say, and try not to judge Tor too much—being married to an MP, she is reduced to getting her pleasure at someone else's expense.

"Well, I really hope she's not been rejected," says Tor.

"She's not," I say firmly, and imagine pushing Tor's taut face into Sophie's dip. "Anyway, if the letter doesn't turn up, I'll see the headmistress on Monday."

"I'm so glad I'm not involved," says Aisha cheerily. "We're saving all our stress, and cash, for eleven-plus entry."

"Of course you are," says Tor. "I expect money's quite tight with Ranni's noble commitment to the NHS."

"Well, you can't do heart transplants privately," says Aisha. "Organs can't be bought and sold."

"Not in the UK, anyway," says Tor, and then offers her sage advice. "If he'd gone into cosmetic surgery, you could afford a house in Hampstead and prep schools for all three."

"We're happy as we are," says Aisha, her anger almost undetectable, but the readjustment of her leggings is telling.

Tor stares as if Aisha is mad and resists a retort, but she can't resist a little shake of her head in my direction.

"How's Ellie?" asks Tor, moving targets quickly. "She must be super excited. I knew some scholarship girls at my school and they actually coped quite well."

"She's on cloud nine," says Sophie, her head tilted back in fear of someone biting it off.

"It's so good to be aspirational, but it's such a gamble too," says Tor.

"What's the gamble?" says Sophie, her calm demeanor breaking slightly.

"If Ellie's set her heart on the place and doesn't get a scholarship, she'll be heartbroken," says Tor with a faintly sinister smile.

"She knows Adams can only happen if we get funding," Sophie says firmly, and stabs a slice of red pepper. "Anyway, we've applied to four other schools."

"Good for you. Not every child is happy in an environment like Adams," declares Tor.

Sophie looks like she's about to swing at her, but her fist opens out and her nails tap in irritation on the tabletop.

"Ellie's super bright. They'd be mad not to offer her a place," I say, which is simply a statement of truth, but Sophie's face melts with delight, and I realize why I'm always nice to her. She's like an emotional slot machine that always pays out.

"Are you still excited about your other news, Sophie?" says Aisha.

Sophie's been regaling us all again about Paolo's proposal. Two days into her engagement, she's already shared a date for the wedding and asked us to keep our diaries free. Aisha instantly asked for her wedding list, while I immediately wanted to book a holiday. Weddings bring out the worst in me; they always seem to end in violence or inappropriate sex.

"I'm so excited," says Sophie. "I'm a fiancée for the first time in my life!"

"Did you have to think about saying yes after such a long wait?" inserts Tor to deflate Sophie's enthusiasm.

"I had no doubts at all," says Sophie smugly.

"So nice to have such simple emotions," says Tor. "I thought long and hard before I said yes to Law, but the promise of a wedding at Westminster Abbey swung it."

"I thought you were married at St. Margaret's Church," I gently correct Tor.

"Which is in the grounds of Westminster Abbey," she replies emphatically.

"I don't care where we're married, I'm just happy," says Sophie. "He loves me, he makes me laugh, he can cook, and he's hung like a horse—what more can I ask?"

We laugh so loud that people turn and stare.

"Ranni was upset by an article he read in the *Observer* the other day," says Aisha quietly. "It said the average penis size in the UK had grown by half an inch in the last twenty years."

"Why was he sad?" says Sophie.

"He said, in two decades, he's lost his hair, gained twenty-two pounds, and his penis is now below the national average."

"What about you, Tor? Does Lawrence satisfy your needs?" says Sophie as the laughter subsides.

"Oh, there are few needs that I leave Law to satisfy," says Tor.

"I bet you have a man who comes in to do that for you, don't you?" teases Sophie. "Your own sex butler."

"I do not," says Tor, quite firmly, and we all burst into fits of laughter again.

"I bet the British make terrible sex butlers," I say.

"I'm not joining in," says Tor, keeping a straight face with some difficulty.

"'If madam would be so kind as to allow, I would like to provide some additional stimulation on behalf of his lordship, who is currently experiencing a slight detumescence in his private estate,'" says Sophie in a refined English accent.

We shriek too loudly again, which attracts several annoyed

glances. It's a raucous united release from our various anxieties about Adams, aging, children, marriage, and, of course, murder. I laugh, too, but part of me is mimicking again and I envy their immediacy and unbridled joy.

As the laughter subsides, a bell jangles loudly, the door of Sable d'Or swings open, and Cait appears, wild-eyed and tearstained.

28

Insurance

"I thought you were at your mother's?" says Tor as Cait arrives at our table looking gloomier than ever.

"I had to come back," says Cait, her voice trembling. "Police called me."

"What's the matter?" says Aisha.

Cait starts to cry before she's seated, and she's soon blubbering inconsolably. If this is about Owen, I'm going to be quite annoyed with her. You shouldn't cry over a little spilled blood. Not of a man like that.

I try to hug her but it's not the least sincere as I'm trying to avoid her tears getting on my D&G floral print blouse. Aisha takes over, shushes Cait quickly, sits her down, and strokes her hair, which could do with a good wash and blow-dry.

"Tea with honey," commands Aisha, with a nod to Sophie.

Sophie's eyes are wet with sympathetic tears and she doesn't move. There's emotion again, making her experience things that haven't happened to her. I turn to Tor. She's not even feigning interest and is distracting herself with her phone.

"What's happened? Are the girls all right?" asks Sophie.

"Yes, they're fine . . . fine . . . they're with Mum," says Cait, gulping.

"Is it Owen?" I ask, trying to move us to the point more quickly.

She shakes her head. I let out a little exclamation of mild surprise.

"My house burned to the ground," she splutters.

"Oh god. That was your house!" says Sophie. "We've all been talking about the fire."

"I only went there to collect clothes for the girls, but it was damp, so I put the heating on. I must've forgotten to switch it off."

"Well, you've had a lucky escape if the boiler blew up," says Sophie.

I'm not unsympathetic, but I do think it's a good thing that her house was incinerated. Not only was it a poor example of Edwardian architecture, but it removes so many unsavory memories. People find decluttering the past so difficult and this gets the whole thing done in an instant. It's a completely fresh start for her.

I return from the counter, having ordered the tea with honey myself, to hear Cait relay her tale of woe as Sophie and Aisha comfort her in a pincer movement. Tor, meanwhile, is looking at Cait in the manner of a mother looking at a friend's child who's just reported a severe case of head lice.

"Was it an old boiler?" says Aisha.

"Only thirty years old," says Cait, and looks around the table. "Are you okay, Lalla?" she says, which takes me aback.

"I'm fine, Cait, why?"

"There's a bruise," she says. "On your neck."

My hand rises automatically to rearrange my scarf. Owen's abuse has made her notice these things.

"Stephen's autoerotic games again. He just can't get enough," I say with an ironic raise of the eyebrows. It's an awkward enough statement that people shy away from further comment, but Aisha's expression tells me I've been inappropriate.

"Is there anything you can salvage?" says Sophie.

Cait's little head moves from side to side. "I'm not even allowed near it. It's unstable."

Aisha says how fortunate it was that Cait and the girls weren't at home when it happened, and Cait bursts into fresh tears and has to retreat to the loo to wipe the black smudges from her face.

"Do you think Owen did it?" says Tor as soon as she's gone. "Come on, I know you're all thinking it."

"More likely to be the boiler," I say, nodding toward Aisha, who nods back. Sensible people think sensible things.

"But he was in her house," says Sophie. "She said so at Nathan's party. And she wouldn't give him the money he wanted."

"If it's Owen, Cait could be in real danger now," says Aisha. I want to dispute this but choose to keep silent.

"More importantly," I say, "Cait's homeless situation is now permanent, and she's got no belongings. We all need to help."

Everyone agrees solemnly. In order to suggest these kinds of things, I just ask myself what Mother Abbess would say.

Cait returns from the toilet looking only slightly more presentable. She sits and puts both hands flat on the table to steady herself.

"The house will probably have to be demolished," she says, clearly still wanting to dwell on the fire. This touches a nerve or two, and Sophie sheds another tear, although she's lost nothing at all.

"Surely buildings insurance will cover it," says Tor, which is what she once said when we were discussing people losing their homes in the floods in Sudan.

"Yes," says Cait. "Owen did all that. I'm sure it's just on direct debit."

"*His* direct debit?" asks Aisha. "I thought he was in desperate need of money."

Cait freezes, and for a moment it seems like the whole of the café holds its breath.

"Fuck," she says loudly.

To-do list:
Buy concealer for bruises
Find old clothes and toys for Cait
Book meeting with Adams headmistress
Check buildings insurance

29

Ponchos

Monday, November 25

I receive a deeply insulting letter from Adams in this morning's post and feel a desperate need for a murderous visit to the head, which would probably help neither of us. What really stings is the false tone of the letter with its smug, throwaway empathy and insults veiled as compliments. I feel volcanic urges bubbling beneath my skin and know that only one thing will calm my rage—a nourishing marine body wrap followed by an energy of the glaciers facial at the Dorchester spa.

I am not wrong. I drive home from Highgate station in a better state of mind, but when I turn into our road, any residual calmness from my spa treatments evaporates. I spot DS Birch and DC Mattoo speaking to number 61.

I make a cup of mint tea and try to rationalize, but with our neighbors telling the police all the comings and goings of Ennerdale Avenue, and the Adams letter sitting there on the kitchen island, I smash my favorite mug, sending tea across the floor, and find myself sitting on the floor and holding my head.

Aimée appears in the midst of this meltdown and looks down at me. I peer up through my ruffled hair and she lets out a long sigh of disgust, steps over me, takes an avocado, steps back over me, and walks out.

"I'm fine, thank you," I shout after her.

"I didn't ask," she shouts back.

I stand up, take the Adams letter, and put it in the wastebasket. No need to be reminded of life's disappointments. There are two other letters on the counter, both still untouched. One is from a real estate agent offering us the fantastic and unsolicited opportunity to have our house valued; the other is handwritten and addressed to Mrs. Stephen Rook, which annoys me as this is not a Jane Austen novel.

Now is not the time to let pettiness rile me. I need to focus. Jason Mercer's phone and car key fob are still in my desk. I realize that I have to get rid of them. Even a detective with the investigative powers of DS Birch might find their presence suspicious. I go to the living room and pick up his belongings.

My plan is to drive to King's Cross, and turn on his phone for a short time in the hope that the police are still tracking it, and that it sends them down another avenue. I leave by the front door in hat and gloves. The police are still speaking to our neighbors, but they have their backs to me, so I walk by quickly.

I get in the blue Toyota and head along Muswell Road. The late afternoon sun dazzles me, and I flip the sun visor down. As I do so, a small blue notebook falls into my lap.

I pull over and quickly open it. There are four pages filled with dates, locations, and what look like hours. The locations are all ones I recognize, including my friends' houses, the Grove junior school, the preschool, my favorite cafés and shops, and my gym.

I breathe deeply and look around as dog walkers and strollers pass by. This is a record of my life. Mercer was stalking me and keeping a record of the time he spent doing so. It only makes sense if he was employed by someone, such as Madeleine, but what could she gain from knowing my movements? She wants background information, not a list of where I eat and drink. I wonder who else might want me followed. Someone from the past, no doubt. Someone I need to find and stop, as I would hate for the past to rob me of the future.

The last page contains two slightly odd names, "MonkeyWarrior" and "Ponchos," with seven scribbled numbers below:

MonkeyWarrior
Ponchos
12-3 13 14

I take my phone out, type *Ponchos* into Google, and I'm swamped by images of rainwear. MonkeyWarrior is worse—models of monkeys in samurai costume with swords. I look back at the number. It's too short to be a phone number but could be a code for a safe or lock of some kind. There seems to be a pattern that intrigues me.

I write the numbers in several different ways and end up nowhere. The only thing that makes sense is that it's a passcode to his phone, as the last four digits are simple to remember: 13, 14.

I know from the dates in the notebook that Mercer was following me for at least three weeks. I presume that MonkeyWarrior is some kind of nickname. The kind of name you might use on social media. Ponchos sounds like a place name, especially if it had an apostrophe before the *s*. I decide to change tack. This is more important than King's Cross. I put the notebook in my pocket, park the car, leave the phone in the glove box, and return home.

In my study, I open my laptop. If Ponchos is a place, it's likely to be a location Jason Mercer is familiar with as there's no address. It sounds like a bar or restaurant. I try various iterations in Google—*Ponchos restaurant*, *Ponchos café*, and *Ponchos bar*. There are results for all three, but even more results for *Panchos*, and looking back, I realize that it might be an *a* rather than an *o*. I search for Pancho's and come away with a long list of Mexican bars and restaurants.

I stare up at the window and shut the laptop. The annoying letter to Mrs. Stephen Rook is still on the kitchen island. I have about five minutes before Aimée returns with Nathan and he describes his day to me in exquisite detail.

I open the envelope. Inside, there's a folded piece of paper—a photocopy of a newspaper article from 1999. I feel a sudden jolt, as if someone's hand has ripped through the fabric of time and grabbed my throat.

The OXFORD Mail

July 2, 1999
By Reece Gunn

Local Man Stabbed, Wife Arrested

A local man is critically ill after he was found with multiple stab wounds in his home late yesterday evening. Emergency Services were called to an address in the village of Wroxton, near Banbury, following reports of screams from the property.

Mr. Brian Wells, 46, a council worker, was discovered unconscious and bleeding on the floor of his kitchen. A police statement confirms that his wife of 14 years, Margaret Wells, is in police custody on suspicion of attempted murder. Mr. and Mrs. Wells's 13-year-old daughter, who was in the property at the time of the incident, and who cannot be named for legal reasons, is currently under the care of social services.

A friend of the family described Mr. Wells as a reserved but well-respected member of the community. A close neighbor reported signs of family tension: "I'd hear raised voices now and then. Some arguments like all families, but no one could've expected this. Makes no sense at all."

Detective Chief Inspector Malcolm Critchley, who is heading up the investigation, said: "This is a tragic event, and we hope the victim pulls through. We are continuing our inquiries to establish the facts of the incident and have no more to share at the current time. We would like to appeal to members of the public to come forward if they have any information pertaining to this case."

There is no message.

30

Burnt

Tuesday, November 26

A successful marriage is a joy solely for the happy couple; a failing marriage, however, is a pleasure for all to enjoy. We arrive at Aisha's house, as planned, with bags of clothes and various household items to help Cait rebuild her life. But as soon as the door opens, we know that something is wrong.

"Oh my god," says Sophie, standing beside me and staring at Aisha. "What is it?"

"It's Ranni," says Aisha, tears streaming down her face as she stands in the doorway.

"God!" says Sophie. "Is he ill?"

"No, no," she says. "He's gone mad. Completely mad! Come in. I don't want the neighbors to see me like this."

We follow Aisha into her super-modern town house made of steel and untold quantities of glass. Every line is squared off, every light fitting recessed. There isn't a curve or decorative flourish in the whole house.

"Please sit down," she says as we enter the kitchen. "Sorry, it's such a mess."

Sophie and I stare. Admittedly there is a single glass on the side and one of the chairs is askew, but it's otherwise spotless.

"Sounds like drinks are needed. Don't worry, the cavalry has arrived!" says Sophie, removing a bottle of wine from her tote bag.

"We had a blazing row last night," Aisha says. I presume this means they didn't end each sentence by rubbing noses. "And he left this morning without a word. It's beyond comprehension. The children are happy here. I'm happy here."

"Is he sleeping with someone?" I ask.

"It's worse than that," she says.

Aisha pulls a tissue from her sleeve and dabs her eyes, which she finds difficult as she's shaking her head in disbelief the whole time.

"He wants to destroy our family," she says, and looks like she's about to break into tears again. "He wants us to move to Abu Dhabi."

There are gasps of shock, as though she's told us that he's leaving her for a nurse.

"When?" I ask.

"He leaves in three months. We're supposed to join him in September."

"How did this happen without you knowing?" says Sophie, unscrewing the cap on the wine bottle.

"Oh, he went off alone to the UAE for a series of interviews. Told me it was a conference and came back with our new life all mapped out. Said he didn't want to get my hopes up. They've offered him the post. I don't want to live in a cultural and actual desert," says Aisha, a sudden defiant tone in her voice.

"They have a Louvre franchise there now," I point out. "And it's so sunny."

"At least we know the price he puts on his family," she says.

"Is it just about money or is it a promotion?" says Sophie.

"It's a lower position, but he can earn three times his current salary, and it's tax free. Financially, it's a no-brainer. But I don't want to bring up my children in the UAE."

"He can't make you move," I say.

"He's made an executive decision. He's resigned from his position at the Royal Free."

"Wow," says Sophie, and gulps half a glass of sauvignon blanc.

"What about your interior design business?" I ask.

"Oh, don't worry, I can just set up over there, apparently. Yeah, dead easy. Just pull a new client list together, work like a madwoman to rebuild my reputation, and find a new set of talented colleagues while trying to get Hari, Ajay, and Ria settled into new schools in a new country, while missing all my lovely friends."

"How about planting drugs on him?" I suggest. "You can't work in the UAE with a drugs conviction. Simple sabotage is sometimes the best thing for a marriage."

"Sure, and he won't be able to work anywhere else either. We'll be destitute," says Aisha, wiping her eyes, when the doorbell rings. "Oh no, that'll be Cait. Please don't tell her about this. I don't want to cry about having too many homes when she's lost everything."

We've each brought enough spare stuff to tide Cait and the twins over. Tor was supposed to contribute toys, but she's gone missing again, claiming an urgent podiatry appointment, which is probably a euphemism for something to do with black-market Ozempic prescriptions.

"Bloody men," says Sophie as soon as Aisha's out of hearing. "They ruin everything."

"Oh, dear, what now?" I realize that I've been so caught up in my own problems I've probably missed several obvious signs that Sophie's no longer dancing in the streets.

"I found Paolo texting a woman. A friend of his dead wife. And he slept with her."

"When?" I say, genuinely shocked, as Paolo has always seemed so rooted to his sofa.

"Twenty-four years ago. It was before his first marriage, but why's he texting her now?" she says, slurping wine liberally.

"Might be innocent," I say.

"Ha! The moment he proposed to me, he starts missing his wife and reconnects with her best friend."

"You might be overreacting," I suggest calmly. I fear this is not her first drink.

"Oh, did he write your script for you? That's exactly what he said."

I shake my head. She's worked so hard on this relationship and with Ellie that it's sad to see her sabotaging her own happiness because of alcohol-induced paranoia. I am about to lecture her when she throws her arms around me.

"I'm a fucking idiot, aren't I?"

"I'm sure things can be mended." I pat her gently.

We stop discussing Sophie and Paolo's courtship rituals as Cait enters the room with Maeve and Orla. Our children are at preschool, but Cait isn't letting the twins out of her sight.

Sophie and I fetch our bags of clothes, and within twenty minutes, everything is spread out on the kitchen worktop. Aisha cleverly spirits the twins off to Ria's room to play with her toys, returns, puts her own troubles to one side, and sits down next to Cait.

"So, how are you, you poor thing?" she says.

"The police came round again," says Cait. "They've started an investigation into the fire."

"Was it the boiler?" asks Aisha.

"It wasn't," says Cait. "But they don't know what it was yet. They can't get to the first floor as the beams burned through, but the fire dog smelled something on the stairs. They think it was an accelerant."

"Do they think someone started it?" says Aisha.

"I don't know," Cait says.

"Have you told them about Owen?" says Sophie.

Cait looks down to her lap. "The thing is . . . they know I was there that evening. I told them I was."

"Oh, what? They think you did it?" says Sophie.

"Why would I burn my own house down?"

Cait is about to add something, but she stops and stares ahead as if lost for words. Too much stress is clearly bad for her skin as I can see two or three spots around her mouth.

"Are you looking after yourself?" I ask, feeling pleased at how this fire business has stopped her going on about Jason Mercer.

"I can't eat or sleep," she says. "The doctor gave me some antidepressants."

"How about the insurance issue?" asks Aisha. "Did you check?"

"I'm trying to argue with the insurers but they say he's not paid and the policy has lapsed," says Cait.

"If you want some legal advice, I know someone in Hari's class," says Aisha.

"Yes, that's helpful, thank you," says Cait, and picks up a blue sweater. "This is nice."

We're all sipping on the matcha that Aisha insisted we try (I've never tasted anything so awful in my life), when Cait's phone goes off. She scrambles through her bag and finds her old iPhone.

We watch as Cait listens, nods, and answers with single words. Her pale skin seems to shrink against her skull, and her hand clenches tighter and tighter.

Cait drops her phone to her side and stares blankly ahead. "They've found a body in the fire. They want me to try to identify the personal effects that didn't burn to a cinder. The remains of a watch, and..." She pauses, then looks up at us blankly. "A wedding ring."

31

Hammer

Wednesday, November 27
I stop by the hairdressers to make an appointment as my roots are already showing. The receptionist with thick makeup and chewing gum manages to look up from her phone, which is commendable for such a young person. We agree on a suitable date and she writes it down for me on an appointment card. Not something I need, but I think all writing practice will help.

I take the card and look down to see that she's avoided words altogether.

> 11-30, 4—5p.m.

As I'm walking home, something in my mind connects. I sit on a bench, take Jason Mercer's notebook out of my handbag, and find the code:

> MonkeyWarrior
> Panchos
> 12-3 13 14

I rewrite the number underneath:

> 12-3, 13-14

If I'm right, and this is an appointment, it means Jason Mercer was due to meet MonkeyWarrior at Pancho's on December 3, from 1 p.m. to 2 p.m. That's in six days' time. And if they've met there before, I know a way to find out where that might be.

I head to the blue Toyota, press the key into the slot, and the car wakes up. I find my way into the information system. It takes a bit of searching, but I soon find the tab for "recent destinations." There are forty-two addresses in the car's memory, but if the car was stolen, it had to be in the three weeks before he died, while he was following me. I scroll through slowly, reading the destinations one by one.

Pancho's is the seventh entry.

I check my watch. I can't be late for my appointment at Adams. It has taken the words *serious safeguarding complaint* simply to get to see the head. She behaves like an archbishop rather than an over-promoted religious studies teacher.

I sit outside the dark wooden door of her study, with its brass nameplate, and can't help memories appearing like vampires from the graves of yesteryear. I find head teachers reliably triggering.

"You asked to see me," says Mrs. Pembury.

"Yes, I want to discuss your offer," I say as I sit in the low chair opposite hers.

"I understood that this was a safeguarding concern."

"It is. Nelly's well-being has been seriously compromised by your offer."

"She didn't get an offer," says Mrs. Pembury. "We enjoyed meeting her but don't think Adams is the right school for her."

"That's what I want to discuss. You've made an opening offer, I'm here to counter," I say.

"That's not how admissions work, I'm afraid," she says, smiling benignly. "And as this isn't a safeguarding matter, I think you should speak to admissions."

"I'd just like you to give this vulnerable child a chance to prove herself, and let her sit for the entrance exam," I say.

The carefully coiffed headmistress looks at me for a time, then says, "It is in consideration of her vulnerability that we're suggesting Nelly will be better served by another educational establishment."

"And what does that huge mouthful actually mean?"

"We don't think Nelly fits in here. She excludes herself from friendship groups, she doesn't respond to nonverbal cues, and she has difficulty following instructions."

"She's shy, that's all."

"During the activity day, Nelly convinced another girl to act as a physical bridge between two chairs so that she could reach her seat without touching the floor."

"It's a touch of OCD. No harm meant."

"We don't think pupils should walk across each other."

"It sounds as if Nelly was being creative, innovative, and bold. Three of your golden skills."

"At the expense of understanding, kindness, and empathy."

"Did you see her wonderful dolphin?"

"No, I did not."

"She's an extraordinarily talented and creative child."

"I'm concerned about her behavior, Mrs. Rook. My teachers are concerned. I've not yet had the report from her primary school, but she's been flagged."

"'Flagged'?"

"They haven't been specific, but along with our observations, I have to be perfectly honest and tell you that Nelly is not the right sort of girl for Adams."

"She's an Adams girl through and through," I say, knowing that Nelly is nothing of the sort but now feeling strongly that they deserve her.

"Now, I have a meeting to attend."

"She's a child. She has so much to learn. What if I made a significant donation?" I say, opening my bag.

"No, no, no . . . Mrs. Rook, please."

"Happy to contribute. If Adams needs a new brass plaque to celebrate your commitment to child well-being, or perhaps I could pay the cleaning bill for the girl's clothes—please let me do my part."

"Mrs. Rook, it's not in Nelly's best interests to go through to the second-round assessment. Nelly would find the rules and approach here too challenging."

"Education's all about being challenged. I want to know my daughter's true capabilities," I say as earnestly as I can, but the woman is made of stone.

"I'm sorry, Mrs. Rook."

"I need a tissue," I say, and open my bag. I rummage and take out my compact mirror and place it on the desk, then my purse, a packet of Nurofen Express, mascara, hand sanitizer, and a sixteen-ounce claw hammer.

"Aha," I say, pulling out a small packet of Kleenex from the bottom of my bag. "The tissues."

I proceed to take out and unfold a tissue as the headmistress's bright blue eyes focus on the hammer sitting on her desk, the steel claw shining in the late sunlight from her beautiful mullioned windows.

"You know what I think?" I say, dabbing the corners of my eyes as I've seen people do whose eyes have become moistened with tears (mine are bone-dry). "I think that children like Nelly need the understanding of the best people."

I take my things up from her desk and return them to my bag, one by one. The hammer is the last item. I pick it up and feel its weight in my hand.

"I too had phases as a child," I say, pointing the hammer at the headmistress. "Phases when I acted a little outside of the norm, but my school provided me with the love and attention I needed and, because of that, I was able to succeed."

She gives me that inscrutable look she's so fond of bandying around. I'm not sure she believes my lies but she says nothing.

"So I ask, do you have it in your heart to give this gifted child the benefit of the doubt?" I say.

"I don't think so," she says softly, pushing her chair back from the desk.

I stand up before she has a chance to get to her feet, and I peer down at her, the hammer hanging loosely in my hand and swinging gently to and fro. Her eyes watch it, like a cat tracking a piece of wool. My grip tightens around the rubber handle and the hammer stops. I lift it to shoulder height.

It might look as though I'm about to strike, or simply using the hammer as a point of emphasis. The headmistress has a short time to discern which it is, and my unblinking gaze is probably not helping.

"Mrs. Rook," she says, but her voice croaks and she suddenly looks like a rather frail middle-aged lady, her pomposity and assumed superiority punctured and leaking out of her like air from a balloon.

"A chance is all I'm asking for," I say. "Like Jean Valjean is given by that priest in *Les Miz*."

To an observer, my response may seem exaggerated, but I can think of nothing worse at this moment than leaving the room with the thought of telling Nelly that her dream is irreparably broken before she's even had a chance to want it.

I hit the hammer down firmly on her desk. It makes such a sound that she jumps backward and her knee thumps the underside of the drawer.

"I'll get her some therapy. Would that help appease your concerns?" I stare at the headmistress. She holds my gaze. I count eleven seconds.

"Yes, I think that would help," she says finally, her voice quavering.

"Have some water." I lean over and push her glass toward her. "And thank you for your understanding."

32

Austen

Friday, November 29

I phoned the real estate agent twelve times yesterday and was told Esmae was out all day, so I left several voicemails. As if by magic, she returned my calls today to say that they'll accept our offer but as they've had two other offers at that level, she won't take the house off the market. I argue my point but she is insistent. It's fortunate that it's a phone call, and that I don't have the opportunity to express my dissatisfaction in person.

"What do I need to do to secure the house and get it off the market?" I say quite sternly.

"You could try a holding deposit," she suggests, her voice sounding distant, as if she's distracted by something more interesting.

"How much?"

"Five percent might work. It would need to be nonreturnable. You have to show your commitment." Her once-charming singsong voice is now deeply annoying.

"A four-hundred-thousand-pound deposit?" I say, struggling with the sheer audacity.

"Or just wait and see."

"Fine. I'll make a five percent deposit," I say, and end the call.

I don't have four hundred thousand, but that is the least of my problems. We don't have the additional million in cash needed to raise the five million mortgage, our house is not even on the market, and Stephen doesn't know I've made an offer. But apart from these minor obstacles, all is well—I just need several miracles or a good to-do list. The latter is more practical.

First, I'll sell our house off-market without Stephen's knowledge, which Foxtons have offered to do at an extortionate 3 percent. Second, I'll raid Stephen's secret savings account. This should provide half of the nonreturnable deposit. Third, I'll redouble my efforts to ensure that a rather deflated Stephen makes partner. Fourth, I'll try to stress Stephen's mother so much that she has a terrible accident. Fifth, if that fails, I'll see if I can use my persuasive power to make her change her mind and help us with the loan of a million. And finally, concerning the other two hundred thousand for the deposit, I'll have to do what I've always done in such circumstances—beg, steal, or blackmail, and I don't mind which.

Having written it all down, I feel better. I have an inkling that Madeleine is behind the poison pen letter and the newspaper article. If she is closing in on some truths about my background, I will have to work harder at the fourth option.

On a much more heartwarming note, we received a letter from Adams with the wonderful news that the school has reviewed Nelly's activity day contribution and is pleased to report that she is successfully through to the next round. Hurrah! I think this might be down to the dolphin, but I may be wrong. I'm delighted. The pain I felt when I thought that Nelly would be denied her chance of a future was like losing a loved one. Or how I imagine that might feel, at least.

I told Stephen about Adams, and he cleared his throat and nodded. I asked him if he was happy about it, and he said that he wasn't unhappy, which is an odd thing to say, but to be honest, after the slight improvement in his mood recently, as evidenced by an extra gym session and the odd furtive glance at Aimée's bare midriff, he's dipped again quite dramatically and is walking about like a miserable eunuch.

He was on the phone for at least an hour last night, I presume to his mother as it was so heartfelt, and, well, if that's not going to make you suicidal, nothing will. The sooner the "widowhood effect" kicks in, the better. They wouldn't have much difficulty digging out the grave again as the soil won't even have fully settled yet.

I hope I helped a little by calling her three times throughout the night (at the expense of my own sleep pattern, I might add), pretending to be a rather assertive woman asking to speak to her husband and hinting at a long-term affair. When Madeleine informed this woman that he was dead, she asked if he left her the French gîte in his will as he'd promised. She was so distraught, I slept like a baby afterward.

In the evening, I catch Stephen reading a classic novel. Not Le Carré (acceptable) or Lee Child (more acceptable), not Len Deighton or Ken Follett. For heaven's sake, even the Thomas Harris I bought him for his birthday is untouched.

"What on earth are you reading, Stephen?" I inquire.

"Just a book."

"What book?"

He shows me the cover. I tilt my head and read the title.

"Jane Austen? Since when were you into romantic literature?" I ask, shocked.

"It's not really romantic literature . . . I mean it is, but it's much more than that."

"Well, I hope you don't tell anyone in your investment bank that you're reading Jane Austen," I exclaim, as this will do nothing for his future career.

"It's so good. You should try it. You'd like Fanny Dashwood."

"I suppose that's some kind of veiled attack."

"I didn't veil it at all," he says. "She's just another ruthlessly self-interested woman."

"Really? I've basically put my life on hold to suckle your children, provide sexual favors on demand, massage your frail ego, and support your stalling career—how is that self-interest?"

Stephen closes his book and walks out. An hour later, I find him asleep in the living room with the book across his chest and decide it's time for action. I take the tube of testosterone gel that I sourced on the internet and rub it on his arm. Some say it can turbo-boost the libido. No point in Aimée pressing the accelerator if there's nothing in the tank.

33

Madeleine

Saturday, November 30

With my hair newly colored, I stare up at the symmetry of Madeleine Rook's Kensington mansion. This elegant combination of stucco, bricks, and stone is the epitome of heritage, wealth, and power. One day soon, we might own this, too, and the thought pleases me immensely.

    I am dressed for the occasion in a black Alexander McQueen suit with a red enamel brooch; I look a little like a black widow spider. Not intentionally, I might add. The door opens and a maid in a traditional white apron and black dress invites me in and takes my coat. I thank her and hand her a large bunch of foxgloves for Madeleine. I'm shown into the drawing room, gestured toward a seat, and asked for my preferred beverage. I state a strong preference for herbal tea on this occasion.

    The room is tasteful and harmonious. Dark blue walls, Louis XVI marble clock, Regency rosewood table, a pair of Chippendale armchairs, and portraits of dead people and dogs.

    The maid returns with my flowers beautifully arranged in an Imari vase. She smiles as she leaves and returns a few minutes later with a teapot and two china cups on a silver salver. The maid asks if she should pour, and I tell her that I will wait for the lady of the house.

    Once she has closed the door, I take a small white envelope from my handbag. Inside it are several foxglove leaves that I removed from the bouquet earlier and cut up like tea. I open the teapot, slip the leaves into the water, and stir.

Madeleine appears a moment later, dressed impeccably in a cream-and-navy vintage Chanel suit dress. I am again surprised at how small the woman is, given how large she features in my thoughts.

"Good afternoon, Lalla." She pauses at the doorway and with a steady glance and slight arch of her eyebrows indicates that I should stand.

Against my better judgment, I get up and offer my hand. She looks at it with an almost imperceptible shake of her head, indicating that I've made another error. With a finger she points to her right cheek. I lean in and make the sound of a kiss.

"How's life in the provinces?"

"We're all coping with the drudgery," I say.

"Oh, good, and to what do I owe the unusual pleasure of your company?" she says with an impatient flourish of her hand, indicating that I should sit, which I do. She stands, framed by two enormous windows, and looks down at me.

"I brought you some flowers. I thought you might need cheering up. Stephen says the anniversary has hit you hard."

"No, I don't think so."

"He seems to think you're inconsolable with grief."

"I don't know any woman who'd consider herself worse off if her husband died. I have all his resources, and none of his annoying habits."

"I'm pleased you're so rational about it," I say, although she clearly paints a different picture for Stephen.

"Now, you didn't come here for my welfare. Either someone's terminally ill, or you need money, which is it?"

"We need a million to secure the house in Hampstead, and Stephen wouldn't ever ask you himself."

"Because he's got class, while you're quite shameless." She peers at me from under hooded eyelids.

"I'm simply trying to ensure your son and grandchildren are suitably homed. You've always detested Muswell Hill."

"I'm sure," Madeleine says and walks from one piece of ornate furniture to the next as she contemplates my request. "I could help you, of course, but I wonder what you might do for me."

"Anything within reason," I say.

"Leave him," she says.

"Why would I do that?"

"Because you're not who you say you are, are you, Lalla?" she says, and smiles. This is not going to plan.

"What does that mean?" I say, trying to buy time to think.

"Presumably, you received the old newspaper article in the post?" she says, watching my response closely.

"I did and have no idea what it's about," I say.

"I thought that's why you were here," says Madeleine. "Smoked out of your den."

"I don't know a thing about it," I say.

"Roger once bought a Monet without provenance," she says. "I advised against it, of course, but he was taken in by the traumatic history of the painting, which included a Nazi theft, tragic deaths, and forty years hidden in the loft of a farmhouse."

"And was it real?"

"Absolutely not. A complete fake. No provenance, you see. Worthless, just like you. You say your parents died, you went to a school in Geneva that since closed, you've lost touch with all your relatives, and you had that accident that wiped your memory. If you were a painting, I'm afraid Sotheby's would put you in a bin sale."

"Is this a feature of your declining faculties, or do you simply have too much time on your hands?"

"Who are you, Lalla? When Stephen fell under your spell, I wanted to check you out, but Roger stopped me. I always wondered what you had over Roger. Did you offer yourself to him in exchange for protection?"

"I think Roger was just delighted that Stephen was happy, because he'd never managed to find love and happiness in his own marriage."

"Anyone can see you're not from money, and certainly not

educated at an elite Swiss school. You're leaking sawdust all over the carpet."

"Have you been poisoning Stephen with these lies?" I say.

"Lies, are they?" she says, puffing herself up like a peacock. "You know how I found out? Your greed. I found a series of payments to someone called Lola Wells in one of Roger's bank statements after he died. He kept everything, you see. They appeared around the time of your engagement to Stephen."

"Just another woman he was sleeping with for comfort, no doubt."

"I thought so, too, but I asked a private detective to do some work for me to find Lola Wells," she says, which immediately makes me think it was her who hired Jason Mercer. "Not an easy task," she continues, "until I realized I had another piece of the jigsaw. Once I gave him your date of birth, things started to open up. He found the birth certificate of a girl called Lola Wells, born on the same day as you, in Banbury. Her parents were called Brian and Margaret Wells. They later appeared in this rather sordid news story, when their daughter was taken into care. She'd be thirty-nine today. I couldn't find a photo of her, sadly. She disappeared from records after the murder. I expect she changed her name and made up a new one."

"You've wasted your money. That's not me," I say with a dismissive laugh, but I feel as if I've been punched hard in the gut. "Why are you so determined to split up a happy marriage?"

Madeleine laughs. "Happy? Have you seen your husband lately? I'm going to share my research with him and let him draw his own conclusions. You do understand that you're on borrowed time now, don't you?"

"You're delusional," I say.

"I don't think so. I'm quite sure that I'm on the right track."

"Tea?" I say.

"How civilized," she replies, and takes out a cigarette from a silver case. As she lights her cigarette, I open the teapot, stir vigorously, then pour carefully into the two delicate cups.

"I know it's naughty to smoke, but I only ever have one to celebrate," says Madeleine, and she puffs a large cloud into the room.

"Milk?" I ask.

She shakes her head. "It's herbal tea, Lalla, not Tetley. I expect you'll find it quite bitter."

"Oh, I'm used to that, Madeleine," I say, and pass her a cup.

Madeleine puts her cigarette down, sips her tea, then smiles broadly at me. "Not drinking yours, I see?"

"You were right about the bitterness," I say. "It's not to my taste."

34

Cocktails

Sunday, December 1

I've known for some time that Tor is hiding something. She's been curiously absent from several events, deeply unhelpful with Cait, and a little more spiky than usual. I ask if we should get a drink in town, and even though it's a Sunday, she jumps at the idea, insisting that we should meet alone, which is quite out of character as I'm not important enough for one-to-ones.

According to the website, the Filthy Fours cocktail lounge is "a celebration of mixology known for its undeniably zany interior with downward-growing trees, hammocks galore, and cosplay bar staff." As far as I can determine (and I don't claim to be an expert), it's an underfunded pantomime serving sweetened cocktails in a drafty warehouse with music at a volume to make your ears bleed, but the youth seem to like it.

"How's Cait?" says Tor, dressed as though she's been at an event at Kensington Palace. "Sorry to have been so out of it. I've been so busy with the building work."

"Did you hear they found Owen's body?" I say.

"Bloody hell! Owen! That's quite gruesome, isn't it. Burnt to death. How awful."

"Yes, but it means Cait can move on now."

We order negronis and talk about nothing in particular. I sense she has a secret as Tor is extremely tense—tightly crossed legs, suspicious glances, and rudeness to the waitress.

By the third negroni, Tor's legs uncross, her arms reach across the back of the velvet banquette, and words start to tumble from her expensive veneers and plumped lips. In order to master the role of the confidante, it's important to model vulnerability yourself and reveal your own weaknesses.

"We all have problems, Tor," I say. "We often hide them away. I know I do. Stephen and I don't have sex anymore."

"What, never?" She looks at me momentarily like a vulture might regard roadkill, then she quickly smiles. "Same."

We laugh, but only for a moment. Her face suddenly sharpens as she catches herself in the mirror. I start to put the pieces together—new face, new clothes, new diet, sexless marriage.

"Are you and Lawrence okay, besides the lack of bedroom activity?"

"As well as anyone, I imagine," she says. "He's deeply committed to his constituents. I don't know how he does it."

I listen carefully, but there's no resentment there, no gibe or aside or tone. If anything, she's far too kind to that portly self-indulgent Tory who has twice had to pay off junior advisers after some indelicate HR issues.

"I've been worried about you," I say. Tor is naturally suspicious and deeply uncomfortable talking about feelings, as with most of her milieu.

"Me? Why?"

Now is the key moment. She can take the bait or close it down.

"In the summer, you seemed happy and full of the joys of life, and now, you seem really on edge."

"I thought I was hiding it well."

I sit back and open my hands. "I'm here for you. I'm a good listener."

"Lawrence is having a midlife crisis. He's taken up with someone again," she says. "But that's not the problem."

"So, what is?"

"I'm having a midlife crisis too," she says. "He's called Zac and he's twenty-six."

I lean forward, unsure whether I'm jealous or feeling just a little salacious. "A boy toy?"

She nods. "It's embarrassing, I know, but deeply, deeply satisfying. The energy of the man."

"How long have you been seeing Zac?"

"Since the summer. I've always been an absolute sucker for dark hair and blue eyes. I shouldn't be superficial, but he's bloody poetry to look at, and he's got the body of a Greek statue."

"It's completely understandable, Tor." I indicate two more cocktails to the waitress.

"It's not something I could tell the others. They're quite moralistic. But I always get the feeling you're more worldly-wise."

"We've all got to find a way to get by," I say, although I now know she chose me because she has so little respect for the views of Cait, Sophie, or Aisha. But why tell anyone? There must be something more.

"Is everything going well with your dalliance?"

"Well, actually, not really. I made a mistake. Something you must never do if you stray. I fell completely and madly in love," says Tor, and she clasps her gold-entwined fingers together and holds them to the place where a heart would usually sit.

"Oops," I say. I conclude that Zac is unusually good in bed and she thinks it's love. Easy mistake to make.

"Head over heels, Lalla. I wasn't in Switzerland, you know. I was in bloody Madrid with Zac, having the most glorious time."

"Well, it's clearly as good as a spa, because you were glowing when you came back."

"He makes me feel amazing. I know there's an age gap, but it feels so right. I think I love him." I look at her and wonder what this word *love* means to an overprivileged woman like Tor.

"So what's the issue? You want a divorce?"

"No, there's something worse."

She is about to reveal her secret when my phone rings. I take it out, apologizing, and see Stephen's name. I shake my head, silence the call, sip my drink, and stare intently at Tor.

"It's only Stephen. He's probably lost a sock or something. Do go on," I say, but I wonder if the testosterone gel has got him into trouble with Aimée, or Madeleine has told him about my visit.

Tor smiles nervously, drinks the rest of her negroni, and says, "I'm being blackmailed."

Although I've learned to control my expressions, my eyebrows rise in delight.

"Tell me more," I say.

Tor is about to reveal all, when my phone pings. Stephen's messaged me, and it makes my pulse race:

Urgent. Please come home. Bad news.

35

Mother

Having rushed home in an Uber, trying to get in contact with Stephen most of the journey, I am not in the best of moods. It's not the most thoughtful of messages. It's liable to create all kinds of worries, if you are prone to such things.

I have only one thought—Nathan and Nelly. I know I'm not as traditionally connected to them as most parents, but if I had to save anyone in the world, it would be them first. Well, not first. But once I'd ensured Purdy was okay, it would be Nelly first, then Nathan, then Sophie, and Stephen would be next.

I am also drunk, which means that I am not as clear-minded as I usually am. At home, I find Stephen rushing from room to room, looking quite disheveled.

"Are Purdy and the children okay?" I ask immediately.

"Yes. Yes. The children are fine," he says. "Couldn't give a fuck about the cat."

"Unkind," I say.

"Well, priorities, you know."

"Your text said it was urgent. I sent you several back."

"I've been on the phone since." Stephen stares. His face is not obviously sad, but there's a dilation to his pupils and a slight pallor around his eyes.

"What is it?" I ask.

"Mum's had a stroke."

"Oh, no, how terrible," I say, thinking that my little visit has worked miraculously well and so quickly too. As I was leaving, I did pop into the kitchen to thank the maid for the tea and was pleased to see the teapot and cups stacked in the dishwasher. I asked her if she could tell me what was in the herbal tea she'd used as it was so refreshing. As she headed for the larder to fetch the tin, I located the compost bin and found the mulch of toxic leaves. I took the whole bag, tied a knot, and placed it in my handbag, leaving absolutely no evidence of my herbal concoction.

"She's bad, Lalla," he says, and looks completely lost.

"Oh, darling, I'm so sorry. How worried you must be." I bite my bottom lip in mimicry of someone stopping themselves crying. If I've helped bring on a stroke, there's hope of an additional bereavement, which would release much-needed funds to secure Hampstead. I won't clap my hands just yet, though. She's a tough old bird.

"She's in intensive care at the Royal Brompton in Chelsea. Mrs. Dekka called the ambulance."

"And is she conscious?" I say, crossing my fingers.

"They didn't say. I'm going to see her now. I need to pack a bag."

"What for?"

"I'll stay at the house, so I'm close."

"How long do you think you'll be gone for?" I say, thinking of his savings account and my need to get five minutes alone with his phone.

"How would I know, Lalla?"

"Of course, but the partner interviews are happening next week."

"At this point in time, I don't give a shit about being a partner."

"I understand," I say, throwing my arms around him to give him an enormous hug. This enables me to appear gracious but also allows me to lift his phone from his back pocket.

"Tell the kids I'll see them soon. Aimée put them to bed. I just need to be with Mum."

"Don't worry. Everything will be fine here," I say. Of course I'm also thinking that Foxtons have three interested buyers, and with

Stephen away, I'll have a clear run to try to get an offer. I make a mental note to get a cleaning company in to spruce up the house.

"Thank you," he says.

At this point Aimée enters in a short T-shirt and, it would appear, an absence of anything underneath besides a thong. She stands there, hands on hips, and stares at Stephen.

"Can we help?" I say.

"I can't find my trousers," says Aimée, and smiles coyly.

"I'm sure you have other trousers," I say, wondering if this is normal in France.

"I need my velvet trousers," she says, staring at Stephen. "They hug my figure so well."

"I think you look fine as you are," I say.

"Do you know where they are, Stephen?" she says, and plays with the hem of her T-shirt.

Stephen is confused. I am envious of her endless and blemish-free legs but I reassure myself that age will get her eventually.

"I have no idea," he says.

Aimée laughs. "Oh, Stephen, you are so funny!"

"Oh, for goodness' sake, Aimée, not now!" I say, realizing that this is her crude attempt to flirt with the man.

Aimée shoots a look of defiance in my direction and shrugs as if to say, *You asked for it.*

"Your trousers are in the airing cupboard on the landing. It's the door you never open."

Aimée lets out a guttural growl and walks toward the radio. "Would anyone like to dance?" she says, turning on the radio. She looks back over her shoulder through a cascade of hair and starts to sway rhythmically.

"My mother's just had a stroke," says Stephen, so well trained in avoiding corporate sexual harassment claims that her presence in the room is causing him to sweat.

"I think you really should go upstairs, Aimée," I say.

"I'm just following instructions," Aimée says.

"What's going on?" says Stephen, and he stumbles out of the room.

In an instant, Aimée drops the entire act, expresses disdain with a release of air from her lips, and turns to me. "That's two hundred pounds, would you like the same next week?"

"That might work in France, Aimée, but an Englishman would never see that as flirting," I say.

"Too much?"

"Oh no, you would have to be a lot more direct than that," I say, furious at having wasted a good amount of testosterone gel, as well as £200.

Aimée leaves with one long sigh. I sit down, open Stephen's phone, as I've long known his passcode, and transfer £200,000 from his savings account to our joint current account. As it's an internal transfer, there's no upper limit, which is helpful. I wait for the notice to ping on his phone. Approve, then delete. If I make a payment to the estate agent while he's focused on his mother, he won't even notice.

I smile at myself in the bathroom mirror. Madeleine half dead, Hampstead half secured. I feel that everything is falling into place.

36

Pancho's

Tuesday, December 3

Pancho's is a nondescript, low-rent Mexican café. The outdoor tables are rather weather-beaten and the whole ambience of the café is shabby without being chic. It is highly visible, and not a good place for an assignation as there is at least one camera that would record us.

I arrive early as I want to scope out an alternative meeting point. My plan is simple. I'll see who this client is (if indeed a client) and work out how they're connected to the deceased police officer, and what they want from me.

Second, I want to gauge his or her size. This will help with later considerations. I am not keen to be lumbered with a heavy and difficult-to-move corpse twice. I find a seat in the window of a Starbucks across the road, which allows me to keep tabs on the café. It is far enough away to avoid being seen, but close enough to identify the client.

I buy a newspaper, a touch spylike, but it's also helpful to pass the time. I order a latte, then all I do is keep an eye on my phone and read about the various conflicts around the world, which can be depressing.

It gives me time to think about Cait. I saw her after she had identified Owen from a couple of nonflammable belongings. She seemed upset. I was expecting song and dance, elation, and gratitude, but all I got was regret, recrimination, and sadness.

I also mentioned that she was now free of worries about Owen getting custody, so she could stop worrying about the *other* dead body, and she started shaking quite violently. I expect it's just tiredness, and she still doesn't look as though she's eating well.

I look at my watch. It is ten minutes to one. The café opposite is not full. There are two women in office attire, a group of laborers, a man in a wheelchair sitting on his own, and an inexcusably jolly woman with two spoiled children. No sign of anyone I know. I wait until two o'clock. Nothing. I decide to give it ten more minutes. At five minutes past, a man arrives on his own, wearing a baseball cap, which looks hopeful. He glances around him, looks at his watch, and then sits down. He takes out his phone and starts to scroll.

I don't recognize him. I want to be patient but I'm quite angry about being stalked by a dodgy copper, so I decide to make my move. I head out, cross the road, and walk up to the café, shades and rather elegant cashmere twill baseball cap providing enough of a disguise. I approach the lone man. I'm about to take the seat opposite him when a woman enters from the other direction and he rises up to embrace her.

Disappointed, I glance around. The laborers are laughing at their own jokes. The woman with the two children is wiping yogurt from the table, the women in suits are chatting intently, and the man in the wheelchair is peering at a laptop, looking at cars.

I decide that I must've missed some other communication that's changed or canceled the plan to meet. I head to my car. I've walked about twenty steps down the street when something stops me. What is it? A thought tugging at my memory banks. I turn around and stare up the road at the café.

I walk back toward Pancho's, trying to filter my thoughts and find the one that is reverberating. I suddenly see it. A single sticker sitting among several other stickers.

I turn into the café and take a position across from the man in the wheelchair, hidden by the awning. I stare at a small image of a chimpanzee holding a samurai sword on the back of his Apple laptop. *MonkeyWarrior*.

I can't see his face, as he's bearded and wearing a low baseball cap with the words *Western Bulldogs*. There's a shudder when I read those two words, but it can't be, I tell myself.

His hand moves to the keyboard, and I see four small black tattoos on his knuckles—a star, a cross, a heart, and a mountain. My stomach lurches.

My heart rate has risen, but it's impossible. He types and then picks up his coffee and I see his face.

Sitting there is my husband, a man I killed ten years earlier.

PART THREE

Reconnect

And sometimes I have kept my feelings to myself,
because I could find no language to describe them in.

JANE AUSTEN, *Sense and Sensibility*, **1811**

37

Rocks

Wednesday, December 4
After carefully following my Lazarus-like spouse in his wheelchair back to his sad little flat yesterday, I returned home. I wasn't much company and even failed to read the children their bedtime story. Quite unforgivable, but it's hard to focus when you've been visited by a ghost.

Today, I think about Hollis, my former husband, as I untangle gym socks, vests, and various pants. I was quite sure he was dead. I pushed him off a high ledge in the Alps myself. I watched him fall, heard his sad, plaintive cry and the thud of his body against the ice.

I then staged my own fall, smashing my climbing hat with a rock and throwing my backpack into the ravine. I made my way down the mountain feeling the wonderful freedom of a super-fast divorce.

I manage to get through the washing before Nathan is due home, and I shut myself away in my office. I do not, as a rule, look backward. I like the past to be past, I like the dead to be dead. Only the future interests me—what I want, and what I need to do to get it.

If, for instance, Stephen were to tell me that his mother died today, I would think how wonderful for him to be free of that shrinking and costly organism, whose sole role seems to be ruining other people's happiness by digging up what should be buried. I know it's not fashionable to say this, but we all think things that would cause alarm if we said them in company. More than half our world is left unsaid.

And that's how Hollis and I got into difficulty. Too much left unsaid, hiding beneath the surface, lowering my boiling point. I see him now on my laptop screen. Matthew Hollis. I always just called him Hollis. Who'd want to be called Matt? It's either a color without sheen or a place to wipe your feet.

He's smiling out from my screen in an old article with a photograph provided by his family, I imagine. There were no such photographs of me. I've always been careful about that. The Google translation reads "Couple Missing on Mont Blanc."

There are three more articles: "Storm Hampers Rescue Attempt"; "Married Couple Feared Dead"; and finally, "Rescue Called Off After Three Days." And that was it. A simple story in four acts. The story ends there. No curiosity, no investigation. The French authorities simply put it down to yet more inexperienced tourists climbing without knowledge or skills. After all, we were on the Goûter Route, which is known rather helpfully as the "corridor of death."

I stare down at his photo and imagine him crawling his way to safety in unbelievable pain, and I feel something. What is it? Regret? Guilt? No, I know what it is. It's disappointment at a job half done.

So, let's recap—my first husband is not frozen to a rock face at thirteen thousand feet above sea level, in a deep, inaccessible ravine covered in thick snow. He somehow found it within his optimistic antipodean nature to transform into one of those survivors worthy of a Netflix documentary, which is surprising for a man who couldn't wash his own socks. Three days he survived on a flapjack, his own tears, and his passionate love for his wife, slowly climbing out of the ravine inch by inch, carrying his shattered legs behind him, until he made it back to the path, when he realized that his wife must've fallen, too, and was probably dead.

And yet, here he is, which means that at some point later Hollis must've come to the belief that I was miraculously alive and dedicated his life to finding me. I am almost moved. But that's not the story. This is the story of a botched, capricious murder attempt. He was annoying me. He'd eaten all the Kendal Mint Cake. He was explaining how I could improve my climbing technique while repeating his dismal utterance of "Love you" at irritating moments.

I was homeless when I met Hollis, running away from a life of rampant drug and alcohol abuse. He took me in, and I found myself married to this random Australian who didn't ask questions, had a job, a home, money, and never judged me. The thing is, I found his mindless optimism and endless emotional support a little too much in the end. It's not reality that kills you; it's the lack of it.

After Hollis fell, I ran away again. I was presumed dead, and I liked being dead. I returned to London, assumed a new name, and returned to poverty and homelessness for a time, secure in a world that didn't love me because I couldn't love it back.

And I thought that was it, but Hollis survived and that presents several rather knotty problems. Not least, that I'm currently married to two different men, which is not only excessive—it's illegal.

I consider my options vis-à-vis Hollis.

Option 1: I meet him. I explain that I thought he was dead and I've sadly moved on. We recall old times, share a memory or two, and then agree to let sleeping dogs lie, get a quick divorce, and I help him find another woman to simper over.

Option 2: I ignore him. I bury my head and hope he will go away. I engage in some light risk-taking to get it out of my system and pretend he doesn't exist.

Option 3: I get rid of him. I appear at his door, declare that he has found me, wrap my arms around him, and weep with joy. We celebrate, drink a bottle of wine together, and I garrote him in his half-drunken state and leave.

My preferred option is Option 3, and I find myself playing this scene out, as it has aroused something within me. However, self-gratification aside, this option does present a potential problem. There is a link between me, Jason Mercer, and Hollis. The police don't know that yet, but if I kill Hollis and the police connect me to Hollis, and Hollis to Mercer, I will become the common denominator in the disappearance and death of two missing men, which makes getting away with either murder a more significant challenge.

After some reflection, I go for Option 2. The past is a hindrance and I fear that if I engage with it at all, it will entangle me. I like the unclouded vistas of the future, not the disappointments of life through a rearview mirror.

To-do list:
Book additional tutoring for Nelly
Pay for a bereavement therapist for Cait
Book the floor sander for living room
Secure Hampstead

38

Bob's

Thursday, December 5

In the morning, I meet Tor in Bob's Café on the Broadway. I can't wait any longer to hear more about the blackmailing, but I'm not in the best of moods. Tor and I manage to get a reasonably private booth (a table for four, which causes some distress in the café), and we're soon enduring glasses of healthy green juice.

We quickly catch up about Cait (sad face), and I tell Tor about Stephen and Madeleine. Tor is both sympathetic and envious.

"I don't think he's over his father's death, to be perfectly honest, and this has hit him hard," I say.

"I would love to lose just one of my mothers! But seriously, is there anything I can do to help?" says Tor, sipping her green juice.

"No, we're just waiting. She's responsive, thank goodness."

"What a terrible time we're all having," says Tor.

"So, back to blackmail..." I say, my spider senses tingling all over.

"Well, a couple of weeks ago, we were at Zac's apartment in Mayfair. The sex was great but even I felt it was a little more performative than usual. I'm sure you don't want the saucy details."

"Mirrors?"

"Exactly. I know men like the more visual stuff, so I didn't think about it at the time, I was just on a wave of adoration. I thought—'This must be how the younger generation does it these days.' Then, I found out a week ago that he had secretly filmed the whole thing."

"No!" I say, in mock outrage, although I'm impressed with the young man's industry.

"He'd set up cameras in advance and he'd been manipulating the whole scene to get good shots," says Tor, glancing around to check no one is listening in.

"How did you find out?"

"He showed it to me one evening, telling me he'd made it in secret as a sexy gift for me. I was really angry. I mean, it's a bloody liberty. Who wants to be filmed like that? I'm not twenty-one. He just laughed and said it'd spice up our relationship. Then he kissed me, one thing led to another, and I forgave him."

"So he's not blackmailing you?"

"Zac? No, Zac's in love with me."

"Then who?"

"I asked him to delete the film, and he said he'd do it, and then he went away on business for a few days. And just after he got back, I got an urgent call. I rushed around and he showed me his computer screen. There was this huge ransomware notice in red and black saying, 'Your accounts have been encrypted and downloaded. Your private content will be shared with your contacts unless you deposit £50,000 into the following Bitcoin account within two weeks.'"

"Christ, Tor. When was this?"

"Ten days ago. And now I've only got a few more days to deposit the money or I'm bloody ruined." Tor buries her head in her hands.

"How do you know it's genuine? I mean, there are scams like this everywhere."

"I thought that, too, but some of his photographs were sent to all his contacts. I received them, too, so we know they've got access." Tor is getting more and more distressed, and her face seems to be tiring from displaying such a range of expression.

"So, you're cheating on Lawrence with a boy toy who made a sex tape that is now in the hands of a blackmailer who wants fifty grand from you?" I want to ask if she's not read the code of conduct for Tory wives, which would probably frown on at least two of these actions.

"It's not cheating," she says angrily. "Lawrence is seeing someone too. It's just . . . how we are."

"Are you going to pay?"

"What else can I do? Imagine the shame if these get out there. And Law's position will be untenable."

"I can only imagine the horror," I say, wanting to write the headlines myself.

"I'm so furious with Zac. He's put me in an impossible position."

"It's certainly backfired," I say, wondering why Tor hasn't the faintest suspicion that Zac isn't everything he seems to be.

"When I told him how cross I was, he started to cry," she whimpers.

"Yes, I imagine he did," I say, picturing him crying all the way to the bank.

"Oh, Lalla, you never want to imagine your family seeing such things. It's so completely degrading. And I don't want to lose Zac."

"You're sticking with him after he took advantage of you like this?" Zac is clearly fleecing her and doing it rather well.

"It was a little mistake and we love each other. Anyway, the thing is, Lalla, I've only got £40,000 at the moment, and I'm £10K short. My money's not accessible, and I can't ask Law."

"Oh, right," I say, realizing I, too, have been duped. This isn't a friend confiding in me. She needs hard cash, and she's looking into my eyes.

"Please," she whines.

"Anything for a friend," I say, as I'm sure there's leverage in this somewhere.

She throws her arms around me. I can feel her desperation and understand why she's been acting so strangely of late.

"But I want something in return," I say, pulling back.

"Yes, of course, anything," she says, although she doesn't have the faintest idea of what I'm going to ask for.

As we leave the café my phone pings twice in rapid succession. I look down at two texts from Aisha:

Cait's been arrested

She's at Tottenham police station

I type:

Terrible news. What have they arrested her for?

Owen's murder

39

Vampires

Saturday, December 7

Just two minutes from Hampstead High Street, four real estate agents, in their mid to late twenties, are sitting in large ergonomically designed Herman Miller chairs at sleekly curved black-and-cream workstations, staring attentively at their double-size screens, scrolling and tapping.

I'm staring at Esmae, who's looking back at me without blinking. I sometimes wonder if the best real estate agents have sociopathic qualities. This one certainly does. I have two hundred thousand pounds deposited courtesy of Stephen's savings accounts, and she is smiling in a way that is not exactly reassuring.

"The rest will come," I say.

"Sorry, I can't take it off the market," she says, turning a pencil in her fingers.

"Two hundred thousand doesn't do that?"

"Four hundred is what they need. They've been burned before."

"Not by me," I say. I look up at the wall behind her. A large map of Hampstead is surrounded by old photographs of bygone times. They are selling nostalgia at eight million a pop.

"Your offer has been accepted, but you know, timing is everything."

"This purchase is worth about fifteen thousand pounds to you, I expect," I say.

"The thing is, Mrs. Rook, things fall apart all the time. The best-laid plans of mice and men, and all that. House sales fall through, offers are withdrawn. There are a multiplicity of factors. In this case, the vendor wants assurances."

"But this is also about trust," I say, and pull the annoying pencil from her hand.

"Trust is best expressed via a nonreturnable deposit," she says, and grabs it back.

"Have you shown it to anyone else?" I move my hand toward her and she pulls back.

"I have four viewings booked for next weekend, but this is what I'll do for you. If the other two hundred thousand is transferred by Friday, close of day, I'll cancel those viewings." She gently strokes her lips with the end of the pencil.

"What if I were to feather the nest?" I say. "Would that extend the timeline? I just need a few more days. How does ten thousand pounds sound?"

"It sounds like a financial inducement to perform my duties improperly, but I'd hate to think that you were trying to bribe me."

"Not a bribe, a down payment," I suggest.

"I don't need to be a criminal, Mrs. Rook. Selling houses is more profitable than that."

"Then I'll have the two hundred thousand in your account by Friday," I say, standing up. I'm about to leave the office, but I can't. I turn, walk across, grab her pencil, snap it, and put it on her desk.

I walk down Hampstead High Street feeling better. Three people have already viewed our house while Stephen was visiting his sick mother, so that's one positive. But how do I get two hundred thousand pounds in five business days? I've already cleared out our savings, and even if Stephen's mother dies, fingers crossed, probate will take forever.

After dealing with one bloodsucking vampire, I visit another. Divorce lawyers are smart creatures. I can see from the look in her eyes that she's excited because I've dressed to look both powerful and wealthy. Divorce lawyers can smell money and I need someone keen enough to provide free advice.

"My husband and I have been married for seven years and have two children and a house in North London," I say as she stares at me with cold, calculating eyes. "He's an investment banker. His family are wealthy. His father died recently and his mother's just had a stroke. I don't know the prognosis but I'm hopeful. I'm hoping to explore the best options, financially speaking."

"May I ask the general cause of the breakdown of your relationship?" she says, pressing the fingers of her hands together to make a pyramid.

"What do you mean, exactly?"

"Is it adultery, unreasonable behavior, or has the marriage just broken down irretrievably?"

"None of the above," I say. "I rather like him, actually, which still surprises me."

"But you want a divorce?" she says, somewhat idiotically, given her specialism.

"Advice, in the first instance, about a small issue, which is probably quite unusual."

"It's often the case. There are rarely simple cases when unraveling two lives," she says, and swivels quite dramatically on her chair.

"Three lives, actually. I've been married before. My first husband died in a tragic climbing accident, or so I thought. I have just discovered that he is alive and well."

Her eyes widen.

"Officially, I'm a bigamist, I suppose, but it's not intentional. Who would burden themselves with two incompetent men when one is often too many?"

"That does muddy the waters of divorce proceedings slightly," she says, and takes a sip from her glass of water.

"How slightly?"

"Well," she says, and eyes me slyly. "I presume that you had good reason to believe your husband was dead."

"He fell into a ravine in the Alps. His chances of survival were minimal."

"And was he unable to find you, once he did survive?"

"I changed my name."

"And does your current husband know about this previous marriage and the accident?"

"Absolutely not."

"You didn't tell him about your first marriage?" she says, leaning back in her chair.

"I'm not a sharer. And I didn't want to be seen as a widow. Something old and to be pitied."

"Right," she says, with a pinched mouth.

"You look doubtful."

"I am just here for legal opinions, but it does look as though your second marriage may not be on firm ground."

"But I thought my first husband was dead."

"Did you file for divorce or get a death certificate?"

"Neither."

"In which case, I would suggest that legally your current marriage would be considered void."

"Surely not."

"Not in life, but in law, it would be treated as if it never existed," she says quite cheerfully.

"Oh, but it does exist. We have two children and a house in Muswell Hill."

"The relationship exists, but the legal contract of marriage is not valid, because you weren't entitled to enter into another contract and, unfortunately, you failed to reveal your true situation."

"And how does that affect divorce proceedings?"

"Your husband can just walk away. There's no contract between you," she says, as if this is a marvelous thing.

"And what about financial recompense? Would I still get half of everything?"

"You could try to argue, but case law suggests that there's no legal grounds for any financial remedy."

"Nothing?"

"Nothing."

I leave with great disappointment, loss of faith in the legal system, and a new sense of purpose. It's absolutely clear what has to happen now. If Hollis doesn't agree to Option 1 (secret divorce and bonhomie), I must move to Option 3 (murder and less bonhomie).

40

Hollis

Monday, December 9

Trying to get a second with Cait at the police station over the weekend was impossible. She was allowed a lawyer, one phone call (to her mum), and a psychologist. But friends and family—no. The closest I got was a conversation with a duty sergeant via an intercom at some awful holding facility.

We all rallied on Sunday and found her a better solicitor as she only had a court-appointed one and everyone knows how overworked and underwhelming they are. Anyway, the new attorney told us that the police applied for an extension to keep her in custody. If they don't have sufficient evidence, she may be released under investigation, or on precharge bail. Whatever happens, they have to release her or charge her today, so we'll know one way or another soon enough.

I now make my way up the gray concrete ramp to a row of flats in one of the many three-story blocks that make up the Meadows. The only remnant of a meadow that I can detect from the balcony is a small diamond-shaped flower bed devoid of all plant life in which a large Staffordshire terrier is crouched down with a concentrated look on its face, while its owner dedicates his attention to his phone.

There are seven near-identical doors along the corridor. One has been finely decorated with graffiti, another with a large hole that reveals the cheap plywood-and-foam construction. The door I stand in front of boasts a large sticky puddle of dried urine.

I ring the bell. After a minute or so, I hear the sound of bolts and chains being drawn, and finally, the door opens.

Matthew Hollis, my undead first husband, is sitting in front of me, smiling.

"Long time no see," I say, deciding to keep it casual.

"What?" he says, searching my face. He doesn't recognize me for a moment as he's looking into the light, but as I move forward, his eyes show recognition and he stares up as pathetically as any drowned kitten swimming to the surface from an ineffectively tied sack.

"Lola!" he splutters, as all the memories and emotions come flooding back to him. "Lola! Is it really you? Bloody hell! I hardly recognized you."

"I've changed a little," I say. It feels strange to be called Lola again. It carries too much of a world I rejected. I didn't just push Hollis off a mountain, I realize; I pushed *me* off a mountain, too—at least my name, my marriage, and my past. I thought I'd been completely reborn, but all the time, my old life was here, waiting for me with all its dark corridors.

"You're so different! You look like you've become respectable. Where's the dyed hair, the eyeliner, the ripped clothes?"

"We've both changed. You're in a wheelchair," I say. "And you have a beard."

"The beard makes me look cool," he says, which is a matter of opinion. "Legs were smashed to pieces."

"In the accident?"

He nods and looks at me. "What happened to you? You weren't hurt?"

"I was lucky, I guess. I'm sorry about your legs."

"Oh, it's not so bad; you get used to it. And my arms are totally ripped now," he says, and flexes his biceps.

"It's good to see you, Hollis," I say, feeling the force of his optimism wash over me again. There were good times too. In the beginning.

"How did you find me?" he says. "I've been looking for you for years and you just show up on my doorstep!"

"You had someone follow me. A man named Jason Mercer. He gave me your address."

"Oh, right. I'm sorry about that. I hired him to try to find you because he had access to police files. He said he'd found someone who might be you—different name, different appearance, so he wasn't sure. I asked him to find out more, and then it all went quiet."

"I think he's done a runner. He was in the papers. Not a nice man, apparently. Had a court case pending. Police are looking for him."

"Oh god, sorry again. I suppose he's bound to be dodgy if he's moonlighting as an investigator. I was just so desperate to find you."

"I thought you were dead, Hollis."

"I thought you were dead, Lola," he says, and his face crumples into something tearless but definitely sad.

"What made you look for me?" I say.

He looks at me and says, "I had this feeling."

"A feeling?"

"Yeah. In my heart. I just didn't feel you were gone. A year after the accident, when the weather was better, I got a team together to search the ravine where we fell. Couldn't find your body. It gave me hope that maybe you'd also climbed out of there. I had this horrible picture of you wandering the earth, having lost your memory. It broke my heart to think of you alone in the world."

Hollis was always one to overromanticize our relationship. He felt we were destined to be together, like two imperfect stars colliding. His capacity for projecting his feelings was overwhelming. I got wrapped up in it at the start because I had so little else in my life, but after a while, I drowned in it.

"Please sit down," he says, but I remain standing, and we stare at each other. There is so much to explain or invent. My mind is racing, but he doesn't want explanations just yet. He only remembers the good parts and wants the reunion scene. He reaches out to me from his chair. I lean forward, bending at the hip. His arms enfold and crush me as my legs jam against the footplate.

We stay like that for over a minute as he hugs and blubbers into my neck. His upper body strength was always impressive and even now leaves me slightly breathless, but as his wet face slides against mine, any residual loin-quivering stops abruptly.

Clearly, I can't share the joy of this momentous occasion with Hollis. I'm angry with him because his existence currently voids my marriage, but I'm more angry with myself. When you set yourself a task, you complete it. I failed, and this is the result.

We untangle from our embrace and he wheels himself up the hall, explaining how lucky he is to get this raised ground-floor apartment because there's a ramp.

"Stairs are the curse," he says as he pushes open the door to the living room. He offers me a cup of tea. I look at the state of the kitchen. I'd rather drink bleach.

"Yes, thank you," I say, deciding that I'll just hold it. The warmth might help as the flat smells damp. Hollis was a man whose ambition always outstripped his ability. He always had a new tech idea that would revolutionize something, and then it would fail and he'd start again. It looks like he's decided failure without ambition is easier. Same result, less effort.

Seeing him reinforces my belief that you should never return to your former lives. The past should be on the Foreign Office's "do not travel" list. It is full of unresolved conflicts and liable to flare-ups.

Hollis is adept in his wheelchair and makes two cups of tea with ease, zipping expertly from fridge to cupboard to kettle and back again. He explains with unbridled enthusiasm how he's learning pistol shooting and wants to compete in the Paralympics.

"I can't believe any of this. It feels unreal!" he says as he hands me the tea. "After ten years, you're actually here. This is the best surprise ever, and it's not even Christmas yet."

"I know," I say, holding the warm mug to my chest.

"Tell me what happened. What the fuck! You fell, I fell . . . We both made it out. I can't get my head around it. How did you get out of that ravine? We found your helmet, it was smashed to pieces."

"More importantly, how did you get out, with your legs like that?" I say, hoping to distract him.

"I just thank God." He pauses and looks at me, his eyes wet. "I was lying there unable to move. I was so cold and I'd accepted that I was going to die, and then I stopped thinking about me and my pains and thought about you. Love gave me the strength to crawl back up the mountain."

Exes are the worst, but exes who don't realize that they've survived a murder attempt and still believe you're in love are worse still. He leans toward me and takes my hand.

"Did you climb out? Where did you go?"

"I don't know what happened to me," I say, realizing I should've come up with a backstory. I stare blankly.

"What do you mean, you don't know?" he says, his eyes darting with interest.

I shrug and look blank. His eyes search my face.

"Oh god, you did lose your memory, didn't you?" he says ecstatically. "Just like I imagined."

I nod slowly with appropriate solemnity. There is one thing worse than thinking about the past, and that is having to speak about it. I look down and compose myself, as if I'm experiencing strong emotion, but all I feel is my stomach rumbling because I've forgotten to eat again.

"I don't know who found me. I was unconscious. A coma. Must've hit my head badly. Some climbers carried me down the mountain. I woke up three months later in a hospital. Frontal lobe damage from the fall," I say, and show him a scar on my head that I had from when I was twelve. "I couldn't remember anything. Not even my name."

"That must've been terrifying," he says. A moment later, he lurches forward and squeezes my arm.

"I guess it was," I say. "But you just fight on."

"What a journey we've been on, and then we find each other again." He leans across and gives me another wet-cheeked hug.

"Amazing, isn't it?"

"Which hospital was it? I searched every hospital in France," he says.

"I was taken to Italy," I lie.

"So that's why there was no record of you. I've racked my brains for years trying to work out what happened to you. And you call yourself Lalla now? Where did that come from?"

"I thought it was my name. I suppose it's similar," I say, and whimper a little for effect.

"Oh, don't cry, Lola! I can help you."

"No one can help, Hollis. That part of my life is gone. It's a blank. I've got a new life now."

"But this is destiny, I can help you to remember everything. I can fill in those blanks for you. Every moment we shared."

"Do you think you could?" My stomach churns but I don't think it's hunger this time.

"I've been quite fanatical about it. I've pieced together everything about us. We can go through it all, day by day."

"Every single day?"

"We can relive our whole marriage," he says, as if this can ever be a desirable prospect.

I look at him, stunned, which is genuine. I make a mental note to find all such material and destroy it.

"And what's your life like now?" he asks. "Jason Mercer said you were married."

I nod.

"I knew you would be. I mean, why wouldn't you? You're more beautiful now than ever! You've got kids too."

"Yes," I say. "Two. Girl and boy. Nelly and Nathan."

"I'd love to meet your kids," says Hollis, smiling benignly. "Little versions of you. I bet they're amazing."

"Yes, that'd be nice."

"What about us?" he says.

"Us? I'm married now."

"To me first, though, right?"

"There's so much to take on board, Hollis. We need to just slow down." I realize at this point that Option 1 (a quick and quiet divorce) might not be possible—Hollis clearly wants me back—and Option 2 (ignore it) is now impossible.

Things are feeling a little too close for comfort, so I tell him I'm overcome with emotion, and we agree to meet the following week. Life was simpler just four weeks earlier, and now, as well as killing a policeman and incinerating Cait's husband, I have an additional husband who could void my own marriage in an instant. I don't tend to be a blamey person but I do feel that all of this is Hollis's fault.

At home, I sit at my desk and turn to a perfectly blank new page in my Moleskine notebook. I write the date and then the simple two words: "To do." I look out at the garden. A blackbird is jumping from spot to spot, jabbing at the lawn. I'm momentarily distracted. The bird finds a worm and tugs it hard until the worm is out of the ground and curls itself around the blackbird's bright orange beak in a last desperate attempt to live. I look back down at my page and write:

Pick up dry cleaning
Phone Nelly's school for reference
Secure Stephen's partnership
Kill Hollis

41

Charged

Tuesday, December 10

Birch and Mattoo pull up in their white Ford Focus as I'm heading down the steps toward my car. I hope to make it past them, but they're surprisingly quick to emerge from their seats and intercept me.

"I'm in a real rush, I'm afraid, can't it wait?"

"We thought you'd want to know what we found out," says DS Birch, intentionally blocking my path.

"I've enough on my plate, actually. My daughter needs a good reference for her next school, so I'm buying flowers for her head teacher."

"I think you might need to know what we've uncovered about Mr. Mercer," says Birch, looking at me archly.

"Well, go on, then, but please be quick," I say. "None of this slow insinuation you've learned from watching too much TV."

"It might be better if we went inside," Birch says rather pointedly.

I give her the wide-eyed stare that I usually reserve for the children.

"I see. Well, Mrs. Rook, I'll be direct. We've got one witness statement saying Jason Mercer was here on November fifteenth, near your house."

"He was probably walking along the street, which most people are permitted to do freely." I sidestep her and head to my car.

"That's not all we have," she shouts.

I wave my hand in the air and beep my car; it welcomes me with an elated flash of several lights.

"He took photographs of you," she calls out. "Quite a few. All in different locations over a few weeks."

I stop and turn. "So, not my lover, then?"

"Why might Jason Mercer have been following you, Mrs. Rook?"

"You'll need to ask him, but given his court case, he seems to enjoy sexually harassing women, so perhaps I was his next victim."

"Maybe, but to my eye, it looks like he was . . ." She screws her face up and pretends to be thinking. I wait until the charade is over. "Investigating you."

"The plot thickens," says Mattoo with a nod.

"Can you think of any reasons someone might have you investigated?"

"My life is made up entirely of looking after my husband and children. They are of little interest to me, let alone anyone else. So I'll be reassured when you've found him and locked him up with your other dodgy colleagues."

"Well, when we do find him, Mrs. Rook, we're sure to discover his particular interest in your life," says Birch, her mouth in a twisted smile.

I am about to say more but this will only prolong matters. "Thank you for your time, Officers," I say, and head to my car, which I realize is still crawling with Jason Mercer's DNA should they care to look.

After buying flowers, I drop them off at the school with a note to Mrs. Nnadi that says, "A good reference is cheaper than a legal challenge." I quickly head over to Tor's, where we've all agreed to an emergency meeting to talk about Cait. I feel the pang of jealousy whenever I arrive at Tor's house. You have to embrace jealousy if you want to aspire to anything. I just pray that Stephen will work harder to make partner instead of hanging about his mum's hospital bed like a punctured Oedipus complex.

Tor shows me into the thirty-foot living room, all muted blues and grays. Sophie and Aisha are already ensconced on the vast white sofa. There's a photorealistic painting of a shark over the fireplace, and I can't help staring at it, speechless.

"Oh, that's a gift from one of Law's cash cows!"

"And is such an image flattering or insulting for a politician?"

"It's from a lobbyist, so it probably means he's doing a good job, and it pays well in the long term. These companies don't forget their political allies."

I glance out of the window. There are now bricks on top of the concrete footings and several men looking industrious, which is reassuring. I've also booked my car in for an "Executive Sanitization Valet," which I hope will remove any last traces of Mr. Mercer from the trunk.

Tor sits us down and presides. "So, what do we know?"

"I thought she'd be out yesterday, but I've heard nothing," I say.

"The police have charged her," says Aisha, referring to a notepad on her knee. "She's on her way to prison."

We all stare in silence. I'm genuinely surprised. The inadequacy of the police has again outdone my expectations.

"What does that mean, exactly?" asks Sophie.

"It means it's serious," says Aisha. "And she could be in prison until her court case."

"Bloody hell, that could be months."

"Law's lawyer friend, Dominic, is on the case," says Tor. "He thinks he can get her released on bail. There's some hope, as she's not been charged with murder. So there's a bail hearing soon."

"I thought they arrested her for murder," says Aisha.

"They could only charge her with manslaughter in the end, as they found CCTV of Owen buying the petrol himself," says Tor, nibbling a pink macaron. "So it's difficult to argue that it was her intention to burn him to death."

"But why manslaughter? I thought it was suicide or an accident," says Sophie, getting upset.

"He had a knife wound in his throat, and there was no knife found at the scene." Aisha taps her notebook. "Which, if I'm not mistaken, means there was someone else there."

"Oh god, really? So he was stabbed first?" says Sophie.

"He could've tried to cut his own throat and bottled out," I say.

"That's a good argument," says Tor. "I'll mention it to Dominic."

"He owed people money," says Sophie. "If he was murdered, couldn't it be one of them?"

"Yes, of course, but there's a big fat elephant sitting in the room," says Tor. "Cait was at the house that evening before she went to her mum's. She said so herself. And the timing of his petrol purchase suggests he might've been waiting there for her."

"Oh, poor Cait!" says Sophie. "So she might've found him in her house and had to defend herself."

"But she said she left the house and never saw Owen," says Aisha.

"But she would say that," says Tor. "Sorry, I'm just trying to be objective."

"Objectionable, rather," I say.

"Look, it's best to think the worst, but hope for the best," says Tor.

"Christ," says Sophie. "If she went to the house on her own, she's got no alibi, has she?"

"Look, no one here thinks Cait did it—do they?" says Aisha, staring at each of us in turn.

"It doesn't matter if she did or didn't do it," says Tor, stumbling upon an insight. "It matters that they can argue that she did. He might've provided the means, but she not only had the opportunity, she had a motive—he was threatening her and the girls."

"You know she was cautioned for threatening him with a knife when they still lived together?" I say.

"That's true," says Sophie. "Oh god, yes, that's not going to look good in court."

"It can't be her," says Aisha. "She'd never do anything to risk losing her girls."

"Sometimes even sane people risk everything," says Tor. "A moment of madness built on years of self-restraint and frustration."

We all look up at Tor, who is speaking with uncharacteristic clarity and passion.

"Are you okay?" says Aisha.

"Well, a person can make a mistake, can't they?" Tor smiles and then bursts into tears and walks out.

We all stare at her. Then we stare at one another. Sophie's eyebrows are raised in astonishment.

"It's like the moment in *The Wizard of Oz* when the Tin Man cries," says Sophie.

As Aisha jumps up and rushes to get Tor a glass of water (why this is needed in an emotional crisis I do not know), I think about the likelihood of Cait telling the police about Jason Mercer and decide I need to feel more confident of her continued cooperation.

I am the last to leave. This is not due to my love of company but because I need to see Tor alone. As she shows me to the door, I hold her hand and say, "I've got the money for you."

"Oh, that's great. Thank you, Lalla. I owe you."

"But I'll need to see Zac for myself before I send anything to him or this Bitcoin account."

"But why?" she says, immediately suspicious of my motives. "Don't you trust Zac?"

"I don't know Zac, so, no, I don't trust him, I'm afraid. I want to know this will end things for you and you won't be asked for any more money."

"Thank you," she says tearfully. "But it's not him, I promise you."

"I'm just making sure. Now, please arrange to meet him. Somewhere public is better, and I'll show up in your place. Surprise will prevent any preparation, and if I'm reassured that Zac's not scamming you, I'll transfer the money and make sure those videos are really deleted."

"I'm so grateful," she says, and her face contorts and reddens like a child's.

"You'll get through this, Tor, I promise. I'm your greatest supporter," I say. As I look at her, I realize what it is I'm going to ask in return. And she's not going to like it one little bit.

42

Bronzefield

Thursday, December 12

HMP Bronzefield is a squat, purpose-built concrete-and-steel construction with the capacity to house 527 inmates. Since the demise of HMP Holloway it is Europe's largest female prison.

Caitlin O'Donnell, prisoner number A3412JX, has now been formally charged and sent here on remand. I don't mind saying that the location is quite inconvenient, given that we are in the run-up to Christmas, and besides the normal festive preparations, I have several quite pressing deadlines, including but not limited to getting pregnant via an absent husband, finding a further £200K down payment to secure our new Hampstead home, getting Nelly to study for her prep school exams, dealing with Tor's lying lover, outwitting the police, and, of course, exploring how to manage a permanent separation from Matthew Hollis without either of my husbands finding out.

However, friendship is about giving as well as receiving, and it's important to help those in need, especially when they are also unstable and know incriminating information about you. For these reasons, with my car being valeted, I find myself on a train heading out toward HMP Bronzefield, reading about its esteemed history of caging violent and deranged women.

Access to prison is not all that different from visiting a poorly run doctor's office. It took several hours on the phone on Tuesday and Wednesday. The building itself is reassuringly familiar in terms of cheap decor, worn-out posters, deformed plastic chairs, and uncivil receptionists. There are various restrictions on entry, including a body search and a metal detector, but this is no worse than the entry procedure for the House of Lords.

The restricted-items list runs to two pages, and I assure the stern and glum guard that I do not have a nail file, firearms, or a spare prison uniform about my person. I'm allowed no more than ten pounds in cash, with which I am told I can purchase refreshments from a vending machine. I'm almost certain that I will not make use of this facility.

I'm led by another surly guard (it's clearly part of their training) to the secure visiting unit, which is run by volunteers. I wipe the chair with a cloth I've brought for the purpose, but the stains are indelible, so I refrain from putting my whole weight on the seat. I'm blessed with strong thigh muscles and work weekly on my core, so while inconvenient, it's not uncomfortable.

I see Cait walking toward me. I have to say that the prison uniform does her slight frame no favors at all, and she doesn't look like she is sleeping well or eating sufficient quantities of fruit and vegetables.

"How are you, darling?" I say, expecting more gloom and self-pity.

"I'm pretty good," says Cait, and she actually smiles.

"Good?"

"They all think I killed my abusive husband and set him on fire. They clap when I walk by."

"Clap?"

"Yes, and whoop. It's quite nice. I've even got a nickname."

"Which is?"

"*Flame*. It's a reference to burning Owen to death but also to my hair, obv."

"Clever," I say.

"Funny, isn't it?" she says, looking directly into my eyes. "You killed a man and you're free, and I didn't kill anyone and I'm in prison."

"But you'll plead innocent," I say, though this defense is probably the tried-and-failed approach of all 527 inhabitants of Bronzefield.

"I didn't shank him," she says. I raise one eyebrow. She's obviously cohabiting with someone who's taught her the required lingo.

"Of course you didn't. We presumed he'd killed himself."

"Me too. But my solicitor tells me Owen couldn't have done it. There was no knife at the scene. Whoever did kill him was a rank amateur or they didn't care. They should've put the knife in his hand, if they wanted it to look authentic."

I'm about to explain how difficult to achieve that might be if the knife in question was contaminated from another murder, but I realize this might compromise my position.

"Not everyone has your professional knowledge of police procedures and autopsies," I say.

"No, you're right there," she says. "I've already helped three women in here with their cases. These women know nothing about forensics and the police, Lalla. They're taken advantage of."

"Well, you've always been community-minded, Cait."

"Worst thing is, I don't have an alibi. They've got me at the scene. And they have all those threatening texts he sent me. I just don't understand how he died."

"Oh, Cait, there must be a way to find out what really happened."

She nods. "I know. They say he bought the petrol, but . . . this is the bit they went on and on about. One of his testicles was completely ruptured."

"What? What does that mean?"

"It means they think he attacked me, and I defended myself, then cut his neck and burned him."

"Christ."

"If it does look like he was with some woman . . . on my bed. Do you think he was trying to make me jealous? I don't understand it at all."

"Unless, someone was there to hurt him," I say. "Someone he owed money to."

Cait's eyes brighten. "You mean someone threatening to kill him?"

"Exactly. A gangland boss who wants to make an example of him. I'm sure the police will look into his gambling debts."

"They've no interest in looking for someone else. I'm a slam dunk," she says, and sniffs like an old convict. I also think there's a new estuarine twang to her diction.

"But no one can seriously think you could've done it," I say to reassure her.

"Why not me? He could've pushed me to it. I hated him enough."

"But you didn't kill him," I say.

"The papers think I did it. Pushed to it by years of domestic abuse. They know about the time I had to use a knife to protect myself against him. They've already been to my family, school friends, work colleagues—scoured social media. Trial by the public, it is. One of my school friends told the journalist I threw a net ball in her face once. They reported it as evidence of *bouts of rage*."

"Sporting incidents aside, Cait, a jury will see that you're a gentle soul."

"Not sure I like that version of me anymore. In here, I'm a killer." She stares at me, her teeth gritted. "And it feels good to be that person, you know—rather than the victim again."

We sit for a moment in silence as Cait or *Flame* continues to try on her new identity. It's not impossible for me to imagine. I transformed myself too. I was homeless, penniless, and depraved. I screamed into the void. But it doesn't do you any good in the end so I made a decision. It's your story. You decide which character you play, so you don't have to choose the victim; you can choose the hero.

"My solicitor thinks I might've even been framed. That someone connected with Owen tried to make it appear like a lover did it."

"Look, Cait, just so I know—did you tell anyone about the other little incident?"

She shakes her head.

"Thank you."

"It wasn't for you, Lalla. I tried to tell my solicitor about it, and he put his finger to his lips and said, 'If you tell the police about another violent incident you're involved in, it certainly will not help your case. Don't incriminate yourself.'"

"Good advice," I say with some pleasure. I had no idea my improvisation would work out so well, although I do feel a pang of something in my gut when I see Cait's situation.

"Exactly. So, I can't tell them, can I? It's just so weird," says Cait. "Two dead bodies, both stabbed. One in your house, one in my house. What are the chances of that?" She looks up at me and her pupils suddenly dilate. I fear that simple-minded Cait has just joined the dots into the shape of yours truly.

"What is it?" I say, as casually as possible.

"Maybe the deaths are connected," she says, jabbing a dirty finger at me.

"I don't see how," I say.

"Maybe Owen's the link. Or they're both linked to someone else. Or something else." She pauses. Something is swirling in her mind.

"What are you thinking?" I say.

"Secret crime syndicate," she says, casting glances left and right and speaking in a low tone. "My cellmate, she knows everything. Been in and out for fifteen years. She's an assassin for a crime syndicate. That's totally confidential, by the way."

"It's unlikely that they've bunked you up with an assassin, Cait. She's probably in for nicking a pack of fags."

"She's a killer, Lalla."

"Well, regardless of her crime, you didn't tell her about Jason, did you?"

Cait shakes her head, then unhelpfully says, "Not directly. I just suggested that there might be another body somewhere."

"I wouldn't advise taking old felons into your confidence, Cait."

"Listen," she says. "She doesn't think Jason Mercer was a burglar at all. She thinks he was a leg-breaker."

"A what?"

"Owen owed money to some bad people. He said something

might happen to him. I think Jason Mercer was the muscle trying to track him down to get the money."

"Right," I say. "But in this scenario, why was he in my house, not yours?"

"I think he might have been following me to find Owen."

"Okay," I say. "But Mercer died before Owen. Doesn't that kind of destroy the theory? A dead man couldn't have killed Owen."

Cait stares at me in silence. Her mouth curls up a little. She nods. "Shit," she says. "I thought I'd solved it."

43

Nativity

Friday, December 13

The small school hall is decorated with lanterns made by the children, covering Christmas, Hanukkah, and Diwali, in addition to other light-loving winter festivals. There is a single line of green tinsel across the front of the stage, and the teachers are wearing Christmas jumpers and reindeer-themed headwear. Mrs. Nnadi is wearing a Mrs. Santa Claus hat and a dress covered with a mistletoe pattern, which I feel is a little inappropriate.

The old public address system is playing a recording of the children sweetly massacring many Christmas favorites, and we are served "delicious nonalcoholic mulled wine"—Ribena made using the hot tap.

By the time I arrive with Sophie and Aisha (Tor is otherwise engaged in saving her reputation, and Cait is in custody), the first five rows are packed with parents (mothers mostly) and grandparents. They're all sitting in their coats, lined up on low gym benches of the kind that I remember from my own school days. I am not in a good mood as I've failed to raise the deposit and Esmae is showing four couples around my Hampstead house tomorrow.

There's a ripple of chatter and side glances as we walk down the central aisle to find a seat. Many faces stare up at us with closed-lip sympathy or high-eyebrowed fright as we're now known notoriously as "Cait's crew." I smile back and give a few little waves. Aisha is horrified, but with Nelly's rather unusual habits, I'm used to these looks.

I know it's a children's performance but if you pay for a play, you expect, at the least, for the actors to know their cues and lines, and that they don't keep acknowledging the audience. My expectations are not high.

"Do you think Cait might've done it?" whispers Sophie.

"Cait couldn't kill anyone," I say.

"People can surprise you. I wouldn't blame her. I mean, Owen was a bastard," says Sophie.

"He broke into her house. I'd kill someone if they threatened my kids," says Aisha.

"What about Ranni, is he still thinking of moving?" I ask.

"Oh, I've stopped being amenable. I do what he's done for fifteen years. I leave for work at five thirty a.m. and return at eight p.m. I ask no questions, I offer no help, I throw my underwear on the floor, expect feeding the minute I get in, and always take the car."

"Good for you!" says Sophie. "How's he coping?"

"He's had to take time off, of course, and he's exhausted and confused."

"He drew first blood," I say, and she stares back and nods fiercely.

A trumpet sounds and the whole school troops onstage. And regardless of breaking the fourth wall, at least three-quarters wave at their parents.

A hundred phones rise to capture the performance, which the head has told us are not allowed due to safeguarding reasons. The acoustics in the freezing hall are also noticeably shoddy, and although I know the outline of the Nativity story, I can't follow this version at all. There are several characters I don't remember from the original, including SpongeBob SquarePants and what looks like a unicorn.

Nelly is not waving. She's dressed in a white sheet with a cord around the middle, and two large cardboard wings painted white with the outline of feathers. She is, as she told me at dinner, *an angel*. I explained to her that angels don't drown hamsters, but she can appear to be one if she wishes. She stabbed a fork into my leg and said quite firmly, "I am an angel."

"Oh, isn't it lovely," whispers Sophie as the head gets up to bore us with her welcome. "I love Christmas. And we really need it this year. We're back on, by the way."

"Back on? Paolo's dead wife's friend and former lover notwithstanding?"

Sophie laughs. "She's actually nice, and happily married. I think I overreacted. I'm giving up drinking in the new year."

"Well, suspension of disbelief is in order."

"I can do it if I put my mind to it," she says.

"I don't mean you," I say. "It's the paper beards and the girl on her iPad in the back row."

"Oh, I hadn't spotted her. I think she has problems with her lines," says Sophie.

"And with acting, I might add."

A mother in the row ahead shuffles and I receive a passively aggressive backward glance. I jam my knee in her lower back, lean forward, put my hand firmly on her shoulder, and say, "I'm so sorry, it's quite a squeeze in here."

"Like mother like daughter," she hisses back.

"Isn't Nelly doing well?" says Sophie.

"You mean she hasn't attacked anyone?"

"She seems really in role. What an angelic expression."

I look at Nelly, who is superconcentrated. I feel a little twinge. Motherly pride? No, this is because I know from the look in her eye that the angel is about to turn devil.

"Ajay!" shouts Aisha, half standing and waving as the head moves offstage and the lights dim.

"Shhh," says a deliberately loud pedant from two rows behind us. I let it go; the soloist deserves our attention, and I listen to a surprisingly sweet rendition of "Away in a Manger." Some of the words are wrong, but you have to forgive at Christmas.

The narrators appear and start to tell the story of the star. Nelly's arms are behind her back now, and she's wriggling. It looks like she's stuffing both her hands down her pants. I raise my eyebrows. Not now, Nelly. Please.

I watch as Nelly retrieves something from her pants. It looks like a roll of paper. I'm slightly concerned but hope it's got something to do with the play.

"Oh, this is the big number. Ellie's in it," says Sophie, jiggling to get a better view.

"What's Nelly up to?" says Aisha.

I lean right to see what she's doing. Adams will soon be requesting references for her, and we're only just over the hamster incident, so I need her to be good.

"Oh, that's beautiful," says Sophie as three girls (one of whom is Ellie) and a boy appear in full snowmen costumes and start to sing "Santa Claus Is Coming to Town."

"Oh, there's Hari," says Aisha with emotion in her voice. Hari is in a huge Santa costume with a cotton wool beard and bright red suit. Sophie squeezes Aisha's arm.

Meanwhile, I'm staring at Nelly, standing center stage, angel wings in the spotlight, unfurling the banner that she's grasping in her hand. She holds it above her head, and we all read:

SANTA'S DEAD

The audience goes silent. Everyone exchanges glances, several in my direction. And then she turns the banner over:

HARI KILLED HIM

"Hari told Nelly that Santa doesn't exist, and she's taken it to heart," I say as she glares at Hari. She looks sweet striding toward Santa in her angel costume. I have a vague hope this is in the script, but the confusion on the faces of the children suggests not.

Santa pulls open his sack and takes out a present as the song reaches its crescendo. Nelly walks directly in front of Santa Claus and shoves him so hard that he tumbles across the stage and into the cardboard Nativity scene, toppling the crib. The baby Jesus hurtles toward the edge of the stage and falls off.

There's a huge gasp in the audience. Children start crying. Hari has so many cushions tied around him that he can't get up and flails about like a dying insect. A teacher rushes to pick up baby Jesus, but his swaddling unravels and he disappears under the benches.

A major search for baby Jesus is underway as Nelly jumps on Hari and starts pulling his Santa outfit off in disgust at his duplicity.

Several parents look at me, their eyes screwed up in fury.

"We can just hope that it's all planned?" Sophie whispers as Nelly holds Hari's beard and hat in the air triumphantly. Several mums rise up, outraged.

Nelly puts on Santa's hat and shouts, "Santa lives!"

"This is a disaster," I say.

"But her handwriting is impressively neat," says Sophie kindly.

44

Feet

Sunday, December 15

"I've been thinking more about the killings," says Cait, her voice amplified by the empty concrete corridor where the pay phone is bolted to the wall.

"Please, do go ahead," I say, popping a piece of mango in my mouth. "I'm getting my feet done."

"You're in public?"

"No, no. Ying's come to me," I say, and smile at Ying, who's preparing my pedicure. It's a treat because I'm too upset about Hampstead.

"I think that's her surname, Lalla. Her name's Fen."

"She told me it was Ying Fen."

"In China, they give the surname first."

"Well, that's confusing."

"Not really, just different."

"Hold on," I say, and ask Ying Fen if her first name is actually Fen. "Right, well, Fen agrees with you, but she can't talk. She's concentrating on my feet, so do go on."

"She might hear something."

"She doesn't seem to understand a word I say about nails, so I doubt she'll pick up the finer points of our judiciary system. Don't they record your calls anyway?"

"Yes, but they don't listen to them," says Cait confidently.

"You're sure about that?" I say.

"Hairy Mary who works in the admin block said they only listen to high-risk prisoners and a tiny random sample. She says she can make sure mine isn't chosen."

"Who's Hairy Mary and why would she do that for you? You're paying her in sexual favors, are you?"

"Don't be stupid," says Cait, laughing. "She's my roomie. The assassin. She just wants cigarettes."

"No need to hide the dirty truth from me." Fen looks up at me, but I can't read her expression.

"Look, she's one of my fans. There's a group of women who give me free cigarettes and nice shampoo. They've been pushed around by men their whole lives, and they like what they think I did. They say I've got style."

"Style? You dress like Charlie Bucket's grandparents," I say.

"Not that kind of style—my *stab-and-burn* style," she says. "They're even asking me what he looked like as he was being cooked."

"And what did you say to that?"

"I said the cheap polyester went up like a flare, and they roared with laughter. I'm sorry, I don't know where it came from."

"Well, you sound like you're enjoying being the center of something for once," I say. "How's the bail application going?"

"Good, I think. The fact that I'm a victim of abuse and the mother of adorable twins will work in my favor apparently. So I might be out soon."

"You don't sound too positive about that."

"The thing is, Lalla, it's weird, but I'm not scared in here. For the first time in so, so long, I've not felt that constant nagging sense that some man might say or do something to me," says Cait, then she pauses. "I've been afraid all my life of one thing or another."

"What did you call for?" I say, a little abruptly as I'm not her counselor.

"I just wanted to talk about Jason Mercer," she says.

"Good, so that's on tape now," I say.

"Hairy Mary won't let us down, Lalla."

"And there's my name too! Fantastic."

"Well, you're on the call log anyway."

"Can we just keep names out of it, please? And any reference to anything criminal."

"Don't worry, I've got it all covered. I just worked out who killed Owen."

"Oh, good," I say, and wish I had popcorn instead of mango.

"Jason Mercer didn't kill Owen, as you pointed out. Mercer was sent out to collect a debt from Owen, but as Owen wasn't at my house, I think Mercer must've been snooping around all my friends to see if anyone knew anything. And that's when he ran into you."

"Yes," I say, trying to keep her from noticing the obvious flaws in her logic. "That seems very plausible."

"And as you rubbed him out, he couldn't return to his crime syndicate. And what are they going to think, would you say?"

"He took the money and ran away?"

"No, that Owen killed him! That's why they put a hit out on Owen. I think I've solved it, right?"

"Yes," I murmur in pleasure, as Fen touches a sensitive spot in the center of my foot.

45

Partnership

Tuesday, December 17

Mirrors do not tell lies. Mine tells me that I'm extremely attractive. Tonight, the bar glistens with glass and gold, and I'm slightly jealous of the people who get to look at me as I sip a martini, elegant as an actress in my silver dress.

I was not always like this. Becoming beautiful has been a carefully stage-managed process, but it starts with what's inside. As a girl I always wore the prettiest dresses, but inside, I was a disheveled creature of dark desires. I felt like a grotesquely stitched-together mismatch of monster and doll.

I was only five when I remember first gaining some control over these mismatched inner and outer worlds. I stole someone's favorite doll, and the pleasure silenced the inner turmoil for a time. I knew, instinctively, that I should keep this secret pleasure hidden from others' eyes, but I kept the doll as a memento of that first feeling. Nelly has it now.

My mother tried to love me, despite these crimes, for which I'm grateful. Children who are easy to love tend not to steal, lie, stab, or disappear from their rooms at night. I think she thought it was all down to him, but I don't think it was only him. It wasn't his hatred that made me weak; it was her love that made me strong. One violent man can do a lot of damage, but one strong woman can do a great deal more.

The man sitting near me at the bar has a buttery complexion, dyed hair, and a shiny forehead that looks like it's been polished with grease. His open-necked baby-blue silk shirt is so taut it gapes around his belly button. Even from the distance of two barstools, I can smell his musky perfume and vape smoke. In the mirror, his bleach-whitened teeth shine like warning beacons, and his heavy gold rings glint with menace.

His name is Josh Krill. He's not a crime boss but an influential partner at Stephen's bank. According to Stephen, his word can make or break a prospective partner. We're both drinking expensive cocktails in the Rivoli Bar. He bought one that cost £120. This is merely part of his courtship display.

He might say the same about my flattering low-cut dress that almost falls from my shoulders, and the glittering platinum-and-emerald necklace that dances on the smooth skin between my neck and chest. Every now and then his eyes glance over at me as if I'm wearing an all-you-can-eat-buffet sign.

I don't mind the Ritz. Their drinks are well mixed, their bar staff impeccable, and their waiters most attentive. It's the customers I object to. Setting this up has been no trouble at all as Stephen told me that Josh was particularly attentive to the interns, so I messaged Josh via a fake LinkedIn account to ask for advice on getting an internship. I used a rather beautiful photograph of Aimée as my profile picture, and Josh was quick to reply.

We went back and forth on a professional level; then he suggested we move the conversation to WhatsApp, where things became more casual and even a little flirty. Before I knew it, and in response to my desperation to learn from him, he suggested we meet privately to share his wisdom, adding "and anything else that might occur between consenting adults."

Well, I'm only human, and my fake self was overwhelmed by the heady mixture of gladiatorial preening alongside the kind suggestion of an illicit relationship with an older man in exchange for his hand on my arse as he pushed me up the corporate ladder.

I replied with emojis to suggest my current state—prayer hands along with shivers of excitement, although in truth, I was patching up Nathan's grazed knee after a fall. I reminded Josh that I was only a recent graduate and explained that I couldn't pay him anything for his advice. Josh's response to this was so honest and caring that I was quite touched:

I'm happy with payment-in-kind. 😉 xxx

In the lead-up to this exciting date, I did a little research and discovered, all via his own boasting, that Josh has five children, a stunning wife, a villa in Tuscany, a boat (not quite a yacht yet), three cars, a pilot's license, a love of rugby, and a huge pile in Surrey. All to display his fertility and status.

His fake date is already thirty minutes late. Josh has downed two cocktails and is getting annoyed. He glances my way once or twice, but I'm not his type by at least eighteen years. He texts Aimée, which I read surreptitiously and then reply. Aimée tells him she will be half an hour late because she wanted to wear something special for him and has been out shopping. He texts back to say she doesn't need to wear anything.

After his third vintage cocktail, and increasingly annoyed texts to Aimée, I text on her behalf to say that I have to cancel. He texts back with a slur reserved for women who are believed to have promised something without providing satisfaction.

"Been stood up, have you?" I say.

"Not a bit," he says, turning to me. "Just been enjoying the view in the mirror."

"Do you make a habit of taking advantage of interns?" I ask.

"What are you talking about?"

"Aimée. A prospective intern. I understand you suggested sex in return for a career opportunity."

"What's it got to do with you?" he says.

"I'm her mother," I say, and although it galls me to say this, I'm pleased with his surprised reaction.

"Don't know anyone by that name," he says, and turns away from me.

"I'm also a friend of Natalie da Costa. Do you remember Natalie? Left your firm quite suddenly in 2014."

Josh swivels in his chair. "I don't know who you are, but I've got nothing to say. And neither does Natalie da Costa."

"Is that because you sexually harassed her, paid her off, and made her sign a nondisclosure?"

"You can't say that."

"Or Simone Farrell? She left in a hurry in 2018 after working under you. Another payoff?"

"If you keep making accusations you can't prove, you're going to find yourself with a fucking big lawsuit."

"There are three other women, do you remember their names?"

"I'm leaving," he says, and waves to the barman for the bill.

"I understand you booked a room for your meeting with Aimée. I asked at reception. Rather presumptuous," I say, and smile. "A standard double too. Not even a deluxe room. That's a little cheap, don't you think?"

"Fuck you!" he says, waving a gold card at the card reader without looking at his bill.

"I'm thinking of writing a story and sharing it with the press. I have all these details of strange departures—and Aimée's messages of course."

"Listen to me carefully," he says, balling his fist. "Don't fuck with me. I'm not someone you fuck with."

"Why not? It might lead to fifty thousand pounds and an NDA. I've even shaved in anticipation."

"Funny, ha ha," he says, taking his jacket from the back of his stool and throwing it over his shoulder.

"You want to comment?"

"If you're a journalist, you can't print this. Not one of those women will say a word against me."

"Because nothing happened, or because they've legally given up their right to call you an arsehole?"

"I can afford the best lawyers money can buy. Just give me your name, and I will end you," he says.

"There's another young woman in your company who is not currently legally bound. She's also very happy to talk. It's enough to get this story out there."

"You're bluffing."

"I have connections in your bank, and I believe there are a number who have yet to speak up, but it's amazing what happens when one breaks the ice."

Josh stops and looks at me, his face red and puffy.

"You can avoid all this trouble, though."

"What do you want?" he says, and sits down.

"A small favor. An associate of mine wants to be made partner. I want you to make that happen. It may just save your marriage, and even your career."

46

Memories

Wednesday, December 18

Christmas lights make driving much less aggravating. There are none in this flat, however, and even the bright red poinsettia I brought as a gift looks sparse and lonely. It doesn't help that I'm staring at a pistol with a heavy wood-effect grip and angular green barrel, and I'm not entirely sure why.

My main preoccupation as I sit here in Hollis's flat is that I lack the additional two hundred thousand for the estate agent, although, fortunately, none of the four families that viewed it have made an offer. It's partly because I spent Saturday sitting outside the house as they looked around and left information on each of their windscreens pretending to be from a neighbor, explaining the undeclared moth infestation that has led to the owner's swift departure.

Stephen, meanwhile, is no help to anyone. His mother didn't even have a stroke. It was merely a sudden drop in blood pressure. Her heart did stop for a minute or two, but once they put her in a coma, it started right up again, and yet she's acting like she's had triple bypass surgery and is playing him like a violin.

"It's a .22-caliber Pardini SP," says Hollis in that way men have of valuing technical data over narrative.

"A gun," I say, a little concerned as this was a man I shoved off a cliff face.

"I'm a competitive shooter now," he says, turning it reverentially.

"It's a lovely color." It's clearly not the response he's after.

He puts the gun down and picks up a photograph of a dog.

"This is Malory," he says.

"Yes, I know."

Hollis stares at me. "You remember Malory?"

I'm flummoxed. An early mistake. "I do, but I don't, if you know what I mean?"

"Not really." He shakes his head.

"It's odd," I say, covering the obvious tire tracks. "It's as if I have memories, but they're not connected to anything. If I'd seen you in the street I would've known your face, but I couldn't have told you why or where."

"Huh," he says. "Isn't the mind an amazing thing? It's like your brain knew there was a problem when you fell and did a quick backup, but you can't access the memory because you've got no RAM."

"Absolutely like that." I have no idea what he's talking about but he's pleased with himself, so I smile. I remember how proud he used to be if he'd managed to defecate in a public bathroom. Well done, Hollis, I used to say.

He approaches me with two cups held in indentations on a plastic tray that fits to the front of his wheelchair. He stops by my side, and my drink alights (I think that's the right word) at my table.

"It was a nightmare before I got this tray. You know, the little things can really stump you, if you're new to it all." He looks up at me, a dreamy look in his eyes. "You never realize what you've got until it's gone."

I don't share his sentiment. I knew exactly what he was long before he was gone.

"Which was the worst thing to lose, Hollis, your legs or your wife?" I say, partly because I'm faintly interested in his answer.

"Come on—you can't ask me that! You know the answer. It's you, every single time, even if I had four legs."

"Thank you," I say, glancing at my watch as surreptitiously as I can, as I do find him curiously boring. It's not his fault; it's just that he's got no relevance to my future.

"Now, on to the main event," he chimes, and wheels himself to a glossy white IKEA bookcase. He flicks through various notebooks and pulls one out. "The beginning!"

"Whoopee," I say. I do remember how we met, where we met, what his hands did, what mine did, and the rest. It sits undigested in my mind, emotionless, as all memories do. Hollis, being a control freak, recorded everything as if we were some fairy-tale couple.

"Listen to this! 'I met a strange girl today. Looked like she'd dressed in a charity shop. A ripped tweed jacket, bright pink tights, a tiny leather skirt, big old army boots with not much in the way of laces, a T-shirt that said "RELAX," and a red beret.'"

"You were quite observant," I say.

"I know," he says. "'She was actually begging at the time. Or I thought so because she held her hat out as I passed. I put a quid in there and she said the funniest thing.'"

"What did I say?"

"You don't remember?"

"I genuinely do not remember," I say. He still doesn't realize that it wasn't a good time for me and I didn't have what he would recognize as *choice*.

"You said, 'That'll only buy you a quick feel, mate.' And I said, 'How much for a slow feel?' and you said, 'If you so much as touch me, I'll break your nose.' I laughed my head off."

"Nothing coming back, Hollis."

"Oh, you must remember this, you said, 'Do you live near here?' I said I did, and you said, 'Make me a cheese sandwich and I'll get you off.' And that's what we did. Never met anyone like you before. Unreal."

"So I'm the girl you took to bed for a cheese sandwich? That's romantic, Hollis," I say calmly, but I don't like this version of myself. It belongs in a ravine, hidden under snow.

"Yes, it was just banter."

I want to tell him that he's wrong. It was a negotiation. I was hungry, so I had sex with him for a cheese sandwich. I had no feelings for him, or anything for that matter, and he thought it was just modern dating.

Hollis offered a way out, and although I had nothing at the time, I realized later that I'd priced myself well below market value. But on that afternoon, as I was devouring that cheddar, white bread, and margarine sandwich in a reasonably warm flat, I felt like I was the one who'd bagged a bargain.

I learned two important lessons based on my experiences on the street. The first is that without bricks and mortar, every day is a losing battle. The second is that in terms of a pleasure-versus-pain ratio, you can do a lot worse than establish yourself as an upper-middle-class banker's wife.

"And then you just stayed. And I made you a cheese sandwich every day, and we got to know each other." He winks at me. "'Her name, she tells me, having slept with her three times (unusual order, but she said she can't tell me intimate things like her name until we get all the pleasantries of fellatio, cunnilingus, and sodomy out of the way) is Lola. She's so funny, my stomach aches.'"

He used to laugh every time I was just being honest. If I said I wanted to break into a shop at two a.m. because I wanted Marmite, he'd laugh, and then when I did that exact thing, he was in absolute awe.

"I won't read the next bit," he says.

Which is, I hazard a guess, the bit when he asked if I wanted to meet his family, and I told him if he ever asked that again, I'd kill his dog. He realized I might be telling the truth and stopped. I wouldn't have hurt his dog, mind you. I have enormous respect for a dog's ability to manipulate its owner and live a life of luxury with minimum contribution.

I sip weak coffee as Hollis regales me with our exciting and dramatic life together. In truth, I can see how it felt dangerous and adventurous for him, but that's men for you: they only see the world in terms of their own pleasure centers. I laughed as much as he did, but I was just about surviving.

"Hollis," I say, stopping him. "It all sounds so sordid and tawdry."

"But it was real. Our little flat was the whole world and when I was at work, I just wanted to get back to you and our bed. You were like nothing I'd ever known."

"That's just sex talking, Hollis."

"No, it's much more than that. You lit up my world."

"Really?" I say, as that certainly wasn't what happened to me. Perhaps I'm just better in bed than I imagined. I should've charged more on the street.

"You were an anarchist, a narcissist, a nymphomaniac, a thief, a rebel, and you were so unkind to me, it blew my mind. And the sex..." Hollis stops and looks at me with some kind of expectation.

"No, Hollis," I say.

"Too early?"

"Too late, actually," I say, and reach into my tote bag.

I consider our relationship with hindsight. I wasn't fully conscious of it at the time, but I didn't like the generous things Hollis did for me. I felt his gifts, his romance, the endless love, were all a way to own and control me. And that's how it was in the end. In the beginning, I confessed my world to him, and in the end, he used it all against me.

"You look so sorted now, I can't get used to it," he says, looking at me with a longing expression.

"I suppose I am, yes."

"I don't know, I'm not a psychiatrist. I'm just thinking that maybe the knock on your head when you fell put something right," he says, and I notice that his chair is creeping closer to me.

"No, you're clearly not a psychiatrist."

He smiles, and with the mere flick of a finger his chair rolls to my side and he takes my hand. I pull it away from him.

"I want you back, Lola. I want to start again." He snatches my hand back.

"Sadly, Hollis, it doesn't work like that." I smile at him fondly, then get up. I move behind him and slip my hand into my bag. I grip the handle of the hammer. It's now or never.

"I know I'll have to win your heart all over again, but I'm going to try," he says as I put one hand on his shoulder. "You were worth more than life to me."

"I was never worth that much, Hollis. No one is." I move my hand to his temple. It probably feels like affection to him, but I'm adjusting his head so that I can get a good connection and do what Mont Blanc should've done all those years ago.

"I never stopped loving you," he says, reaching up and putting his hand on mine.

"I know, and, in my own little way, maybe I never stopped loving you too," I say. "But I'm married to someone else now, Hollis. I don't want to go backward."

"He doesn't love you like I love you." His voice is plaintive now.

I slide the hammer into my palm and feel a rush of desire. I step back slightly and widen my stance. He has no idea as his hand strokes my free hand affectionately.

"Why did you search for me for so long when I treated you so badly?"

"If you love a tiger," he says, "you know that one day it'll bite your head off, but you don't love it any less, because you've always known it's a tiger. You were my tiger."

I look down at him. I feel a piercing beat in my head, the pitch rising and rising. I need this. I need this now. I need to stop the past recurring. I need Hollis dead. To secure my future, I need to kill my past. It's completely rational.

I try. But my arm won't move.

47

Beaufort

Thursday, December 19

The Christmas tree in the lobby of the Savoy is so beautiful that I could stare at it for hours. Sadly, I have an assignation to get to. The Beaufort Bar is dimly lit and decorated in jet black and shining gold. It is sleek, sexy, and expensive, a little like yours truly. I am draped on an art deco sofa, ensconced in velvet cushions, listening to a jazz standard played on a baby grand with an attentive barman smiling at me. It has the feel of one of my favorite fantasies.

Tor first met Zac at the American Bar, but that's not for me at all—too shiny and light. I like a room with dark colors and hidden corners that you can disappear in. A room for whispering.

Tor believes that Zac is a victim like her. She emailed him at my request to say that she has the rest of the money but wanted to see him in person to check the details before she sent it.

Apart from mere lust, Tor's background might explain this risky affair. Her parents were cold. She spent most of her childhood in boarding school. She wasn't given love and hasn't learned what it feels like. And she has so many staff running her home, she needs a release from the stress.

Zac is her opulent rebellion against her parents' absence and the compromise of her love-free partnership with Lawrence. I can't object to her methods, but her judgment is off. By all means, sell your soul for personal gain, but choose a partner who inspires trust. Neither Law nor Zac would fall into that category.

The silk-crepe halter-neck Valentino gown I've chosen has a ravishingly high split skirt that gives tantalizing glimpses of my legs. I have accented this outfit with bold earrings and a chunky gold necklace. I'm channeling excessive wealth and the promise of promiscuity.

It's not difficult to understand men like Zac Estall. He probably found himself in a relationship with an older, richer, married woman at some point in his life and realized that it could be quite lucrative. He's a planner, but he also has an opportunistic streak, and I'm guessing that he won't be able to resist an attractive woman of indeterminate age alone in beautiful surroundings with luxurious bedrooms so close by.

I see him surveying the room like a predator. I feel his eyes linger on me, move on, then return. He takes a seat near the bar, orders something without looking at the cocktail menu, and interacts with the barman as if they are old friends. His charm is tangible, and his suit is beautiful. I can feel the Zac Estall effect immediately deep between my legs. He is movie-star gorgeous and looks like a bad boy. Tor did him a disservice in calling him handsome. I have to remind myself I'm working and not here for pleasure. But it's hard not to want when the offer is so unhusband-like.

I order a seasonal sour, which arrives on a silver tray and is placed with an elegant flourish on the table in front of me alongside a small bowl of olives. I sip, turn to the room, and note his eyes boring into me. Not lust yet, although there's a hint of desire. He smells the money. It's eight o'clock already. Any moment now, Zac will receive a message. I turn away, relax back into my seat, and let the music flow over me.

Ping.

Tor's message will tell him of a fight between her and Lawrence over the money. She can't make it. She's terribly, terribly sorry. This was my plan, and I insisted Tor follow my instructions. What else could she do? Zac will message her back in soothing, forgiving words, although he'll be annoyed by her lack of ability to deliver what he wants.

Now it is all about me, so I rise from my seat and head to the piano, stand beside the pianist, and listen attentively. All the time, I can feel Zac watching, trying to work me out. I return to my seat with an appreciative but brief glance in his direction. You must disguise the hook as you draw the fly through the water. Impressively, Zac does not approach me for twenty minutes. Perhaps he is merely cautious. But I feel him glancing and calculating as I slowly become his mark.

At 8:25 p.m., a barman appears at my side. "The gentleman at the bar would like to offer you a cocktail. What might madam prefer?"

"A man who can choose the right cocktail for me," I say. Four minutes later a cocktail appears on my table with a new bowl of olives. I look at it.

"Peas in a pod," says the waiter.

I take the glass, turn to Zac, raise it, and sip.

The tall, dark, ravishingly good-looking Zac Estall stands, adjusts his jacket, and walks imperiously to my table.

"It was presumptuous," he says. "After all, you might just be here for the music, but I've been stood up."

"I wouldn't say I've been stood up," I say. "Rather, I've been let down."

"Would you mind if I join you? Maybe for a little character assassination?"

"Why not? Killing people is always preferable to killing time."

Zac sits opposite me in a velvet armchair. He leans forward and appears panther-like in the darkness.

"It's a beautiful dress," he says. "Special occasion?"

"Well, I wouldn't wear this just to meet a friend," I say, smiling.

Zac laughs. "Not unless it was a special friend."

"And what's your story?" I ask.

"Dating by app. Digital disappointment."

"I'm glad it wasn't around in my formative years," I say, wondering if he's actually attracted to older women or just sees them as easy prey.

"It's a perfect example of overpromising and underdelivering. I'm looking for a deeper connection, even if gloriously fleeting." His blue eyes stare into mine, and I nearly gasp. He is, quite simply, edible.

"How fleeting?" I ask.

"Oh, you know. More than a swipe and less than a proposal."

"I'm Lalla, pleased to meet you."

"I'm Zac, and inordinately pleased to meet you."

"I'm married. And you may think me depraved that I was here waiting to hook up with an old flame, but it's purely to support my fragile ego, which has been ravaged by age."

"I think your ego needs to look in the mirror."

"That's very kind, but life has a way of chipping away at you," I say, and sip my cocktail.

"And serendipity has a way of putting the pieces back together."

"Is this serendipitous?"

"Two disappointed voyagers thrown together. Two peas in a pod."

"Or ports in a storm."

"In any weather at all."

The next hour rushes by. I feel younger, more wanted, more intelligent, and, most of all, desired. Although I'm over ten years his senior, Zac manages to keep the conversation buoyant with his flirtatious wit. I can see how he found his way past Tor's icy defenses.

Now and then, his hand rests gently on my leg for the briefest moment, but the touch is enough to make me hunger for more. At 9:30 p.m., his eyes hold mine, he takes both my hands (his are soft and warm), and he says, "I know this is an incredible liberty, and that we've known each other barely an hour, but you are exquisitely beautiful, effortlessly brilliant, and extraordinarily brazen, and I have this insistent desire to kiss you."

48

Zac

It's only Thursday evening, and I'm in a black cab whizzing through the bright and busy streets of Mayfair, the warm buzz of a cocktail in my head, an attentive and beautiful companion silent at my side, with nothing but the anticipation of forbidden pleasure ahead.

The visceral frankness of our purpose excites me. Zac has played me well and I feel as though my body is lit up with Christmas lights. He kisses me softly as we drive slowly up the Strand and by the time we reach his apartment, we are already intimately acquainted, fueled by months of marital disappointment.

In his sleekly designed living room, we drink a beautiful Meursault, and he tells me he deals in art and antiques. He speaks passionately about Fra Angelico's frescoes and Donatello's *David* with such insight, I'm sure he's recently looked it up on Wikipedia.

On his plush velvet sofa, he runs his hand down the back of my head and kisses me again. Having been let down by Stephen so often, I don't think it's unfair of me to enjoy a little pleasure while helping a dear friend.

With his lips on my neck and his hand inside my dress, he suggests we retire to his bedroom. I whisper "Yes" and he leads me theatrically through a set of double doors. The bed is like a stage set—crisp linen, ruffled velvet throw, and subdued lighting. Opposite the bed is a large mirror. I can't help it: I want him with every single cell of my body.

I nod coyly and head for the en suite. The bathroom is impersonal and scattered with high-end products. I wonder how to manage the next part of my operation. I'm feeling so awakened after the drinks, the blue eyes, the kisses and roving hands, that if he wasn't liable to video our session and blackmail me, I'd probably let nature take its course. Tor speaks highly of his ability.

But Zac is masking—something I know all about. He's faking it, and although he's good at it, I can feel the lizard below the surface and see the cold reptile eye of the predator.

He will make light work of my soft flesh. I feel myself tingling. However, business must come first. I put on perfume, reapply lipstick, adjust my hair, and return to the bedroom.

Rather self-confidently, Zac is lying completely naked on the velvet throw, a wide boyish smile on his face.

"Presumptuous," I say.

"Just a little warm," he replies.

I take in his body, not without pleasure. He's clearly worked hard on it and such endeavor does deserve admiration. It's admirably honed, but I'm more taken with the velvet throw, which is a subtle duck-egg blue. Perhaps this is a sign of age, when the quality of fabrics becomes more interesting than the shape of a body.

"Do you do this often?" I ask.

"No," he lies. "I just feel a real connection with you, and that doesn't happen often."

"No, it certainly doesn't, and does the age gap bother you?"

He scoots across the bed, puts his arms around my waist, then slips his hands down to my hemline.

"I think it's super sexy. Wisdom and beauty perfectly in tune. And you?"

He doesn't really want to know what I think. I don't like to be duped by anyone, and the fact that I want to let him take advantage of me annoys me.

"Do you like to play?" I say, taking control of my feelings and pinching his lips with the nails of my forefinger and thumb. My sexual desires are suddenly replaced by a strong urge to keep pressing my nails until they break through his skin. I resist. "Maybe just a little tie and tease?"

His head tilts, his smile broadens, and he makes an appreciative sound. I can see him calculating the additional value of this fetish when he shows me the video. I open his wardrobe, pull out a selection of silk ties, and hold them up. "Does sir like floral or stripes?"

"Oh, stripes, I think," he says. "As long as you don't leave any marks."

Zac doesn't realize what's happening because he thinks he's the predator. He's felt invulnerable his entire life, and women have no doubt added to his godlike sense of self.

I tie each limb to the bed at wrist and ankle, using knots that Hollis taught me for climbing. Once he is incapacitated, I use the fifth tie as a blindfold, then I leave him and return to the living room to look around.

He calls me back and I explain in a seductive tone that I now control the tempo and he will have to wait for me. There's nothing else in the apartment. Nothing personal in any drawers. If I were to hazard a guess, I'd say this is rented under a false name solely for the purpose of bedding and blackmailing wealthy targets.

I find his laptop on his desk and open it. It is locked with a password. I walk back into the bedroom with the laptop in hand.

"Why are you keeping me waiting?"

"It's part of the process of domination, Zac," I say. "And from now on, please do not speak unless you're asked to, do you understand?"

"Oh, come on, I'm desperate for you."

I lean over him, as if to stroke his face, and slap him hard. He cries out, which I enjoy more than the slap.

"No screaming, either, Zac, except with my express permission."

"You hit me!" he shouts, and pulls hard at his restraints. "What the hell are you doing?"

"Not a quick learner, are you?" I say, and slap him even harder.

"I've stopped, I've stopped," he says.

"Remember, it's just a game, Zac. You like games, don't you? It's just that it's usually you who's in charge. Now let me lead."

I take his hand, which is firmly tied to the bedpost, stroke it gently, then isolate his thumb and press it against the fingerprint reader on his laptop.

"What's that?" he says.

"A little toy," I say as I go into the settings to add my own fingerprint. This requires his thumb one more time to authorize, and after that, I pull his blindfold off.

"Your laptop doesn't seem to be encrypted. Therefore, I have some questions about your relationship with a friend of mine called Tor. I want to know if you have a compromising video of her on your laptop. You may speak now but please be brief."

I watch Zac's expression. He tugs hard on the ties. His vanity and pride, which give him such an oily veneer, are replaced by a pallid sheen reminiscent of a boy who's been caught stealing sweets.

"I don't know what you're talking about. I don't know anyone called Tor. You've got the wrong person. I'm just here to have fun," he says, but his voice has lost its confidence now.

"Oh, Zac, that's disappointing. I'll give you one more chance to be honest."

He tells another lie.

"Right, I'm going to boil a kettle now. It'll give you time to consider telling me the truth."

I walk to the kitchen. I can hear him struggling. The bed is shaking and the ornaments on the sideboard are rattling. I fill the kettle, stand there waiting for three minutes, pick it up, and walk back to see Zac.

I hold the kettle directly over his crotch.

"No!" he cries out. "No, no, no!"

"The truth," I say.

"Okay, right, okay . . . We did have a relationship. I met her a few months ago, and I did film her, but she knew all about it. And my computer really was hacked."

"I think this is a scam."

"It's the truth," he says. "I can't get into any of my files."

"Lies, again." I stare at him coldly, tip the kettle over his groin, and watch him shriek in pain.

49

Video

Back at home in my study, I copy Zac's considerable backlog of illicit files as Stephen snores loudly from the bedroom. Each video is identified by a set of initials and date. There are over twenty in all, but I quickly find the one labeled with Tor's initials.

With some trepidation, I watch a little of Tor's premiere. It's not something I want to do, but if it gives me something I can use against Tor in the future, it will be worth the pain.

Although Zac is a complete shit, I admire the way he throws himself so enthusiastically into his work, and Tor is a natural performer. Much more submissive than we're all used to, and she's kept herself impressively in shape. There's an eyebrow-raising moment when she pretends to be a cat, but who doesn't push one's boundaries when the opportunity presents itself?

While watching, an idea comes to mind that might give me the additional leverage I need for what I want from Tor. I screenshot a suitable image, crop it to remove any identifiable features, and create a mysterious and sexy edited version. After setting up a fake Facebook account, I post the picture, then tag all the mummies in Hero's class under the headline: "One of These Mums Is Not Like the Other Mums."

I think about Zac, all tied up in his bed, and wonder how he's coping. It took him about ten seconds to realize that the water from the kettle was ice cold rather than boiling hot. The most he suffered was a slight shock and loss of pride. Even so, I had to hold a boiled kettle over his crotch before he would tell the truth. It only took three little stinging drops of boiling water, and he was desperate to tell me the whole story.

Zac agreed to my two conditions. First, to cut all ties with every single woman he'd abused and exploited, including Tor, and stop his abuse. If he reneged on this condition, I explained that his laptop, containing evidence of all incidences of blackmail and illegally obtained videos, would be handed over to the police.

Second, to pass all the proceeds of his wicked deeds to me. With his direction and passwords, I withdrew everything from his Bitcoin wallet and transferred it to my account. This upset him immensely as it came to £150,000. This wonderful and unexpected gift means I only need fifty thousand to secure the Hampstead house.

Not only had I increased my bank balance and freed those women from extortion; I'd done a good deed for anyone who might have fallen victim to his wiles in the future. I was about to leave, when Zac, showing an undiminished commitment to his craft, asked if we might finish what we'd started.

I was surprised but he seemed turned on by a woman tying him up, ruining his little business, and extracting money from him. I understand that financial domination is a niche fetish, but he seemed eager.

Call it an indulgence or an act of charity if you will, but despite our differences I was happy to oblige, once I switched off the cameras, and we left on good terms. With this memory, I decide on one further act of generosity. I call the concierge at Zac's apartment block, explain that I was called away in the midst of a sex game, and ask if they might possibly visit Zac to untie him.

Feeling physically aroused from my recent escapade, positive about my improved bank balance, pleased with Madeleine's heart condition, and happy about Stephen's partnership prospects, I decide to watch a few more of Zac's videos to remind myself of his astonishing body.

In my fourth video, Zac is wearing leather chaps, a cowboy hat, and nothing else, which is not my taste, but intriguing nonetheless. He pulls a whip from the wardrobe and is standing there in a domineering pose when the en suite opens and his next victim walks in, dressed in a leather waistcoat and cowboy boots.

The thing that catches the eye, however, is not the fancy studwork but the fact that this nearly naked cowboy is male. And not only is he a man—he's a man I clearly recognize.

50

Bail

Friday, December 20

It's a remarkable feature of Muswell Hill that killing your husband is not the social faux pas that it perhaps once was. While no one seems to believe Cait is innocent ("dark horse," "it's always the quiet ones"), everyone is extremely understanding, especially in the supermarket. The woman at the self-service tills in M&S, who knows I'm one of Cait's friends, even asked what advice Cait would give to someone looking to unburden themselves of a partner past his sell-by date. She told me she was asking for a friend.

Tor and I spoke briefly about Zac last night. I told her I was satisfied that the ransomware was genuine and had paid the additional money as required but that the laptop hadn't yet been unencrypted. She seemed pleased but quite jealous of my time with Zac, and asked several questions about him as he's not responding to her texts. Of course, I've not told her that he's now committed to breaking all ties.

This morning, we're at a small and quiet coffee shop just at the top of Muswell Hill, where Tor, Sophie, Aisha, and I are sipping skinny lattes, staring longingly at the homemade cakes, and trying to work out how best to help Cait. The breaking news for the day, we're all delighted, surprised, or disappointed to find out, is that after her Crown Court hearing, Cait has been released on conditional bail. Apparently, as the charge is for manslaughter not murder, the evidence against her is circumstantial, and as she's a domestic abuse sufferer and sole carer for her girls, she's not a risk to anyone. However, the downside is that, as she's no longer living rent-free at taxpayers' expense, there's the issue of accommodation.

"It would look poor for us to host a criminal," says Tor, clicking her new nails on the table. "Papers would play merry hell with it."

"She's not a criminal, she's your friend," I say, placing my hand over Tor's to stop the anxious tapping, no doubt coming from being denied her route to sexual satisfaction.

"And she has to live somewhere—her house is a burnt-out shell," says Sophie, who arrived flustered from school, bemoaning some boy in her class who keeps climbing out of the window.

"Can't she stay with her mother again?" says Tor. "Isn't that what families are for?"

"What, like Christmas and criminal charges?" says Sophie. She's marking as she speaks, which appears to involve writing "Where's your homework?" across blank pages.

"Yes, but she wants the twins to keep going to preschool in Muswell Hill, so they experience as little change as possible," says Aisha.

"But the optics, politically," says Tor. "Especially if they link this to Lawrence."

"Tory Politician's House of Sin," I say, and smile at Tor, which she does not appreciate.

"It wouldn't be the first time," says Sophie.

"She's not been found guilty." Aisha makes this statement in bright yellow-and-blue leggings that she says are for Ukraine, which is a nice way to help the war.

"But she's hardly innocent," says Tor. "We all know she had a good enough motive."

"We're all innocent until proven guilty," I declare, which makes me as innocent as anyone. It makes you wonder about who invented that little statement.

"No one would blame her," says Tor. "But we've all got to think about the risks."

"What risk?" says Sophie, glaring now.

"Having a killer in your house is a risk." Tor glares back.

"Cait is not a killer. She was abused for years," says Sophie. "We need to show compassion."

"Indeed," I add. "She never tried to stab or burn any of us."

"But what if she did do it in a moment of madness?" says Aisha. "You know, we all snap at some point."

"So you won't have her either?" I say to Aisha.

"I don't think it's fair to Ranni," she says. "He might see it as a veiled threat, you know. We're in stage three of the battle—our troops are deployed and fully engaged."

"You lot! I'd have her if we didn't live in a cupboard," says Sophie.

"And I'd have her at mine, but with Stephen's mother's condition being so touch and go . . . it's just not possible." I look down at the table, blink several times with a sharp intake of breath through trembling lips. Two hands reach out and comfort me.

"We've got to acknowledge that she's mentally disturbed and needs professional help," says Tor.

"Well, here's to mentally disturbed women everywhere!" says Sophie.

"She's better off at her mum's," says Aisha. "Anyway, a group of pre-school parents have petitioned the management committee. They don't want Cait on the premises under the current circumstances."

"She's banned from picking up her kids now?" Sophie throws her head back and swears at the ceiling.

"They think it would cause too much disruption, and the press would be hanging off the railings to get photos." Aisha plays anxiously with her wedding ring.

"Shit, if your mates won't stand by you when you kill your fucking husband, who will?" says Sophie.

Tor crosses her arms defiantly, and Aisha closes her eyes meditatively.

"Look, don't worry," I say. "I'll explain the politics to Cait. I'm sure we can pick up the girls between us."

"I'd be happy to," says Aisha. Sophie nods.

"Ditto," says Tor. "Ask my nanny if you need help."
"We mustn't fall out over this," I say.

After our coffee shop meeting, I walk back to the car and receive three messages from Stephen. He apparently needs to speak to me urgently—again. His mother's dragging out her near-death experience by convalescing in a private hospital, although I'm sure there's nothing wrong with her anymore. All I can hope for is that she's suddenly croaked. While I only need another fifty thousand for the house deposit, we still need a million in cash to raise the mortgage.

I call him as I walk up the Broadway to the unbearable din of traffic, children, sirens, and shop refurbishments.

"What?" I say, clasping the phone to my ear.

"The police called me today."

"About what?" This is not what I want to hear.

"About that missing man, Jason Mercer. They're asking if I know him. And if you might. Do you?"

"No," I lie.

"They want to know if I had any worries about you?"

"What kind of worries?" I say, taken aback by this intrusion. It comes to something when the police, who can't spot a murderer at five paces, are seeing cracks in our marriage.

"They wanted to know if I thought you were having an affair."

"They asked me that too," I say.

"Why would they think you're sleeping with a corrupt policeman?" he says.

"Perhaps I'm just the most eligible prospect because they know you won't fuck me," I say, a tad tense perhaps. The group standing at the bus stop turn and stare. I smile and nod.

"They asked if I ever thought about having you followed."

"I'd be flattered if you were that concerned about me," I say.

"They also asked if I've ever paid anyone in Bitcoin."

"Bitcoin?" I say. Why would they ask about Bitcoin? Do they know about the money from Zac? Were they watching my bank accounts? I feel a flash of self-recrimination for treating the police so lightly. They might look stupid but perhaps it's an act.

"Ah! I know what it is," I say, realizing what DS Birch is getting at. "They think you paid Jason Mercer to follow me, because you thought I was having an affair."

"It's all a bit weird, isn't it?" says Stephen. "Anyway, they need to catch this guy. He sounds like a horrible bloke. Oh, and I told them about the..."

"Hold on, can't hear you," I shout, then I dart into a charity shop and close the door.

"What was that?" I ask.

"I told them about the anonymous letter. The one saying you're not who you say you are."

"Listen to me, you idiot," I say firmly. Then I have to say sorry quickly to the nice old lady at the till, who looks a little shocked.

"Calm down," he tells me. This does not calm me down. "I thought it might be from this Jason Mercer. They want to see it."

"If you give them that letter, Stephen, I'll . . ." I seethe into my phone, then stop. I feel a wave of dizziness and put my hand on the counter. A smiling reindeer stares up at me from the woman's sweater.

What will I do to stop my husband giving them the letter? Withdraw my affection? Stop sexual favors? Stop sharing my thoughts? In the middle of Crisis, I realize I've lost any hold I had on my husband. I'm his childminder, diary manager, social secretary, and cook—all replaceable services.

"Are you all right?" Stephen asks.

"Yes," I say, quietly, but I'm not. If I don't have a heart, why does it feel as if something is breaking?

51

Fog

Saturday, December 21

Back at Hollis's dingy flat in Hackney, we sit on either side of his kitchen table. He suggests a meal out or, worse, a visit to the pub. I don't feel like it after more weak coffee and another revisionist history lesson about myself.

"Tell me about your kids," he says. "You always said you couldn't have kids because you were scared you wouldn't feel anything for them."

"We've grown attached," I say. "But it doesn't come easy, it just takes time, and routine."

"Come on, you must dote on them?"

"I like their company and they need me. I like their independence. I like Nelly's rebelliousness. She's like I was at her age—a mystery to herself. I want to get her out of her current school. It's already labeled her as a misfit, and she's doing all you can do once you're labeled—you lean in."

"What about your Nathan?"

"Nathan's funny. He's as loving as a puppy. When he wants a hug, he takes my arms and wraps them around him and tells me to squeeze. When I let him go, he looks at me and says, 'That's good for a beginner.'"

"Sounds cute," says Hollis.

"They're mine, you know, but I still wade through fog to find them."

"That's how I always felt with you," he says. "You weren't ever with me totally. I was jealous of not being the center of your world. I loved you hard, but you're hard to love. You don't really love back."

"You never wanted to find someone who would love you back?" I say.

"I suppose I'm selfish. I get to do all the loving."

"Or you're an obsessive who sees it as a fucking challenge," I say.

"That might be true," he says, then sips his coffee and asks, "Does Stephen know about me?"

"I told him I had a climbing accident, and that I lost my memory, but nothing about us."

"Why hide it?" he says sharply. He's clearly offended.

"I didn't remember enough to talk about it," I say.

"So he doesn't know you're still married?"

"Look, I didn't know I was still married until two weeks ago."

"Do you remember the accident at all?" he says, with a nervous twitch in his left eye.

I shake my head.

He looks at me closely. "Nothing at all? You shouted 'Rocks.' You tried to grab me. Anything?"

I shake my head and look down. I can smell the damp from the carpet. Hollis moves closer.

"You can't be married to two people at the same time, you know."

I nod. "Sadly, bigamy is still illegal in the UK."

"You're going to have to choose who you really want to be with and forget about bureaucracy for a moment."

"It's been a long, long time, Hollis. I've moved on. I'm not that girl."

"When you did remember bits and pieces, did you ever think to look for me?" he says coldly.

"I did, but I saw those articles about the accident and presumed you were dead."

"But there were other articles. Stories about my miraculous journey."

"I stopped looking. I focused on the future. I just thought that part of my life was over. I had to make a new life for myself."

"Why did you disappear? Why did you change your name? It makes no sense to me. Like you were hiding."

I look at him. There are too many questions here that can't really be answered. And he's been dwelling on them for years and years. You can see that when he talks—an etched frown and a twitchiness around his eyes.

"You know I carry a lot of baggage. This was the chance to start again."

"But you can't start again. You can't reject the past just like that. We're still legally married, for instance," he says. He seems to enjoy the difficulty this puts me in. "You're essentially cheating on me with Stephen."

"Come on, Hollis. I thought you were dead."

"Do you love him?"

The question catches me off guard. I hesitate slightly and look up. "He fits into the shape in my head. Our lives are entangled."

"'Entangled'? What, you share a mortgage and bills? We had real electricity."

"Electricity is unstable. Unstable compounds tend to explode," I say.

"An explosion sounds like fun." He reaches across, holds my hand, and looks into my eyes. I feel a tiny flicker of static electricity spark between us like a pinprick.

"I want stability," I say, and pull my hand away.

"Well, in that case, I probably need to tell you something that Mercer found out as he was following you. I wasn't going to mention it, but now I feel I have to."

"And what's that?"

"Your stable husband is cheating on you," he says.

52

Unfaithful

Sunday, December 22

With term now ended and Aimée about to depart back to France, I'm looking ahead to trying to manage Christmas preparations and full-time childcare while investigating Stephen's potential infidelity. This requires multitasking, which is why I'm clicking away at an Excel spreadsheet as Cait sits opposite me, talking at length to Sophie about prison as if it's a magical fairyland where wonderful things happen and you make friends for life.

We can hear the children fighting over their Jellycat cuddly toys in the playroom, and the air is beautifully scented with Dettol, as Purdy has not covered herself in glory. Sophie loudly refrains from accepting my offer of wine. She's trying to mend things with Paolo, and being sober is part of their negotiations. I understand, in return, he has to stop being so Italian, which seems fair.

"What's that thing on your leg?" Sophie asks Cait. I haven't asked as I know what it is, and most people would wear wide-legged trousers to hide it, but not *Flame*.

"It's a requirement of the bail," says Cait proudly. "I'm not allowed out after seven p.m."

"No serious partying for you," I say. "Shame, as it's Christmas party season."

"I don't care, as long as I'm with the girls."

"I expect they see you as low-risk, as you don't have any more husbands to kill," I say, and continue to tap away, although Cait and Sophie do go a little quiet. Hollis's revelation about Stephen has been playing on my mind somewhat. On the one hand, I know he's just trying to drive a wedge between us. On the other hand, he did have me followed for three weeks, and Jason Mercer might have seen something.

I asked Hollis for evidence and he said he didn't have any, which wasn't helpful, so I thought I'd try to see if I could find any. I'm tabulating our sexual intimacy from my diary to see if there are gaps where he's likely to cheat, hence the Excel spreadsheet. All I've found out so far is that we do it less than we used to, but I'm sure that's true of all marriages.

"Are you having any therapy?" says Sophie.

"I don't need therapy. I need to find out who killed Owen."

I look up from a dispiriting tally from October and give Cait a conspiratorial look.

"How are your wedding plans going?" says Cait.

"It's off," says Sophie. "I mean probably. We're negotiating. It's brought out a lot of hidden anxieties—on both sides. Complex thing, merging families—love and grief."

Cait nods sympathetically.

"Like a motorway junction," I say. "The issue is that everyone's going different speeds."

A shriek emanates from the playroom and Sophie has to go to check on the children as no one else moves. Cait comes round the kitchen island and stands at my shoulder, so I shut the laptop.

"What have you found out?" says Cait.

"I found details of a meeting between Mercer and someone called MonkeyWarrior in a notebook in his car," I say, as I know Cait needs something to keep her conspiracy theory alive. Otherwise, she might just realize I'm the missing link.

"Wow, that's a lead!" she says eagerly.

"I'm going to go check it out. If Jason Mercer was working for some syndicate, this might be the connection."

"Can I come?" says Cait excitedly.

"I'm not sure you should," I say, pausing a moment to find a way to dissuade her. "I mean, if it turns out to be Owen's killer, he'd know your face."

"But I want to do something," she says, her body tense.

"Let me find out more first."

After Sophie and Cait depart, I return to my sex spreadsheet and tally the columns. The evidence of a serious problem with Stephen is staring me right in the face. The weekly average for sex over the last seven years has shown a chronic decline, even discounting time either side of my pregnancies for the sake of statistical integrity.

In our first year together we were averaging 3.1 encounters per week—which is impressive. By our third year, it was down to an acceptable 2.3. By our fifth year, a lackluster 1.4. That we've dropped off is no surprise—the unstable chemical compound finds stability. Lust becomes duty. Life takes over.

More noticeably, the last twelve months have shown a severe falling off. I'd presumed this was due to the bereavement and other stresses, but it could also indicate extracurricular interests.

There are also certain days when the overall frequency of sex drops off completely. I have cross-referenced with our calendar to account for absences and other issues (death of fathers, surgery, children, holidays, urinary infections, guests staying in the next room to ours), and there is still something to note. For instance, in the last twelve months, we've never made love on a Sunday or Friday. Stephen goes to the supermarket on Sundays and the gym on Fridays, but it may be more than that.

It upsets me to find out that we've entered into negative equity. In the last twelve months, we had sexual intercourse less than once a month, and for the last few months it is probably not even statistically true that we have had sex at all.

Currently, I'm more likely to die of a shark attack than have sex with my husband.

53

Identity

Monday, December 23

Eyes swivel and glance, then look away quickly. Some brave souls raise their phones and snap surreptitiously. On the icy pavement, couples part and strollers move aside. I'm enjoying being out with a Muswell Hill celebrity. Cait, however, who is the subject of all this furtive interest, is hiding her face in a thick scarf, which makes her look even more criminal.

Despite Cait's gloom, the shop windows are festive and bright and I'm a little smug that my Christmas preparations are almost complete. Presents all wrapped, Christmas pudding prepared, deliveries of consumables locked in with Ocado, and I've ordered a goose from the Hampstead Butcher as a change feels right. Picking up the turkey is Stephen's sole contribution to this annual event, but he makes such a song and dance about arriving home with the bird as if he's killed and plucked it himself that, this year, I'm getting it delivered.

Cait's moaning that her stint in prison has put her preparations behind, but the truth is, Cait is very last-minute, arrest or no arrest. And she's not the only person with challenges this Christmas—but you don't find me making a fuss about dealing with two murders, the reappearance of my first husband, Madeleine's reluctance to die, and the fact that the police are stalking me. Thoroughness can sometimes feel close to persecution, and I've made an official complaint about DS Birch.

Hollis's accusation about Stephen is still rumbling in the back of my mind. I'm not a suspicious person, but Stephen's coldness and absence (he's been at his mother's bedside for days at a time) is now even more distressing—I like a warm body in my bed, not a cold shoulder. One husband is pushing me away, and the other is trying to drag me closer.

"I don't want to be away for long," Cait says. "It took an hour to get here and I want to spend every second I can with the girls."

"I know, but I've got some really good news," I say with a big smile.

"What? You got your house?" says Cait, which is really generous, to think of my problems when she's got so many of her own.

"No, I've not quite managed that yet. It's about Owen's killer. I think I've found him!"

"What?" shrieks Cait and stops in the street. It causes all kinds of mayhem on the pavement and a minor pileup outside M&S.

"Yes," I say, and then notice even more people staring at Cait. They've clearly seen through her disguise. Fortunately, people are too polite to shout "Mummy Murderer," but they do shield their shopping from her rather obviously.

"Who is it? When did you find out?" she says, oblivious to the crowd and their prurient interest.

"All that matters is that I've actually found him," I say quietly.

We dart into Crocodile Café and find a corner seat. The young woman serving has a pleasingly round face with rosy cheeks, like someone you'd expect to see serving apples in a medieval fair.

"Just take me through this slowly," says Cait. "And don't leave anything out."

"I went to the meeting with MonkeyWarrior. It was at a café in Islington. I waited until the contact arrived."

"How did you know it was him?"

"He was wearing an *I killed Owen* T-shirt," I say.

"Ha ha."

"Well, stop interrupting! He was alone, he looked shifty, and when I followed him, he went to his car and I recognized it. It's quite distinctive. I was desperately trying to remember where I'd seen it."

"And?"

"I'd seen it in your road. I can't remember when exactly, but it was definitely before the fire."

"That's evidence, Lalla. Should we tell the police?"

"No! We should make sure first. We can't let the police mess this up."

"Did you find out his name?" she says, nodding with enthusiasm.

"It's Matthew Hollis," I say.

54

Wolseley

Monday, December 23—Evening

The Wolseley is my favorite restaurant, sitting so elegantly and undemonstratively between its more showy neighbors, the Ritz and Fortnum & Mason. Over the past few days, I've been sending Stephen loving and slightly flirty texts, often with up to seven kisses, but I'm not convinced that my charm offensive is the sole reason for our night out.

We walk in silence along Piccadilly, our hands clasped together. Since my research I've concluded that his sexual reluctance is down to grief. Besides work, he only goes to his mother's, the supermarket, and the gym. He simply can't be seeing another woman as he doesn't have the opportunity.

I've chosen a rather daring dress and even more daring underwear. It's rather breezy, but I'm willing to endure minor irritations for my husband as I'm hoping that this evening is the start of things to come.

I've been trying so hard to control my impatience and be nice, as I'm sure my nagging has pushed him away and left him at the mercy of Madeleine, who is clearly poisoning his mind from her hospital bed. And I have to say, it feels like I've made a breakthrough. When Stephen arrived home last night, he seemed happier than he'd been in months. And this evening, he's been enthusiastic and even quite boyish.

The smiling doorman in a bowler hat holds open the door as if we're old friends and wishes us well. Inside, a dark-haired woman in a waistcoat and white shirt appears and takes our coats. I feel a shiver of pride that he attracts admiring glances as we walk to the table.

My suspicion is that this dinner is the outcome of my candid little conversation with Josh Krill. Stephen has been given the nod at work and will be made a partner. The dream of Hampstead and our new life feels closer than ever.

We sit almost side by side on a soft banquette. Two glasses of rosé champagne appear, followed by sparkling water, crisp bread, and French butter. We drink, eat, and order. Stephen is charming and attentive. When his hand brushes my arm, I feel an intense shot of electricity. We eat oysters together with a bottle of Chablis Grand Cru and it almost feels as it did before the children arrived to drive out pleasure from all its hiding places.

I wait for the moment. When he asked me to marry him in a charming restaurant in Paris, I had to wait until coffee before he proposed, so I'm used to his tactics to keep me hooked until the end.

I'm proud to have helped secure his partnership. And hope to discover later this evening that those daily dabs of testosterone gel and Aimée's admiration have had an impact. I have rebuilt him, inside and out. Being made partner has made him like a man again—desirable and powerful—and he's come back to me.

"So, Lalla," says Stephen, as the coffee arrives. "I expect you're wondering why I brought you here."

"Such elegance needs no purpose," I say.

"No, but as you've always said, if someone were to have news, you'd want it done beautifully, right?"

"Why share wonderful things in ugly surroundings?" I say.

Stephen nods, picks up his coffee, and drinks. He looks to the door almost involuntarily.

"Lalla, we've been married for seven wonderful years."

"And what good years they've been," I interject.

"Our children are monsters, of course, but delightful and adorable. And you're truly a unique and special person."

"Thank you, Stephen."

"What I'm trying to say, Lalla, is that it's been great. We've been great." He pauses.

I notice a fly land beside my spoon. It's one of those winter flies that are clearly already half dead. I turn to Stephen. "Go on."

"I've been thinking about us."

"So have I," I say. "Almost nonstop."

My hand rises above the fly and hits down hard. My palm presses it flat to the linen tablecloth.

Stephen jumps as the teaspoon flips in the air and clatters down.

"Missed it, huh?" says Stephen.

I raise my hand. The half-dead fly is stuck to my hand with its innards on display, while its legs cycle helplessly in the air.

"Just tell me," I say. "Stop teasing me, Stephen."

"No, I'm not teasing."

"Come on, I know what this is about."

"You know?"

"Women's intuition, and, well, you've been so stressed about everything, and now your mood's improved, I imagine there's only one reason."

"What reason were you thinking?"

"Becoming a partner!"

"This isn't about that." His eyes fix on mine, and his forehead creases. He takes one of the gold-wrapped chocolates and puts it back.

"I thought this was a celebration."

"I'm so sorry," he says, looking down at his lap.

I wipe the fly off my hand with the white linen napkin and stare at him. "You didn't make partner?"

"No," he says, and looks up at the high dome of the ceiling.

"Then what's the news?"

He shakes his head. "You're so funny, so clever, but you always have difficulty understanding the simplest things."

"In which case, blame the English language, not me," I say. "Now tell me!"

"I'm sorry, Lalla. I want a divorce."

PART FOUR
Revive

It never will rain roses: when we want
To have more roses we must plant more trees.

GEORGE ELIOT, *The Spanish Gypsy,* **1868**

55

Christmas

Wednesday, January 1, New Year's Day
Christmas came and went without anyone being murdered, which shows great restraint on my part. Our Instagram reels portrayed an ostensibly Happy Christmas—reading "The Night Before Christmas" together by a log fire on Christmas Eve, the children jumping up and down in matching red-and-white pajamas with their stockings, Stephen and me singing "Here Comes Santa Claus" in jolly Santa hats, and gasping as the Christmas pudding was set aflame with brandy.

So many pictures that jar so violently with my memory. Between these homely images, I cut holes in the crotches of Stephen's suits, superglued his MacBook Pro shut, and dumped his Patek Philippe in the toilet bowl. Petty, of course, but felt good.

We argued when time allowed, but I didn't mention the specter of divorce at all, although the thought of it left me feeling quite sick all week. He doesn't know a divorce could leave me with nothing if he found out about Hollis and our voided relationship.

I'm sure the children sensed the tension because Nathan wasn't sleeping and Nelly pulled all eight tentacles off his brand-new Jellycat octopus. Nathan had a wee on Nelly from the top of the stairs in revenge. Not much landed on Nelly, but it did hit a socket and blew the fuse. Stephen scolded everyone, then disappeared to the place men go when they find a little puddle of pee too much to bear.

When he came back he lost the plot again because he discovered I'd bought a goose, not a turkey. He told me that his mother would never have done such a thing to his father, and he left again, claiming he was going to buy a turkey, at 1:00 p.m. on Christmas Day.

I assumed he was on his way to mope at his mother's bedside as she would probably equal his outrage at my culinary detour. However, he'd consumed three-quarters of a bottle of Baileys by midday and called not long after he left, having driven into a tree just outside our house.

I told him that his actions were unbecoming of someone hoping to become a partner as the final deliberations would happen early in the new year. He told me that my goose was cooked, which annoyed me because I knew it was—I'd put it in the oven myself.

Even though the children enjoyed Christmas, Stephen's mood remained sour. He blamed our ruined festivities and everything else (including the new dull Quality Street wrappers) on my unilateral decision to abandon tradition rather than his decision to abandon his family. He even asked me if the goose was some kind of "perverse revenge" for the divorce, and I assured him that spending four hours preparing and cooking a Christmas roast did not qualify as revenge, and if I did punish him, it would be far more painful.

On reflection, showing the children how to flambé a Christmas pudding with brandy was not such a good idea, as Nelly and Nathan ended the day by pouring brandy all over one of the knitted Christmas pudding tree decorations and setting it aflame.

Stephen and I had to stop slandering each other in the kitchen as the scream from the living room was truly ear-shattering. Cait could learn a thing or two from Nathan in the bloodcurdling cry department. We found a considerable-size Christmas tree fire in the living room. Nelly did not need my support but Nathan did, so I took him in my arms and cuddled him, which felt quite rewarding.

It's in moments such as saving a child from a burning tree that I feel my motherly instincts are at their strongest.

Our Christmas Day ended with the fire brigade dousing everything in water, but they were better company than Stephen and complimentary about the cold goose. The living room is completely wrecked. On the plus side, it does mean that we will have to press ahead with a full redecoration, and I'm sure the fire will have destroyed any residual traces of DNA.

There were lovely moments on Boxing Day, because I used the excuse of feeling sick to refuse to drive the family to visit Madeleine. Stephen had to go alone to see his steadfastly undead mother. That left the three of us to renew the bond of mother and child, which we expressed through baking.

We enjoyed a joyous three-hour baking and decorating marathon. Nathan and Nelly were particularly keen on making the marzipan leaves and berries for the cupcakes. To a background chorus of "Rudolph the Red-Nosed Reindeer," Nelly added the red color dye for holly berries, and Nathan added the green for the leaves.

The late afternoon was spent eating cupcakes and sitting together to watch a movie. Our favorite is *Nativity!*, which makes both children howl. When you consider divorce, putting aside income, a convenient companion at social events, and use as a bed-heater in winter, you're really not all that worse off. That's not to say I'm giving up. The announcement of a divorce isn't final; it's an opening jab, nothing more, and I used the opportunity of New Year's to devise some resolutions to save my marriage.

New Year's Resolutions
✗ *Tend to the physical*—Increase testosterone gel dosage.
Build shared goals—Lie about being pregnant.
Connect emotionally—Buy a puppy (?).
✗ *Show your kindness*—Send his mother a "get well" card.
Satisfy his deeper needs—Buy him track day at the Nürburgring.
Remove the financial pressure—Ensure Josh makes him partner.

Allow him to be a hero—Break the toilet flush so he can mend it.
Retain a mysterious allure—Send flowers to myself anonymously.
Gain his commitment—Secure mortgage on my dream house.
Build trust in the bedroom—Offer him a threesome.

56

Stalking

Thursday, January 2

Hollis has been away for Christmas visiting his mum and dad in Melbourne. He called me several times and I just ignored his calls as I have enough to deal with. He did ask me to join him shooting today, which is why Cait and I are now at Blackheath Rifle Club, in the middle of nowhere, which is located on the outskirts of Surrey.

The lane is so narrow that the car brushes hawthorn twigs as we creep between two overgrown hedgerows, good for wildlife but not for a large SUV. I don't mind a little bit of nature if it's clipped or caged, but to be perfectly honest, it's just a relief to get away from the house.

"Are you sure he's here?" says Cait, brimming with eagerness. I'm doing my best to keep her investigative enthusiasm under control. She now blogs quite openly about her experience of domestic abuse, which is a sign of progress, and has garnered a large online following.

"This is where he comes to practice shooting," I explain. "It's what assassins do."

"I'm ready for him," declares Cait, and opens her large, ill-fitting anorak (donated by Sophie, who's a giant in comparison to Cait) to display a John Lewis carving knife still in its plastic sheath stuck into her belt.

"What's that for?"

"Protection," she says. "And don't worry, I bought it for cash. No trace. If he goes for one of us, I'll shank him."

"It's not an easy thing to do," I say. "Especially if you hit cartilage or bone. The knife can get stuck and it's quite messy."

"He's ruined my life, Lalla," she says. "I think I'll manage."

"That's the spirit," I say, and pat her leg.

We park the car, obstructing a footpath, but there's no other option unless we use the rifle club's parking lot, which is not a good idea as we want to remain hidden.

I open the trunk of my car to retrieve my backpack, Barbour, and wellies. "I've got my gloves, balaclava, and binoculars in the bag."

"I don't have anything," says Cait. "Not even gloves."

"Well, just keep hidden," I suggest.

We trudge down the lane, climb through a hedge, and skirt the clubroom to reach the outdoor ranges. I find a tree with a low branch and start to climb. Cait follows but makes a terrible racket.

Sitting in the tree, we stare out over the undulating countryside. Fields of brown earth and grass as far as the eye can see. I put the binoculars to my eye and scan the rifle and pistol ranges.

I spot Hollis sitting in his wheelchair with a .22 pistol. He's wearing a green padded vest, flatcap, and earmuffs. He's firing rapidly at a target some fifty-five yards from his chair. I look through the binoculars at the target. Impressively, he's hit the bull's-eye repeatedly. I hand the binoculars to Cait.

She puts them to her eye. "What am I looking for?"

"The man shooting with the flatcap."

"They've all got flatcaps."

"Right . . . well, the one in the wheelchair."

"He's disabled?" says Cait.

"It's a disguise," I say.

Cait shakes her head. "That's despicable. I really want to hurt him now."

"You go, Flame—get it all out."

Once we've ascertained Hollis's presence and Cait's expressed more of her murderous rage, we climb down and head to the car lot, where I point to Hollis's smart BMW.

"That's his," I say. I don't tell her that I planted a surprise in the trunk last night that I hope will keep her engaged and excited.

"What should we do?" she asks.

"We need to prove he did it, so I think you should search for evidence."

"Me?" she says, suddenly showing caution.

"If you want to keep out of prison," I say.

Cait steels herself, looks left and right, then creeps across the car park toward Hollis's car.

I look up at the two CCTV cameras overlooking the rifle club parking lot and the back entrance to the clubhouse, which are recording Cait as she opens the car trunk, which he's left unlocked. She starts to search inside, and I await the moment.

"Ah! Lalla! You won't believe what's in here."

Cait pulls out her phone and takes a dozen photos of the contents of Hollis's trunk before running back.

"What did you find?" I say.

"Rope, petrol, bin liners, gloves," she reports, panting with excitement. "Hidden in the spare wheel. The whole lot! We've got him, Lalla."

"You got him, Cait," I say.

"What now? Call the police?"

"No, we can't. They'll arrest you and send you back to Bronzefield."

"What for? I've found the killer."

"Breaching your bail conditions. You're not allowed to investigate your own crime, or break into cars. They'll say you planted it."

"Shit, you're right. Then what do we do?" says Cait.

"We need more. At least we know it's him now, but we need something that ties him directly to the murder."

"The murder weapon?"

"Yes, or something that connects him to Owen. We should see if we can search Hollis's apartment."

"Seriously?" she says.

"Yes, and if we get this right, you'll not only clear your name, you'll be known as the woman who caught a contract killer."

For the first time since her release, Cait smiles.

57

Revenge

Friday, January 3

The first icicle of the new year hangs from the gutter of the Grove Café. I've spent the morning with a doctor, discussing my fertility. The nurse took more blood than seems decent as I pretended my marriage is not on the rocks. Although it's not pretense, it's determination. A baby is just what's needed to save it.

Tor is huddled into a parka, her hands wrapped around a hot chocolate. Although the temperature has dropped to below freezing, we're sitting outside with rugs over our knees as the Italian owner swoops from table to table, singing operatic arias and spreading joy.

"How are you bearing up?" I ask.

"Nothing like the terror of being exposed as an adulterous slut to add a little spark to your life."

"You haven't heard anything about the tape?"

"Zac is ghosting me. Completely. I've no idea what's going on."

"What an inconsiderate bastard."

"I know, I fucking hate him, but I'm also having severe withdrawal symptoms."

"Well, choose your outlet more carefully next time."

"It's all shit at the moment. Even the pool house is on hold."

"Why?"

"The foundations haven't set properly. One of them is completely cracked and they're going to have to dig it out or something."

"Poor you," I say, wanting to ask more but fearing that too much interest in her concrete will appear odd. Another problem I have to solve as it won't help anyone if the builders find Mercer's body.

Aisha arrives at the end of a run and sits, panting. "How's things?"

"Bloody marvelous," says Tor. "And talking of shit shows, how's your move abroad going?"

"Ranni's still convinced it's best for us all. Isn't it clever of him to know what we all need and feel without asking a single question? I'm just in awe of the man's intuition." She opens her water bottle and drinks.

"Cut up his passport," says Tor.

"But leave it till the last moment so he can't get a replacement," I add.

Sophie appears with a huge smile on her face. She pulls back a chair, throws herself down, and lets out a long breath.

"Scandal afoot!" she says. "Of the best possible kind."

"Where? Spill the beans," I say as Aisha tuts.

"Well," says Sophie, leaning in. "I've just been speaking to the other mums, and do you remember that saucy picture someone posted online before Christmas?"

"The one on Facebook?" I say.

"Yeah, well, someone's posted it again, with a challenge. It says—'Guess Who I Am. You have twenty questions. I will answer "yes" or "no" to one each day.' The mums are like a gaggle of schoolgirls!"

"What picture? I didn't see anything," says Tor, her paralyzed frown lines desperately trying to reanimate.

"It's a picture of the back of a woman facing the crotch of an impressive young man with beautiful abs!"

"And those women are playing twenty questions with someone's life?" says Aisha.

"Yes, and as much as I deeply disapprove, it's quite intriguing," says Sophie.

"It could be some awful man who wants to shame his wife or girlfriend," says Aisha. "I've read all about revenge porn, and it's absolutely horrible."

"Let's see it," I say, with a glance at Tor, who's looking uncomfortable.

There's an enjoyable frisson around the table as Sophie takes out her phone and finds the latest post.

Sophie turns her screen to us. There's a sculpted male torso and hairy thighs, framing the back of a woman's head.

"He's got a six-pack so it's definitely not someone's husband," I say.

"It's just a complete joke and obviously fake," says Tor, who is leaning back and looking into the clouds above.

"Unusual earring though," says Aisha, pointing to a pair of mother-of-pearl and diamond earrings.

I'm not looking at the phone. Instead, I'm watching Tor's face turn so pale that it looks as if someone has just given her an electric shock.

58

Divorce

Sunday, January 5

Aimée puts her rucksack down and immediately starts complaining to me about the divorce. I haven't told her anything, so clearly Stephen informed her on the way back from the airport. Nice touch.

"How was your family?" I ask, trying to divert her.

"I told you this would happen if I flirted with him," she says.

"I don't think it was you, Aimée."

"I dance with him one time, and he wants to leave you. I have power, you see."

I stare out of the front window and nod. Stephen hasn't yet appeared, and for some reason, I feel anxious. Do I miss him or am I anticipating how it might feel if he simply stopped coming back?

"And who's going to get me?" she continues. "I don't want to go from house to house. I need space, and I like the privacy of the loft."

"I can assure you, you will be our first thought when we come to a settlement."

Stephen finally appears in the window and I feel a telltale flutter of excitement. He's so uncomplicated I find it grounding, and it could all end, just like that. He takes hold of the gate, then stops and looks to his right. He nods, then says something, and I conclude he's talking to someone.

I knock on the window, as I am impatient when I feel I'm the person who should be the center of attention.

Stephen glances across at me, puts up his hand and waves, then turns back to his invisible interlocutor, speaks, listens, and then laughs.

"I think we need to think about my wages if there are two houses," says Aimée.

I ignore her, as I'm feeling a pang of what might be jealousy, but it feels to me more like a shot of icy anger. I tap the window again, firmly this time. Stephen waves his hand toward me, but this time without glancing.

"Fuck you!" I say, which makes Aimée sigh and leave in a huff.

I decide that I'm going to punish Stephen's insolence by having a public row. I head for the front door, but Nathan is already rushing down the stairs calling "Daddy" in a way he never calls "Mummy."

I open the door, and Nathan trundles down the steps, shouting. Stephen turns immediately, of course, and his face breaks into a huge and genuine smile full of warmth and delight. A face I've not seen myself for some years.

"Hello, darling!" I say as Stephen heaves Nathan high in the air and kisses his belly.

"Hi," he says.

As I arrive at the gate, I stop dead. The out-of-sight subject of Stephen's interest is a man sitting in a wheelchair. A man with a beard, carrying a bunch of flowers.

Matthew Hollis looks at me. I look at Hollis and grit my teeth. I am wondering what he's said, why he's here, and what I'm going to do to him, all in a single moment.

"And who's this?" I ask, feigning ignorance.

"I'm just looking for an old girlfriend," says Hollis, holding up the flowers and smiling at me as if he's practiced at such deception.

"Apparently, she might've lived in our house at one time. I told him we've been here for years. Do you remember the name of the woman we bought it from?"

"No, but I do remember she died soon after," I say, and glare at Hollis.

"Really?" says Stephen, with Nathan now upside down, dangling by his ankles.

"Good luck with your search," I say, taking Stephen's arm and tugging him through the gate.

Stephen pulls away from me and swings Nathan upright. Nathan squeals in delight and they chase each other up the path into the house.

I am left standing there with Hollis.

"You don't answer my calls," he says.

"There's a good reason for that. Stephen's divorcing me," I say. "So I've been a touch preoccupied."

"Shit," he says. "I didn't know. But that's good news for us, right?"

"Yes, I suppose it is, but I've got a lot to think about, and none of it is helped by you turning up in the middle of my life like this. Okay?"

He nods apologetically and hands me the flowers.

I head back to the house, stuffing the flowers in the trash on the way in. Stephen has Nathan on the floor and he's tickling his feet with his stubble. I pick Nathan off the floor and tell him to hide in the playroom and Daddy will try to find him. Nathan runs off, giggling.

"Your mum called while you were out," I say. "She's taking some time to recover, isn't she?"

"It takes time."

"Have you discussed euthanasia?"

"Lalla," he chides, as if I'm joking, which I most certainly am not. I doubt that Madeleine is remotely ill now, but it serves her purpose to draw him away from me.

"Are you all right?" he says. "Shouldn't we start talking about the whys and wherefores?"

"About what?"

"The divorce," says Stephen, showing a little frustration.

"Oh, I thought that was a joke. A response to the stress of your mum and dad and maybe even work too."

"It's not stress. It's what I want."

"Oh, don't give me that hangdog expression, Stephen."

"But I want a divorce."

"No."

"What?"

"We're not getting divorced. It's not in the plan. We'll rekindle our love instead."

"I'm not in love with you anymore, Lalla."

"That's just your opinion."

"No, it's not an opinion," says Stephen, looking shocked.

"Well, it's not a fact, is it? Love is a feeling. Your feelings may be wrong."

Stephen seems about to say something but just puts his head in his hands, which gives me the perfect opportunity to share my thoughts.

"We're just on different ships at the moment, and we need to steer in the same direction. If you want to take up cycling, walk the Camino de Santiago, or have separate bedrooms, I'm happy, as long as we're on the same path together."

"Lalla, I'm just not—"

"Trying hard enough?" I add quickly.

"Happy. I don't want to be a partner. I don't want a house in Hampstead."

"Don't be ridiculous. I refuse to be punished because you can't manage the simple task of keeping yourself happy. Here's an idea. We don't get divorced and you start making an effort."

"I find this all really, really draining," he says. "You've changed. I've changed."

"Well, it's no surprise, is it? I didn't have children to care for. You used to be quite independent too. You used to be able to wash your own clothes, book your own dentist appointments, plan holidays, pay your council tax, cut your toenails, make social arrangements, even make a woman orgasm. It's a little galling to then claim I've lost my sparkle. I'll fucking sparkle if you want me to, darling! Just stay at home and look after everything, and I'll be your firework."

"I empty the dishwasher," says Stephen.

"Sadly, darling, like sex, even that is a rare delight these days."

"Well, you don't know what it's like to earn the money to keep this all going," he says. "I feel like I'm being drained, like all my energy is being siphoned off. Like there's a syringe in my arm taking everything."

"Fine, if that's how you feel, let's get on with it. Have you thought about practicalities?" I say. "Where will you live?"

"We'll sell the house. I'll get a flat and you can get a smaller house for you and the children."

"Children? What do you mean?" I say, feeling the anger rise in my throat. "If you want a divorce, you can have the fucking children."

"Pardon?" he says, his eyes wide now.

"I've no interest in them. What for? They belong to our marriage. If that dissolves, it's all off. You think providing money is tough, you should try providing motherhood. If you're closing your wallet, I'm closing mine."

"Don't you want your children?"

"Certainly not. I don't want to be reminded of their weak-willed failure of a father, who jumps the moment it all feels a little strained."

"I knew you'd confuse the fuck out of me."

"Oh, sorry, did I make your divorce uncomfortable?"

"We can go for dual custody. We could have them half the week each."

"Not interested. You leave me, take your stinking children with you. I'll be the one who lives exactly as I want, without any responsibility. You don't get to win, Stephen."

59

Law

Tuesday, January 7

Lawrence agrees to meet me in the House of Commons, which is a rare treat. He put me off, or his PA did, until I told him it was a private matter that was potentially going to wreck his chance of being a cabinet minister. After that, I received an invitation within the hour.

When he meets me, rather than the taciturn, distant chap I've so disregarded at various evenings at Tor's, I see the pompous, power-hungry politician, using his sweaty palms and smarmy words to get his way. He tours me through the halls of Westminster with many a well-worn comic anecdote and becomes a little teary at the statue of Margaret Thatcher in the Members' Lobby.

We sit together in the corner of what looks like a bar. It's just past midday. Lawrence sips cognac, while I have English breakfast tea. The whole feel of the place is unmistakably male and privileged, and it puts my teeth on edge.

He asks about me, which is kind, and I flatter him with well-chosen words. I praise his recent statement on the radio about the government's position on badgers.

"You know, these walls have seen so much, and they never tell tales," he says. "But out there in this modern Babel, anything can be said and will be said. Our great country was built on reserve, and we need to return to some old-fashioned values."

"You sound so regal, Lawrence."

"Well, I'm the parliamentary undersecretary for rural affairs and biosecurity."

"And soon will be staking your claim for a cabinet position, no doubt."

"I've always hoped for such an honor," he says, modestly picking his ear. "The cabinet is awash with the overpromoted, or those appointed by positive bias. It needs balance, and people like me have been part of this country's democratic process for decades."

"Hear, hear," I say, and sip my tea. "Rousing stuff."

He nods, tells a sexist joke, guffaws loudly, leans forward, and before I know it, his hand is on my knee.

"I like you. I've always thought of you as the special one among Tor's coterie. You're . . . I don't know, what is it?" His face is so close to mine, I can almost taste the cognac.

"Female?" I suggest.

"Oh, I don't mind what you are, as long as you're game," says Lawrence, and he squeezes my knee, then downs his drink. I reassure myself that it's nothing personal, just a deeply ingrained disregard for other people's personal space and integrity.

"So, has Tor got herself into a muddle?" he says, picking up a napkin and wiping his mouth.

"A little, yes."

"Fucking around, is she? Excuse my French. I tell her to be careful, you know. What's she done now?" His face seems to freeze as he stares at me.

"Got herself a boy toy."

"Well, she's obsessed with antiaging products!" Lawrence waves his jowls at me, pulls the two sides of his old-fashioned suit jacket together around his large middle, takes a sausage with his fingers, and pushes it between his lips.

"The problem is that the young man is blackmailing her," I say, trying to ignore the grease emerging from the crease at the side of Lawrence's mouth.

"The shit! Really, do these people have no morals?"

"He secretly filmed their trysts," I say.

"Oh god, Tor, you silly ass!" says Lawrence with loud laughter. "Is he a foreigner?"

"He's not."

"I thought he might be Russian for a moment."

"He's quite establishment, actually. Harrow, Cambridge, civil service, then opportunist sexual blackmailer."

"Oh, well, Harrow, there's your problem right there. Chip on his shoulder."

"He wants fifty thousand," I say, and give him a sympathetic expression.

"Bloody hell, fifty? Will this money get rid of the problem? Such a thing could ruin my chances, you know?" he says, and looks really quite upset.

"And that would be a great shame and a terrible loss for this country," I say.

"Wouldn't it?" he says.

"Tor doesn't know I'm here, Lawrence. She'd be embarrassed if she knew I'd spoken to you."

"Of course. Once more, I'll just have to bear the consequences of my wife's indiscretion." He sighs. It's comforting, like the sound of a wood pigeon in a copse.

"I've been her go-between with this scurrilous individual," I say, smiling conspiratorially.

"So you want money to pay him, is that it?"

"Tor's paid him already, actually, but the thing is, he wants another fifty thousand."

"Well, it's cheaper than a divorce, I suppose. But why does he want paying twice?" he says.

"Oh, no, this is for another tape altogether," I say, and gently remove his hand from my thigh.

"What do you mean?" Lawrence doesn't change his expression, but fear shows in his eyes.

"There's a tape of Zac Estall with a man wearing nothing but cowboy boots and a leather waistcoat who looks the spitting image of you."

60

Mother-in-Law

Thursday, January 9

At this dark and cold time of year, with the lights of Christmas back in their boxes and stowed away in the loft, it's heartening to see delicate white snowdrops appear from the frozen earth. It gives hope for a brighter future and is a sign that our deepest wishes can emerge, fragile but unbroken, even at the darkest hour.

There are swaths of these bright white flowers beneath the bare beech trees and across the manicured lawns of Glynburgh Private Hospital. I imagine that the patients take a great deal of comfort from them. I've arrived a little early and take a walk in the grounds to pass the time, admiring the soft yellow stone of the house, and the large, landscaped lake.

At 10 a.m. I'm at the teak reception desk, where a smiling woman in a dazzlingly white tunic greets me. I doubt she's a nurse as she looks about eighteen years old; however, it's all about giving the impression of clinical expertise, even at check-in.

"Lalla Rook," I say. "To see Madeleine Rook—she's my mother-in-law."

"Of course, it's good to see you. Is this your first visit to Glynburgh?"

"No, it's not. Sadly, I was here to visit her husband last year."

"Oh, well, I hope he's better now."

"Not really," I say. "He's dead."

"Oh, sorry," she says, the mortification glowing on her cheeks.

"We all go sometime," I say and smile.

She clicks away at her Apple computer, deciding to avoid further small talk, and suggests I take a seat. A nurse arrives within minutes, shakes my hand, and walks me to a well-appointed suite. Once she was out of the emergency room, Madeleine generously insisted on no longer being a burden on the NHS and came to Glynburgh to convalesce in more comfort. She's been here for almost a month.

"You may be surprised by her condition," she says, touching my arm. "If you've not visited her before."

"Oh, has it deteriorated dreadfully?" I ask, with a hopeful expression that seems to confuse her.

"No, not at all. She's much improved. She's a fighter."

"Isn't she?" I say.

The nurse opens the door, and her voice rises to a volume she clearly uses for the more senior patients.

"Hello, Madeleine, dear, I've a visitor for you today."

"Is it Stephen?" she says from her bed, her voice rising in hope.

"It's your daughter-in-law."

I arrive in the doorway to watch her frown appear. It's probably harder to disguise your disgust when you're recovering from what I now understand was simple heart failure rather than a stroke or heart attack, but Stephen was always one to exaggerate.

"Can you stay?" Madeleine asks the nurse, reaching a hand out toward her.

"We'll be fine," I insist, and hold the door open until the nurse feels obliged to slip out.

I feel Madeleine's cold eyes on me as I wander around her room silently. I pick up her cards and read the anodyne messages from well-wishers. I smell the roses in the vase on her bedside cabinet and read the chart at the end of her bed.

"Heart's not so strong, is it?" I say, tapping the chart. "Must be so worrying. I mean, one shock and it might pack up for good."

Even though she's stronger than Stephen suggested, without her makeup, fine clothes, and elegant house, Madeleine looks much older. Her skin is so thin that you can see every contour of the bone beneath.

"Where's Stephen?" she says. "I don't want to speak to you."

"But I do want to speak to you, Madeleine, on a delicate matter, so Stephen doesn't even know I'm here," I say, and sit down in the rather upright chair at her side. "Lovely place here. Do they treat you well?"

"I want to see my Stephen," she says, her sharp eyes on me as I inspect her drip.

"I have a couple of questions. That's all. I want an honest answer—just a straight yes or no, okay?"

Her eyes widen as she stares at me. There's something about her sunken eyes and sharp bones that gives her an ill-deserved grandeur.

"Question one—did you convince Stephen to divorce me?"

Madeleine looks to the window, which is both rude and revealing.

"A simple yes or no will suffice, Madeleine."

Her mouth puckers and tightens. I don't feel I have much time, so I reach across, take her wrist, and quickly pull out the cannula. She lets out a small cry, more of shock than of pain.

"Sorry, I thought you were finding it difficult to pay attention. Yes or no? I doubt Stephen has the imagination to come up with this himself."

She rubs her arm and starts to pick off the remaining surgical tape. This suggests guilt, but I need to hear her say it.

"I've devoted several years of my life to making Stephen happy and raising our children. And yet, he spends time with you and comes back saying he wants to leave me. Anyone would think you've poisoned his mind against me, or worse."

"Worse?" she spits.

"I suspect you threatened to disinherit him."

"None of your business what I do with my wealth," she says firmly.

"So that's it. You told him he'll get nothing if he's still with me," I say.

She swallows and looks down at her hands.

"You're a parasite," she says, staring at me coldly.

"We never really bonded, did we?" I say, although she's spot-on with her description. Age hasn't wearied her perception at all.

"You stole him from his fiancée." Her body leans forward, showing more determination than I imagined she had. "He loved her. I loved her. She was from better stock."

"Eugenics is frowned upon these days, Madeleine. And she was sleeping with one of his friends. Not so classy."

"Liar," says Madeleine, trying to shift herself onto her elbows. "You made it all up, as you always do. I know what you are."

"And what's that?" I say.

"A nothing from nowhere," she says, her eyes twinkling with delight as she looks me up and down. "A charade. But I found your shadow. I found Lola Wells. The poor girl taken into care with a murderer for a mother."

"My name is Lalla Rook."

"Is it, indeed? You made up this fantasy of who you are and fooled everyone. But not me, and now it's all coming apart at the seams," she says.

"We're all inventions, Madeleine. Some are born with their masks on, others have to create one to survive. We all strive for more. You're no better than me."

"I am better than you. I don't need to lie and cheat to find a husband. I'm going to tell Stephen all about you, and then we'll see what happens. Would've done it already if I hadn't had heart failure."

"I think you've been suffering heart failure most of your life, Madeleine. You'll convince him I'm someone else and you think, along with your threat to disinherit him, that'll be enough."

"Seems like checkmate, Lalla."

"Actually, I find it quite reassuring. If he was leaving me because he'd found someone else or had fallen out of love, I might worry, but if it's just due to your lies and money, then I can do something about it," I say, taking her wrist and squeezing it until she squeals and pulls away.

"He's never loved you, Lalla, because you're not real. You're a set of reflections. Now, you have a choice. You can agree to a divorce on amicable terms and avoid public humiliation, or I'll not only tell Stephen, I'll release everything I know to the press and prove he married you under false pretenses. You'll get nothing."

"You shouldn't threaten me, Madeleine."

"Oh, I believe I just have," she says with a smile. "And let this be a warning—I've only just scratched the surface with you. I know there's more. I daren't think what I'll find next if I carry on scraping around in the mud, so your best move would be to disappear and take your funny little children with you."

"Pardon?" I say, my stomach lurching. "My children?"

"Everyone knows, Lalla. Everyone talks about them behind your back. Nathan's sweet but he's a bit of a simpleton, and Nelly is just strange. God knows how Stephen has stayed so long. I always told him not to mingle his genes with the lower orders. Use them for fun, but don't bloody breed with them."

I have to stand and turn away or she'll see my distress. I feel my legs weaken as I take two small steps to the window. I want to feel strong now, but I don't feel any strength at all. I want to curl up and lie on the floor. In the face of attack, I've always been able to punch right back harder, but I can't focus now. This wasn't how this was supposed to go, and I can't think.

I steady myself on the windowsill and feel the cold stone against my hands. Outside, I can't quite see the lake anymore as it's lost in a layer of mist.

"Just go back to whatever hole you came from," she says, "and I won't dig any deeper."

61

Headmistress

Friday, January 10

Mrs. Pembury is resplendent. She's hosting a secondary school evening at Adams, where heads from the key senior schools give a sales pitch about their hundred acres of parkland, Olympic-size swimming pools, and Michelin-starred catering teams to the parents of current Year 5 and 6 girls.

I'm not interested in secondaries as yet. I just wanted to have a word with the head and she didn't get back to a single one of my thirty-four emails, which I find unprofessional. I have to sit through four generic monologues, and my boredom is only slightly alleviated by one gorgeous headmaster that all the mums talk about.

I don't drink too much of their Chilean sauvignon blanc (they could do better), and I don't ask difficult questions. I just stare at Mrs. Pembury from the audience, which seems to put her off-balance.

I wait by the door as she goes through her clever social interaction with each and every parent. I'm probably the only non-Adams parent present but one of the best dressed. They're all parading luxury loungewear with Ugg boots and cashmere sweaters, but I've made an effort.

When it's my turn (and I do ensure I'm last in the queue), Mrs. Pembury's seemingly endless stream of graceful smiles dries up.

"Hello, Mrs. Pembury. Lalla Rook," I say, and hold out my hand.

Her eyes are pebble-hard and her lips pout. "This evening is for current parents, not prospective parents."

"I like to get to know a school, inside and out," I say. "And it was most informative."

"I'm pleased that you enjoyed it. Good evening." She turns away before I can reply. An expert in cold-shouldering. She is half out of the door when I grab hold of her arm. She turns, glaring at my hand.

"I wouldn't mind a quick word about Nelly. Do you remember Nelly?"

"Please direct your questions to our registrar, and I'm sure she'll be only too pleased to assist."

"But I've tried and, if I can speak plainly, it's like talking to the back end of a bus. All you get is exhaust fumes. I thought I'd go right to the top. I'm just trying to get some support."

"Well, I can't help you," she says, removing my hand.

"She finds the experience of examinations quite challenging. She has special needs. Would it be possible to give her extra time and I could provide evidence of her specific condition later?" I stand in front of her to prevent her leaving.

"No, Mrs. Rook, we must be fair and act only where there is an actual diagnosis, not where there is merely a suspicion," she replies, and steps to the side. "You must use the resources you have. Now, I've said my final word on this matter. And furthermore, please do not send me any more gifts." She must be referring to the Harrods hamper she received at Christmas.

"Everyone deserves a chance," I say.

Her eyes blaze, but she quickly douses the flames with controlled calm and says, "Good night, Mrs. Rook. Good luck in the tests."

I'm left standing alone in the hall, with the cleaner trying to get in. I just want Nelly to do well. Clearly, she will not do well without help, which leaves me feeling, I might as well admit it, vulnerable.

I return home deeply dissatisfied. Stephen isn't there. Instead of a husband, I find a note telling me that he's staying in his mother's house in Kensington until Sunday morning, to give me "space," and he asks for the name of my solicitor so that we can start to discuss a deal. Charming. He wants to force me to accept a reduced settlement. I don't need space or a lawyer. I need the opposite. I need firm arms around me. I need to stop spinning.

The bed is cold and my mind is racing. Words like *simpleton* and *strange* keep circling like vultures. I get up, look in on Nelly and Nathan. I sit on the edges of their beds and stroke their foreheads. I'm a mother, aren't I? Even if I don't... even if I'm not... and they deserve the best, don't they?

I think I must fall asleep in the chair in their bedroom, because I awake suddenly to the image of Jason Mercer clawing his way out of wet concrete and pulling trampoline plastic from his face. Except it's not him at all. It's Nelly's face gasping for breath.

I sit bolt upright, sweating. I rush to Nelly, but she's sleeping. She's not a maniac. She's just a girl who can't quite conform. I kiss her head. Her smell smothers me. She's the past as well as the future. Why do I let people insult my children and do nothing?

I suddenly know what I have to do for my children. Ten minutes later, I'm driving toward Barnet in my pajamas and dressing gown. I stop at an ATM and use four different cards to withdraw as much cash as they allow. Various passersby give me rather odd looks. Of course, I realize I don't look my best, but that's not important now. I get back into the car and stuff the cash into an envelope.

I park outside the house and march up to the door. There are no lights on, but it is after one in the morning. I press the bell and wait. Nothing happens, so I keep my finger on it for a full minute, until a light goes on and a figure appears through the frosted glass.

"Who is it?" calls out a frightened voice.

"It's Mrs. Rook. Nelly's mum."

"What are you doing here?" says the voice.

"I need to speak to you," I say.

"I can't speak. Go away," says the voice, with a gulp of panic.

I take the envelope of cash from my dressing gown pocket and stuff it through the mailbox.

"I hope this helps. We all need extra in January."

"What are you doing?" she squeals. "You can't do this. You can't give me money."

"You said I should use the resources available to me. I didn't realize what you meant, and then it just came to me."

The door opens on the chain, and Mrs. Pembury holds out the envelope with a shaky hand. "Mrs. Rook, you can't give me money. I only meant that you should focus on Nelly's strengths rather than seek extra time."

"You have it. Clearly, you need it more than I," I say, indicating the house.

She pushes the envelope farther through the gap. "Go away, take your money, you can't harass people like this," she says, her voice breaking.

"Please," I say, grabbing her hand. "I want you to help Nelly. She's not a bad child."

I see her eyes through the gap in the door. "Let go, let go," she shouts.

I let go of her hand. She pulls it back through the narrow crack and tries to slam the door, but my foot is wedged in the gap.

Mrs. Pembury is breathing rapidly now. She says quite slowly as though trying to remain calm, "How did you know where I live?"

I don't want to tell her that I followed her home once, so I just stare at her.

"Please, you have to go. I'll call the police."

"Why won't you help me?" I say. "I want you to give Nelly a chance. If she had extra time, she'd really surprise you."

"My husband is upstairs," she says, then calls upstairs. "Malcolm!"

"But you don't have a husband, Mrs. Pembury," I say. "He died five years ago."

"I'm calling the police," she says. "This is harassment, and I won't stand for it."

"You'll have to let go of the door to do that," I say. "And these chains break easily."

She looks over her shoulder. A small dog appears from the kitchen and lowers its head submissively. Not the guard dog she was hoping for.

"Can I just ask one question? Then I'll go."

"I'm not answering any of your questions."

"Do you think it's worth getting Nelly an autism assessment? It's three thousand pounds, so I don't want to waste money unless it will do some good."

Mrs. Pembury tries to kick at my foot.

"Please don't make me angry, Mrs. Pembury. I would hate to have the loss of a leading educationalist on my conscience. I just want some advice about which disability to choose."

"You can't choose a child's disability," she shrieks.

"But hypothetically, would you say that strong dyslexia trumps mild autism?"

"Go away," she says through the gap.

"Do you think you can add them up? You know, if she has dyslexia and autism? I suppose I could just apply for both."

"Don't ever come here again," she says.

"Do consider my request, Mrs. Pembury," I say, and remove my foot. The door slams shut. I walk back to my car and sit there watching the house until the lights all go off again, then tiptoe back to the front door.

"Just a little thank you," I whisper, take the thick envelope out of my pocket and push it back through her mailbox.

62

Supermarket

Sunday, January 12

The little green dot on Find My Phone moves away from our house, makes its way up Alexandra Park Road, stops, waits for several minutes at the junction, then turns right onto Colney Hatch Lane, continues all the way down, crosses the A406, then turns left and stops in Tesco's parking lot.

I've regained some composure over the weekend, as I decided not to talk to Stephen about his mother's background checks or threats. At least, not until I have a plan to remove her and all her evidence from Planet Earth. Instead, I put my head in the sand and played happy families, which felt nice.

This morning, however, Hollis called. He apologized for turning up at my house and said he's desperate to meet now he knows we're divorcing. I told him that we're not, and that Stephen's current preference is only based on his mother's threats of disinheritance. There was a long pause on the line.

"For someone so smart, you can be so dumb," he said.

"Because I'm willing to fight for my marriage?" I asked.

"Because he's cheating on you, Lalla. I asked Mercer to follow him because I wanted to know if you were happily married. He meets a woman every Sunday."

I threw my phone against the wall, and when I had calmed down, I decided to find out the truth for myself. The only place Stephen goes on a Sunday is to the supermarket. He started just after Nathan was born as payment for never getting up for night feeds.

He always comes back with a trunkload of shopping, so unless he's fornicating somewhere between the vegetable aisle and the checkout, I think Hollis is lying.

I am relieved to see the dot still in the parking lot half an hour later, but something does bother me. The dot is not moving. I reassure myself that this is either due to a lack of a signal inside the supermarket or he's left his phone in the car. I continue my ironing.

Another thirty minutes later, I've abandoned my chores and I'm about to drive to the Tesco lot when the doorbell rings. I open it without looking, just as I'm putting my coat on, and who do I see standing there?

"DS Birch, and the odd man who is always with her," I say impolitely.

"Mattoo," he says, and smiles brightly. I find him charmingly disarming.

"On your way out?" says DS Birch.

"You are brilliant," I say. "Was it the coat that led to this breakthrough?"

"We just want a word."

"Can't you call in advance and book an appointment?" I say.

"This won't take long," she says, and takes out her notebook. "I presume you don't want us inside?"

"Cleaner's just mopped the tiles, sorry," I say, and start tapping rather exaggeratedly on the doorframe.

"Well, could you explain a recent £150,000 transfer to your bank account from an anonymous Bitcoin account?"

"You've accessed my bank accounts?" I say, horrified.

"We obtained a court order to access your financial records as we have reason to believe that you're helping Mr. Mercer. Now, can you explain where the £150,000 came from?"

"Not really," I say.

"We believe that your husband may have paid Jason Mercer to

have you followed," she says, with a face that suggests she's terribly pleased with herself.

"You really don't know Stephen, do you? I could conduct an affair on our kitchen table and he wouldn't care less," I say, realizing that I'm losing grip of my normally clear boundaries.

"Your bank records also show payments for drinks at the Savoy and the Ritz. We checked their CCTV against the time of those bills, expecting to see you with Mercer, but you were with two different gentlemen. It would seem that Mr. Rook has good grounds to suspect adultery."

"How dare you!" I shout.

"It's a priority case, Mrs. Rook. The reputation of the Metropolitan Police is important, and we're under significant pressure to find Mercer, so please just tell us where he is."

"I have a right to meet male friends where and when I like. I also have a right to receive loans from other friends. It's for a house purchase. You can check with the real estate agents, if you like."

"Do you have the name of this wealthy friend so we could tick this one off?" says Birch.

"No," I say. "You can't. This is an invasion of privacy. I want you off my bloody porch."

"We think you found out that Mercer was following you and demanded money from him to keep quiet."

"Oh, please, do I look like someone able to blackmail anyone?" I pull the door closed and walk between them as quickly as I can on my heels.

"One more thing," says Birch as I reach the gate.

"What?" I shout. "I'm not having an affair or helping anyone abscond from court. I'm just trying to save my marriage, get my daughter into prep school, and move to Hampstead so please leave me alone."

A mother passes with a stroller. She avoids my eye.

"It's just that you have a pair of pants stuck to your leg," she says.

I look down. A red thong from the washing basket is clinging to my trousers. I pull it off, curse Aimée, and push it into my pocket.

"Good luck," says Mattoo.

I get in the car and start the engine. It's only a matter of time before my bank shows a deposit of £50,000 from Lawrence and they come back with more questions. I don't really know where this will end, but I need to find a solution.

At the entrance to Tesco's parking lot, I look down at my phone and try to stop DS Birch's voice circling in my mind. The green dot remains motionless, so I drive toward it and park close by. I get out of my car, look around, and then cross over to Stephen's car. I put my face to the window and there it is. Mystery solved. His phone is sitting there in the central console on his wireless charging mat. Hollis is lying. Stephen and I can still work.

I know it's childish but I let the air out of all four of his tires and return to my car. I'm about to leave when a blue Audi A3 drives up and stops just beyond Stephen's car. To my astonishment, Stephen gets out of the sporty Audi, flicks open its trunk, and then proceeds to move several Tesco shopping bags into his own car.

I stare, confused, as Stephen notices one of the back tires and the Audi takes off at speed. It's as if I've watched a county-lines drug transaction. I put the car into drive and power away, skidding on the tarmac, but turn the wrong way up a one-way lane and meet another car head-on, only just avoiding a collision.

I beep wildly. The woman in the car points to the arrows, and although she's in the right, I edge up to her until she loses confidence and moves backward. I skirt around her car, speed out of the parking lot and up the road to the lights, my eyes peeled for the blue Audi, but it's nowhere.

I cross two lines of traffic to a succession of beeps and drive home with my mind racing. My god, I thought he was being unfaithful, but if he's been cheating on domestic chores, this is even worse.

63

Blackmailing

Tuesday, January 14

First thing in the morning, I find a man at the door with a huge bouquet of flowers. There's also a small package addressed to me on the doormat. The flowers I sent myself are beautiful (even if I do say so myself) and have a mysterious note attached that just says, "from an admirer xxx." I place them as ostentatiously as possible on the kitchen table for Stephen to see; divorce and domestic betrayal notwithstanding, there's still much to play for.

The package is less welcome. It contains two thousand pounds, with a note from Mrs. Pembury's PA, saying that I mistakenly posted this through her mailbox the previous Friday evening, and that she informed the police about the incident as it was a considerable amount. The letter also had a postscript that said she will file a harassment complaint if I ever visit her house again. What a devious woman!

I'm not displeased to get my money back, of course, but I'm not even sure I've achieved my aim of convincing her to help Nelly. I suspect that applying any more pressure will lead to a formal police complaint, which DS Birch would no doubt find a way to use against me.

At lunchtime, Nelly is sent home from school. Aimée has to collect her and tells me with unnecessary venom that she's not "on shift" until pickup. Aimée's wearing a new outfit, courtesy of her additional money for trying to flirt with Stephen. It galls me to pay for incompetence, but she looks amazing.

"What did you do, Nelly?" I say as I'm cooking fish sticks (minus points for nutrition but plus points for happiness). Nathan stares through the oven window and reports on progress. I can't help thinking of what Madeleine called him every time he calls out, "Not ready yet."

"Nothing," says Nelly, already changed into her full ballerina costume and practicing positions.

"She stapled a girl to her seat," says Aimée.

"Did you staple someone to their seat, Nelly?"

Nelly scrunches up her face. "Yes. But I said I didn't, so I shouldn't be told off."

"That's how it works in court but not in school," I say, with the word *strange* reverberating. "Anyway, I'm sure it was an accident."

"I did it on purpose," Nelly says, moving through fourth and fifth positions quite elegantly.

"Well, at least pretend it was an accident," I say.

"I did pretend, but she didn't pretend with me," says Nelly, attempting an arabesque that needs significant improvement, but now isn't the time.

Nathan interrupts. "Fishy sticks have cracked open!"

"Thank you, darling. You keep a close eye, it's ever so helpful."

Nelly crosses over to Nathan and kneels by his side to look into the oven, then comes to me and rests her head against my arm. I'm touched. She rarely touches anyone. I reach my hand down and stroke her soft cheek.

She bites me.

I yelp and she howls with laughter.

"Fishy sticks ready!" cheers Nathan.

I've spent years trying to calm my internal chaos, but this chaos is different. This moment, this treachery of teeth, this stapling of friends, this fascination with exploding fish sticks, this unbridled and raucous laughter—if I could stop time now, I would be happy, I think.

As soon as I realize I am feeling a kind of contentment, I fear that I'm losing all of it. Whatever becomes of Stephen and me, it will not be this.

I kneel down and take Nelly's hand. "Don't bite or staple, Nelly. I know we're all annoying, but try not to hurt other people."

"Okay," says Nelly and continues her ballet. I know that inside Nelly there's a void as deep as my own, but she can't say. I couldn't when I was her age either. When your heart feels so empty you fill it with sensation, just to stop the silence.

"You must punish her, or she'll be confused," says Aimée.

"There are worse things in life than stapling someone to a chair," I say.

Aimée lets out a puff of French air and flounces out. Later I have to pay her extra to look after the children for the afternoon, when I leave to visit Tor.

She's not the Tor of old, and the latest perturbations have clearly left their mark. The charts on her fridge appear to have been neglected and there's an unwashed plate by the dishwasher.

"It's absolute bedlam here," she says, and throws up her hands.

"I can see, it must be terribly hard."

"They're getting closer and closer."

"Who is?"

"The Facebook group! Whoever's doing this is torturing me. They already know the woman in the photograph drives a four-by-four and has blond hair. Hello?" she says, and pulls up a strand of her hair.

"I'm sure it will blow over," I say.

"Why are they doing it? They've got the money."

"I can try to contact Zac again to see if he has more news."

"Oh god, that's what makes this so awful. I miss him so much. He must be so worried too."

"Yes, I think he must," I say, knowing that Zac will be off planning new schemes.

"If it gets out that it's me, I'm ruined."

"I think I know the problem," I say.

"You do?" says Tor, suddenly erect and attentive.

I nod and sit on one of her Carlos Cane swivel barstools. She has six. Each one costs a thousand pounds, which is a lot for a stool. It is comfortable, though.

"You may need a stiff drink."

"Oh, fuck, is it that bad?"

"Look, I don't think there's a third party in this situation, Tor," I say with my most serious expression. "In fact, I doubt there ever was any ransomware."

Tor gets up and places her hands flat on the shining white surface of her breakfast bar. "What do you mean?"

"I know you'll find this hard to take on board, but I think it's Zac who's scamming you."

"No," she says with strains of a dying heroine.

"I think he targeted you, researched you, faked his interest, and seduced you." I watch her reaction and can't help feeling some pleasure in her distress.

"But he loves me." Tor holds her head in her hands and whimpers. I have a sense that she suspected this. She's an intelligent woman. You can listen to the ache of lust, but the mind continues to speak the truth.

"He's gone, hasn't he?"

I nod. "He stole fifty thousand pounds from you, and, for some reason, is now taunting you via Facebook. He'll probably ask for more money when they get close to guessing your identity."

"Bastard," Tor shouts, then throws her carefully constructed bowl of kiwis across the kitchen.

"I expect he's done this to other middle-aged women."

"I'm not fucking middle-aged!" she shouts loudly.

"Sorry," I say.

Tor opens a cupboard door, takes out a bottle of gin and a glass, goes to the freezer to get ice, finds a lime. In her distressed state, Tor makes herself a large and elegant G&T, adds a sprig of fresh mint, then sips.

64

Laboratory

Friday, January 17

The Laboratory Spa and Health Club by the lake in Alexandra Palace is at the more expensive end of gym membership and is frequented by those seeking to avoid the teenage crowds of Pure Gym and too many familiar faces in the Muswell Hill Club.

I've tried to make sense of what I saw in the supermarket parking lot. It may be that Stephen gets his kicks out of deceiving me to balance our relationship and heal psychic wounds, but I expect it's laziness. I bet Stephen orders the groceries online, has them delivered to a friend's house, and when I think he's at the supermarket, he spends time watching football.

All in all, I'm impressed that someone would go to such lengths to try to avoid a chore. I do, however, have a question mark about the nature of his friend, the owner of the blue Audi, so suspicions remain, which is why I've followed him to his sacred Friday gym session.

I'm in the health club's parking lot, having watched Stephen arrive. His phone is with him. After a quick walk around Alexandra Palace, I'm halfway through devising my third plan to rid myself of Hollis, when I see Stephen emerge from the gym, alone. He skips across to his car, looking revitalized and refreshed. Hardly the depressed, grieving character that I get to spend time with at home, but on a positive note, he's not lying about the gym.

I wait until he's left the lot, then press the ignition. I'm about to pull off when I see someone who looks strangely familiar. I can't quite place her, as her face is half concealed by her hoodie, but it's her walk that I notice.

As she turns, I recognize her immediately. It's a face I first saw about a year before I married Stephen. She's changed her hair and is a little more athletic, but otherwise she's still pretty in an inoffensive way, still has an upturned nose and too many teeth.

This is Georgette Mallenberg, or Georgie, Stephen's first fiancée, a woman I'm told he actually loved. The daughter of a baronet. The woman his mother preferred and who I had to remove from his affection in order to free his heart for me. My first love rival.

My hackles are definitely up. I get out of my car, zip up my coat, and walk toward her. I stare at her until she senses something and glances in my direction. She sees my face, and her post-gym expression of physical satisfaction evaporates. She never did like me, but why would she? I befriended her to get to know Stephen (an old ploy) and then poisoned his mind against her by planting evidence that she was cheating on him.

"Hello, Georgie," I say.

"Lalla?" she says, looking like a meerkat that's just spotted a vulture.

She, no doubt, considers me cruel to have broken up their engagement, but a successful marriage requires dedication and determination—little things like love stand in the way of genuine happiness.

"I didn't know you were a member of this gym," I say. "I thought you moved to the Middle East?"

"I did, but I came back," she says, fiddling with her hair and glancing behind her.

"Still married?"

"He wasn't what I thought he was."

"They rarely are, Georgie. Where do you live now?" I say.

"Not far from here, actually. Highgate. I didn't know you lived here. Are you and Stephen still together?"

"Oh gosh, so together," I say, and touch her arm. "Have you found anyone?"

She nods. "I met someone really nice."

"So pleased for you. It must be a relief at your age," I say.

She glances at me, stung slightly. I find it difficult to know if she still blames me for what happened. She takes out her car keys. An indication that she'd like to draw our conversation to a close.

"I know you must dislike me, Georgie, and we really tried to fight it, but love is love. It finds a way, doesn't it?"

"It hurt," she says. "But only for the first five years."

"Children?" I ask.

She shakes her head.

"Oh, to be child-free, what a perfect life you must have."

"I have a lot of freedom," she says.

"We have two children," I say. "Six and four. A handful, as you might imagine."

"I'm sure they do you proud," she says, and glances again toward the exit.

"Have you ever seen Stephen here?" I ask. "He goes to this gym. I would've thought you'd have crossed paths."

"I only do classes. Not many men in Pilates," says Georgie. "I've got..."

She can't think of anything, and I don't help her out. She looks like someone frozen on Zoom.

"Anyway, must go," she says. "Nice to see you."

"We must do coffee," I say.

She smiles briefly and scurries away quickly. It's so dark that she soon disappears into the shadows of the row of leafless trees.

I head back to my car, reminding myself how far I've come, from that young woman in a stolen dress and someone else's shoes with a pieced-together story trying to find her anchor in the world.

I hear an electronic beep as Georgie presses her key fob. A car flashes its orange lights, and two bright headlights startle the darkness and half blind me. I shade my eyes as she drives toward me, heading for the exit. I watch it go and wave, which is when I notice the car—a smart blue Audi A3.

65

Surveillance

Saturday, January 18

Cait meets me at Pret. No one in our circle comes here. The counter staff don't speak to you, and everyone looks like they're waiting for a bus. It's the first thing I mention to Cait when she arrives.

"That's the point, Lalla—we can speak privately here," she says in a hushed conspiratorial tone.

"So what did you find out at Hollis's flat? You're looking tired. I presume you stayed late?"

"I had to. It's his address, but there's no way I could get in. He was there the whole time, so I just watched him from one of those industrial bins. I could see right into his living room."

"Brilliant work, Cait, and did you find anything out?"

"He's good-looking, isn't he? And he's so committed to the wheelchair thing. I didn't see him stand once. I really got into it. I think I like stalking."

"Well, it's nice to see you broadening your interests."

I sip my coffee while Cait retrieves her notebooks and tries to find the right page. The coffee is surprisingly good. Cait casts another suspicious look around the café and says, "The police knew I was there."

"How?" I say, about to throw my coffee over her, as the last thing I need is the police talking to Hollis.

"I have to report to the police station every week. It's a condition of my bail, and I didn't realize they monitor my location. They told me off for being out after curfew and asked what I was doing."

"Christ, Cait, you've got to be more careful. Did they ask for a name?"

"No. They just said they'd rearrest me if I was out again after curfew."

"How are the twins?" I say, trying to move her onto less dramatic topics as the woman next to us is staring. We speak about children for a good ten minutes. I explain how Nelly is getting on with her exam practice (not well) and how Nathan is teaching me how to speak worm (apparently worms only use vowel sounds and the letter *w*). Cait explains that living with her mum is difficult, as her mum thinks she spoils the girls, but she's quickly back on her favorite topic—London's underground crime bosses and Matthew Hollis.

We share a millionaire's shortbread (shouldn't have bothered) and part company. I watch Cait pull her scarf over her mouth and slip into the stream of pedestrians. With the potential divorce ahead, I need to be rid of Hollis or I won't even get the house from Stephen. I think that framing Cait is the best way forward, as she's going to be in prison anyway, and her electronic tag will now have recorded her presence both at Hollis's flat and his shooting club. Also, her DNA and fingerprints are all over his car.

As I'm finishing my coffee, I have a call from an unfamiliar number. I imagine it's the real estate agent again, as I've transferred Lawrence's fifty thousand to secure Hampstead. I know it's crazy, given what Stephen has been doing, but I'm pushing ahead with my plan on all fronts, regardless.

It's a female voice, but it's not Esmae's. The woman tells me that she's the receptionist at the Harley Street Health Centre, and she's called to arrange a conversation with the doctor, as the results from my fertility tests have arrived, which seems a little bit bloody late.

I ask for the results, and she says the doctor wants to speak to me. I tell her I'd prefer not to, as I don't have much time. She says it's protocol. I tell her that women have been denied unmediated access to information about their own health for centuries, and she repeats the whole conversation from the top until I am browbeaten into accepting a telephone appointment.

Around dinnertime, with no word about Stephen's partner nomination, I call Josh Krill. I've been trying to get in touch with Josh for days, but he's not been answering my calls.

"Why the fuck are you calling me?" he says, charming as ever.

"I wonder if I could get an update on our agreement," I say.

"My wife's listening," he whispers.

"I'll be discreet," I say. "Now, tell me, is Stephen Rook in line to be made partner?"

"I recommended him, all right, which made me look like a prick. What more do you want from me?"

"I want more than a recommendation. I want certainty."

"He's third-rate, at best. He's nowhere near the cut. How could I make him a partner?"

"You have influence. You manage to silence anyone you abuse. You work it out, or I'm going public with my story. My contact is keen to speak her truth."

"I've done what I said I'd do," he sneers. "Can't do more than that unless you offer a little sweetener, if you know what I mean."

"As kind as your offer is, I believe I have enough leverage. Your career is worth millions, so I think you're getting quite enough. You have one week, or this goes public."

66

Georgie

Sunday, January 19

Highgate is halfway between Muswell Hill and Hampstead in terms of both geography and prestige. The fact that Georgie lives there is annoying. She went to Downe House, was brought up in the Cotswolds, had several horses, and can ski. Unusually for a woman, she inherited the title of baronetess when her father died, as the title had a special provision that enabled succession through the female line.

She is also the anchor to the past that Madeleine and perhaps Stephen seem to yearn for. I email her, pretending to be a client for her PR firm, and ask to meet at the media-friendly Dean Street Townhouse in Soho, just across from the walk-in STD clinic. I stand under the gaudy awning of a gentleman's strip club and watch her arrive.

I leave it a few minutes, then enter. Georgie sees me approaching, and I spot the bristling of her shoulders as I take my seat.

"What a coincidence," I say, and hold out my hand.

"Sorry, I can't speak now, I'm waiting for a client," she says, and I can see she's made an effort with her outfit to look a little bit hip, which she isn't.

"I'm the client," I say. "I need some PR advice about how to destroy a rival without ruining my reputation. Do you have any experience in that field?"

"I don't want to speak to you," she says, shrinking from me.

"Then at least listen." I remove my coat and notice some of Nathan's breakfast on my blouse and sigh to myself. I did want to make a powerful impression, and soggy Weetabix slightly undermines it.

I turn to the waitress, who has the insouciance of a model.

"How may I help?" she manages to squeeze reluctantly from her lips.

I hold her gaze for a second to reset the relationship, then smile. "I'll have a decaf skinny latte, and my dear friend here will have the same, is that right, Georgie?"

Georgie smiles politely. I know she'd hate a scene in front of her kind of people. Me, I have no kind of people, which renders me quite dangerous.

"What do you want?" Georgie says as the waitress departs.

"That's rather unwelcoming," I say. "And bold, considering you get your groceries and grope in the same weekly shopping trip. Saves on petrol, I suppose."

Her face crumples. "Does Stephen know you're here?" she says as if in control, but there's a layer of sweat on her upper lip already.

"I think it's better to keep men out of business deals, don't you? They tend to get emotional," I say, and hold her gaze.

She stares. Her blue eyes are less beautiful than they once were. They have a watery quality now, no doubt from too much pleading.

"I don't think there's anything to discuss, actually. Love is love. It finds a way, doesn't it?" she says, falling back on her PR training, but I sense it's only skin-deep. A prod with a fork would puncture her.

"You're fucking my husband. Don't you think that merits a conversation?"

"I love your husband. He loves me. It's sad that he doesn't love you anymore, but false love withers, while true love doesn't die, it just hibernates." Georgie's face brightens as she says this, which is sweet.

"I bet he says that to all his mistresses," I reply, and watch her closely for any doubts, but there are none. Aristocratic confidence. I might need to increase the pressure.

"He's never stopped loving me. I'm sorry about that, but as you'll remember, I was here first." She gives me what is, I presume, a fake sympathetic smile.

"What he feels isn't of any importance, Georgie. I don't rely on emotion when dealing with important matters like love. We have a contract. You're trying to break that contract."

"Just let us be together, Lalla. He would've left you some time ago but he didn't want to hurt the children."

"How kind of him to consider his children. By my reckoning, you've been together on a regular basis for about twelve months."

"Four years," she says with a small smile she can't hide.

"Since Nathan was born?" I say, feeling my heart sink again.

"Just before, actually," she says, her smile broadening. "While you were heavily pregnant."

"Well, that shows a ruthless streak I didn't know you had," I say, smiling back. The hit, though, is very real. I've been truly duped. It's not jealousy or sadness I feel, it's shame. I slip my hands beneath the table, so I can pinch myself hard while my face remains impassive and calm.

"It's not how I would've wanted it to happen. We met by chance. We had a few nights together, and then he felt it was wrong, and we stopped for a month, but the feelings we had were too strong. You can't swim against the tide forever."

"If he's failed to leave me for four years, what makes you think he will now?"

"The children are old enough to understand now."

"It's all about the children, is it? Well, they'd be so thrilled to know daddy is fucking some woman on the side but not leaving mummy because he doesn't want to be seen as a bastard."

"It's not like that," she says.

"He likes having his cake and eating it, that's all. I don't mind as long as there's a good salary coming in and he doesn't bring any diseases home with him, but he's not leaving me. I absolutely forbid it."

"I don't think he's eating cake with you anymore," she says, rather snidely.

"Is that what he tells you? Well, believe me, he's still got a sweet tooth."

"I don't believe you. He's told you he wants a divorce," says Georgie, glancing nervously at the other tables.

"That's what these men say for years and years, but do they actually leave?" I stand up. I'm talking so loud now that the waiters start to confer on the best course of action.

"Let's be civilized," she says.

"You're being misled. So I'm going to set out your options. Option 1, you leave him, and I don't harm you. Option 2, you carry on, and I do harm you."

"You can't threaten me, Lalla. We're not animals," says Georgie. She picks up her coat and places it across her lap. "I love him. You split us up once. I'm not losing him again. Everything's planned already. The house. The wedding."

"The wedding?" I say, another feeling of being punched in the gut.

"We've chosen the Cotswolds, in late summer, as soon as the divorce is through."

"Madeleine knows, does she?"

Georgie shrugs neatly. The waitress arrives and places our drinks on the table. She retreats quickly. Neither of us takes our eyes from the other.

"Well, I presume he's told you that I'm pregnant again," I lie, feeling it's the only way I can return the blow. "So your wedding might have to wait."

67

Favor

Monday, January 20

Three builders are surrounding me. It seems that they are keen to drill out the footing that contains Jason Mercer, as it's cracking badly. I'm keen they don't. They want to understand why, and I tell them that I'm representing Tor, and she wants to sell the house soon, so it's imperative the pool house is built without delay.

They talk about insurance and I say that I don't give a fuck about insurance, I just want Tor to have her pool house. The only way of curtailing the endless conversation with these persistent men is to offer them five thousand pounds. It is an expensive business, burying the dead, but the builders are happy with the deal and agree to inject some resin to strengthen the footing instead.

I find Tor inside shouting at various staff. I try to explain that I've contained the situation, and the pool house will go ahead on time. She doesn't even seem grateful about the builders, but as soon as I reach out to comfort her, she lunges and hugs me.

"Thank you," she says. "I'm sorry. I'm such a fool, a bloody, bloody fool. I'm finished."

"What's happened now?" I ask.

Tor reexplains the situation with Zac and canters through the various stages of her grief—denial, anger, bargaining, self-flagellation, and acceptance—with impressive efficiency.

"It's not you, Tor. He took advantage of you. He's ruthless."

"He's still doing the Facebook thing. I don't understand why," she says, pushing me away and stomping around her kitchen island.

"He wants more money," I say, with one of those empathetic tilts of the head that people so enjoy.

"He's been in touch?" she says, and grabs my arm.

I nod and gently unpry her fingers.

"He's not getting a penny more," she declares firmly.

"But you want the Facebook image gone, right?"

"Of course," she says, adding gin to a large ice-filled glass for what is, I presume, not her first of the day. She holds the bottle out toward me but I shake my head as she heads for the mint.

The doorbell rings, and Tor, who would usually leave it to her maid, for some reason feels that it might be relevant and rushes off. I can't help thinking she's imagining Zac arriving on a white charger to take her away from all this wealth and privilege.

In her absence, I take out my phone. The mums on the Facebook group have asked their next question after some intensive debate. I decide to give them an answer.

Their question is: "Does her first name start with a vowel?"

It's such a good question, I'm impressed.

"No," I write and send.

Tor returns with a package from Net-a-Porter and puts it on the countertop.

"You okay?" I say, with the low tone people use when supporting others.

"No," she says. "But shopping doesn't stop for scandal."

She glances at her phone, which she's left out. A notification is sitting there. She reaches out and picks it up. A moment later, she is silently shaking her head and cradling her gin.

"What is it?"

"My name starts with a consonant, I'm fucked," she says. "The bastard's going to ruin me."

"I can try to help," I say.

"How? He wants to destroy me and I've got no money left. What will my children think?"

Tor is now where I need her to be. Imagining her ruin in garish colors.

"I'll pay it for you," I say. "I'll make him delete everything."

"You'd do that for me?" she says, her eyes wide with hope.

"Of course I would, Tor. I can't let you be ruined by someone so deceitful."

"You're the best friend in the world," she says, throwing back half her G&T and embracing me.

I peel her bony arms from my shoulders, then I ask if she would be willing to do me a little favor in return.

"Anything at all," she says.

"You sure?"

"Ask away. I'll do anything for you."

I smile. "Don't be cross."

"I won't be. You've saved my life."

"Yes, I have. Please sit down."

"Why?"

"I think you'll want to be seated, that's all," I say.

Tor eyes me suspiciously, then flops onto a stool and folds her arms.

"In return for solving your persistent problem, I was just wondering if you wouldn't mind swapping Hero's admissions number with Nelly's," I say, looking out toward the garden.

"What do you mean?" barks Tor.

"The candidates are given anonymous candidate numbers, which they put on their desks to enable blind marking. If Hero and Nelly swapped numbers, then whatever Hero answers on her test would be marked as Nelly's effort."

"Right," says Tor, her eyes narrowing. "But then Hero would get Nelly's marks."

"Yes."

Tor is open-mouthed. "But Hero's brighter than Nelly."

"She has a more measurable intellect currently, if that's what you mean."

"I mean she's bloody smarter, Lalla. You want Nelly to take Hero's place at Adams? You want to cheat my child out of her place?"

"I'm just trying to help you, that's all."

"You manipulative, conniving bitch. I can't believe what you're asking me to do."

"It's a small sacrifice to save your reputation," I say, staring coldly and unblinking.

"The answer's no," she says defiantly.

"You're one question away from being exposed. The press would be camped outside your door. Lawrence's political career would be up in smoke, and you'd be the *middle-aged* woman seduced by a boy toy who took you for a ride, in both senses of the word. Adams wouldn't accept being associated with such a scandal."

Tor stares hard. Her head is shaking. "Did you plan this? You and Zac? Is that why you wanted to meet him?"

"Not at all, Tor, I'm just seeing an opportunity."

"I'll never forgive you," says Tor.

"Luckily," I say, "that's not something I've asked for."

68

Resignation

Tuesday, January 21

I've locked Stephen in the cellar. He's upset but, in my defense, so am I. All he wants to do is talk about the divorce, which is really irritating me as he doesn't know that I know about *her*, and he's trying to tell me that we've just "drifted apart."

Georgie clearly hasn't told him about our meeting either, or my *pregnancy*, which either suggests that she's scared that he'll end their relationship, or that they're not all that close, let alone suitable to live in the same house till death parts them.

At the moment, I can't deal with Stephen as I've got to focus on Nelly and her examinations, as she must believe she got in on her own merit. We've just completed one set of practice questions, when Nelly asks to go to the loo. I hear Stephen, who clearly has no dignity, begging through the cellar door for his daughter to free him. Bless her, she refuses, but I don't realize this is only until he offers an inducement.

Minutes later, Stephen appears in the kitchen with a mustache drawn on his upper lip. This was the cost of his freedom. Nelly thinks it's hilarious and dashes upstairs in case I don't find it funny. She's wrong, however. Stephen with a fake curly mustache paints the picture of this tin-pot lothario extremely well.

"You think that's funny?" he asks.

"It is," I say. "I think it's the curls. Humor is all in the detail."

"Not the bloody mustache, locking me in the cellar."

"Stephen, I know that when emotion is involved, you feel it gives you additional rights in the world, but it doesn't. A carrot with feelings is still a carrot. I'm planning our future. It's rather complex and, quite frankly, much easier to manage if you're locked up and can't spread your vile ideological nonsense about divorce."

"I want to talk to you properly!" he says, stooping unattractively.

"I know you do. And I know what you'll say. You're going to say that you love me, but that you don't love me like that anymore, and you're going to use the fact that I find accessing emotion hard to label me as cold and tell me you need space to find yourself. Am I right?"

"No, Lalla," he says firmly, then goes quiet. "Well, yes, actually."

"Love doesn't mean thrilling each other every day, Stephen. Love means committing to a future together, forming a shield against the world. Love is a plan, not a feeling."

"But without feeling, it's all meaningless."

"Children, houses, and history are not meaningless. I've formed an attachment, and I don't make attachments easily. And this is the thing, Stephen. I even feel affectionate toward you, which, given the amount of different things I have to balance, is an achievement."

"But that's how my parents existed, Lalla—attached but without love. I want more."

"So did Oliver Twist, and he ended up with Bill Sykes, so watch what you wish for."

"I want love and affection," he says, banging the table dramatically.

"You have Nathan for one," I say, "and your mother for the other."

"You know what I mean—romantic love."

"You want romance but you don't want sex with me?"

"I don't want sex with you because there's no romance," he says.

"Are you sure that's why?"

"Yes," he lies.

"Right. Romance. Certainly," I say. I go to the cupboard and take out two candles. Then go to the fridge and return with a bottle of wine. I light the candles as he shakes his head at me.

"Now can we have sex?" I say.

"Lalla, that's ridiculous. I want something real."

"Believe me, Stephen, being real is on my to-do list, and I will get to it when I can."

"I don't want to be someone's to-do list. I want to be someone's priority."

"I can make you my priority, darling. Just give me the word." I throw a lighted candle at his head. Stephen flinches.

"I want someone to love me."

"Good god, Stephen, you sound like the heroine of a Mills & Boon romance."

"We see things differently. We've gone as far as we can go," he says.

"Then let's agree on a way forward," I say. "You get made partner, borrow some of Mummy's money, we buy the Hampstead house, and if you give me the house and half your salary, ad infinitum, I'll consider the balance paid and let you go."

"That's not possible, I'm afraid," says Stephen, and he looks at the floor, which usually means he's done something silly.

"Why not?" I say, stepping toward him and folding my arms.

"I've left the bank," he says, stepping backward.

"What? When?" I shout.

"Today," he whimpers back.

"That's not possible," I insist. "You were about to be made partner."

"What are you talking about?" he says, edging for the door as I pick up the vegetable knife.

"Josh Krill recommended you for partner," I say, and point the knife at him.

"I don't know where you heard that, but he didn't, Lalla. He actually did the opposite and gave me the worst reference I've ever seen. They let me read it, and I thought, enough is enough."

"He did what?"

He stares at me and suddenly starts to cry, which makes it hard to stab him. Even a flesh wound would feel a little vicious.

"Okay, I'll stop threatening you, but what have you done?" I say.

"Resigned," he said.

"You cheating bastard!" I shout. Stephen thinks I'm talking about him and cowers.

"I don't want to do this anymore," he says, like the fatigued victim of a melodrama.

"You need to go and beg for your job back, right away," I say, approaching him.

"I don't want that job. I want a different life, Lalla. My mum says she'll support me."

"Your mother? Is that wise, Stephen? You really should be weaned by now."

"It's a short-term thing, while I rethink. I might have a go at craft beer brewing."

"And who's going to pay the mortgage?" I say.

"We'll sell and downsize. We can get two flats."

"And Hampstead?"

"It was never going to happen, Lalla. It's your delusion."

"Women are forever being told that their dreams are delusions, Stephen. You're not taking my dream away from me. So grow up and get your fucking job back!" I feel a sudden jolt, like someone's plugged in an electric current. I lean back against the counter. The only way that I might get a settlement from this now seemingly imminent divorce is if no one finds out that I'm already married. If they do, I'll be left living with Hollis in Meadow Estate with urine-stained doormats, surrounded by dog feces and youths in hoodies.

"Don't panic," he says "We've also got savings. We can survive until the divorce."

"We don't have any savings," I inform him.

"We have two hundred thousand."

"I used that for the deposit on the house," I say. He is about to shout, but he just puts his hands on his head and makes a moaning sound. "Nonreturnable, I'm afraid. It's a sellers' market in Hampstead."

"You forged my signature?"

"I just used your phone. It's all digital these days. On the bright side, if you return to work, ask your mother for your inheritance, and we sell this place, we can still achieve Hampstead and nothing is lost. Never say never, Stephen."

Stephen stands and walks to the window. He looks out and shakes his head. Without turning around, he says, "I'm in love with someone else."

"No, you're not," I say.

"Lalla, I'm sorry, but I am."

I stare at him and he stares at me. There are tears in his eyes. I think about my ten-point plan and feel a sense of sadness that it's failed.

"What is love, Stephen? The dopamine hit you get from having a sordid affair and lying to your family, or is it this unique piquant feeling that is always here and curiously pleasurable and painful at the same time—Nelly, Nathan, me, us?"

"It's not like that. It's someone I've known a long, long time."

"Look, I know about your sad reunion with Georgie, but that's not love, that's the only delusion here. You're escaping into the past. And tomorrow is Nelly's test, so today we must stop being selfish and think about her, okay?"

"We can't afford Adams," he says. "She can't go."

"Take that back, you useless, cowardly fuck," I shout as I jab the knife at him.

"We can't afford it!" he shouts back, and foolishly grabs my arm. "You've even fucked up our savings. The gravy train is over, Lalla!"

"It's not about money, it's her future," I shout. He tells me to drop the knife. I switch it to my free hand and scowl at him. I'm better at this than he is. He's now screaming at me, but my pulse remains slow. I pull my arm back, and I'm about to thrust the knife into his leg, when my phone rings.

I stop, glance across, and look at the number. It's the doctor who wants to discuss my fertility test results. I look up at the clock. Surprisingly, they're right on time. That doesn't bode well. Bad news always arrives promptly.

"Sorry, Stephen, I've got to take this," I say, put the knife down, and take my phone. At which point Stephen, who is quite cross at being nearly stabbed, throws a vase on the kitchen floor. He can be so childish sometimes.

69

Test

Wednesday, January 22

The day circled several times in red on the calendar has finally arrived. According to the weather app, it's going to be fine, with zero chance of rain. Stephen is sleeping in the guest room, which is actually a relief.

I walk into his room, pull open the curtains, and tell him to get up and go to work. He grunts and turns over. This is not what I married, I tell him. I know this won't help him to fall in love with me again, but I'm losing patience. I pull the duvet off him and throw it on the floor. I want to hurt him, but there are things that have to be prioritized above bludgeoning your useless, adulterous, jobless husband to death.

I head upstairs to the attic and yank the duvet from Aimée's bed. I see Luca, my gorgeous gardener, lying next to her, stark naked. I tell him that this kind of slovenly behavior is not going to get the garden ready for spring.

Luca informs me that it's 4:30 a.m. I explain that I've been up for an hour already, making a fruit compote for Nelly's yogurt, and if people don't start making a contribution, I'll wield the axe or, in his case, the pruning shears. Aimée doesn't even stir, although judging by Luca's expression I appear to be shouting.

I open the curtains in the living room and am astonished to see

Hollis's car sitting just outside our house. I rush through the door and down the steps to the gate.

"What the fuck are you doing here?" I say in a seething whisper as his window winds down.

"I just wanted to talk to you. It's important. I can't get what happened straight in my head."

"Hollis, if you do this again, I'll never speak to you, do you understand?"

Hollis tries to argue, but I push his head back into his car and tell him he has to go.

"I just want us to be together," he says. "Stephen doesn't even love you."

"We'll see about that," I say, "but today is Nelly's admissions test and I need to focus on her."

"Right, sorry," he says.

I leave him and return to the house. I've put my heart on the line for Nelly. That's what a mother should do for her daughter. Make sacrifices or, as in this case, make someone else make sacrifices for you.

Today, my daughter will get her place. There are several other targets, but today I want to prove to my own adorable little maniac that she can be with the best of them, that she can turn those strange urges into talents and find some peace with the world. I want her to know that she doesn't have to kill hamsters anymore.

I had to wait until I was in my late twenties, when I met Stephen, to recognize I was not merely Hollis's charity case or the sum of my wickedness. I realized that I could be something else if I could harness my emotional detachment and rationality to build something strong enough to hold me.

But the threads to the past weren't cut decisively enough and it's come back. And now, in spite of good planning, clear targets, an annual review, and even murder, things are collapsing. The past is gnawing away at the future, and the future is eating away at the present. It's like salt water surrounding the foundations of a bridge and eroding it from all sides.

Back in the house, I check my dress, straighten my hair, apply my makeup, and inspect Nelly's outfit, which is an Adams uniform bought from their official supplier. This may seem a step too far, but I want Nelly to feel that she fits in.

Stephen emerges with ruffled hair and bleary eyes to ask if the kettle's just boiled. I say, "How the fuck should I know? Am I the fucking kettle monitor?"

He makes his coffee without further conversation. I tell him, as he butters his toast, that I'm pregnant.

"What?" he says.

"Don't you fucking *what* me," I say. "I'm pregnant. You know what it means. We're going to have a baby. I'm fucking ecstatic. I hope you're fucking happy too. It's fucking perfect. Happy fucking families! Nothing like a divorce and baby in the same week. Stuff of dreams."

He stares at me, his mouth open, as I stomp to the doorway and shout at Aimée to get Nelly up.

"You can't be. We haven't even . . ." says Stephen.

"Well, it was the doctor who called yesterday. I'd only gone to see if I was still fertile, and she said, 'Yes, you are, in fact, we're pretty sure because you're up the fucking duff, Mrs. Rook, congratulations.'"

"Is it mine?" Stephen asks.

I'm cutting the crusts off Nelly's bread with a large, serrated bread knife, which is now pointing at him. "Are you questioning *my* fidelity, Stephen?"

In the silence, I hear him gulp, although there was that indulgence with Zac so I couldn't be absolutely sure.

"I thought not. I'm committed to you, to the children, to our family. I've given you everything, and yet you think you can just walk away when it suits you."

"I just don't see how you can be . . . pregnant."

"You were drunk, but it seems your half-hearted effort was enough. A congratulations would be nice. And to be frank, it's exactly what we need. A new baby, Leopold, a new beginning, a new house, a new job, a new school. All we've ever dreamed of within reach. You just need to beg for your job back and throw Georgie off a tall building."

"Leopold, after my granddad?"

"Yes."

"How do you know it's a boy?"

"Or Leopoldine. Doesn't matter to me. Either way, Leo will cement our relationship, so you need to put the past to one side and I'll forgive you this once. Consider yourself lucky to have got your bland and insipid affair out of the way and come away unscathed."

He glares at me. I can see that Georgie didn't tell him about my pregnancy. Probably thought it was a lie. I did, too, at the time.

"Where's Nelly?" I shout at Aimée, who appears alone at the kitchen door. "She's not even had breakfast yet."

"She's not there," says Aimée, looking worried. "She's gone."

70

Gone

"She's not in her bed?" I ask.

"There are two pillows under the duvet," says Aimée, as if it's not her entire fault.

I rush upstairs to confirm that my six-year-old daughter has run away. I've all but secured her place at Adams. All she needs to do is turn up. She doesn't have to write a word. Her lack of marks will be attributed to Hero. I told her it was all in the bag, and she does this to me, to her own mother.

"Nelly's run away," I say to Stephen as I arrive back in the kitchen.

Stephen's face indicates in that tiny moment not concern or fear for his firstborn but censure.

"Oh, I see," I say. "You think it's my fault."

"No. Not at all."

"I can see what you think, Stephen, and if you think that I'm to blame, say it."

"No one's to blame. I just don't think Nelly responds well to pressure."

"No one likes pressure, Stephen, but without pressure we can't breathe. We'd be in a vacuum; we'd lose consciousness and die. Is that what you want for Nelly? To be starved of oxygen in the state sector while you continue to breathe the air of undeserved privilege?"

"We should look for her," he says.

Argument won, I think.

We search the house, top to bottom. Nelly has won every single game of hide-and-seek she's ever played and has an ability to enclose herself in the most extraordinary places. An hour into our search and we're all frantic. Stephen has called the police, who are keen that we update them in the next half hour if she's not found.

Aimée searches like you'd expect her to, by pretending to look, and not pretending very well at all. She glances into each room and sighs, which doesn't amount to looking, as I tell her on more than one occasion.

We extend our search into the garden, including the shed, but to no avail, and regroup in the kitchen. Nelly will miss her exam if we don't find her, and her place will be lost. Stephen is shaking his head. I'm not sure why. I tell him to check the cellar but he's afraid I'll lock him in again and refuses.

We start phoning friends. If Nelly left the house by the back door to avoid triggering the Ring doorbell, where else could she go? One by one, we tell our friends the news, and they respond with shock and fear. No one can do enough for us, which is nice, but no Nelly anywhere.

Nathan sleeps through the whole affair, even when we lift his bed off the floor to look underneath. He finally appears, looking like he's still half in the land of dreams, his pajamas all wrinkled, clutching his toy bunny.

"Nelly's missing," I say.

"She's in bed," he says, yawning.

"No, darling, that's just pillows."

He shakes his head, opens the cupboard in search of cereal, and says, "She's in the pillow."

As Stephen tries to question Nathan, I run up the stairs and open the bedroom door.

"Nelly!" I shout.

I hear giggling from the two pillows lying together on her mattress. Nelly has carefully concealed herself by pushing her legs in one pillowcase and her body in the other, and flipping herself upside down.

"You are . . . annoyingly good at hiding," I say, and she appears with a smile. She likes winning. If she'd have shown anything like this level of application to her nonverbal reasoning, I might not have had to blackmail my good friend's daughter out of a school place.

We arrive at Adams with minutes to spare, but the school has yet to open its gates. This is presumably to assert their power and create an impression of market demand. I'm not impressed as it's freezing, and we pass hordes of parents and children shivering in the cold. Parking is impossible, so I double-park and put my hazards on.

I drag Nelly from the car and stand near the back of the queue until the gate finally opens. We shuffle forward, observing the ballet of parental expectation and ambition being metamorphosed into affection and love as they say goodbye to their darlings, most of whom are trembling as they have prioritized fashion over comfort and are not wearing coats.

I see Tor ahead in the queue and wave. She sees me but doesn't wave back. I don't even get a smile, which is quite rude considering I saved her from ruin. Admittedly, she must feel aggrieved that I've leveraged her mistake, but if friends don't pounce on your errors, then others will, and what would you prefer, a headline in the tabloids or a place on the waiting list? Objectively speaking, she's a winner here.

As they dispatch their dear daughters into the first phase of a long and expensive premium sausage factory, the relatively few fathers give manly bear hugs and the mothers engage in face touching, forehead kissing, and shoulder squeezing. Calls of "Good luck!" tumble through the cast-iron railings as the hopefuls disappear inside.

Sophie arrives even later than we did, which is impressive. She is breathless and Ellie is bright-faced and steely-eyed, a picture of determination and desire.

"Good luck," I say. "She looks the part."

"She's so desperate for this," says Sophie. "Been practicing nonstop. I don't even have to ask."

"Same with Nelly," I say, remembering the practice papers that I found clogging up the toilet.

"Why is she wearing an Adams uniform?" asks Sophie.

"Positive psychology," I say. Sophie nods without a further word. Jealous, I imagine.

As we reach the gate, Nelly tells me triumphantly that she's not got any pens. I open my handbag and produce her transparent pencil case, which I found hidden in the Rice Krispies box. Nelly scowls, takes the pencil case, and heads for the school. No hugs, no tearful goodbyes, no kissing of cheeks. Feet stomping on cold paving stones is our poignant farewell.

"Remember not to write your name anywhere on the paper, darling," I call out as she disappears inside the glossy black door.

I head off feeling satisfied, but only for half a second as I see DS Birch and DC Mattoo on the other side of the road. This feels like a vendetta against the innocent. I try ignoring them and walk directly to my car. By the time they catch up with me, I'm sitting in the driver's seat, and they tap on the window.

"What now?" I say. "Or are you lost?"

"It's good news, actually," says Birch.

"I find that hard to believe," I say.

"We've found the origin of the £150,000 payments made to you. It came from a Bitcoin account and it's not linked to Jason Mercer."

"I thought cryptocurrency was untraceable," I say.

"Not if they use an exchange. That requires a verified identity. This payment was linked to the name David Bunting. Do you know this name?"

"He's an old friend," I say, as I presume this is Zac Estall's not-quite-as-glamorous-or-sexy real name.

"And he just gave you the money?"

"We were good friends," I say. "And, as it has nothing to do with your case, it's none of your business either."

"We did find several payments to Jason Mercer, however, in another name."

"Not my husband's presumably."

"No. They came from an account under the name Matthew Hollis. It's an offshore account so we can't access any more info. Do you know that name?" says DS Birch.

I shake my head. I'm disappointed that Hollis didn't hide his connection with Mercer at all effectively, and I feel goose bumps on my arm as I realize that Hollis has to disappear before the police get to him or he'll tell them what Mercer was doing.

"No, I thought not."

"As your mystery doesn't involve me, can you stop harassing me now?"

"Just doing our job, Mrs. Rook," says DS Birch.

"And so invasively too," I say, and click the window button. The glass rises until Birch's fingers suddenly intervene and stop the window halfway.

"One more thing," she says.

I should be used to this by now, but I still sigh.

"Does your husband know that you received £150,000 from David Bunting?"

"No, but if you want to tell him, go ahead. You can't make anything worse."

71

Teddy

Thursday, January 23

Alone in my car, I feel rather like running someone over, so I call the most obvious target.

"Krill," I say. "My husband isn't a partner yet."

"What do you mean?" he says, as if we've never met.

"It's Lalla Rook, we made a deal. You make Stephen partner and I don't publish these stories about you. You need to keep your side of the bargain."

"But that's blackmail," he says. "And those stories aren't even true. You just tried to entrap me."

"Krill, if you don't want the world to know what you are, make Stephen partner."

"I couldn't if I wanted. The idiot resigned," he replies.

"Because you fucking told him he wasn't going to get it."

"Look, he was desperate for a way out. Some men facing divorce do that to avoid maintenance payments to their vicious ex-wives."

"He's not getting divorced."

"Odd. That's what he told HR. Change of life circumstances."

"I don't think so."

"Well, he's your husband, you ask him."

"Listen, Krill, this story about your abuse of interns is going everywhere unless you backpedal like your life depends on it, get Stephen his job back, and make him partner."

"I'm not going to be blackmailed," he says coolly. "And I don't think any of the girls will speak out against me."

"Creep," I say. "But I've found one who will."

"Are you talking about that dark-haired girl from the north with a Cambridge degree?"

"You'll find her story in tomorrow's papers—along with details of the five women you abused and then paid off," I tell him.

"Six," he says. "She signed an NDA yesterday."

"You're lying."

"You have to accept that there are several reasons that a company will use NDAs, and it's a complex area. You've got no evidence and no one who can speak against me."

"I can make evidence, Krill, don't try me."

"I don't doubt you, Mrs. Rook, but I've got a better story for the papers. It's about a high-flying investment banker who gets his sexy wife to try to blackmail his boss to make him partner."

"You've got no evidence of anything," I say.

He pauses; I hear a click, then my own voice saying, "You've got no evidence of anything."

I've got nothing to come back with and it hurts.

"I've stopped recording now," he says. "The *Sun* is interested in the story. You'd be splashed all over the papers. Stephen would never get another job. You'd be labeled all kinds of things."

"How does that benefit you?" I say.

"I don't like to be blackmailed, Lalla, so I want to show you what it feels like. You meet me in a hotel and apologize properly, and I won't send this tape to the papers."

72

Georgie

It's not been such a good day. The police interfering with my marriage. Krill getting the better of me. Husband keen on divorcing me. On the positive side, Nelly's success is now almost guaranteed. Although Tor continued to squeal at me for the dreadful crime of ensuring my child succeeded at the expense of hers (surely the foundation of her own social class), when we received our children's confidential candidate numbers the day before the exam, she caved in and swapped numbers with me.

Nelly, joyfully, said that she found the examination easy, which probably means she simply made up her own questions. I checked that she put the swapped examination number on her paper, and she said that she did, so as long as she's not lying, her mark will be assigned to Hero, poor thing.

I just need to find a way to delete Hollis, nullify Krill's disgusting demands, and keep Stephen. A problem of being overmarried, overdesired, and underloved, but at least it's a puzzle that I can put right.

These tiny modern houses, essentially one small box beside another, go for £1.3 million. Kitchen, living room, two bedrooms with a bathroom in between, and a minuscule back patio. There are several of them in a row. Once considered modern, with slotty windows like mailboxes, and a child-size front garden, they now look dated.

Georgie's daddy, the baronet, probably bought the house some years back when it was a snip at £750,000—a place just out of town for his darling daughter before he died, and a sound investment too. I imagine she eats salads out of plastic boxes, does home Pilates in full-on Lululemons, and spends the evenings chatting with Tiggy, Cozzy, and Jasper on FaceTime about her latest status symbol purchases.

Having ensured I've not been followed, I sit in the car in a side street just off Southwood Lane, wearing gloves and a beanie. By 2 a.m., the lights are almost all off in the row of houses. I get out of the car and walk to Georgie's house. I look at the locks. A Yale and a mortise. There are two such keys on Stephen's spare key ring, which is in my hand.

I try the mortise. It turns easily and without a sound. The Yale also works, and the door opens quietly. I slip inside and smile at the sensation of being a secret and unwelcome guest. I walk through Georgie's kitchen and open her fridge, which is completely empty, like everything else about her. Her living room is not only small; it's so devoid of character I feel nauseous.

I stop at the shelf built into an alcove. There are several framed photographs of Georgie and Stephen from long before I met him, along with several more recent ones. I am simply an interregnum. From Stephen's haircut and clothes, I can just about date them. Two go back to before Nathan was born and one is not long after, and I thought I was the deceitful one in our relationship. The more I find out about people, the more I realize that I'm the normal one.

At this point, I want to do harm. An emptiness rises within me and then a growing anger. I take each photograph, one by one, and place them face down. I leave my shoes by the door and tiptoe upstairs. Her bathroom is rather messy and there are flecks of toothpaste on the mirror. My pale face looks back at me steely-eyed. I take each precious tube, brush, stick, and case from her bathroom cabinet and put them one by one in the toilet bowl. Each little splash of water fuels my anger.

I draw a broken heart on the mirror in red lipstick, then put the plug in the bath and run the hot tap. I head for her bedroom with nail scissors in my hand and open the door. I stand there, watching her sleep, twisting the razor-sharp scissors in my hand. Her body is long and thin. I doubt there's too much blood in it. I think of it as assisted suicide. Alcohol, pills, bath, and wrists. Standard procedure for someone with a broken heart jilted by their married lover.

I take a bottle of vodka from my handbag and a large container of paracetamol. The bath will soon be ready. I move to her bedside and stare down at her. Even with a to-do list, I've struggled to make Stephen feel how I want him to feel. What does she have that I don't? Is it just that he wants to be needed and I don't have needs? Men are so weak.

By her bedside is a notebook from Liberty decorated with pretty pink and purple flowers. There's a pen beside it. I can't imagine what someone like Georgie has to write about. I open it and immediately realize who it was that sent the anonymous letter to Stephen. In these days of texting and sexting, Stephen didn't even recognize her handwriting. Was this a clever ploy to push him to the edge or even to push me to the edge? It seems too clever for Georgie, who only managed to pass two GCSEs, one of which was PE.

Staring down at her rather innocent-looking face, I see that she's clutching a teddy bear. It's so incredibly threadbare that I can only presume she's had it since she was young. An image of Nelly lurches from the recesses of my mind. I see her asleep with Dolly, clutching something that she knows, as the world around her seems so unknowable.

Without thinking, I reach out and touch Georgie's cheek. I pull back as she stirs and find my eyes are wet with tears. I have no idea why, but looking down, I have a sudden change of heart. I don't want to hurt this woman. I actually think it's Stephen I want to kill right now, not Georgie with her teddy bear and romantic fantasy. She just tried to win something back that she'd lost, that's all. Nothing wrong with a trier.

I reach down and slowly pry the teddy bear from her arms. If I'm not going to kill her, I should at least be allowed to annoy her intensely. It pleases me more than it should. I take the teddy bear, pick up the diary, and leave. Downstairs, there's a large black leather Prada tote bag. I have an identical one. Something tells me that Stephen bought one for each of us, which is another sudden imaginary stab against him. I tip out the contents and drag the scissors through the sides of the bag, leaving three long gashes, like tiger claws.

73

Electricity

Friday, January 24
I feel truly blessed to be pregnant. Despite the daily sickness, loss of reliable bodily functions, and excruciating pain ahead, it's a magical gift. If it is Zac's rather than Stephen's, it's good to know my child will have more get-up-and-go, even if they'll never know their biological father.

Of course, there are one or two obstacles in the way of happiness. Stephen's still going on about the incident in the kitchen with the knife, as if that's the key issue. He's probably upset at having his dream of running away with Georgie questioned. I told him that all couples bicker. And anyway, a sensible wife wouldn't kill her husband because it's a pleasure she could only enjoy once.

My current mark is walking down Fleet Street after work with a large and rowdy group of bankers. He's wearing a three-piece suit and a small pink party hat that he no doubt thinks is hilarious. I'm on the other side of the road, taking care to stay behind the group, in a beautiful deep red cashmere coat.

The group collect around the entrance to a high-end, glass-fronted bar with neon signs and a security man standing guard. They stop to have a loud discussion with the doorman, then pile through the door. I cross the road and follow them inside.

I realize that I have an unfulfilled urge after I wasn't able to murder Georgie and was unable to sleep worrying that I've discovered some kind of internal moral qualm. Josh Krill is not expecting to see me; I can tell that from his expression as he turns to me from the urinal he's pissing into. I've put an out-of-order sign on the outside door of the gents that says: "Raw Sewage—Please Use the Ladies." This should give me sufficient time.

It was galling to watch him and his shiny-suited mates laughing uproariously at the bar, drinking stupidly and poking fun at everyone around them, as if they had not a care in the world.

He looks up and sees me. His eyes widen. "You? I thought our date night was tomorrow? I'm looking forward to getting to know you intimately. It turns me on when a woman doesn't want me. Is that weird?"

"Yes, it's fucking weird. You think I'd sleep with you because of those threats, do you?" I say, closing the toilet door.

"I think you just have to take one for the family. You might actually enjoy it," he slurs, swaying slightly.

"If you're capable," I say. "That's a good strong flow you've got there."

"Three pints in, three pints out," he says, and nods proudly down at the urinal as I approach him. Concealed in my hand is the orange extension lead from our shed, usually reserved for lawn mower use. One end has been plugged into the mains in the corridor outside (minus the circuit breaker that Luca insists on). At the other end, which I am holding quite carefully, the socket has been removed and the plastic stripped back, leaving the copper wires exposed.

"You coming in for a closer look or something more?" Josh says with a wink, but there's a faint sense of vulnerability in his voice now.

"I'm disappointed in you. You think you're untouchable and can do what you like," I say, and move closer, observing that the ground beneath the urinal is sopping wet, presumably because several drunken men have missed the large open ceramic bowl in front of them. Josh's expensive hand-made, leather-soled shoes are standing in a pool of piss. It's quite poetic and rather helpful.

"This is going to hurt you more than it's going to hurt me," I say, leaning in, ensuring I'm not touching him.

"What is?" says Josh.

I push the live wires into the urinal. Instantaneously, the electric current travels up his stream of urine, through his penis and fingers, and up through his body, then down through his legs to the wet ground, forming a circuit.

I smell burning flesh almost immediately. His body does a kind of floppy dance, jittering like a glitchy computer image, and a moment later he's flat out on the floor, urine all over his trousers, fizzing and jerking on the wet tiles.

"You're a sick man, Josh. But I hope those nasty burns will make our assignation impossible, so let's call that quits. Now, I want you to focus on getting the bank to give Stephen his job back. If you don't, I'll find you again and tie your testicles to my car. Do you understand?"

He gulps, his eyes open. He tries to speak, but it's unintelligible.

"I'll follow up with an email to clarify," I say, and walk out.

I unplug the extension, wind the cable up neatly, remove the sign on the door, and head out into the night. I think of my father at moments like this. I walk down the street feeling that state of complete oneness that only electrocuting a bastard like Josh can give you. It's like your whole body is connected at every point to the universe, and pleasure tingles through every part of your being.

I return home. Stephen is out, possibly nursing his bruised ego or wiping away Georgie's tears at her lost teddy bear. I have the chance to complete my read-through of Georgie's rather pathetic little diary. She marks some occasions with a number of stars, which I imagine indicates sex. I presume it's with Stephen because they're always on Fridays and Sundays. She's rather coy even in her diary, which is quite sweet, but Stephen often gets five stars, which means either he's always saved his best for her or, more likely, Georgie has a low pleasure threshold.

It's hard to read all the intimate details of Stephen's affair, but I know it's not a reflection of my attentiveness or attractiveness. He's responding to his feeling of personal deterioration. Happens to all men as age, work, and family life wearies and emasculates them.

They look in the mirror at receding hairlines and increasing girths and feel intense sadness at their failure to get promoted, find fame, or realize their footballing dreams. Men might cry when their teams lose, but it's the lost confidence of youth they're crying for.

We should offer our sympathy, not our censure. No one really appreciates the intense pain of the middle-aged man, so worshipped in youth (by himself) and disabused of his delusions in age (by others), left just with hairy ears, a sports fixation, and a friend from twenty years ago called Dave.

All my to-do lists have been thrown in the air and, although not ideal, I have to plan on the hoof at the moment. However, I'm amazed to have completed some key things:

Get pregnant
Secure Hampstead
Get Stephen his job back

And one or two things still to do:

Remove Hollis
Remove Georgie
Remove Madeleine
Live happily ever after 😊

74

Strand

Saturday, January 25

Hollis arrives at the Strand in his manual wheelchair. He's twenty-five minutes late. Even though it's a bitterly cold evening, he's enjoying the workout as he darts between pedestrians on the pavement.

I feel a little twinge of affection but quickly remind myself that he's an obstacle to my happiness, and if Stephen or Madeleine discover his existence, I may end up with nothing, as no divorce will be needed. Poverty is not an option.

Hollis explains that someone parked in the disabled parking space, so he had to find another spot farther away, having already scoped out the disabled bay on a parking app he recommends. If this indicates the type of conversation he foresees in our future, I have no qualms about cutting things short.

I've worn an all-black ensemble with a hood. You'd find it tricky to identify me from the poor-quality CCTV that records London life from overhead. I've also made my route here purposely circuitous and even used the tube, that large sewer for human beings.

"I never asked how you got by money-wise?" I say as we walk, thinking about how much it would have cost to hire Jason Mercer for three weeks.

"The travel insurance payout helped," he says.

"And do you work anymore?"

"I continue my endeavors in tech," he says.

"I remember your commitment to *Assassin's Creed* and *Grand Theft Auto* well."

"I moved into AI coding and started another company," he says, which means little to me, but my almost inaudible murmur doesn't stop him. "I was quite good at it. AI was growing at the time, and I got in early."

"Interesting," I say. Just what the world doesn't need—another bedroom tech warrior calling himself a CEO because he spent £50 to register a company.

Our conversation doesn't improve much as we eat overcooked pizza in a chain Italian (his choice) and drink in an incredibly busy Wetherspoon (again, his choice). If I had any qualms about committing murder at the start of the evening, I have none at all by the time we're walking along Victoria Embankment beside the river.

I'm entranced by the oily surface of the Thames and the glistening lights. I feel a Dickensian thrill at the prospect of a Gothic ending. We head to a romantic spot by Waterloo Bridge. Why not give him a pleasing view before he's snatched away for eternity?

We reach the metal stairs that I scoped out earlier in the week. During the day this is a ferry stop, but now the steps lead directly to the inky water with only two metal barriers. Earlier this evening, I cut the padlocks off and unbolted the gates. When someone next leans against them, they will fall open. The water should be icy enough to ensure that Hollis dies quickly. He deserves that, I think. I'm not a brute.

He'll experience cold-water shock as he plunges, then a sudden phase of rapid breathing. Freezing water will fill his lungs and his brain will flood with chemicals to subdue the panic, and his last moments will be lived in a momentary ecstasy. The happy ending Hollis yearns for.

"Isn't the river beautiful," I say, my head buzzing with my plan. It's a relatively simple approach. Choose a dark night, find somewhere out of the sight of CCTV, and push him in the river. He's strapped into about forty-four pounds of metal, which means he and his chair should sink straight to the bottom of the Thames. This ferry stop is deep enough for larger tourist boats, so Hollis should rest there peacefully, out of the way of any tidal drag, and enjoy his future as another skeleton in the macabre history of this river.

I'm planning on implicating Cait again. I've suggested we meet first thing in the morning at this spot, as she can't come out at night anymore. She'll turn up, her tracker will show her presence here, and should Hollis's body ever be found, I'll call the police anonymously to say I saw a red-haired woman push a disabled man into the river.

"I could learn to love London on nights like this," says Hollis. "But could you learn to love me again?"

"I think so," I say, and our hands join. I can see in his expression hope for the future and feel a jolt of physical sensation that surprises me. I think it's just unfulfilled carnal desire attaching itself to the nearest male object, but still, it's time to end this before it heads in another direction entirely.

I peer over his shoulder at the steps below. I suggest we move farther forward to get the best view of Westminster and gently edge his chair toward the gate until the two small front wheels cross the lip from stone to metal.

Hollis's wheelchair has brakes and he's got sharp reflexes, so I'll need to be quick. I check left and right. There are so few people around on this cold, moonless night, with only buses and taxis trundling by. I wait for a gap in the traffic and prepare to push.

"I've got something to ask you," he says.

"And what's that?" I betray annoyance at being interrupted.

"It's a bit weird, because, you know, we're already married." Hollis pushes his hand into his pocket and removes a blue velvet box.

"For fuck's sake," I whisper to myself. I really don't want him to propose to me just before I kill him. That seems a particularly harsh response, which will definitely hurt his feelings.

"I never gave you a proper ring, did I? I didn't have the money back then."

"You don't have the money now, Hollis. You live in public housing."

He opens the velvet box. I expect something modest and in

keeping with Hollis's style, but in front of me is an enormous diamond ring.

"That can't be real."

"It is," he beams. "All five and a half carats."

I'm calculating quickly in my head. If Hollis is telling the truth, he's holding about £100,000 worth of solid carbon in his hand.

"It's beautiful," I murmur, feeling the deep emotion that comes from excessive expenditure.

"It's for you. If you'll be mine again," he says, turning and looking up into my eyes.

"How can you afford it?" I take it from him. After all, no point in a good diamond ending up in the Thames.

"I do okay these days," he says.

"Doing what?"

"I run a company."

"You've run lots of companies and they all went under." I put the ring in my pocket as I notice a lull in the traffic. No more delay. I take hold of his wheelchair.

"It's called MHI," he says, enthusiastically.

"Matthew Hollis Industries? So modest."

"Modeling Human Intelligence, actually. It's an AI unicorn."

I take a breath, set my feet in position. Better that he's pontificating on the finer points of AI than noticing where I'm heading, although I dread to think what his last words are going to be.

"Unicorns are a fantasy, like most of your endeavors," I say. He stares up at me and as he's no longer looking ahead, I heave him forward.

"It's what venture capitalists call a billion-dollar start-up," he says.

With the words *billion-dollar* reverberating in my ears, I pull back with all my weight, swivel the wheelchair away from the river, and start a romantic walk along the Thames with my dear husband.

PART FIVE
Renew

The only difference between the saint and the sinner is that every saint has a past, and every sinner has a future.

OSCAR WILDE, *A Woman of No Importance,* **1893**

75

Desk

You work so hard on one marriage only for the other to come up trumps at the eleventh hour.

On the way home, my mind rumbles with glorious cannon blasts and fireworks exploding. Hollis is a billionaire. This failed entrepreneur, who couldn't be trusted to put the toilet seat down, has built a company that's worth real money, and he's in love with me, even after I pushed him off the side of a mountain. Has there ever been anyone as clever or beautiful as I am? I almost want to clone myself so I can experience what it's like to know me.

I turn off the ignition, sigh at the joy of serendipity, and walk triumphantly into what is really now my former home. The lights are all off and the house, despite all the things I tried to do with it, now looks rather dreary and commonplace. You never realize you're in the gutter until you look back down from the stars.

The house feels cold and uninhabited. Aimée is staying with Luca and Stephen has taken the children to visit Madeleine, no doubt to enable a bit of character assassination. I take off my coat and head to the kitchen. Purdy is sitting on the table. Her eyes hold me for a moment, then look away in disgust as I've neglected her all evening. I scratch her chin to ask forgiveness when I hear something upstairs and turn quickly.

"Stephen?"

No response. I reach behind me and pull a small knife from the knife block. I'm going to need a new set at this rate. I walk slowly down the hallway, slip off my shoes, and head upstairs. There is a single shaft of light coming from my study—where I keep my notes and to-do lists. I breathe deeply, steadying myself. I hear someone ruffling paper. The familiar creak of my Eames office chair.

I fear Josh Krill has broken in, seeking revenge, and hold the knife firmly at my side. I push open the door.

No, not Josh.

Stephen, my sometime husband, is sitting in my chair. My desk drawer has been jimmied open with a claw hammer. The wood has splintered. The private contents, including my journal and un-deleted to-do lists, have been tipped onto the desktop.

"What's going on?" I say. "I thought you were at your mother's."

"We came back," he says, with no further explanation.

I fear that Georgie must have told him about the break-in and my threats. He picks up the claw hammer and stares at me with a strangely violent look in his eye that I've not seen before.

"You don't break into someone's house, you fucking bitch!" he snaps. He's not awfully good at venom and it's a little high-pitched, but I try not to smile. Men have fragile egos.

"Is this about her teddy bear?"

"Who are you?" he says, and rises, pointing the hammer at me. "Who the fuck are you?"

"You cheat on me for four years, break a perfectly good desk, and I'm the bitch?"

"Don't be funny with me. You terrified her! You stole her diary!" He holds up Georgie's stolen diary.

"Did she ask you to get it back?" I say.

"Yes, she fucking did, and her teddy bear, where is it?"

"I gave it to Nelly. I don't think it stands a chance."

"You've made me feel like I'm the bad guy, and I find this fucking list. Your fucking scheming!" He holds up my ten-point marriage-saving plan. Fortunately, I shred my daily to-do lists or I'd have a huge amount of explaining to do.

"Everyone needs to plan, darling, or we'd get nowhere. I mean, look at you and Georgie, four years and still fumbling around for five minutes together in a car parking lot."

"Because we're authentic, Lalla. I wouldn't want things planned. Not like this. Every single thing you do. It's all worked out, isn't it? I thought that was really nice of you, but actually it's just part of your game."

"I'm not the most spontaneous person, Stephen. You've always known that. We all have our different ways to cope."

"This is a script, not a life. Testosterone gel, for fuck's sake! Getting pregnant just to keep us together. You can't do that. Nothing's real. All this time, I've struggled with feeling disconnected, and you're planning our life one bullet point at a time."

"Reality is overrated, don't you think? I presume that's why you pretended to be a good husband and father, while betraying the foundations of our relationship?"

"Is it a surprise I found someone else? You're actually a fucking robot. I loved you, you know, but you gave me nothing in return. I thought you were just a little on the spectrum, but this is something else!"

"I gave you everything I had to give. A family. A beautiful wife. Children. A successful marriage."

"Successful? I wanted to feel loved."

"I'm not your mother, Stephen."

"This is why I've been so unhappy," he says, holding up my plan again.

"You think I'm manipulative, do you? You have no idea," I say.

"Idea about what?"

"Do you know why Georgie wants her diary back?"

"Because it's her fucking diary, and you broke into her house and stole it while she was asleep," he says.

"Have you read it?"

"She doesn't want me to read it."

"No, she wouldn't. It would ruin your little fairy tale."

"What are you talking about?"

"You've been scammed, Stephen, and not by me. I was just trying to save our relationship. That's what that list is—the last attempt of a betrayed wife to try to be what you want."

"You're lying."

"No, Stephen. I was willing to try anything to get you back, but I couldn't win, not with those two working against me, playing you for a fool."

"Who are you talking about?"

"Georgie and your mother planned the whole romance, bullet point by bullet point. It's all in her diary. How they schemed to get you two together whenever I was pregnant, ill, incapacitated, or away. How they drip-fed criticism about me. Don't you think it uncanny how she had that knack of always being there with her uncomplicated adoration?"

"That's not true. That's bullshit."

"After Georgie's disastrous divorce, they hatched a plan to oust me and turn your head. Georgie was amazingly always at your mother's house visiting when you arrived. And even had to stay the night for any number of dubious reasons. How they plied you with drink. How she tiptoed into your room because she was feeling so lonely. They made it so easy for you to fail."

Stephen is looking concerned now.

"Did your mother tuck you both up in bed together?"

"That's disgusting."

"The truth is often disgusting, that's why no one bothers with it anymore."

"I don't believe you. I love Georgie. Yes, okay, maybe she worked hard to get close to me again, but that's because she loves me."

"Your mother bought her the house in Highgate."

"What?"

"Didn't Georgie mention that?"

"That's ridiculous," he says. "Georgie inherited her family's estate, she doesn't need money."

"I looked up Georgie's house on the land registry, and it's registered to Madeleine Rook. And there's a nice section in her diary about her financial situation. All she inherited was debts. Three million pounds of debt, after mortgages, death duties, legal fees, and taxes."

"I'm not listening to you."

"Your mother even threatened to disinherit you if you remained married to me, didn't she? Your mother is a sociopath, and like all sociopaths she believes a successful marriage is one you can buy."

"You're wrong about Georgie, you're wrong about Mum. They're right about you, you're a lying bitch," he says, but the anger is gone from his voice. He's realizing, I imagine, what it's like to go from a frying pan to a cold bath.

"Darling, your mother is selling you off to an impoverished aristocrat for a title. Your lover is more interested in money than you. I'm the only honest person in this relationship. It's all in the diary. Read it for yourself. I've marked the interesting pages with Post-its."

He pushes past me and says coldly, "I'm not reading it. I told her I wouldn't and I won't."

76

Bigamist

Sunday, January 26

Nothing better than a Sunday morning run to contemplate the future. I do a circuit of Ally Pally to reflect on yesterday while Stephen takes the children out to the park. Hollis, despite his many faults, is a better option than Stephen, who is jobless, unfaithful, inadequate, and, it seems, quite without backbone.

I decide that I'll have the children, despite their general inadequacies and neediness. I imagine Georgie doesn't want them anyway. Baronetess Mallenberg is, no doubt, intending to repopulate her family line from scratch.

After I shower, I find Nelly alone in my office in the midst of a discarded hammer and splintered wood. There doesn't appear to be anyone else in the house.

"What are you doing here?" I say.

"I don't like her," she says, drawing in one of my notebooks.

"Who don't you like?" I peer over her shoulder. She's drawn a rather good picture of a pretty and glamorous woman. I presume it's me and am quite flattered.

"We met *her* in the park," says Nelly, jabbing at the picture.

"Who?" I say.

"Georgie," she says, almost spitting.

I want to take the hammer to Stephen's head, but that will have to wait. I watch Nelly draw a succession of arrows hitting the woman in her chest and legs and face and realize the picture is not of me.

"Darling, what happened?" I kneel and swivel her chair around. I hold her hands. They seem so small all of a sudden. "I'm your mummy. She's just a nobody. Nothing to worry about."

Nelly swivels back to her notebook, satisfied, draws another arrow right through Georgie's heart, and walks out with Dolly in her hand. I'm not sure the books on divorce advise such honest appraisals but it did feel deeply satisfying.

"Love you," says Nelly at the door, without turning back.

I breathe in sharply. It's the first time in her life that she's said that to me, and I break into a smile. Georgie might be breaking up our marriage, but I have one thing to thank her for.

"Nelly's here," I say to Stephen, pointing at the living room, as he returns frantically from the park.

"Oh, thank god," he says. "We looked everywhere for her. How did she get back?"

"Walked."

"God, I'm sorry," he says, and puts Nathan down. "Go on, go and see if Nelly's all right."

"I didn't find Nelly, but I found this," says Nathan, and he opens his hand to show me a large beetle on a dead leaf. I congratulate him and he runs off shouting to Nelly about his monster find.

"In here," I say to Stephen, and point to the living room with the hammer. The last man I entertained in this room met with a sharp and sudden ending, but I don't mention this. He walks past me like a schoolboy entering the head's study for a caning.

"You took them to meet Georgie. What have you got to say for yourself?"

"It was a mistake . . . Yeah. A total . . . complete . . ."

"Fuckup?"

"Misjudgment. Mum told me that children are much better if you just tell them the truth as early as possible. Nelly just ran off. We were desperately looking for her."

"You're sometimes so stupid it offends me to think that I actually married you."

"It wasn't ideal. Not my best decision." He hits his head with his hand and looks genuinely upset.

"You can have your divorce," I say, swinging the hammer loosely. "Not that you'll need one."

"What?" He sits up, clearly confused.

"I won't fight it, and I don't want anything from you."

He looks at me with a scrunched-up face that denotes suspicion. "That's uncommonly considerate, are you dying?"

"No. But I'm having the children."

"Shouldn't we share them?"

"You don't seem responsible enough. I'll let you have weekends. But you'll have to see them alone for the first year. I don't want Georgie near them, okay?"

"Well, okay, at least until they're used to the new situation," he says, as expected. It's always best to negotiate terms when your enemy is weakest.

"Now, about us. Stephen, you're not the first man to respond to a debilitating degeneration of his masculinity, and the growing autonomy of his wife, by sleeping with a younger woman."

"She's four months younger than you, Lalla."

"Exactly, and you're not the only man in the world either. Actually, you're not the only man in this marriage. Not even the only husband, in fact."

"What's that supposed to mean?"

"I've met someone, recently. A past relationship has reared its head. It presents a good opportunity for me."

"Who is it? Someone we know?"

"Someone I was married to before I met you."

"You never told me anything about being married."

"Thought it'd just complicate things. And anyway, I'd forgotten all about it by the time we met."

"Are you being serious?" he says, his voice all puffed up.

"His name's Matthew Hollis. An Australian. Opposite of you in almost every respect—charming, faithful, fantastic lover."

"Look, I'm really sorry this has happened to us, but you shouldn't do anything on the rebound. You're not planning on marrying him, are you?"

"No need. We're already married," I say. I watch his face melt in confusion.

"You get drunk and go to Vegas last night or something?" He laughs.

"We never formally divorced," I say. "Technically, we're still married. In my defense, though, I thought he was dead."

Stephen stomps from one side of the room to the other, pulling a face and shaking his head as if this is all too much for any man to understand. "What about our marriage, though?"

"Why does that matter to you?"

"We've been married for seven years, Lalla."

"You'll be pleased to know our marriage doesn't exist. It's void." I stare at him and he stares back, open-mouthed. "Of course, we still exist, all our special memories and all that, but it doesn't count. Like a no-ball in cricket—you can score runs but you can't be bowled out."

The cricketing simile captures his attention and he nods. "You always have something. I've never really known you, have I? So how does our divorce work?"

"You don't need one, because we're not married."

"So I can just marry Georgie? I don't even need to divorce you?"

"Yes. I have no claim on you. No legal rights to your money."

"You're not entitled to anything?" There's a hopeful twang to his voice. Not quite heartbroken by this news, it would appear.

"The only child in you quickly rises to the surface, doesn't it?"

"Mum's going to love this!" he says, standing. "Georgie's going to be thrilled." He shakes his head in disbelief, takes his phone out, and leaves. I feel something lurch in my stomach, but I try not to take it too badly that he seems delighted that our seven years together can be popped like a balloon.

I reassure myself that he's lost a great deal more than he's about to gain. I outscore Georgie on beauty, intelligence, wit, spontaneity, humor, physical attractiveness, ambition, drive, and even kindness. She outscores me on only two things—skiing, and resemblance to a horse.

77

Proposal

Monday, January 27

I expect our celebration drink to be somewhere rather special as Hollis sent a car for me, but the Mercedes deposits me outside a dreary pub near the river. I feel overdressed and unimpressed. "The Last Post" is the ominous name that hangs in gloomy light over the door.

I don't really know if the pub is simply run-down or if this is what passes for chic these days. It smells of stale beer with top notes of cider and is populated by bald men watching football on a large telly, sipping at their pints and making unnecessary comments.

I look out of place in my rather revealing outfit and cause something of a fuss. My dress is low-cut, my hair is freshly blow-dried, and I'm looking absolutely drop-dead, red-carpet gorgeous. I wanted to appear to Hollis as a sparkling gift. In these surroundings, I'm more like a Quality Street dropped onto a turd, if that helps capture the moment.

I spy Hollis with his wheelchair tight against a dilapidated table, staring at a pint. I have a feeling that he's expecting rejection. I will try to convince him that I love him, and not because he's a billionaire, but because of the depth of our love.

There are comments and noises from the men as I sashay over the sticky wooden floor. I'm glad to give them something to think about when they crawl back to their illegal dogs and tattooed wives.

"Hello, you," I say, giving Hollis a kiss on his head. "Are we staying?"

"Just for one," he says. "What'll you have?"

"Something from a bottle that remains in a bottle," I say.

Hollis raises a finger to the barman. "A Peroni, no glass." He turns back to me. "You look absolutely stunning."

"I've been thinking about your proposal," I say. "And all the wonderful memories that you've filled in for me, too, but it's so much to get used to."

"I want you so much," he says. His eyes are moist and his hand rests on mine. It's really rather lovely, in a pathetic way.

"Well," I say, wondering if I've resisted enough and made my point. "I want you too."

"You do, really?" His eyes redden and his lips quiver. "Even without working legs."

"Just as you are," I say. Our fingers entwine, tears fall (his, not mine), and we hug over his pint.

"I love you," he says.

There are several things I want to say and I have to suppress them all before I say, slightly choked, "I love you too."

"Drinks on me!" he shouts, and of the six men in the bar, two turn their eyes from the screen and look across. It won't be an expensive round. Hollis kisses me. I kiss back. He's been eating mints, which I find a little presumptuous but sweet.

"I hope you don't mind," I say, and show him my left hand where his ring is glittering in the dim light.

"You've taken off your wedding ring!" he says.

"I told Stephen it's over," I say. "Told him all about us. No more secrets."

"You did that for me?" he says, looking shaken.

"I lost you for such a long time. I feel like I'm getting the chance to live my life over again." I'm such a good actress that I'm even beginning to convince myself.

"Until yesterday, I felt sure you didn't feel the same."

"My feelings are coming back more and more each day. I was so traumatized by losing you that I closed off my heart, but I'm ready for Lalla and Hollis, Season Two."

"This is more than I ever dared dream of."

I can't help feeling this sounds a tiny bit sarcastic, but all declarations of love sound like that to me. A bottle of lager appears in front of me. I thank the barman. He doesn't speak and returns to the bar.

"To us," I say with a broad smile, and clink. I take his hand and squeeze it to reinforce the idea of unexpressed emotion like I've seen on TV.

"What about your children?" he says.

"They come with me, but we can have our own children too," I say, immediately calculating that if we sleep together soon, I could reasonably claim that Leopold or Leopoldine is his.

"Cool," he says, glancing at his pint, which I'm not really sure how to interpret.

"Don't you want children?"

"Oh, yes, I do. It's just . . . my testicles were ripped off during the fall, which makes it, well, tricky."

"Oh, sorry, I didn't know. You should've said. Both of them?" If I was ever going to feel guilty in my life, I guess it would be now, but nothing appears.

"Yeah, both. That little stumble cost me a lot, didn't it? I mean, my legs, my ability to have children, even my wife . . . for a time."

I nod in a manner I hope is grave enough to honor a man's lost testicles but privately I'm wondering how I'll cope with another man with low testosterone levels.

"But you have your wife back now, and we can have my children. I'm sure they'd like you. Nathan would love your wheelchair, and Nelly would be fascinated by your legs. She disables all her own toys." I decide to leave out any mention of Leo until we're fully back together.

"Thanks, that's appreciated," he says, in a tone I'm not quite able to read.

"You sound sad. Having second thoughts?"

"No, of course not. It's just. It's been a long chase. Feels like *Moby-Dick*, you know," he says and empties his glass.

"A man hunting a whale in revenge for taking his leg? Not a flattering analogy."

"It's been a long search," says Hollis reflectively.

"I'm not always right in reading people, Hollis, but you seem less like a man who's finally found his true love again, and more like a man who's got the weight of the world on his shoulders. You think I'm just in it for the money?"

"No, of course not. There's something else," he says, looking away and tapping the table.

"That sounds ominous."

"I'd never written a will before, you know. And, well, I was so worried about your turnaround that I wrote one last night, Lalla, and you're not in it. You'd get nothing if I died."

"I was going to suggest it myself. I want nothing from you," I say, my pulse almost stopping, but it won't take long to conjure up a plan to make him change his will back in my favor. "I presume your cheap little flat was also a test?"

"I didn't want you to like me just for my money," he says.

"Well, I'd love you if you had nothing," I say. "After all, I once did. I'm not someone who cares about all those status symbols."

"That means so much," he says, and smiles warmly. And we stare into each other's eyes for what would feel like far too long even if I were in love.

Hollis grabs both my hands. "Look, if we're going to start again, I want us to be able to be completely honest with each other."

"Yes, of course," I say.

"Call it an amnesty," he says. "Whatever you tell me now doesn't count, right? We say it all and then we move on."

"But there isn't anything to tell you."

"Yeah, I totally get that," he says, then smiles. "But I want to talk about the day I fell."

"What for? It's not something I remember at all."

"Yeah," he says. "It makes me wonder if you blocked something out."

"Like what?" I look at him struggling with his thoughts.

"Something you did that you don't want to think about. Something you can't face."

"Like the trauma and pain of it all?" I say.

"No, before that. Before the fall, in fact," he says.

"I have no idea," I say, looking as innocent as possible.

"I remember it in two different ways, and I've been thinking over the years that maybe I joined the dots wrong," he says. "Trauma can do that. You fill the gaps."

"As interesting as this is, Hollis, don't you think we should go home to bed?" I say, although I'm wondering if sex without testicles is even possible. I decide to google it later.

"Look, I know I'm struggling a bit," he says, and holds my gaze. "I've got these two versions in my head of what happened the day I fell."

"Go on, then, what are they?"

"In the first one, I hear you shout, 'Watch out, rocks!' I look up, lose my balance, and stumble. You try to grab me, and I fall."

"And the other version?" I ask.

"That's even harder to imagine. Maybe so hard, I suppressed it."

"What are you getting at?" I say.

"That you shouted, tried to grab me, and it was only then that I stumbled."

"Meaning I tried to help you, but I made it worse? Oh god, that's a terrible thought," I say, and raise my eyebrows as sympathetically as possible.

"Yes, but that's not even the most terrible thought," he says, and stares at me.

78

Push

We walk and wheel in silence alongside the river. I check my phone. There are eighteen messages from Cait about her investigation, but I'm not in the mood to engage with her delusions. I make a note to myself to convince her to move the focus from Hollis, as he must be my future now.

We arrive at our romantic spot with views of Westminster and the London Eye. The place I was going to kill him and where he proposed. We've said little, and I'm buttoned up against the cold. I put my handbag on the arm of his wheelchair and push my hands deep into the pockets of my Prada coat.

He looks up at me, expectant. If it's honesty Hollis wants, then I can be honest, but people rarely enjoy it when they get what they ask for. If Hollis's will is not in my name, it means there's no advantage to killing him. A necessary precaution for a billionaire, and quite a helpful impediment to the murderous urges that used to punctuate my relationship with Hollis. I'll try to enjoy his wealth, at least until I find a way to convince him to change the will.

"I've got no evidence, Lalla," he says. "You can just walk away now if you want. But I love you, and if you love me, you'll tell me the truth."

"What exactly do you suspect me of?"

"I know what you are. You told me all about yourself and your deeds during your drunken rambles, and I loved you more for it. But there's been this doubt I've had for a long time."

"Then make the accusation, Hollis."

"Did you push me off the mountain?" he says, and stares at me fiercely.

I pause. I've rarely been confronted with the things I've done, and I'm not sure of the best response.

"What would I possibly have gained from killing you?" I ask.

"Not all crimes are about satisfying material needs. Some are more psychological."

Hollis stares at me in silence. I see him try to swallow. I feel the gulf between us.

"You seem to remember all the good things about us, but it wasn't all good," I say.

Hollis loved me in the beginning. He even loved the rage, anger, and transgression. It allowed me to feel free and I told him things I'd never told anyone in my life. And then, day by day, comment by comment, he slowly started to hold it against me. He used it to cut me off from other people, remove my freedom, take away access to money, until the noose was so tight around my neck, I either had to beg for air or push back.

"You forced me to stay with you, that was the truth."

"You were free to go whenever you wanted," he says.

"You threatened to tell people what I'd told you in confidence. That's not freedom."

"I didn't threaten. I just said you needed looking after. I was trying to keep you from harming yourself again, or someone else."

"When we arrived in France, I wanted to leave you. We talked about it. You said I couldn't. You took my passport away."

"Where would you have gone, Lalla? You had no money, you were..." He looks up at me, silent for a moment. "You were a danger to yourself."

"I just wanted to be free," I say.

"So you pushed me off the mountain," he concludes.

"You suffocated me," I say.

"So you smashed my legs to pieces and left me for dead!" he shouts, and indicates his legs and missing scrotum with a dramatic sweep of his hand.

"This isn't getting us anywhere, Hollis. The past is the past." I frown and bite my lip a little, which I hope shows regret.

"And will there be other mistakes? You know I'm rich now too. Must be tempting."

"You asked for the truth. I told you. I don't know if I wanted to kill you or not. I just wanted to escape. Don't you ever feel like that?"

"I don't push people off mountains," he says.

I look at him. The smile has disappeared, and he's staring at me with something that looks a lot like hatred.

"What?" I ask.

"You're a liar," he says.

"What do you mean?"

"You planned to kill me on Saturday," he shouts, then wheels up to me, grabs my lapel, and pushes me backward with one arm. I can't pull away from his grip, and he shoves me against the barrier. It swings open, but he doesn't let me go. He holds me there, leaning backward. If he pushed me now, I would fly down the steps and into the river.

"Stop!" I shout.

"You were going to do it right in this spot until you realized I was rich. I saw that the padlocks had been cut. Not enough to try to kill a man once, heh?"

I'm lost for words. I feel a horrible, dawning realization that Hollis has gotten the better of me. With his free hand, he pulls his shooting pistol from the side of his wheelchair and presses it into my stomach. I feel an almost visceral shame at being duped by someone feigning to love me. Why did I not see through all his games?

"Are you going to kill me?" I ask. "You knew what I was, Hollis, and you tried to destroy that side of me, but I won't be tamed by you or anyone. And I'll always fight for my life."

"I want people to know who you are and what you've done," he says. "I want your husband, children, and friends to know you're a cold-blooded killer. I want to see you ruined and humiliated."

"Every man's dream," I say, and spit in his face.

This is a mistake. He shoves me hard. My feet fall off the step, and I lose a shoe. I'm leaning backward, staring into the barrel of a gun, with his one fist keeping me from the icy water, when he says, "Watch out, rocks!"

79

Fate

The Thames is a beautiful river. I know it's full of sewage effluent and probably a few dead bodies, but the surface is glittering with reflections from the city's lights and looks like it's plated in gold. The last time I was here, I was about to murder the man beside me. Now he is about to murder me. How quickly things change.

I have no fear of what might happen to me. But then I imagine Nathan hugging Georgie's legs, and Nelly stabbing her with a knitting needle, and I feel something deep within. It's like someone drumming urgently on a closed door. I feel sad about Stephen momentarily. No matter what, I feel sure that Stephen would never try to kill his wife.

I look across the road beyond Hollis, desperate to spot a CCTV camera, but I chose this location so carefully. I see someone on the pavement opposite. They're only partly visible as they're hidden in the shadows. A witness, standing and watching. They've got their phone out too, recording the scene. It might just buy me time.

"Hollis," I say, seriously now. "There's someone filming you, and if you let me go, and I hit that freezing water, then you're going to prison, not me. You'll lose everything you worked for. And you don't deserve that."

Hollis looks at me suspiciously, then glances quickly over his shoulder. We both stare out across the road and see the figure take a step toward us, a phone held up in front of them.

"How long have they been there?" he says.

"Since you attacked me," I say, and I quickly raise my hand and shout, "Help! Help!"

"Say another word and I'll drop you," he says.

In response to my call, the figure runs into the road and tries to cross. As they're lit up by headlights, I see they're dressed all in black, a hoodie hiding their features. My only chance is to delay.

"Call the police," I say. "Let me confess to them. Let the police do your work for you. I'll lose everything. I'll be imprisoned, shamed, and humiliated, just as you want."

Hollis turns again to see the black-clad figure now running toward us.

"Shit," he says, and jams the gun hard into my gut. "You're going to do exactly what I say."

The figure tries to dash across the lanes of traffic as cars screech and slam on the brakes.

"Stop!" shouts the figure in the road. As soon as I hear the voice, I know who it is. I grab on to a railing with one hand while Hollis is preoccupied and hold as firmly as I can.

As Flame sprints directly toward us, Hollis looks up at me. "Just tell them it was a misunderstanding and I'll let you live."

I sway back and forth, his fist and my one arm holding me in place. I feel as if I could tumble into the dark river any moment.

"Help! Cait!" I shout.

Cait leaps onto the pavement and darts toward me, but at the last moment she sees the gun Hollis is pointing in my direction, veers suddenly to the left, grabs Hollis's wheelchair, and pushes him with all her might toward the river. He says something inaudible and hurtles past me. The side of the wheelchair clatters into my legs and I start to fall. Cait follows quickly, grabs at me, manages to catch my dress, and hauls me back.

We turn together and see Hollis's wheels hit the first few steps with a loud clang. The chair flies into the air, along with my bag, flips completely, hits another step, and lands with a splash. Almost at once, the water closes over him.

I glance at Cait, then at the water, where Hollis and his chair have been replaced by a ripple of concentric circles, and my billionaire husband's last breath is a series of small bubbles reaching the surface of the water.

"You okay?" says Cait.

"Another dead body, another ruined dress," I say, looking at the torn red silk. "But otherwise fine, thank you."

"He was going to kill you," she says.

"He's deranged," I say, then I realize that there's something urgent that I have to do. Something that my whole future depends upon.

"Cait, you've done so much, but could you do one more little thing for me?"

"Shouldn't we try to rescue him?" she says, as two cars stop and their drivers approach us, asking us what happened.

"No, leave it to these people. You need to go."

"Where? To hide, you mean?"

"No. You need to go straight to Hollis's flat, find his will, and destroy it."

"Why?" she asks.

"If you want a new house, Cait, just do as I say. I'll tell you everything as soon as this is over."

It's only when Cait's gone, the passersby have hauled Hollis from the water (my Prada handbag having caught on the last step, preventing him sinking farther), the police have arrived, and I'm in an ambulance that the enormity of the situation hits me. I suddenly feel physically sick as I realize I've lost two husbands and a handbag in the space of a single day.

80
Hospital

We arrive at St. Thomas's under the dramatic flicker of red and blue lights and the occasional burst of a high-pitched siren. If it wasn't for a torn dress, grazed knees, and a filthy coat, I'd feel like a star.

Five minutes into my stay, I'm still at the entrance to the emergency room, sitting in a queue due to a lack of free beds. I tell the first nurse I see that I need priority treatment as I'm pregnant. She takes me right past everyone. I'm quite sure I'm the only one in Prada in the whole place, and I receive what I take to be admiring glances despite the torn fabric.

In the triage area, the nurse checks for broken bones, dresses my shins, and makes admiring comments about my one shoe. I tell her the story of how my husband tried to kill me, and she tells me I'm not the first and won't be the last.

After the treatment, I text Stephen to tell him I've been "nearly killed" and he needs to pick me up if he can tear himself away from his floozie. The problem I now have is that I'm not married to anyone, and Stephen knows he owes me nothing. Despite several texts, I have no idea if Cait made it to Hollis's flat or if the police picked her up on the way. Several drivers described a Ninja-like figure with long auburn hair pushing a disabled man into the river, so she won't be difficult to find.

As I'm waiting for Stephen, the furrowed brow of a uniformed police officer appears from behind the thin blue curtain, followed by his inappropriately grinning subordinate with his helmet in his hands. I'm really not in the mood for a police interview and sigh quite visibly.

"I know you won't feel like speaking to us," says the police officer. "We won't keep you long. We just need to ask some details about the incident tonight at the river."

"Yes, my wounds are fine, thank you," I say, making a necessary point.

The police officer stares at me as if the idea of asking after my well-being is making him physically uncomfortable, but he finally says, "We've spoken to your doctor about your injuries and understand they're not life-threatening."

"No thanks to the police, I might say. Luckily, my friend was around to save me."

"We understand a man was pushed into the Thames by a woman with red hair."

"That was my friend Cait. She didn't mean to kill him. She was trying to save my life."

"Oh, he's not dead, madam. He was hauled from the Thames, but he's in a critical condition."

"Not dead? Surely, he's . . . I mean, he must've been in the water for several minutes."

"It's cold-water hypothermia, we understand. He's in a coma. This man was your husband?"

"Yes," I say. "And he was trying to kill me. I hope you found his gun. I'm sure Cait has it all on her phone."

"Do you have this woman's surname?"

"O'Donnell," I say. "She's on bail for manslaughter, so she's in the system. She will have broken her bail conditions, unfortunately, but she was following me, you see. I think she sensed I was in danger. I hope you'll look favorably on her actions."

The PC writes all of this down, which takes some time, then he sits on the blue plastic chair and says, "In your own words, could you tell us exactly what happened?"

Having had some time to consider how to play this particular scene, I explain as succinctly as possible that my estranged abusive husband tracked me down, even using an investigator (I mention DS Birch here), and when I told him I'd remarried and couldn't have him back, he said he'd rather see me dead than living with another man, threatened me with a gun, and tried to push me in the river, whereupon my friend Cait saved my life, and in the scuffle, he fell down the steps into the water. I also told them to look for the severed padlocks as I believed the cunning bastard had removed them in advance, which clearly indicated an intention to murder me.

They ask all kinds of additional questions, but I try to keep the story as simple as possible—another jealous husband attacking his wife because he can't accept he's not wanted anymore.

They tell me they'll need a formal statement and disappear into the night. Stephen arrives an hour later looking guilty. Nothing like being in bed with your mistress when the mother of your children is being nearly murdered to make a man question his priorities.

81

Results

Tuesday, January 28

As the press are rehashing Hollis's and my relationship as a tragic love story with some help from me, I await the postman. My shins are still sore, not that anyone's asked. Hollis is still in a hypothermic coma and seems determined not to die, which is probably the worst of all worlds.

I hope it's not uncharitable to wish for brain damage in the area responsible for language and memory, if he does pull through. If he survives, I'm unable to inherit a penny of his considerable wealth and am entitled to nothing from Stephen.

If he dies, things are somewhat sunnier. Cait did manage to break into Hollis's flat, find his will, and burn it, clever girl. If he now dies, he dies intestate, which should mean I'll get everything as his legal spouse. On the less positive side, Cait's been arrested for the attempted murder of Matthew Hollis. I strongly believe that her video of him dangling me over the Thames while holding a gun means that they won't charge her. However, as she breached her bail conditions again and is clearly a lethal threat to abusive men everywhere, she's back in Bronzefield until her trial for Owen's manslaughter.

I watch the road from the front room. The mail carrier's a nice chap, quite mature, with a limp and a large wheeled cart. Always manages a smile, but he is slow. I head upstairs to the bedroom for a better view and spot him five houses down from ours. I look at my watch. I just want to run and grab Nelly's letter.

I decide to indulge my impatience on this occasion, rush downstairs, grab my coat, and shout to anyone who's interested that the post is here. No one in the house responds, least of all Nelly, who's hiding again. We no longer search for her. I think one of those trackers that Cait has attached to her ankle might be the only solution.

I open the door and I'm confronted again by DS Birch and DC Mattoo coming through the gate. It's almost as if they know I won't answer the door and wait to ambush me.

"Mrs. Rook," says DS Birch. "Looks like you've recovered from your injuries."

"I nearly died. Most of the scars from that incident will never heal, Detective," I say.

"Yes, I'm sorry. Mrs. Rook, we just need a further word with you."

"If this is about that Jason Mercer again, I can't help you. You've got to learn to find people by yourself."

"We understand that Matthew Hollis paid Mercer to track you down," says DS Birch. "It explains a great deal."

I stop, partly because they've blocked my path but mainly because of the expressions on both of their faces. I glance from one to the other. Constipation? It's a strange look for a police officer and it suits neither of them.

"Could we come in?" says DS Birch. "There's something important we need to discuss."

"I'm afraid not, I'm just trying to catch the postman. Just say what you need to say right here." I look over their shoulders at the postman as he reaches number 40.

"It's about Matthew Hollis," says Birch.

"Hold on," I interrupt as I slip in between them and head for the postman.

"Mrs. Rook, did you hear me?"

"I don't see what I can add. He attacked me. I'm a victim—look at my bandages. Isn't it time the police stopped persecuting women for protecting themselves? Now, I've got to catch the post. He's missed number forty-two. They rarely get letters, actually."

"Mrs. Rook, we're not investigating the incident at the river. That's not our case."

The postman arrives at the gate and I wave at him enthusiastically.

"Mrs. Rook, please," says Birch loudly.

"One minute," I say, and walk to the postman. "Hello, anything for me?"

The postman nods his head, then gives me a look and points his nose toward the police officers.

"Oh, my husband tried to kill me," I say.

"Sorry to hear that," he says. "He always seemed so nice."

"Oh, not Stephen, another husband," I say.

"Takes all sorts," he says, and gives me a quizzical look as if I'm part of a throuple.

"I'm expecting good news, actually," I say, as he flicks through a handful of letters.

"Just the one." He hands me a beautiful, weighty envelope inscribed with the Adams crest.

I press the envelope to my chest and turn back to the door. "Important letter," I explain to the police officers, whose expressions are still quite somber.

"I'm afraid we've got some bad news," says DS Birch.

I stare down at the envelope. It's a gorgeous thick ivory paper. Like something from Buckingham Palace. I can't imagine that they would send a rejection in such a fine envelope. I nod to the police officers as I pull out the letter. It's folded so exactly that I delight at the execution. These little touches really matter.

"Matthew Hollis died in the early hours of this morning," says DS Birch.

"Right," I say, hardly listening as I unfold the letter and read. I scan it quickly and feel my organs all seize up at once. I stagger forward. DC Mattoo has to reach out to stop me falling, then I let out an almighty scream.

"We're sorry for your loss," says DC Mattoo, with a kindly hand to my shoulder.

ADAMS PREPARATORY SCHOOL
Hampstead

Dear Mr. and Mrs. Rook,

We so enjoyed the pleasure of meeting Nelly over the course of the admissions process. She's a remarkable young lady with such strength of character and talent. We were particularly impressed by her beautifully sculpted dolphin and her passionate interest in Mary Poppins and taxidermy.

The examination consisted of a mathematics test and an English test. Our decision is also based on other important factors, such as Nelly's school reference and her social interactions.

It is with enormous regret that we are unable to offer Nelly a school place for 7+ entry. We are grateful for your application and all the work that Nelly has put into her preparation. She should be justly proud of herself.

Although you may be deeply disappointed by this news, please may I take this opportunity to share my personal good wishes for Nelly's future education.

Yours sincerely,
Penelope Pembury

82

Gloating

"Dear daughter-in-law!" says Madeleine, standing on my doorstep, leaning in to kiss my cheek, her teeth flecked with lipstick as if she's just come from tearing flesh off a carcass.

"Oh, I'm so sorry. You're not actually my daughter-in-law, are you?"

"You've come to gloat? How kind."

"Not at all. Simply come to offer my sincere condolences. I understand your actual husband died."

"Quite tragically," I say as she hands me her coat.

"While trying to kill you, I hear." She smiles.

"Tea?" I say.

"Absolutely not," she says, staring at me with what can only be interpreted as an accusation of some kind. "Life can be so unpredictable at times, can't it? There I was, changing my will, and all the time you're a bigamist and would get absolutely nothing anyway. And now, I'll get a baronetess for a daughter-in-law."

"We're both social climbers, I see."

"Well, you're more on the descent, I feel. Stephen and Georgie are currently ensconced at an undisclosed London hotel, paid for by yours truly, planning their big day free of worries about divorce and divorce settlements. They've been able to bring the date forward by six months, thanks to your little oversight."

"I'm happy for them," I say. "The three of you deserve each other."

"And we're all terribly sad that your husband wrote you out of his will. So you're penniless, husbandless, and homeless. If that's not karma for poisoning my tea, I don't know what is. I'm aware of what you tried to do, you know. I'm not stupid."

"How do you know about his will?" I ask, ignoring her unfounded accusation.

"When Stephen told me the news about your other marriage, I presumed, based on your essential narcissism, that it was a more viable economic option, so I looked up Matthew Hollis and discovered that he was a significantly wealthy man. I saw your game, Lalla, and I called him."

"What exactly did you do, Madeleine?"

"I thought it only fair to advise him that you'd recently tried to poison me for my inheritance, so he should watch his back. He seemed interested in that. I also advised him to change his will."

"You know, Madeleine, for years I thought we were alike. But I never delighted in other people's destruction. It was always just a practical necessity for me. We're actually worlds apart."

"Indeed, I am who I am, and you're a girl from nowhere who'll do anything to get her way."

"But you taught me something important about people."

"Oh, I do apologize. I only wanted to teach you a lesson." She readjusts her Alice band.

"You taught me how to outflank my enemies." I lean back in my chair. "Hollis did rewrite his will as you advised. But it seems that he never submitted it, or even had it witnessed, which is reassuring as there's no one left to verify it, and I feel sure that it won't be found in his possessions."

"You destroyed it?" she says, her chin shaking visibly.

"Perhaps he simply decided that he loved me."

"I doubt that," she says, but I see that the light has gone from her eyes. "Even if you have someone else's money, there's one thing you don't have and that's my son. And if you try to harm his new relationship, I'll release all I know about your sordid little life."

"Of course, Madeleine. But it's Georgie you should be worrying about, not me."

"Georgie's not going to do anything to jeopardize her future."

"How much did you pay her to get back with him? Aside from settling all her debts?"

"Our affairs are none of your business."

"But they are Stephen's business."

"Stephen will enjoy the fruits of our arrangement, he does not need to see the details."

"There's one more small thing I ought to share," I say. "Georgie has an unfortunate habit. She keeps a daily diary and is absolutely scrupulous about recording every minute detail. What she eats, what she buys, who she sees, who she sleeps with, and the details of all her meetings with you. Every single one."

Madeleine's face goes pale. "And you have this diary, do you? Is this what's called mutually assured destruction? We either both release what we have and destroy each other, or we agree to keep things private."

"Yes," I say. "Except that I've already given the diary to Stephen."

Her eyes widen and her mouth slowly opens. "You're lying, Lalla."

"I'm afraid not. He hadn't read it, last I heard, but I did text him this morning to say that he really should."

"If he finds out about my payments to Georgie and all our plans, I'll tell him everything about you. I'll send it all to the *Mail*. They'll pull you to pieces."

"I realized that I've been hiding my background for so long because I've been ashamed of it, but there's no shame in being from a broken home, getting in trouble with the police when I was young, or marrying an abusive man. The papers seem to like that version of me, so I've already told them everything. It seems that they see me as the heroine of this story, and that means they'll be looking for a villain. Now, where shall I direct them, do you think?"

83

Letter

Wednesday, January 29

Dear Lalla,

I hope you and the children are all doing well. It's difficult back in prison, especially being away from the girls, but I can't tell you the reception I'm getting in here. God, when I think about returning to Muswell Hill and all those entitled women jumping on the bandwagon, compared to the ecstatic cheers I got arriving back here! They call me "Cait Two-Time" now because they think I've killed two abusive men.

This time, I actually did kill someone, but I only stopped that bastard throwing you to your death. Fucking men! All the police and social workers keep asking me is whether I regret it. I have to say I do, but I don't. I enjoyed pushing him in the river. It was incredibly cathartic after everything with Owen. It was such a bloody rush.

Thank you for explaining on the phone about Hollis and your secretive past. I can't believe you kept all that hidden for so long, but I understand why you would want to hide from such a brute. It was a bit odd that you didn't recognize him at the rifle range, but I suppose with his wheelchair, flatcap, and beard, he must've looked so different.

Oh, and I got two marriage proposals today. Both from serial *killers, but still, a proposal is a proposal. The best news is that I've got a newspaper that wants to tell my story and there's even a publisher interested. They say that if I set up a trust fund for the girls, I could get a big lump of cash just by telling people how I fought back against abuse. I'd have to tell the prosecution's version of how I killed Owen as there's much less money in it if I tell my version, but it might do some good if I inspire women to feel that they can fight back, albeit not with petrol and knives.*

Mum brought the girls today. No point hiding anymore, I'm a hardened criminal. Everyone was lovely to them in the visitor center. Mum's going to get them ice cream on the way back too. I feel more in control of my life than I ever have before.

And it's all down to you, Lalla. You helped me turn off the fears and anxieties in my head. Showed me how to be the kind of woman I want to be, and I'm free now. I want to kill more abusive men. I really do. We should set up a club! There's some girls in here who'd definitely join.

Oh, and I've met someone. People go on about prison being the worst, but I love it. It's got everything you could ever want.

Love to Sophie and Aisha, too—please come visit me anytime.

Two-Time xxx

While Cait is communicating well, Tor is not answering her phone, WhatsApp, or email. I am keen to know what happened in the Adams exam. I really hope that Nelly didn't lie to me. I go to Tor's Instagram account and find a post with a photograph of a triumphant Hero holding her offer letter above her head. She's also wearing a tiara.

I call Sophie and ask how Ellie got on. She says that Ellie is almost peeing herself with excitement but she doesn't get mail until the afternoon. I decide I need answers so I head across to Hampstead and make my way directly to Adams Prep, with Nelly's failure on my mind and Tor's gloating in my ear.

I stand at the beautiful reception desk and ask to see the head. I am asked what it's about, and I tell her that there's been an error in the offer letter. I'm asked to sit. The waiting room is like a gentleman's club with trophies adorning the walls and shelves. I don't have to wait for long before a tall, glamorous woman seats herself opposite me and asks how she can help.

"My daughter, Nelly Rook, she's not been offered a place, and I think there's probably been an administrative error."

"Mrs. Rook, thank you for coming in. I've had a look, and I know how sensitive an issue this is, but unfortunately the data seems to be correct. It's been the most competitive season we've ever seen, and you and Nelly mustn't see this as any judgment on her abilities."

"She didn't get in? You're sure?"

"I'm afraid to say that she just missed out."

"I think there must be some mistake."

"No, I'm afraid not, but it is most upsetting when children set their sights on something important to them."

"No, Mrs. Whellam," I say, reading her badge. "I think this is a genuine slipup. The headmistress assured me that Nelly would get a place. I want to see the head."

"Mrs. Pembury's not here today."

"But she must have said something about Nelly. We had an understanding."

"Sadly not," says Mrs. Whellam with an artificial smile. "I know that parents can sometimes misinterpret meetings with the head."

"I didn't misinterpret," I say, and grab her arm.

"I wish Nelly all the best," she says, and yanks her arm from my grip.

"Did you check the candidate numbers?"

"Of course. In fact, on the day of your daughter's exam, we had to double-check all the candidate numbers because we received an anonymous call that morning, informing us that some parents had been pressured into swapping their daughter's candidate number."

"An anonymous call?"

"Yes, and you'll be pleased to know that we found out that your daughter had the wrong number. Thank goodness we did check!"

"Yes, thank goodness," I say.

I sit in the car outside Adams and open Facebook. I paste a clear still of Tor and Zac in flagrante delicto and type:

My name is Tor, I'm a lying bitch, and this is my boy toy, Zac.

I wait for eight seconds before the first response. Soon there is a tidal wave—about 50 percent moral outrage, 30 percent prurience and lust, and 20 percent feminist solidarity.

I head straight to WH Smith. They don't have any paper quite as pompous as Adams, but I buy the best I can, go home, and type the content of my rejection letter onto the laptop with variations more suitable to Ellie. I copy the coat of arms from their website and paste it at the top of the letter. I print it several times to get the right placings and colors and after half an hour I'm quite satisfied. There's a job for me as a forger if all else fails.

I use a little bit of steam and pry the address label off Nelly's envelope, then it's just a matter of printing Sophie's address on a new label and sticking it on. I fold the letter and use the iron on a low setting to achieve the pristine lines, then pop it into the envelope, use a bit of Nelly's Pritt Stick, and seal it.

I race down the road and arrive just as Sophie's mail carrier is nearing her house. I run ahead of him to hang around Sophie's front door in a proprietorial manner. When the postal carrier arrives, I walk toward her and hold out my hand. She glances at me as she clearly knows I'm not Sophie, but my gaze suggests that questions are not welcome.

"I'll take those in," I say.

She puts a small bundle in my hand. I watch her leave and head to Sophie's front door. I find her letter from Adams, replace it with Nelly's rejection letter, and pop it through her mailbox along with the other mail.

As I leave, I hear a thunder of footsteps and then Ellie cries out, "Mum, the post's here!"

84

Acceptance

The evidence suggests that I might love my children. I give so much to them while getting nothing in return, which suggests something more than just a transactional relationship. My actions are no different from my friends' except I'll go the extra mile to ensure things work out well for them. Perhaps in feeling less, I even love them more.

I'm standing alone in the kitchen with Sophie's letter. I feel a sense of excitement that I've purloined this potential golden ticket. I slowly peel open the envelope and take out the perfectly folded letter. I've prepared myself for bad news, but I don't know what steps I'll take if Ellie has also been rejected. I might have to hound them into changing their minds with a malicious social media campaign.

I hold the letter in my hand and slowly unfold it. I see the beautifully embossed school coat of arms and the first line, "Dear Mr. Caldas and Ms. Hills." I close my eyes momentarily, then read the first word. "Congratulations."

I have an Adams offer letter in my hand. Admittedly, it's not for Nelly, but I feel the same enthusiasm and joy as if it were. I read the rest of the letter and discover that Ellie has been offered a 50 percent scholarship. I feel so proud of her. She must have worked like an absolute demon.

I make myself a cup of Earl Grey tea, thinking through the options. I sip and mull. I wonder about the relationship between the

Admissions Department and the senior staff and whether data changes are shared. I imagine not.

I find the telephone number on the letter and call Adams.

"Hello, this is Sophie Hills, I've just received an offer for my daughter, and I'd like to accept," I say.

"What's your daughter's name?"

"Eleanor Caldas," I say.

"Well, congratulations. I've noted that now, and you'll receive confirmation by letter. Is Eleanor pleased?"

"She's absolutely delighted."

"We're so happy that she'll be coming to Adams."

"As are we," I say. "Just one more thing. I need to inform you of a slight change of our details?"

"Of course," she says.

"It's a delicate situation, actually. Mr. Caldas and I are splitting up, but Eleanor doesn't know anything about it yet."

I wait a moment as she types away at her keyboard. I am banking on there being no information about parents' marital status. I know that it was not something they asked for on the application forms.

"We certainly won't break any confidences," says the woman's low and sympathetic voice.

"I've had to change my contact details. My husband's not behaving well, and it's for the children's safety." I put a little touch of desperation into my tone for good measure.

"Of course. Shall I put you in touch with our safeguarding lead?"

"I've done that already, but thank you. I just want to make sure that he doesn't get any letters or communication. He even stole my email password, you know."

"Gosh, how awful for you," she says in a breathy whisper.

"Well, you know how some men are, don't you? Charming for a while, then simply beastly."

"I'm so sorry," she says, sounding entirely genuine, which is nice. It's a horrible feeling when you fake bad news and people are unsympathetic.

"First, can you update our address? It's forty-four Ennerdale Avenue. Eleanor will be with me in my new address," I say.

"Yes, of course. I've put that in the database now."

"And please delete my previous address. I don't want any mistakes."

"Of course, it's your data, you've got a right to say what we keep. Anything else?"

"Well, as I say, the email you have is compromised. Can you delete it and put my new email in?"

"Of course, no problem."

I give her my email, which is one of my pseudonyms that I use for online accounts.

"There, that's all done for you."

"Thank you, that's so kind. I can't tell you how helpful you've been," I say.

"We're here to help," she says.

"Oh, I nearly forgot. Eleanor won't be using her father's surname. She's going to take a different name so she can't be found."

"Oh, this does sound awful. Right, let's get this set up. What would her surname be?"

"Rook. She'll be known as Eleanor Rook."

"No problem at all, I can change this right now. I know how difficult these things must be."

"And can you also note that she prefers the name Nelly to Eleanor?"

"Of course, no problem. That's all changed for you."

"So pleased, and do please keep these changes private. He's a violent man and I would hate for any indiscretion to put my daughter at risk."

"Fully understood," she says.

I put the phone down and smile. Of course, there's a residual chance that someone will recognize Nelly and ask questions, but as Adams has over a thousand applications, I think this is a small risk worth taking. Anyway, I plan a new haircut for Nelly before September, so that should confuse any curious minds.

It's only Mrs. Pembury I'm concerned about—she would remember Nelly, I'm sure—but her absence from school suggests that the evidence of financial impropriety that I've sent to her governing body has had the desired impact.

It was quite simple really once I had her bank account details (purloined from a bank statement found in her recycling bin). No one is concerned about security when you're putting money into an account, and I just transferred three separate payments to her using a new Bitcoin account. I sent copies of these payments, and of three anonymous emails of thanks for her generous support, along with a letter accusing Mrs. Pembury of taking bribes for school places, to the chair of trustees, along with a suggestion that they talk to her PA about any cash changing hands.

Of course, Mrs. Pembury would deny it all, but evidence speaks volumes and schools hate scandals. She would have deleted the anonymous emails, of course, but they'll be in the system, and once they initiate a search, well, it'll look rather like a cover-up.

The English hate financial impropriety even more than they hate queue jumpers, so I don't think we'll be seeing Mrs. Pembury again. It's a shame, really, as I think we would've gotten on well, given different circumstances.

I also receive a phone call from my solicitor, and although it'll take months for the will to be executed, she gives me positive news about Hollis's will. He did indeed die intestate, and as his wife, I am the sole heir. If this isn't challenged, I'll be able to afford to buy my Hampstead house. I feel newly rich and head to Harrods in the afternoon to spend some money. We were there before Christmas and the children had enormous fun. I buy a large panda for Nelly, which costs nearly £600—a lot for a soft toy—but what price love? Nathan's cuddly octopus is £700, the additional price probably due to extra limbs—or tentacles, as he would tell me.

I'm not completely altruistic as I manage to spend £4,500 on a dress for myself. I'm not even sure if I like it, but that's what being rich is all about: not having to care. I get a taxi all the way home and find Aimée reading to Nelly and Nathan in French. It is rather an idyllic scene and I think she's bonded with them rather well. Even the most inadequate person can surprise you.

I give them their gifts, which are popular, and hug them. I don't know why, but I don't want to let go. Our idyllic moment is ruined, however, when the police appear. I know what they're going to say, so I stand in the doorway and allow DS Birch to elaborate.

"We found Mercer."

"You did?" I say, worried momentarily.

"Well, we found his phone and notebook, and his blood was all over his phone."

"Where?"

"Matthew Hollis had a rented flat in Hackney. We didn't know anything about it but got an anonymous tip-off. Someone must've seen his picture in the papers."

Yes, I think to myself, *I wonder who that was.*

"By the look of things, Hollis might have killed Mercer and thrown him in the Thames."

"Like he tried to do to me."

"People repeat patterns," says DC Mattoo, nodding.

"They were probably in a dispute about money. We just wanted you to know."

"I'm grateful, Detective. I expect his body's been dragged out to sea by now."

DS Birch stares at me. There's a hunger in there still undiminished. An instinct that she can't quite itch.

"Anything else?" I ask.

"No, not for now," she says.

"It's been nice getting to know you," says DC Mattoo.

I watch them head back down the path and feel a sense of peace and inner satisfaction.

85

Reader

One of my favorite places in Muswell Hill is the bench beside the ancient oak tree in the Grove. Look one way and you can see the whole of London spread out against the sky. Look the other way and you see parkland and an avenue of limes. History has it that Dr. Johnson himself once walked along this avenue. These days, there is a constant stream of water from some unplugged leak and a cattle drive of buggies, dogs, and toddlers.

Stephen joins me and hands me a coffee from the Grove Café. He's dressed in his most casual attire, and I can't help feeling a simple attraction to him, like two magnets drawn together. I want to hold him and be held by him. I have this feeling of comfort in his company. Perhaps it's my pregnancy, but given our recent interactions, feeling anything positive is an achievement.

"You wanted to meet," I say, looking into his clear blue eyes.

He says, rather sheepishly, "I read her diary. Beginning to end."

"Well, it looks like we've both been taken advantage of by scurrilous lovers. I had mine killed, what did you do with yours?"

"I suggested we break it off," he says. "She plans on going back to Dubai. Finding a wealthy partner in London since the Russians left is a nightmare, apparently."

"Death or Dubai has a ring to it, don't you think?"

"I've been a fool, Lalla. I had no idea how manipulative she is, or more importantly, how weak and stupid I am. I don't know what to say."

"I've heard the done thing in such circumstances is to say sorry."

"It's not really adequate, is it?" he says, and sits down next to me. "But I am sorry."

We both stare out across the London skyline. Behind us a father plays football with his daughter and their dog. Their cries of joy and disappointment punctuate our conversation.

"I can't expect you to forgive me, but I wanted to tell you that I know I got it wrong," he says.

"We all get mixed up sometimes. I'm sure I'm not an easy person to live with. I never felt it was over between us, you know. Not in my heart of hearts, wherever that may be."

"I suppose it's a midlife crisis, of sorts."

"Next time, buy a Ferrari."

"It felt like something real, but at the same time I always knew it wasn't..."

"It's the past. It calls to us all. Feels like it might offer certainty when the present doesn't. It's best not to listen. The past lies something terrible."

"She still wants her diary back," he says.

"I bet she does. Who'd want evidence that they're a mercenary narcissist shared around? Anyway, she wasn't much of a writer. I hope the sex was better than her descriptions." I smile. I've never been jealous like that. It helps sometimes not to feel. It allows you to care less.

"No comment," he says. "But she's going to troll you online for ruining her makeup and stealing her Prada handbag if she doesn't get her teddy bear back."

"Well, I'm happy to settle with the bear—minus two arms."

"How do you feel about everything?"

"I'm sure your mother's malign influence was partly to blame. Georgie seems quite an impressionable forty-year-old."

"I haven't told my mum that I know what she did. Paying Georgie a fortune to get back with me. It's outrageous, but I think she's too frail."

"Oh, I think you should, Stephen. There are precious few means available to legally kill a parent, it'd be terrible to waste the opportunity."

"Now, now," he says, and sips his coffee. "But the thought did cross my mind too."

We sit for a moment in silence. I'm imagining an order of service for Madeleine's funeral, opening with Beethoven's "Ode to Joy." I'm not sure what Stephen is thinking of, but then he turns to me and says, "You had a lucky escape at the river. I was terrified when I heard. I was so scared of losing you. We've got a lot to thank Cait for."

"I just hope the jury agrees with you."

"God, what a mess I made of something so good," he says, and puts his hand next to mine on the bench. "I suppose we run away when things are tough."

"There's no future in hiding. Ask Nelly. You always get found eventually. Better to face the present."

"Hear, hear," he says, and we clink paper cups.

"To you and me," I say. "Whatever that might look like. Nelly and Nathan deserve a little longer with us, and Leo needs a family."

Stephen's hand moves over mine. We sit for three whole minutes in silence, and I'm not sure what happens in that silence, but by the end of it, I know we have a future and so, I think, does he.

"I got my job back," he says.

"That's good to hear."

"Josh went out of his way to help. He's a good guy."

"He sure is," I say.

"And I've got something else to tell you."

"Georgie's terminally ill?"

"I'm a partner. Just heard."

I look at him. The power of a to-do list and electrocution is truly inspiring. "Well done, you, and all on your own merit. And it means we can afford Adams."

"She got in?"

"Your daughter is a clever girl."

"That's great. Wow. I expect several challenges ahead."

"She'll be fine," I say. "She just needs boundaries. That's what we all need."

Somewhere behind us, parakeets screech, dogs bark, and a little girl scores a goal. Times change, and we have to change with them.

"And what about us?" says Stephen, looking down at our hands. "I can't imagine being without you."

"Then don't," I say, and smile.

Epilogue

86

Claridge's

Sometime later

Gloriously sparkling tiles, ornate chandeliers, shimmering art nouveau mirrors—afternoon tea at Claridge's is a welcome delight. And I have to say, I feel I deserve it. For someone without a great deal of empathy, to do so much good is surely reason to celebrate. I feel like someone very noble, such as Evita Perón. I've done so much for my people.

Tor is released from her terribly demeaning affair with a blackmailer; Cait from the stinging tentacles of an abusive husband; Georgie from the clutches of a deplorable old witch; Madeleine from gnawing guilt at having destroyed her son's happiness; Mrs. Pembury from the stress and strains of headship; and Nelly from a future of polyester uniforms and low expectations.

The handsome waiter in a white dinner jacket and bow tie asks if I am expecting company. I tell him that I'm waiting for my fiancé and ask for the champagne afternoon tea for two as the grand piano starts up, accompanied by a violin.

I'm wearing a strapless magenta crepe gown with a beautiful satin-twill train. It's definitely too much, but it has an hourglass shape and makes me feel like an old-fashioned movie star, even with my bump. While waiting, I have time to recollect the last few months from the vantage point of a job well done.

Of course, sadly, I ended January without a single husband. One dead, one voided. In fact, men in general had not had a good time of it. Hollis, Mercer, and Owen all lost their lives; Hollis also lost the love of his life; Lawrence lost the whip when Tor's scandal emerged; Stephen lost his childhood sweetheart and the delusion that his mother was ever good to him; Josh lost half his penis due to third-degree burns; Zac lost his blackmailing career; and Ranni lost his dream job in Abu Dhabi. Only Nathan remains unscathed. He has his worms and he's happy.

Ranni's passport didn't go missing at the last moment. It didn't need to. Aisha found her own simple strategy. She stopped arguing with him, wished him well in his new life, and refused to leave the country. Resistance conquers all, even a husband's erroneous belief that his patriarchal position is a right, not a duty.

Aisha is delighted and has resigned from her position as PTA chair since she's just taken on a high-profile client who's taking all her time. This left an opportunity for someone. I was just in the right place at the right time. Another little tick on my to-do list.

Fortunately, my formal marriage to Hollis, so tragically brought to an end by his sudden death, was validated by lawyers, and as no one challenged my status as his legal spouse, I was the sole beneficiary of his fortune. I've been able to buy the Hampstead house and am already planning various improvements.

Sadly, when Stephen ended his relationship with Georgie, she took it badly and started making all kinds of accusations about me on social media. Fortunately, before she could do any serious damage, she was hit by a blue Toyota Corolla just outside Highgate station—a notoriously busy junction. The combination of emotional and physical injury has been hard for her and she headed back to Dubai. The past will come back to haunt you if you don't smother it with a pillow, as I've found out to my cost.

Stephen has come to better appreciate the underlying strength and simplicity of our transactional and uncomplicated love after Georgie's mercenariness and his mother's manipulation. He said he's always felt a pressure to be happy, but he now realizes he doesn't need to be and is much more content with being successful. Our current intimacy rating is 2.4 times per week and increasing all the time, which bodes well for the future.

Anyway, we remain a permanent port for each other in a stormy world. In the end, we're a team and although we've faced challenges, we're now stronger than ever. And with little Leopoldine on the way (gender now confirmed), Stephen's already designing a new nursery. Of course, the baby might be Zac's, but life isn't about origins, it's about destinations, so I'm not even all that curious. But if she is Zac's, she will be so beautiful the world will be lucky to have her.

As the Hollis tragedy revealed, Stephen and I were never legally married, so we've decided to wed again. Everyone's so supportive and the whole saga makes for a great dinner party story. Hampstead is going to love it as it makes us seem quite bohemian. I decided to put Hollis's diamond ring to good use and gave it to Stephen to use as our engagement ring. Sophie and Paolo also finally agreed on marriage after Sophie gave up drinking and realized drink was the problem, not Paolo. It's going to be a double wedding, of sorts. We're getting married in a fabulously lavish Scottish castle, and the following week, Sophie and Paolo will be married at an approved council venue in Wood Green.

Following the wedding, the baby will be born, and Nelly will start at Adams, which gives me great pride. Nelly was so happy when I told her she'd passed that tears fell from her eyes. You see, people often fail themselves in advance by claiming not to care, but in reality it's because they have no hope of their own success. It takes others to have that confidence for them. I'm hoping the rules and routines of a private school will help to rub off her harsh edges and violent outbursts, or at least teach her how to disguise them better, as it has with the aristocracy for centuries.

There was a small funeral for Hollis, which I chose not to attend, as there seem to be some residual feelings of blame coming from his coworkers and family. Apparently, they think I sought him out once I found out he was rich—oh, the irony! I understand his mum and dad couldn't make the trip, so I arranged with the vicar for the ceremony to be live-streamed to Australia. It's the least I could do.

Cait is still in prison awaiting trial, but thoroughly enjoying the infamy. Her old podcasts have gone viral and she's delighted. It's a strange coincidence that she killed my husband, and I killed hers, but what are friends for if not to help rid you of undesirable partners?

Anyway, as there are eyewitness accounts of Hollis's sad ending, Cait will be charged with involuntary manslaughter as she was only trying to protect me. Quite unexpectedly, however, she has decided to plead guilty to killing and burning Owen. She told me that she wants to own it, and she likes her new nickname, Two-Time. Her lawyer was furious about her change of plea, but her literary agent suggested it'd work wonders for her book sales.

She's a beacon of hope for survivors of domestic violence everywhere, and she really does look good on it. She's had her hair cut to give it more body and her skin has even cleared up. She's still with her new girlfriend—another murderer, as it happens—but shared interests are bound to lead to romance in such confined spaces.

I've used Hollis's money to pay for an excellent firm of lawyers for Cait and will honor my promise to buy her a house for when she gets out. There's a vocal campaign in support of her, and the lawyers are hopeful that she will be treated leniently by the courts. I'm sure she'll be back at home before the twins reach secondary school, so it's good to know they won't be without their mother for too long.

Not wanting to trumpet my generosity, but I did repay Tor the money she paid to Zac. I told her that I'd managed to force it out of him with threats. Tor loves money more than anything, and she was genuinely pleased. We're on good terms again and planning for Adams together. She still thinks it was Zac who released the photo, which helps. She was also rather surprised by the response. After the initial censure from the other mums, she was soon overwhelmed with praise for her sculpted body and time management. She also received several requests for Zac's number.

Everyone loves a happy ending, and here we are. No damage done, and lots to be grateful for. A Hampstead house, a successful marriage, a child in a good school (the new head looks a great improvement on the last one), a baby on the way, and me as PTA chair. I feel blessed. Even Ellie seems better off. She was offered places at every other school she applied for and accepted a prestigious 100 percent scholarship at another good school. I've personally saved that family thousands, but I won't ask anyone to thank me. It's the little unrecorded acts of kindness that make the world go round, as George Eliot so famously wrote.

One would think that I could now rest on my laurels. However, as Hollis's will should pass everything to me, in addition to considerable private wealth, I will soon own a billion-dollar AI company. I've never been a CEO before, and the challenge intrigues me. It'll require a whole new wardrobe, of course, and I'll need to study the ins and outs of being a successful female CEO to get things right.

And although we've just moved in, who knows if Hampstead is my forever home or just another stepping stone? I found myself looking at properties in Kensington the other day and I have to say there was one particular house that piqued my interest.

Acknowledgments

Most importantly, thank you to my incredible wife and our wonderful children. Not just because they are lovely, talented, and brilliant people, but for being such endlessly optimistic and generous supporters, and such insightful readers of many early versions, and also for providing the essential honesty and humor that is the special preserve of family members. Without you, it is no mere cliché to say none of this would have been remotely possible.

For picking this manuscript up from the slush pile, reading it in double-quick time, and contacting me in response via an actual telephone call while I was in the supermarket, thank you to the super-supportive, endlessly dynamic and brilliant Felicity Blunt, who has continued to call to share ideas throughout the whole process of readying the book for submission and beyond. Such admirable, old-fashioned adherence to speaking in person should be worthy of an award. And also a nod to Stanley Tucci, for glancing at the title of the book as Felicity read it and saying, in his inimitable style, "Sounds about right."

Thanks to the whole Curtis Brown team, who made the complexity of the process so simple and were always there to explain things to me without making me feel like I was actually that stupid. Thanks to the indefatigable, cheerful, and forensic Flo Sandelson, and to the fantastic rights team of Sophie Baker and Katie Harrison, who kept sending me lovely messages of auctions in far-off lands and helped with everything that was so alien to me.

Thank you to my three wonderful editors, Julia Wisdom at

HarperCollins UK, Iris Tupholme at HarperCollins Canada, and Kaitlin Olson at Simon & Schuster US, for their collective vision, insight, and ambition. I feel so lucky and privileged to have such expert and accomplished editors looking after and championing my book.

My first calls from my new editors arrived while I was walking in the Dolomites with my family. It was a surreal moment of feeling and almost being on top of the world. They also work with really great teams at HarperCollins and Simon & Schuster. I'm indebted to everyone who worked so hard on this book. Special thanks to Lizz Burrell and Ife Anyoku, who masterminded so much of the journey to publication; Felicity Denham, Libby Haddock, Megan Rudloff, and Molly Ketcheson, the incredible and knowledgeable PR experts; and Maudee Genao, Lipfon Tang, Adam Humphrey, and Amy Ruffhead, in marketing, who made sure the book makes a splash.

Thank you to my wonderful US agent, Gráinne Fox, at United Talent Agency, for her endless enthusiasm and selling skills. And the Film and TV team at United Talent Agency, especially the ebullient and also understated Jason Richman and his superb assistant Daniel Beracha, who arranged no fewer than twenty-eight Zoom calls with different production teams, most of them crossing several time zones, which felt very glamorous. And thanks to the wise and supportive Jazz Adamson at Curtis Brown, who provided a clear and sane voice as we were dealing with so much TV-speak.

An enormous thank-you to all the folk at ABC Signature, and the fabulous team at Best Day Ever Productions for taking up the option on the book. Working with Liz Tigelaar, the showrunner, and Stacey Silverman and their team has been a creative joy. They are so open, dynamic, and determined, taking meetings at all times of night and day. The story is safe in their hands, and I'm delighted that they were so keen to see Lalla brought to life.

Part of becoming a writer is getting help, support, and advice. I'm very fortunate to have been on a number of writing courses, with Faber & Faber, Curtis Brown, and even the Royal Court Theatre.

ACKNOWLEDGMENTS

Thank you to the inspiring course tutors at Curtis Brown Creative (CBC), especially Sarah Hilary and Erin Kelly, and all my fellow writers on those courses. I'd also like to thank the CBC team led by Anna Davis, and particularly Abby Parsons and Jack Hadley, who were so helpful and responded to every one of my many questions.

And a big shout-out to the amazing debut author Sarah Harman, who was such a source of savvy and sage advice and encouragement, even as she was going through the same process herself.

Thank you, finally, to Muswell Hill and the many wonderful people and places that make up this little North London enclave, a place so difficult to leave but fortunately so easy to return to. To all our friends who have been such great supporters in the various trials and tribulations of life as well as writing: thank you. I do apologize for Lalla's acerbic commentary and, by way of an all-purpose disclaimer, any and all offense is definitely down to her, not me.

About the Author

M. K. Oliver is a former English teacher and headteacher originally from Liverpool. He long dreamed of becoming a writer and after many years of working in schools, he took the exciting decision to put down the whiteboard marker, take up the keyboard, and give it a go. He enjoyed writing courses at Curtis Brown, Faber & Faber, and the Royal Court Theatre and now lives with his family and talkative cat in North London.